PRAISE FOR DiA

TRACE OF DO

"A well-researched and intimate story with some surprising twists along the way. In *Trace of Doubt*, Mills weaves together a tale of faith, intrigue, and suspense that her fans are sure to enjoy."

STEVEN JAMES, award-winning author of *Synapse* and *Every Wicked Man*

"DiAnn Mills took me on a wild ride with *Trace of Doubt*. . . . Filled with high stakes, high emotion, and high intrigue, *Trace of Doubt* will keep you guessing until the thrilling and satisfying conclusion."

LYNN H. BLACKBURN, award-winning author of the Dive Team Investigations series

"DiAnn Mills serves up a perfect blend of action, grit, and heart with characters so real they leap off the page. *Trace of Doubt* takes romantic suspense to a whole new level."

JAMES R. HANNIBAL, award-winning author of *The Paris Betrayal*

"*Trace of Doubt* is a suspense reader's best friend. From page one until the end, the action is intense and the story line keeps you guessing."

EVA MARIE EVERSON, bestselling author of *Five Brides* and *Dust*

AIRBORNE

"When DiAnn Mills started writing suspense novels, she found her niche. They are strong stories that keep the reader guessing. *Airborne* was filled with twists and turns."

LENA NELSON DOOLEY, bestselling, award-winning author of the Love's Road Home series

"Mills keeps getting better with each novel."

LAURAINE SNELLING, bestselling, award-winning author of *A Blessing to Cherish* and the Home to Blessing series

FATAL STRIKE

"DiAnn Mills has done it again! *Fatal Strike* captivates the reader from the first to last page. Deliciously detailed, this fast-paced romantic suspense novel creates an emotional roller coaster that keeps the pages turning as quickly as they can be read."

REBECCA MCLAFFERTY, author of *Intentional Heirs*

"*Fatal Strike* is a fascinating and page-turning suspense novel with fabulous characters and a touch of romance. Five stars from me! . . . The plot was full of suspense and plot twists and I was left guessing at every turn!"

SARAH GRACE GRZY, author of *Never Say Goodbye*

BURDEN OF PROOF

"DiAnn Mills never disappoints. . . . Put on a fresh pot of coffee before you start this one because you're not going to want to sleep until the suspense ride is over. You might want to grab a safety harness while you're at it—you're going to need it!"

LYNETTE EASON, bestselling, award-winning author of the Elite Guardians and Blue Justice series

"Taking her readers on a veritable roller-coaster ride of unexpected plot twists and turns, *Burden of Proof* is an inherently riveting read from beginning to end."

MIDWEST BOOK REVIEW

"Mills has added yet another winner to her growing roster of romantic thrillers, perhaps the best one yet."

THE SUSPENSE ZONE

HIGH TREASON

"In this third book in Mills's action-packed FBI Task Force series, the stakes are higher than ever. . . . Readers can count on being glued to the pages late into the night—as 'just one more chapter' turns into 'can't stop now.'"

ROMANTIC TIMES

"This suspenseful novel will appeal to Christian readers looking for a tidy, uplifting tale."

PUBLISHERS WEEKLY

DEEP EXTRACTION

"A harrowing police procedural [that] . . . Mills's many fans will devour."

LIBRARY JOURNAL

"Few characters in Mills's latest novel are who they appear to be at first glance. . . . Combined with intense action and stunning twists, this search for the truth keeps readers on the edges of their favorite reading chairs. . . . The crime is tightly plotted, and the message of faith is authentic and sincere."

ROMANTIC TIMES, 4½-STAR REVIEW, TOP PICK

DEADLY ENCOUNTER

"Crackling dialogue and heart-stopping plotlines are the hallmarks of Mills's thrillers, and this series launch won't disappoint her many fans. Dealing with issues of murder, domestic terrorism, and airport security, it eerily echoes current events."

LIBRARY JOURNAL

"From the first paragraph until the last, this story is a nail-biter, promising to delight readers who enjoy a well-written adventure."

CHRISTIAN MARKET MAGAZINE

DEADLOCK

"DiAnn Mills brings us another magnificent, inspirational thriller in her FBI: Houston series. *Deadlock* is a riveting, fast-paced adventure that will hold you captive from the opening pages to the closing epilogue."

FRESH FICTION

"Mills does a superb job building the relationship between the two polar opposite detectives. With some faith overtones, *Deadlock* is an excellent police drama that even mainstream readers would enjoy."

ROMANTIC TIMES

DOUBLE CROSS

"DiAnn Mills always gives us a good thriller, filled with inspirational thoughts, and *Double Cross* is another great one!"

FRESH FICTION

"For the romantic suspense fan, there is plenty of action and twists present. For the inspirational reader, the faith elements fit nicely into the context of the story. . . . The romance is tenderly beautiful, and the ending bittersweet."

ROMANTIC TIMES

FIREWALL

"Mills takes readers on an explosive ride. . . . A story as romantic as it is exciting, *Firewall* will appeal to fans of Dee Henderson's romantic suspense stories."

BOOKLIST

"With an intricate plot involving domestic terrorism that could have been ripped from the headlines, Mills's romantic thriller makes for compelling reading."

LIBRARY JOURNAL

TRACE OF DOUBT

TRACE OF DOUBT

DiANN MILLS

Tyndale House Publishers
Carol Stream, Illinois

Visit Tyndale online at tyndale.com.

Visit DiAnn Mills's website at diannmills.com.

Tyndale and Tyndale's quill logo are registered trademarks of Tyndale House Ministries.

Trace of Doubt

Designed by Libby Dykstra

Published in association with the literary agency of Books & Such Literary Management, 52 Mission Circle, Suite 122, PBM 170, Santa Rosa, CA 95409.

Trace of Doubt is a work of fiction. Where real people, events, establishments, organizations, or locales appear, they are used fictitiously. All other elements of the novel are drawn from the author's imagination.

For information about special discounts for bulk purchases, please contact Tyndale House Publishers at csresponse@tyndale.com, or call 1-855-277-9400.

Library of Congress Cataloging-in-Publication Data
A catalog record for this book is available from the Library of Congress.

ISBN 978-1-4964-5184-2 (HC)
ISBN 978-1-4964-5185-9 (SC)

Printed in the United States of America

27	26	25	24	23	22	21
7	6	5	4	3	2	1

*To every woman who has ever closed the door
on her past to step forward with Jesus.
And to Edie Melson, my sister-friend, who
inspires me to reach the mountaintops.*

PROLOGUE

SHELBY

Would I ever learn? I'd spent too many years looking out for someone else, and here I was doing the same thing again. Holly had disappeared after I sent her to the rear pantry for potatoes. She'd been gone long enough to plant and dig them up. I needed to get those potatoes boiling to feed hungry stomachs.

I left the kitchen to find her. The hallway to the pantry needed better lighting or maybe fewer corners. In any event, uneasiness swirled around me like a dust storm.

A plea to stop met my ears. I raced to the rear pantry fearing what I'd find.

Four women circled Holly. One held her arms behind her back, and the other three took turns punching her small body. My stomach tightened. I'd been in her shoes, and I'd do anything to stop the women from beating her.

"Please, stop," Holly said through a raspy breath. For one who was eighteen years old, she looked fifteen.

"Hey, what's going on?" I forced my voice to rise above my fear of them.

"Stay out of it, freak."

I'd run into this woman before, and she had a mean streak.

"What's she done to you?" I eyed the woman.

"None of your business unless you want the same."

"It's okay, Shelby. I can handle this." Holly's courageous words would only earn her another fist to her battered face.

And it did.

"Enough!" I drew my fists and stepped nose to nose with the leader.

The four turned on me. I'd lived through their beatings before, and I would again. I fell and the kicks to my ribs told me a few would be broken.

A whistle blew, and prison guards stopped the gang from delivering any more blows to Holly or me. They clamped cuffs on the four and left Holly and me on the floor with reassurance help was on its way.

I'd been her age once and forced to grow up fast. No one had counseled me but hard knocks, securing an education, and letting Jesus pave the way. I'd vowed to keep my eyes and ears open for others less fortunate.

Holly's lip dripped blood and a huge lump formed on the side of her head. I crawled to her. "Are you okay?"

"Not sure. Thank you for standing up for me. I thought they would kill me. Why do they do this? I've never done a thing to them."

"Because they can. They want to exert power, control. Stick by me, and I'll do my best to keep you safe."

1

I tightened my grip on the black trash bag slung over my shoulder containing my personal belongings—parole papers, a denim shoulder bag from high school, a ragged backpack, fifty dollars gate money, my driver's license at age sixteen, and the clothes I'd worn to prison fifteen years ago.

The bus slowed to pick me up outside the prison gates, its windshield wipers keeping pace with the downpour. The rain splattered the flat ground in a steady cadence like a drum leading a prisoner to execution. I stepped back to avoid the splash of muddy water from the front tires dipping into a pothole. Air brakes breathed in and out, a massive beast taking respite from its life labors.

The door hissed open. At the top of the steps, a balding driver took my ticket, no doubt recognizing the prison's release of a former inmate. He must have been accustomed to weary souls who'd paid their debts to society. The coldness glaring from his graphite eyes told me he wagered I'd be locked up again within a year. Maybe less. I couldn't blame him. The reoffend stats for female convicts like me soared high.

For too many years, I imagined the day I left prison would be bathed in sunlight. I'd be enveloped in welcoming arms and hear encouraging words from my family.

Reality hosted neither.

I moved to the rear of the bus, past a handful of people, and found a seat by myself. All around me were those engrossed in their devices. My life had been frozen in time, and now that I had permission to thaw, the world had changed. Was I ready for the fear digging its claws into my heart?

The cloudy view through the water-streaked window added to my doubts about the future. I'd memorized the prison rules, even prayed through them, and now I feared breaking one unknowingly.

The last time I'd breathed free air, riding the bus was a social gathering—in my case, a school bus. Kids chatted and laughter rose above the hum of tires. Now an eerie silence had descended.

I hadn't been alone then.

My mind drifted back to high school days, when the future rested on maintaining a 4.0 average and planning the next party. Maintaining my grades took a fraction of time, while my mind schemed forbidden fun. I'd dreamed of attending college and exploring the world on my terms.

Rebellion held bold colors, like a kaleidoscope shrouded in black light. The more I shocked others, the more I plotted something darker. My choices often seemed a means of expressing my creativity. While in my youth I viewed life as a cynic. By the time I was able to see a reflection of my brokenness and vowed to change, no one trusted me.

All that happened . . .

Before I took the blame for murdering my brother-in-law.

Before I traded my high school diploma and a career in interior design for a locked cell.

Before I spent years searching for answers.

Before I found new meaning and purpose.

How easy it would be to give in to a dismal, gray future when I longed for blue skies. I had to prove the odds against me were wrong.

2

During my years in prison, the demons ruled the night. Whenever one of the guards habitually unlocked my cell in the quiet stillness to force himself upon me, I vowed no one would hurt me again. Odd, I felt the same fear when I descended the bus steps at a Shell station in Valleysburg, Texas, as though the residents planned to attack me.

Darkness had long since covered the town in night's blanket. Telltale signs of earlier rain glistened on the ground under the streetlights and cooled the temperatures. The prison chaplain had recommended the central Texas town as a solid place to start over and arranged for me to rent a cabin here. When I explored the area online, I was drawn to the rural beauty and proximity to what I needed for my second chance.

Actually, God had already given me a second chance. This location offered me an opportunity to contribute positively to others while inching forward as a productive member of society. But I was afraid that I couldn't make the transition into society.

Memorized landmarks would be visible in the day hours, especially the location of the parole office on Main Street and a handful of boutiques whose owners might be interested in my jewelry designs. And the right church.

After exiting the bus, I looked for my new landlord, Edie Campbell—also a Realtor. She was to transport me to my new home and hand off the keys. A few people from the bus mingled outside the gas station, including some teens, but no one approached me. I'd described myself as wearing jeans and a blue T-shirt to Mrs. Campbell. Her delay wasn't my fault because my bus had arrived on time.

I scanned the area again and waited twenty minutes. Prison life worked wonders in developing patience, but the unknown picked at my courage. What if Mrs. Campbell had changed her mind about renting to an ex-con? The fragment of me who'd survived prison life now faced reentry into the world, and I felt like I'd spent fifteen years on another planet.

I pulled her contact information from my purse inside the trash bag and walked into the Shell station. A twentysomething, tattooed man worked behind the counter.

"Excuse me, do you have a public phone?" The first words I'd uttered in the free world.

He glanced up. "Didn't charge your phone, huh?"

"I don't have one."

"Bummer. But I get it. I've lost mine twice. I'm such a klutz. We don't have a public phone, but you can use my cell." The man handed me his device.

I smiled my thanks and hoped I could figure out how to use it. So many options. Dad had a new Nokia back in 2004 with a flip cover—nothing like this. "Would you punch in the numbers for me? I've had a rough day."

"Sure. What's the number?"

I gave him the numbers, and he pressed them in while I feigned interest in a candy display, my focus somewhere between lemon sours and bitter chocolate. When he returned the phone to me, it rang twice and a woman answered. "Mrs. Campbell?" I said.

"Yes."

"This is Shelby Pearce. I'm at the bus station—"

"Oh, my goodness! I thought you were arriving tomorrow night. I'm so sorry."

"That's okay."

"Hold tight, hon. I'll be there. Just need to make arrangements for my kids. They're asleep."

"I can call Pastor Emory." My number two contact per the parole guidelines.

"Not a good idea. His whole family has the stomach flu."

"Can you recommend a place where I could spend the night? I'd hate to inconvenience you." I'd earmarked the little money in my jean pocket for groceries.

"Heavens, no. This is my fault, and I want to show you the cabin. Give me about thirty minutes. I'll be driving a white Ford SUV."

"I'll be looking for you. And I appreciate all you've done."

"Glad to help. See you soon."

I clenched my belly to stop this unwanted worry. I was made of stronger stuff than this. After gathering my composure, I placed the phone on the counter and thanked the young man.

"Need anything else?" He pointed to a clock on the back wall. "We close in ten minutes."

"A restroom?"

He pointed to the left rear.

The lights in the building dimmed, and I stepped outside. Rain splashed onto the concrete. The second time today I'd been drenched.

A police car pulled in front of the store. The headlights seemed to shine through my soul as though examining the detestable part of me. An officer exited his car and walked toward me with deliberate, heavy steps. He seemed to be in his forties and losing his hair at the crown, but I could tell little else with his head bent low in the rain.

Heat rose from my neck. Did he plan to arrest me for something? Logic told me cops weren't the enemy, but I still trembled.

"Are you Shelby Pearce?"

"Yes, sir."

"I'm Officer Hughes. Edie Campbell called me. She's on her way. Asked me to look after you until she arrived. Want to sit in my car out of the rain?"

"I appreciate it." My shoulders relaxed.

We hurried to his cruiser, and he opened the door for me. A first. He rushed around to the other side, bringing the rain with him. Once seated, he eyed me squarely. "I speak my mind, Ms. Pearce. Edie is my sister. She's a widow raising two kids by herself while working full-time. I don't agree with her renting out the cabin to an ex-con, especially a murderer. But she has a mind of her own. Believes she's doing the right, Christian thing. As the only family left since her husband passed, I look out for her. The bottom line is, if you break one condition of your parole, I'll escort you back to prison myself."

I expected problems and I'd been instructed how to handle them. "Sir, I assure you I have no intentions of breaking any laws or rules. My intent is to live quietly and earn an honest wage."

"Here's my reminder that you gave up your Fourth Amendment rights as a condition of your parole. Expect me to be at your door often. This community and my family are important to me."

"I understand, sir. So is my family."

"Then tell me why your father called our office—worried about your release. Claims you threatened the entire family. Do this town a favor and leave on the first bus in the morning."

3

My first day in prison, a spider skittered across my cell floor. I knew for sure it planned to attack me, and I had no way to escape. Now sitting in Officer Hughes's cruiser until Edie Campbell arrived, the same panic threatened to paralyze me.

I'd survived the spider. A twinge of comfort rested there.

Why had the officer made such a ridiculous claim about me? "I have no intention of leaving, and I haven't spoken to my family since the judge pronounced my sentence. My father has no reason to fear my release."

"Ma'am, the sheriff told me about the call."

I feigned interest in the dark street. One thing prison had taught me was to curb my actions and reactions. Right now, I wanted to wipe the smirk off Officer Hughes's face. But losing control invited trouble.

"Do you have a job?" His voice broke through the steady tapping of raindrops against his windshield.

"I have a job at a café here in town, and I design jewelry."

"Edie told me about your skills. You gotta be real good to make it in the arts and crafts world around these parts." He frowned. "Folks might not be willing to buy your stuff since you're—"

"I know what I am, Officer Hughes. My jewelry is unique, and it *will* sell." Confidence and uncertainty exchanged punches on my ribs.

"Just sayin' you might have to find other work too. The Winsome Horse Stables is always searching for someone to muck out their stalls."

"Sounds like honest work to me."

"Smelly. But I'm sure you're used to that."

"Is rudeness a way to protect your sister, or do you naturally oppose those who've made mistakes?"

"Fresh starts are for deserving people. I'm—"

A knock on the driver's window stopped him. He slid the window down, the rain spattering inside. "You made good time."

"My neighbor is a saint." An attractive woman with shoulder-length brown hair and carrying an umbrella peered into the window. "Shelby, good to finally meet you." Her smile broke through the gloom. "I'm sorry about my mistake. Has my brother been treating you with Southern hospitality?"

"Yes, ma'am."

"I'm Edie. The *ma'am* stuff makes me feel like I'm a hundred years old."

"Thanks, Edie." I grabbed my bag from the floorboard and opened the door. "Thank you, Officer Hughes, for coming to my rescue."

"Sure thing. Don't forget our conversation."

How could I? "It was enlightening." I exited and shut the door. The chilling rain had more appeal than his company.

Edie dashed around the front of the car. "You'll be soaked. Scoot under my umbrella."

I ducked beneath its wide shelter and hurried to the SUV. I hated climbing into her vehicle and plopping my wet rear onto her seat. "I hope I don't ruin anything."

"Impossible. Don't inhale or you'll get a whiff of dog, greasy fries, and my forgot-to-shower sixth-grade son." Again the wide smile parted her lips.

She dashed around to the driver's side and slid in. "Hungry?"

Genuine and full of life. I liked her.

I hadn't eaten all day. Should I put her out any more than necessary?

"Your hesitation tells me you're starved. I'll drive through McDonald's. Is that okay?"

"It's been a long time since I've eaten anything but what was dumped on my plate."

"Oops. I'm sorry."

I waved away her remark. "No need to tiptoe around me. Where I've been is not where I'm going. I'm starved, and a hamburger sounds delicious."

Edie pulled onto the street, her washer blades reminding me of a hummingbird's wings. At the McDonald's drive-through, I placed my order. She added a Coke for both of us and paid for it, much to my protests.

"I inconvenienced you. Left you in the rain and my brother can be lousy company. He wanted to drive you to the cabin, but his attitude can be intolerable."

She knew him well. "But we're in good shape now. If you don't mind, I have a few questions." When she nodded, I laid them out in the order I'd stacked them in my mind. "Do your children know about me?"

"Enough to know your past is private." She tossed me a mom-look, complete with squinted forehead. "They are to keep family business private with a threat of me skinning them alive. Told them we're being Jesus."

Officer Hughes's comment about Edie not listening to him made sense. A woman with my reputation could be bad news. "I promise you I will not be alone with either of them."

"Thanks, and we've discussed the same scenario."

"Your brother said you're a widow?"

She nodded. "He died of a heart attack. No clue he had a health problem. Went to sleep one night and didn't wake up. It's been four years now."

"I'm so sorry."

"Thanks. Every day gets better."

The drive-through girl handed Edie a bag and two drinks. One bite, and I thought I'd died and gone to heaven. I chewed slowly to savor it all.

"Incredible." I stuck the straw into my Coke and drew in a long, sweet sip. "How old are your kids?"

"Timothy is twelve and Livy is seven. They're good kids."

"Single parenting must be hard."

"Every day gets a little easier . . . until they're teenagers."

I smiled. What a grand feeling to be talking with a normal person outside concrete walls. "Any special instructions?"

"Just common sense around my kids. You've met my family's worst—my brother."

I held up my palm. "Not going there."

"No need. He's like *Good Housekeeping*."

"What?"

"He has years of issues."

I covered my mouth to suppress the humor. Didn't work. "It's been way too long since I've laughed. But I was serious about guidelines around your kids."

"I know you are." She sobered. "After you've rested tomorrow, we can talk. I'll do all I can to help you succeed." She patted my arm. "We women have to stick together."

"I won't disappoint you."

"We have Jesus, and He's done the hard work."

How did one woman say all the right things? "How many people in the community are aware of me?"

"Sheriff Wendall, my brother, Randy, Amy-Jo, who owns the café, the parole officer, my kids, and Pastor Emory. No one else's business. Wanted to tell you the pastor has signed a check for you to purchase jewelry-making supplies."

I startled. "But he doesn't know me."

"Pastor Emory is a kindhearted man. He wants to make sure you have all you need to get started on the right path. I showed him some pics of your designs. He was impressed."

A warm sensation curled through me. The chaplain had complimented me, but her role was encouragement. "I'm grateful, and I'll pay him back. I don't want to owe anyone or be viewed as a charity case. What a blessing."

"You do what feels best, but he's not expecting payment."

"Would you keep the check for me? The jewelry supplies and stones are sold online, and I don't have a credit card."

"Sure. Put together the order, and I'll handle it. Before I forget it, you have a neighbor who is a super nice guy. I've asked him to keep an eye out for you. The cabin is a bit remote."

"What's his name?"

"Denton McClure. He rented the cabin nearest you, about a quarter of a mile through the woods. He's a widower." Edie laughed. "The man would make friends with a fence post."

"What's his profession?"

"High school math teacher."

"Anything I should be aware of?"

Edie waved away my concern. "Not at all. I trust him implicitly. He's done a few repairs for me and given Timothy and Livy riding lessons. Told me he'd taken an extended leave from teaching to sort out what he should do next. Said he'd been widowed for over two years, and it was time to put the grief behind him."

A pop rang out and the right front tire blew, sending the SUV left toward the shoulder. Edie slammed on the brakes, and the vehicle slid and swerved.

"Don't brake!" Years ago a driver's ed instructor pounded the warning into my brain. He followed up with videos depicting what happened to metal and people who had blowouts on wet, slippery roads.

Edie lifted her foot, fighting to keep the SUV under control. But the vehicle ignored her efforts and dove hood-first into a water-filled ditch.

⊙ ⊙ ⊙

The rain had stopped its deluge, but the dark night still held menace. A tow truck disappeared down the road with the SUV. Edie and I had crawled out the passenger side. Now she, Officer Hughes, and I stood on the side of the road like a face-off in the prison yard. Blood trickled down the left side of Edie's forehead.

"Sis, I'm calling an ambulance." Officer Hughes yanked his cell phone from his pant pocket.

"You do and I won't let the paramedics touch me. I'll handle this with a Band-Aid at home. You're getting on my last nerve."

He turned to me. His scrutiny made me crave a shower. "A shooter fired into the tire. Do you know anything about this, Ms. Pearce? My sister could've been seriously hurt or worse."

Anger boiled from my toes to my mouth. "Nothing, Officer Hughes. Edie and I were talking, and I wasn't aware of anyone else on the road."

"Your kind has its ways. Looks to me like you crossed somebody, and they're sending a deadly message."

"Prove me wrong, Officer Hughes."

"I'm sayin' you've made enemies."

"Randy, hush," Edie said. "You're jumping to conclusions. We've talked about this, and I'm giving Shelby an opportunity to put the past behind her. In fact, I think she should spend the night with me. It's late and—"

"That's kind of you but no thanks." I waved away her offer. "I prefer the cabin. My concern is we don't know why someone shot a bullet into your tire."

"Probably just kids."

He leaned into me, nose to nose. "I don't want the likes of you influencing Edie. Neither do I want you around my friends or family. I want you out of our community."

"Stop it." Edie's voice echoed around us. "Pushing your weight around makes you look like a bully on steroids. I want to get Shelby settled into the cabin and then home to my kids. Are you driving us, or do we walk?"

I didn't need anyone to fight my battles, although she knew her brother better than I did. He wanted to protect her from trouble . . . namely me.

"Get in," he said. "I'll take you."

"Not one more ugly word to Shelby. You hear me? I've had enough from the chairman of the unwelcome committee."

Others must have voiced their opinions about helping me.

He scowled and strutted like a rooster to the cruiser. At the door, he whirled around and shook his finger at me. "When I get to the bottom of this, you're heading right back to prison."

Fear coiled around my heart for too many reasons to list. Should I go through with his earlier request to take the morning bus to another town? Two surprises had blindsided me—my dad claiming I'd threatened the family and someone firing a bullet into Edie's tire.

I'd thought of little else but freedom for years. But was I ready to leap into the unknown?

4

Sunlight filtered through the bedroom window above my head, an amenity I'd once taken for granted. Despite the mix of emotions assaulting me about being shot at and a disagreeable police officer, I'd slept in my own bed. In my own home. And wearing soft pale-green pajamas—a gift from Edie. Did she know the color green often signified healing?

Last night after she'd shown me the cabin and bidden me good night, I walked through each of the five rooms, exploring and praying for my fresh start. No spiders caught my attention. Sometime after midnight, the rain stopped. My mind ceased to deliberate the myriad problems ahead and those who stalked me, and I yielded to sleep.

This morning through fog-laden eyes, I admired my rustic bedroom. I stared up from a chunky, four-poster bed to a light pine-beamed ceiling and inhaled the sweet peace that cradled me. Perhaps my joy came from the homey wood, varying textures, and endearing fabrics woven together to create a homespun feel. I drew my fingers over the quilt covering me and touched the threads of the perfectly crafted pieces of a star pattern symbolizing the Lone Star State. Back in high school, my interior design dreams included living in an apartment in New York City with sleek lines and huge windows overlooking Fifth Avenue. Another lifetime. Another me.

The cabin seemed to whisper that I could make it, the same thing I'd told myself since giving my life to Jesus. My fingers gripped my Bible on the nightstand—the only way to start the day. The reading came from Psalm 139: *"O Lord, you have examined my heart and know everything about me!"* Trusting in Him superseded everything else. I finished the passage with more optimism than the depression attacking me the previous night.

After swinging my legs over the bed, I lingered on the scent of freedom and lavender potpourri, a strange but incredible mix that seemed to shake off my trepidation about the future. In the kitchen, I rummaged through the fridge and small pantry. Edie had stocked me with enough to feed a family of four for a week. My favorite luxury sat on a tan-and-cream marbled counter— coffee beans, a grinder, and an upscale coffee maker. Soon the smell of freshly roasted coffee tickled my taste buds.

Before prison, I'd dabbled in the taste of coffee with no preference either way. In prison, I found it disgusting but the caffeine necessary to survive. The smooth, bold flavor of my sip this gorgeous morning sent me soaring into paradise.

Edie's kindness blessed me. How could one woman shine love all around her? She'd lived through tragedy too, not of her own making. For that, we were sister-survivors.

Barefoot, I took my mug outside, and the coffee tasted even better with the sounds of birds and fresh smell of clean air. A robin perched in a tree, singing a crisp tune. Stepping gingerly over the driveway's gravel, I made my way to the grass. Oh, the feel of the soft blades between my toes and tickling my feet. I leaned my head back and let the sun bathe me in delicious warmth. Never again would I take the taste, smell, sound, touch, and sights of nature for granted. Bright. Beautiful. Full of vitality.

I missed my family, but my decision was vested in love.

Back inside, I reached inside my backpack and placed one of my treasured possessions on my nightstand. For my twelfth birthday, Dad had given me a kaleidoscope. He showed me how the pieces of colored glass formed intricate designs. I'd spend hours creating patterns and sketching them until interior design attracted my interest. That kaleidoscope went with me to prison. The intricacy of color helped me process the valleys and mountains of my life journey. I simply applied bright colors in place of dark and gray.

A knock at the door startled me. Neither the sound of tires crunching pea gravel nor a car door slamming had given me any indication of a visitor. I walked to the window and took a look. A cowboy or cowgirl had paid a call. Not Officer Hughes, whom I'd nicknamed Bubba Valleysburg.

I opened the door to a mostly white-haired man, more like premature white because only a few lines fanned from his brown eyes. "Can I help you?"

A smile greeted me, framed by a salt-and-pepper mustache and a goatee. "Hey, I'm Denton McClure. I live on the other side of the woods." A slow drawl rolled off his tongue. "I heard you'd moved in from Edie. Wanted to introduce myself. Give you my cell number in case you need something."

"How kind of you. I moved in late last night." I glanced at my pajamas. "I apologize for my lack of dress."

"It's early, and I'm sure you had a late night." He inhaled deeply. "Oh, I smell coffee. For sure another day. You must have plenty to do, so I'll leave you alone." He handed me a folded piece of paper. "My number's there, and your name?"

Heat rose into my face for not offering it earlier. "Sorry. I'm Shelby Pearce. Pleased to meet you, but I don't have a phone yet."

"Just text me when you do. That way we can keep in touch."

First I needed to buy a phone and figure out how to text.

"We're isolated here," he continued, "and you don't seem to have a car. I believe neighbors should look out for each other."

He said goodbye and rode off on his horse . . . sorta like one of the many John Wayne Westerns I used to watch with Dad. Denton's dark eyes had studied me in a type of peculiar curiosity. *Trust him or beware?* I'd play it safe and not return the good-neighbor persona. The truth about me would rise like smoke signals soon enough.

Someone had laid the foundation for trouble last night with a gunshot. Until I found out who was responsible, Officer Hughes and Denton McClure weren't above suspicion.

5

Prison had given me hours to deliberate life. In my seventeen-year-old naiveté, I had never imagined Dad and Mom's abandonment or a prison sentence. When first charged with murder, I'd thought my age would soften the judge's heart. I'd land a few years in juvenile jail and lengthy probation linked with community service. In essence have my hands smacked. That didn't happen. As the years inched by, I learned my parents protested my parole three times. I might never learn all the reasons why they chose to close the door on our relationship. Although I had confessed to a horrendous crime. Once I'd gotten past the feeling-sorry-for-myself syndrome, I chose to make the best of my circumstances by pursuing an undergrad and master's degree in business.

While the experience with my parents nipped at my heels, it had also shaped me into the woman I am today, sitting in a rocking chair on the front porch of a cabin reflecting on what I'd learned from the past and how I planned to march forward.

I rubbed the scar on my left shoulder from a knife wound . . . inflicted when I was barely eighteen from an inmate who liked girls. That part of my life was over. In prison I expected discrimination and prejudice to shoot poison darts from every direction, but God was my constant companion.

I finished a third mug of coffee and basked in the flavor. The many singing birds and the quiet of nature with its intoxicating scents should have continued to relax me, yet a cloak of darkness threatened to destroy my joy. Instead of a song titled "Sweet Freedom," memories of last night and this morning droned a cautionary tune into my thoughts.

A distinct feeling of someone watching me prickled the hair on the back of my neck, an acquired safeguard from prison gangs and a few sleazy guards. I dismounted the steps and panned the area. "Who's out there? What do you want?"

Was it just my imagination? I'd sensed danger too many times to ignore the signs. I set my coffee on the porch step and walked the perimeter of the cabin. The windows were locked from the inside as well as the rear door. Still, those precautions never stopped a serious intruder. I calmed when I didn't see any footprints in the rain-soaked earth.

But the ground would dry. I gathered pine cones and sticks from the woods and laid them in a pattern no one could avoid. Primitive but that would be my watchdog.

After rinsing the mud from my bare feet with an outside hose, I put my apprehension on hold and indulged in a hot shower. The water massaged my entire body—lavender-scented soap, shampoo, and conditioner delivered the fragrance of a new morning. I stayed longer than I'd been allowed in years. I slathered on real body lotion and body spray that matched the lavender scent, another gift from Edie. She'd used some of the money I'd sent to buy a few clothing pieces, and the jeans and soft sweatshirt against my skin gave me a surge of new normal.

I removed a notepad and pen from my trash bag. On the bus

I'd jotted a list of jewelry-making tools and supplies I needed to get started. Pastor Emory's check helped speed up the process in moving me down the road of self-sufficiency. I must thank him properly and repay him ASAP. On Thursday I'd begin work at a local restaurant, requiring another note of gratitude to Edie and the pastor.

Tears crested. I had to succeed. I would not disappoint my new friends and hoped Officer Hughes didn't discredit me in their eyes.

I wasn't alone anymore. My surroundings proved it.

Tires crunched over gravel. A quick peek out the window showed Edie was right on time, and I met her on the porch. The Shelby before prison would have bombarded her with a hug. But this Shelby asked for permission first.

She drew me into an embrace. "If you ever ask me again if a hug is okay, I might have to smack you."

"Deal. I see your tire's fixed. Have the authorities made an arrest?"

"Not yet. My brother dug a 9mm bullet out of it. He's working on the who and why."

No doubt. "Is there anything I should know?"

"Not to my knowledge." She sniffed. "Do I smell maple syrup? Peanut butter? Chocolate?"

"My first prison-free breakfast was my favorite as a kid and teen—chocolate chip pancakes smothered in peanut butter and warm syrup. Not just any pancakes, but a recipe from my dad." I raised a finger. "Don't remind me of the calories, and yes, I have two left for any taker."

She moaned. "Best keep them for yourself. Peanuts give me hives, and I tend to wear pancakes on both my thighs." She patted her legs for emphasis.

"Coffee? An incredible woman bought me an incredible grinder, coffee maker, and beans that brew an incredible taste straight out of heaven."

"Yes, ma'am. Add a little half-and-half, please."

"Kindly have a seat on my beautiful pecan-colored leather sofa." I gestured into the living area. "Ready to see my jewelry designs and help me with my business model?"

Edie wiggled her shoulders. "I've thought of little else. You hit my hot button with the word *jewelry*."

I reached for a mug inside a cabinet. "Denton McClure stopped by on his horse earlier."

"Good. We all need friends. Last week he visited me while the kids were doing homework. Timothy was struggling with algebra, and Denton spent an hour helping him. Afterward, Timothy claimed no one had explained algebra so thoroughly before. But Denton is a math teacher."

Maybe Denton was a good guy. I handed Edie a mug of coffee the way she liked it. We sat side by side on the sofa while I showed her my few pieces made in prison—six necklaces, five pairs of earrings, and two bracelets.

"These are gorgeous, Shelby. So well crafted. I love the green-and-blue labradorite pendant in antique brass. Oh, and look at how you've woven the wire to look like lace."

"Thanks. I owe your friend, the chaplain, for showing me how to create jewelry."

"Donna told me you were good, but I had no idea how beautiful the design was until now."

"You should have opened the box when she mailed the pieces here."

"Wouldn't have dreamed of it." Edie examined the back of the pendant.

"Every piece has a tiny wire twisted into a cross on the back."

"Is this your logo?"

"Yes. You beat me to it." I turned a few pages in my sketch pad. "Here is an area where I need advice and guidance."

"Don't you have a master's in business?"

"Yes, but not experience." I set the open page on her lap. "With my logo I want women to see how God is in the redemption business through a wired cross that isn't a perfect traditional one. Airy. Whimsical. And imaginative."

She touched the sketch as though it might leap from the page. "The cross is intricate, symbolizing beauty in the ugly mess of our lives."

"We might have to take up preaching," I said.

"Don't get me started."

I giggled like a schoolgirl. "Some names for the business keep running through my mind. Such as Classy-Chic Jewelry Designs, Your Jewelry Designs, and the third is Klassy-Kreations written with *K*s instead of *C*s. But I don't want it to be cutesy either. This morning Simple Pleasures came to me."

Edie tapped her chin. "What about Simply Shelby in a flowing script?"

"Simply Shelby," I whispered. "Sounds like me. Perfect." I flipped to another page in my sketch pad and pointed to my card creation. "On one side of a business-size card, I'd print *Simply Shelby* in the middle with a twisted cross in the left-hand corner and a thin gold border framing it. On the opposite side, I plan to name each design and add a corresponding Scripture verse. That means an investment in card stock because the back of each piece would reflect a distinctive style and verse."

Edie let out a dramatic sigh. "You could tie your name in with all promotional items."

"True. I'm also thinking the online logo could have fluidity to build anticipation for showcasing the jewelry." I turned a page in my sketchbook. "My target buyers are women from ages thirty and up who enjoy one-of-a-kind designs. One thought is to have selections for the younger woman. Another thought is to create smaller pieces for the young teen or petite woman. All medium priced to make this affordable but not to give my jewelry away."

"We need to get you established on the various social media platforms to reach online buyers."

"I need help with the social media part. All of it."

"No problem. I can teach you." Edie gestured for me to continue. "Keep talking. My mind is sparking ideas like firecrackers."

"Perhaps a blog focusing on how each piece is created and tips on how wearing them would create interest. I'd like to stage them, take photos to show versatility. Even videos once I learn how it's done. Of course, I need a website, but that development will need to wait until I have the funds. Do you think my past will hinder buyers?"

"Oh, stop it. Do you plan to announce it?" Her fun personality was fantastic. "We can work around every issue you can toss my way. My web designer is amazing, and he could help you with everything online, including marketing and promotion. And don't forget an online catalog. Facebook, Pinterest, and Instagram are all good for you. Not every person hangs out on the same platform."

I rubbed my palms together. Last Christmas I'd hoped for a new friend who wouldn't mind giving me business advice. Fanciful dreams didn't compare with the excitement bubbling inside me. "I've made out an order. I just need you to call it in."

"Which reminds me, I bought a new phone a few months ago. You can have this one, and you can access Wi-Fi from it too. Randy looked at it this morning and told me it was in good shape." She reached into her monster bag and presented me with a cell phone.

My fingers trembled. "Why are you doing this?"

"I believe in your heart, Shelby. The chaplain and I are high school friends from my San Antonio childhood. She believes in you too."

I rolled the phone over in my hands, holding it like a precious jewel. "Will you show me how to connect and text?"

We both laughed at my helplessness. "I'd love to."

For the next hour, Edie tutored me in how to set up my phone, text, and access the Internet. She jotted down websites for me to learn about social media, marketing, branding, and other foreign topics. "You're a fast learner. Just call—"

A swish near the door turned our attention to an envelope sliding under it. I rushed over and flung the door open in time to see a man bolt into the woods.

"Hey!" I raced after him on a winding path. He wore a ball cap and a black T-shirt. He ran like a deer, and his long stride and pace lengthened the distance between us. My breathing came in short, painful spurts. Dratted asthma. He disappeared into the thick woods, and I stopped to grasp my knees until I gained control of my air-depleted lungs.

Edie.

She could be hurt. Fighting for every breath, I rushed back to the cabin. She stood on the porch, her phone in one hand and the envelope in the other. I swept my gaze over the perimeter and back to the item in her hand.

"Are you okay?" she said.

I gestured my thumb and finger like an inhaler and retrieved it from inside. She followed me in. I inhaled the medicine deeply and waited for my lungs to cease their protest. "I'm all right. He outran me. I feared he was circling back to you."

"You chased him when he could have turned on you?"

"He meant no good, and I acted instinctively."

Her features softened. "Did you recognize him?"

"Never got close enough."

She held up the envelope. "Obviously this was an important delivery."

"Wash your hands before I open it. He could have laced it with poison."

Her eyes widened. "You're kidding, right?"

"Not in the least. I heard a few tales in prison that would make your skin crawl. Scrub for thirty seconds with lots of soap and water."

Her face pale, Edie returned shortly afterward.

We walked several feet beyond the cabin for two reasons— if the envelope held deadly contents, I'd rather contaminate the outside of the cabin than the inside. Also, if the sender watched me, I wanted him to know I'd opened it. I gingerly lifted the envelope's flap and tugged on a folded, typed note.

You're not wanted here.

6

At my trial the prosecutor laid the groundwork for first-degree murder. He alleged that Travis had discovered I'd hacked into his bank account and embezzled five hundred thousand dollars, but the defense claimed a third person had to have been involved. Where would a seventeen-year-old stash so much money? And how? The prosecuting attorney claimed I had an accomplice, but lack of evidence helped to eliminate those charges.

The note shoved under the cabin door threw me back to the days when suicide looked inviting. Depression had stalked me like a shadow for as long as I could remember, and the two incidents since I'd been released coaxed me into a well of despair.

Officer Hughes stepped into my personal space and waved the note in front of my face. He conveyed his contempt without opening his mouth.

He whirled to Edie. "I warned you about spending time with an ex-con. You're risking you and your kids' lives for a stupid be-like-Jesus mission."

As much as I disliked the man, he raised a good argument. "Officer Hughes, I agree Edie needs to keep her distance from me until the issues are resolved."

"More than six feet," he said.

Edie stood from the sofa. "I won't be told what to do."

My new friend had a bit of naiveté going on. "We can't be seen together as friends. You and your children take priority, whether the threats are connected to me or something else."

Her countenance fell. She closed her eyes—not for drama as much as helplessness. "You're both right. I'll stay away until an arrest is made."

"We'll visit in person when this is over. You've been a tremendous source of encouragement, Edie. Because of you, I have a plan and can move forward."

"Shelby, you have a job, and I planned to help with the transportation."

"Never have I expected you to cater to my needs. I have two good legs, and I can take care of myself."

She shook her head. "It's five miles each way, and—"

"I'll loan her my bicycle," Officer Hughes said. "Anything to keep you two apart."

Edie braced her hands on her hips. "You'll bring it today?"

"I suppose."

What a good turn for the day. "I'll store your property inside the cabin until I purchase a lock and chain. And I'll take good care of it until I can buy my own bicycle."

"What about your online research?" Edie said. "We were going to work on your business plan together."

"I'll use a computer at the library, and we have our phones."

Officer Hughes huffed. "Great idea, Shelby." I despised the way he spoke contempt into my name. "That way you won't be imposin' on anybody. Make sure you don't take matters into your own hands, or I'll have to pick you up." He focused on Edie. "You've listened to reason, so wrap this up. We have no idea who could be watching the place."

"Sundays," Edie said.

Officer Hughes and I stared at her for clarification.

"Shelby and I can see each other on Sundays in church. No one will suspect a thing."

"We'll discuss it," he said.

"No, we won't. You have no say in what I do at church, especially since you never darken the door."

He held up his clipboard that had the note attached. "I have my report to submit. I'm waiting here until you drive off. Then I'll swing it by the sheriff's office and pick up my bike."

A bicycle would allow me to report in to the parole officer, explore the town, research at the library, find a printshop, stop by to introduce myself to my new employer, visit Pastor Emory, and even pay a visit at two boutiques. Such a long list. What I couldn't get done today, I'd finish tomorrow.

I hugged Edie. There was so much I wanted to say, but not with Officer Hughes observing me through his microscopic lens. I dreaded the next encounter with him. But I'd be armed with my own stubborn resolve.

I needed Valleysburg. Not sure why, but I believed I belonged here. Someday, if I found favor, I'd call this town home and these people family.

Maybe not Officer Hughes.

7

DENTON

How strange to feel an emotional connection to a horse again. Not since I was a kid had I been attached to such a magnificent animal. Back in those days, my heart belonged to a quarter horse whose speed challenged the wind. Nothing compared to feeling like the horse and I flew as one.

In my twenties I exchanged the horse for a silver Camaro. Finished college. Fell in love and proposed to the most beautiful brunette on the planet. Planned a fall wedding. Joined the FBI. My youngest brother jabbed at my career choice every chance he got. So I committed to nail Shelby Pearce for life. My future slid downhill from there . . .

My life lay in shambles, and I blamed her. My parents wanted me to talk to their pastor, but why? God was using me as a whipping boy.

"Great way to spend the morning." I brushed the sides of Big Red to cool my constant companion.

He shook his head to chase away a fly, but it looked like he agreed.

"What do you think of Shelby Pearce? I'll tell you a few things first. Those blue-gray eyes, long honey-colored hair, and sweet voice might lead a man to distraction. Not me. When she was fifteen, she broke into her high school and vandalized the girls' athletic trophy case. She also had two arrests for underage drinking and took a neighbor's car joyriding. That's just a drop. But I know what she did to her family, and one of her crimes remains an open case."

My brain must have been hit by buckshot to talk to a horse about a string of crimes that happened over fifteen years ago. She'd pulled the trigger on a man, leaving her sister a widow and an unborn baby without a daddy. Add the disappearance of five hundred thousand dollars.

Upon her release from prison, she'd chosen Valleysburg to supposedly begin her life all over. I knew exactly what she planned—sit tight until she could get her hands on the money. No doubt she had an accomplice who worked the sidelines.

I'd been given another chance to prove myself to the FBI, and this time I refused to be defeated. I'd been given an undercover assignment to locate the stolen money. I took up residence in the community and set up my role. Shelby had blinded the parole board, Edie Campbell, and Pastor Emory. But I'd expose her. No one had the right to steal from a nonprofit organization that housed, schooled, and fed African orphans.

My cell phone alerted me to a call from Mom with "Hey Jude." The ringtone always took me back to the days of her at the piano playing and singing Beatles songs. Dad, my two younger brothers, and I learned every word.

"Hi, Denny, this is Mom."

I chuckled. Who else could it be? "What's happening with the fam?"

"That's why I'm calling. Our annual barbecue cook-off is in

three weeks, and I wanted to make sure you were coming. Your recipe always wins, but your brothers are perfecting theirs."

I pictured my dark-haired mom doodling on a scratch pad, her normal manner of doing *something* while on the phone. "Mom, I'm working undercover."

"Where?"

"If I told you, then it wouldn't be undercover."

A sigh met my ears. "I can always ask. Any chance your case will be closed by the cook-off?"

"I have no idea, but we can hope." I hated to disappoint her. "But you can tell Dad, Andy, and Brice they will never beat out my barbecue sauce. Mamaw gave me the recipe with the orders it was to be passed down to the oldest son of each generation."

"Right, and the competition is between the McClure men. You'd think her own daughter would have it tucked away. But I didn't qualify." She huffed.

"You know Mamaw."

"Sweet and sassy. I miss her."

"So do I."

"Does your undercover work let you work with troubled teens?"

"No, and I miss it." I'd been volunteering with Hope for Today's Youth since the eruption in my life years back.

"All right, Denny. I'll let you go, but first I have to ask—"

I laughed. "No, I haven't met a nice girl."

We ended the call. My family meant a lot to me, but between Andy marrying my ex-fiancée and Brice's jabs, my brothers had a way of making me feel like day-old coffee grounds.

A vehicle engine rumbled a familiar sound. Through the barn's opening, I saw Edie Campbell approaching on foot. "Morning, Edie. You doing okay?"

"Better than I deserve. Hey, I wanted to ask you a favor."

I laid the brush on the trunk outside Big Red's stall. "I'm listening."

"I came from visiting Shelby Pearce. Thanks for showing her a warm, Valleysburg welcome."

"No problem. She's a nice lady. I intend to visit again."

Edie moistened her lips. "She's gotten off to a bad start. Someone shot out my SUV tire when she was with me last night, and today someone shoved a note under her door, letting her know she wasn't welcome."

"Why?"

She flushed. "Honestly, she came from a rough past."

"Aw. An abusive ex?"

"Something like that. I'm concerned about her."

"Edie, did she report it to the sheriff?"

"My brother responded to the call."

"If I see or hear anything suspicious, I'll let the sheriff's office know. In the meantime, I'll look in on her."

"Thanks. I need to get back to the office." She drove off.

Shelby was released yesterday and already she'd taken a prime spot on a shooter's hit list. But someone had threatened her more than once. Perhaps an accomplice who wanted all of the stolen cash? Or a person invested in protecting Shelby's family? Or someone taking a stand against crime in Valleysburg?

I'd find out.

8

SHELBY

I stepped onto the porch of my cabin, the lure of freedom pulling me into her spell. I never wanted to take the beauty around me for granted.

I removed my worn journal from my backpack. Settling on a rocker, I opened my journal, an old friend that's always available for conversation, and clicked the pen. The chorus of insects reminded me of childhood days at my grandparents' farm west of Houston. Sweet memories of simpler days.

Four years into prison life, I decided to record my thoughts and emotions, more to help me process my past choices than anything else. In the eighth year, I admitted journaling wasn't filling the hole in my heart. Jesus stepped in and became my mother, father, sister, and friend. A few times a week, I allowed myself the luxury of writing down thoughts and happenings. But never in the light-filled joy I knew this very moment.

I wrote of my experiences since yesterday morning. Enduring resistance and persecution after prison had been on my radar. I'd been counseled about the likelihood and thought I was prepared. Officer Hughes had the hostility gene going for him, and Denton McClure was at the opposite end of the spectrum. But I didn't trust either man.

I headed into my bedroom and returned my journal to its new home, a narrow drawer in my nightstand. A long walk to clear my mind pushed to the surface of my want list. But Officer Hughes hadn't returned with the bicycle and leaving made me look like a coward. Which was partially true.

An oncoming vehicle barreled up the drive. Officer Hughes had arrived. At least he wasn't part of an angry gang. He might be worse if my suspicions were true.

I met him at his cruiser, and he powered down his window.

"I appreciate the loan of your property," I said.

"Thank my irresponsible sister. I'd rather you walked. Make sure you buy a lock and chain. I get real upset when my property's abused." The vertical lines between his brows dug deep. The world must disappoint him on a daily basis. He carried the bicycle onto the porch.

"Would you like to sit and talk?" I hoped his animosity toward me might take a positive spin.

"My favorite place to visit with a killer is behind bars."

I sighed. The rancid heat of humiliation assaulted me. "From your perspective, I had that coming."

"Yep."

"Anyone ever give you a second chance?"

"Never needed it. I'm squeaky-clean."

"Officer Hughes, I'm not your doormat. So clean your muddy boots somewhere else."

"I expect to receive respect from the likes of you."

I refused to respect any bully. "Did you leave the note to run me off?"

He leaned on one leg. So bully typical. "Nope, it would be breaking the law. Did it work?"

"I'm here, and I intend to stay. Does the sheriff have the note or was it destroyed?"

He smirked. "My sister was here when you got it, so she'll make sure he knows about it. But it's hard to nail down where a typed note came from."

"So you're the guilty one?"

He rolled his eyes like I used to do when my parents objected to my behavior. "By the way, the parole officer is expecting you this afternoon. A no-show means a stain against your record." He tipped his hat and walked to his cruiser.

9

The rear bicycle tire flattened about three miles from Valleysburg. The air valve stem cap was missing. I suspected an intentional action on Officer Hughes's part. I walked the bike into town and stopped at a hardware store. After airing up both tires, I bought two stem caps and a chain and lock. The store owner gave permission for me to keep the bike locked there until I finished with errands. The idea of someone stealing it left a sour taste in my mouth. As soon as I had a few dollars extra, I'd flip for my own two-wheeled transportation.

Thirty minutes before the parole office closed, I approached a weathered brick building. A sign above the door read, *Established 1932*. Inside, an arrow indicated various offices on the second floor, and I climbed the wooden steps. Every creak and groan spoke of age and history. At the top, I inhaled a generation gone by and admired the tall ceilings, arched windows, and age-scarred but polished wooden floors. If I owned the building, I'd re-create the era and update only what was needed for safety and convenience.

Not my purpose this afternoon.

The parole office occupied a secluded spot at the end of the hall. There I met a balding man with thick black-framed glasses rummaging through a file cabinet.

"Mr. James Peterson?"

His glasses slid down his long nose, rather comical, but I knew better than to laugh. "How can I help you?"

I extended my hand. "I'm Shelby Pearce."

"Ah, yes. Have a seat, Ms. Pearce. Officer Hughes stopped by and indicated you were eager to see me this afternoon."

I bit my tongue. "Yes, sir. I wanted to make sure I got started on the right foot."

He sat at his desk and brought his computer to life. "I was looking at your file earlier. Do you have any questions about the terms of your parole?"

"No, sir. Do you have noted my job at Amy-Jo's Café? I begin on Thursday."

He nodded and told me he had the verification. I gave him my address, cell phone number, and plans to design jewelry.

"I see you earned a master's degree in business while incarcerated. The education will serve you well with your jewelry endeavor and reclaiming your life." He squinted into his computer screen. "A 4.0 average too. Well done."

"Thank you." I removed my backpack from my shoulders and reached for my denim bag, a gift from my parents on my sixteenth birthday. Inside were two envelopes. "Here are my release papers and cash payment for the monthly parole fee."

He examined the contents of each envelope, then counted the money. "If there's ever a problem in paying the fees, let me know ahead of time. Don't wait until past the due date."

After the formalities and scheduling a weekly appointment, he gave me his card. "Parole is a privilege not a right. My goal is to help you succeed. We'll begin with high supervision for six months, and Pastor Emory will handle the weekly counseling. If all goes well, we'll drop to moderate level. Do not hesitate to contact me for any reason. How are you doing with your family's request for no contact?"

"Their stipulation is one of the reasons I'm in Valleysburg." While he typed, my mind wandered. My family broke contact right after sentencing. My sister and I were raised with the knowledge of unconditional love, but I learned some deeds were unforgivable. How could I fault them?

Mr. Peterson leaned back in his chair and folded his hands over a trim stomach. "What's your biggest concern right now?"

Honesty . . . "Someone wants me out of town in a bad way." I told him about last night and earlier today, omitting my intuitiveness. "I have no idea who did it or why. Edie Campbell has helped me tremendously, and now she could be hurt by association. Officer Hughes gave the note to Sheriff Wendall. If he's in his office when I leave here, I'd like to talk to him."

"The sheriff's a good man. He'll untangle what's going on." Mr. Peterson picked up his cell phone and pressed in numbers. "This is Jim. Shelby Pearce is in my office, and she'd like to stop by. Will you be there for another hour or so?" He paused and laid the phone on his desk. "I'm going with you."

Why was I so paranoid? I hadn't done anything to warrant a nightmare trip back to prison.

"Is there anything I should know before we talk to the sheriff? A threat from inside or outside prison? I see you'd received severe beatings from fellow inmates."

I pushed aside the memories. "I stayed to myself to avoid too many problems."

"Your file says the same thing. Good record, Ms. Pearce. My concern is depression. If you need medical help, don't hesitate to let me know."

Depression could be a formidable enemy. "Yes, sir. Since

becoming a Christian, I'm much better equipped to handle my emotions."

He smiled and stood from behind his desk. "My car's in the rear parking lot."

At the sheriff's department, Sheriff Wendall surprised me with his short, thin stature and broad shoulders, as though he'd stopped growing in junior high. A gray felt Stetson sat on the corner of his desk, just like the cowboy hats in the Westerns I used to watch with Dad. Mr. Peterson and I took chairs opposite the sheriff's uncluttered desk.

"Is there updated information on the two incidents?" I said.

"Well, little lady, we haven't any leads on either one." The sheriff studied me like I was a specimen under a microscope. "We're on it. Looks like you've made an enemy or two."

"If I had a name, believe me I'd give it to you."

The sheriff rubbed his chin. "One thing to consider is the missing money."

"Ms. Pearce wasn't convicted of theft," Mr. Peterson said.

"But plenty of folks believe she stole it."

I drew in a breath to cover my frustration. "Sheriff, if I'd taken the money, would I be renting a cabin outside of town?"

"Doubtful. But someone might see it as the perfect cover-up."

"Do you?" I'd had enough of the once-a-criminal, always-a-criminal status. "I've paid my debt to society. I didn't steal from my sister and brother-in-law. Neither am I aware of what happened to their money. While in prison, one of the gangs did their best to find out about it. I couldn't tell them what I didn't know."

I shook my head. "I've asked Edie Campbell to keep her distance until the problem is solved. Two crimes have been committed against me since my release. They weren't coincidences, and my fear is whoever's responsible has just started."

"What about Travis Stover's family?"

"Last night I checked online, and they are still missionaries in

Bulgaria. He was an only child. No immediate family." I erased suspicions of his family being behind the threats.

"Then we'll hold on to the possibility of someone from prison being responsible until this is over."

The sheriff's impassive stare left me questioning if he and Officer Hughes shared the same mindset.

"My job is to make sure the laws are obeyed and to protect others from harm," the sheriff said. "If your rights have been violated, and it appears so, then I'm out to make an arrest."

Dare I fight the opposition, or should I move to another town? Would my past haunt me forever?

10

No one could ever appreciate the scent of freedom unless they'd been locked up. Wednesday morning, I pedaled into Valleysburg, drinking in the morning freshness. The five miles of nature-infused earth nurtured me, and optimism blossomed like the Indian paintbrush and bluebonnets blanketing the spring fields.

My first stop was Pastor Emory's office. I wanted to thank him for his generosity, but his secretary reported he and his family were still down with the flu. I wrote him a note and included my cell phone number with a request for him to call when he felt better. I also scheduled my first counseling session for the following Monday. I'd dread the session every day until it happened.

My secrets lay buried, and there they'd stay.

I chained the bicycle to a bike stand outside Amy-Jo's Café. A step under the green awning transported me back to the early twentieth century. I walked inside to the sound of a bell tinkling over the door. Tongue-and-groove hardwood floors and tin-and-wood ceilings reflected the original construction, a wall held antique kitchen utensils, and another wall exhibited framed depictions of what appeared to be historic Valleysburg. I asked if the owner was available.

A middle-aged woman with mango-colored hair, purple eye shadow, large-framed pink glasses, and ruby-red lipstick greeted me. I introduced myself.

"Honey, I'm Amy-Jo. Glad you stopped by so we could get acquainted. Can you come in at five thirty in the morning instead of six? One of the girls is down with the flu."

"Must be going around. Pastor Emory and his family are fighting it."

"Nasty stuff. Nothing bothers me." She placed her hands on her ample hips. "Germs take one look at me and run screaming."

"Thank you for this job opportunity."

She smiled. "Nervous?"

"Yes, ma'am."

"Don't be. The past is behind you. You paid your debt and now you have another chance at life."

I blinked back the wetness filling my eyes. "Just what I needed to hear. Do you have time to tell me what I'll be doing?"

"You'll handle the bakery counter. I'll be here in the morning to guide you through your duties."

"I grew up with my elbows in flour."

"Tell you what, when I retired from my old job, I weighed 108 pounds. Every time I missed the fun, I'd either go to the shootin' range or bake and eat. You're too trim and pretty to make that mistake." Amy-Jo walked to the glass bakery case and gestured at the pastry display. "This is a perfect fit for you."

I bent to take in the pies, cakes, cookies, tarts, donuts, various pastries, and a gluten-free section. Oh, the hours I'd spent with my parents in their bakery. "If you need any help with the baking, I'm your gal."

She laughed. "Best news I've heard since you agreed to come in early. I'm always looking for an extra hand and new recipes."

"Most of mine are in my head, but I can write down my favorite ones I remember." Dad had often talked about creating a cookbook, and I hoped he'd published one. "What else can you tell me?"

"The mornings are hectic with folks lined up for coffee and pastries before work and school. Around nine it slows down a bit. If I'm low on waitstaff, I may ask for your help. I provide two shirts, one to wear and an extra. You're responsible to keep them clean."

I glimpsed the two other women wearing jeans and red T-shirts with *Amy-Jo's Café* on the back. I could do this.

"Let me show you my boutique. We expanded last fall, and I'm tickled pink with the results." She led me to a wide entrance on the right. An ornate chalkboard inscribed with *Amy-Jo's Gifts* was mounted on an easel and pointed to another large, wood-floor room. The charm of the old building, probably built in 1932 like the one housing the parole office, complemented the homey displays of quality gifts, small furniture items, and decorating accessories.

"Edie tells me you design jewelry. I've been looking for a feminine line with flair. Would love to see what you have."

Excitement rose inside me, along with a lump in my throat. "I have a few pieces in my backpack."

"Let's do it." She patted a small oak table. "Right here."

I fished out the tissue-wrapped jewelry and laid out the pieces. Amy-Jo touched a green-and-gold labradorite pendant with twisted antique brass wire. Her bubbling laughter showed her pleasure. She selected a few designs from my sketch pad to create. I had no clue why God was blessing me—a woman with a muddy past. But I loved His favor.

"Does your business have a name?"

"Yes, ma'am. Simply Shelby."

She wagged her finger at me. "Simply Shelby, I'm Amy-Jo. Call me *ma'am* when I'm a hundred."

⊙   ⊙   ⊙

I completed my errands and took a look inside a secondhand store for a bicycle. The owner didn't have a thing. Once I paid Pastor Emory, I'd purchase a new bike. Hope-filled dreams surrounded me as I pedaled home. Later I'd call Edie with a list of jewelry supplies I needed and tell her about today's adventure. My fingers tingled with the expectation of creating new jewelry pieces.

Night came all too quickly. The headlights and roar of an advancing vehicle sent me hugging the grassy side of the road. I glanced back. A truck gained speed, closing in fast. I moved farther onto the grass near the ditch and took another look behind me.

The driver of a black pickup headed straight my way. Why? He had the whole road before him. Was the driver blind? On his phone? Drunk?

Or worse?

With nowhere to go on a bicycle that wasn't mine, I screamed. The truck raced past, spitting stones from the shoulder into the left side of my body. The momentum sent me off-balance and into the mud and ditch. Only a fool would call what happened an accident.

Except I'd seen the first three letters of the rear license plate.

Alone and dripping wet, my thoughts darted from anger to fear and back again. I yanked on my backpack for my phone and pressed in James Peterson's number. I despised the title of *victim* as much as I hated *ex-con*.

I'd been easy prey once. Never again. I'd find who stalked me.

11

I'd survived the groping hands of guards and inmates. I'd been beaten twice for standing my ground against a gang who assumed I'd stolen my brother-in-law's money and wanted a cut, a third time for helping a woman defend herself from attackers. Two other beatings were to show who was boss. I believed in justice and truth, and I'd find out who and why someone wanted me out of Valleysburg. Although Officer Hughes seemed to be the front-runner.

I'd stay unless someone became a victim because of me.

I trembled at what my stalker might have planned next.

A vehicle pulled up to the cabin. I flipped on the outside light and viewed Mr. Peterson exiting a Jeep, and I met him on the porch. He eyed me and frowned. "Are you sure you're all right? Wouldn't hurt for a doctor to take a look."

Mud clung to the right side of my T-shirt and leg. The left side stung from the stones hurled by the truck tires. "The water and mud cushioned my fall. I just have a couple of scrapes and bruises."

"Did you walk here?"

"I rode the bike. Like me, it survived." I invited him inside my cabin and gestured to the sofa. "I called Sheriff Wendall and reported the incident."

"And?"

"He's sending Officer Hughes to take my statement."

Mr. Peterson huffed. "Fat chance his response will do any good. I'm sure you've experienced his . . . superior side."

"Yes, sir, and he's not happy about my presence in Valleysburg. Neither does he approve of his sister, Edie Campbell, renting me this cabin and befriending me." I told him about the bicycle and the circumstances surrounding why I was using it.

"Hughes and I have discussed you," he said. "I requested that he tone down his behavior. What's your gut telling you about the hit-and-run?"

"I didn't see the driver. Someone is using fear tactics to try to run me off." I hesitated. "Are you thinking Officer Hughes is behind this?"

"Let me just say I suspect him. His dark-green pickup could be mistaken for black." He rubbed his stubbled chin. "What haven't you told me?"

I'd endured years of secrets. "Nothing that would provide answers." But I'd not sit idly by while someone destroyed my second chance at life. "I don't have a clue what the person wants except to scare me away. He's the one who's a coward."

"Officer Hughes needs every detail for his report, no matter how insignificant it seems. I'll inform Sheriff Wendall that you and I have talked."

"Would you stay until Officer Hughes has all he needs?"

"You bet."

I heard a car pull up and checked the window. Officer Hughes slammed the door on his cruiser. My frustration in dealing with him had to equal his disdain for me.

"My bike okay?" He eyed it. "Why haven't you cleaned it up?"

"I wanted to show you the evidence. As far as I can tell, it's a little out of line."

"Let me check it out."

Mr. Peterson cleared his throat. "Randy, why not investigate the hit-and-run before you evaluate the condition of the bicycle?"

"I'm sure the driver didn't see her. Made a mistake. It's dark and visibility is bad."

"The driver had headlights," I said.

"That means he saw her." Mr. Peterson gave every indication of supporting me, but trust hadn't been earned yet. "This makes the third crime against Ms. Pearce."

"She's got a record, Jim. Murdering an innocent man sets her up for a few enemies. Besides, my bike doesn't have reflectors."

"What's wrong with you?" Mr. Peterson frowned. "Don't you think a little due diligence is in order?"

"Sure, once I inspect my bike. Then we'll take a look at the alleged crime scene." He walked back to his car, popped the trunk, and grabbed tools to realign the bicycle. All without a word. "It's okay for now, but if I have problems down the road, you'll pay for repairs or a replacement."

I rode with Mr. Peterson, and Officer Hughes followed in his cruiser to the spot where I'd fallen. Mud and crushed grass indicated the area. Officer Hughes spent all of twenty seconds surveying the scene. "Nothing here to open an investigation."

Patience with Hughes waned. "I have the first three letters of the driver's license plate—DAT."

"What state?"

"I have no idea, but it wasn't Texas."

Officer Hughes chuckled. "Nothing for me to validate a crime's been committed. Looks to me like you wrecked my property and made up this fool story." He headed to his vehicle. "I have real work to do."

"You're out of line," Mr. Peterson said.

"I'm doing my job."

I watched Officer Hughes speed away. "Thanks for supporting me."

He nodded. "It's doubtful that whatever's going on is over."

At the cabin and again alone, I considered what had happened—the shot fired into Edie's SUV, the note letting me know I wasn't wanted, and the pickup driver's actions. All deliberate. Repeatedly my thoughts landed in the same place.

Someone thought I should have stayed in prison, or I had knowledge about the unrecovered money or both.

The person had a stake in the past, but no one came to mind. How did I fight an unseen enemy? *God, give me strength to hold tightly to You.*

My phone rang. An incomplete number appeared on the screen, so no chance of tracing it. Should I answer?

"This is Shelby."

"You're not doing your family any favors," a distorted voice said.

I breathed deeply to calm my shattered nerves. "I agreed not to contact them, so what's the problem?"

"Give them the gift of suicide."

I shuddered. "Why?"

"They want you dead or back behind bars. No need for taxpayer money to support you."

My parents wouldn't do that, would they? "Who are you?"

"Doesn't matter."

"Let's meet face-to-face. Or are you a coward?"

"You'll see my face when you rot in hell. Tell anyone about this call, and you'll regret it."

I trembled and grabbed my inhaler. "Officer Hughes, to what extent will you go to run me off?"

The phone clicked.

12

James Peterson's warning kept me looking over my shoulder. He doubted the attacks against me were over. But what could I do when Hughes claimed a crime hadn't occurred? The road to and from Valleysburg gave me the chills, especially in the mornings when it was pitch-black. I found a flashlight in a kitchen drawer and used it like a headlight. I pedaled past the site where the truck ran me off the road and worried what might happen next. I wanted to confront the person, see if the problem could be resolved.

I'd encountered enough bullies to risk whatever it took to stop my personal predator.

My second day on the job, I arrived home at three o'clock. So far, working for Amy-Jo had filled my hours with meeting new people and filling pastry orders. I'd forced myself out of cave mode into a new Shelby, who longed to make people smile. The wait-staff and cook were pleasant. I looked forward to the days ahead, anticipating free time at the cabin to create jewelry, explore my surroundings, and read. What more could I want?

I'd been home long enough to change my red T-shirt and wash it out. Nothing new to harm me had happened in two days, and my homemade alarm system of pine cones and sticks remained untouched.

A knock at the door ended my deliberations, and a quick peek showed my friendly neighbor was paying another call. My distrust level rose. The five-letter word *alone* was my best company. Except I'd vowed to find who—

Denton knocked again.

Be neighborly. I opened the door and allowed kindness to lace my voice. "Good afternoon."

He held a border collie puppy in his arms. "I've come begging for a cup of coffee. The smell from the last time has lured me back."

I stroked the puppy's black-and-white head. Why had he brought this soft little creature? I learned a long time ago that people always had a reason for their behavior.

"Hope you don't mind I brought a little girl with me."

I took the sweet puppy's face into my hands. "She's adorable. What's her name?"

"That's up to you. She's yours, Shelby. Once she's a little bigger, her bark will alert you to anyone near the cabin." He paused. "Or if you decide to raise sheep or cows, she'll herd them."

A gasp escaped me but also a hint of alarm. "I have no idea what to say."

"Thank you?" He grinned and held out the puppy. "She still needs a name."

I gathered her soft, fluffy body into my arms, and she licked my face. "I'm in love. Thank you, but border collies are expensive."

"Not really. She's the runt, and I got a good deal. She doesn't have papers, but I understand it's possible to buy them."

"Why did you do this, Denton?"

"Not sure, but she's yours. Cute too." He cocked his head. "I had one like her when I was a boy. She needs a name."

I traced the white streak between the puppy's eyes and around her nose. The rest of her black coat glistened in the light. "What's your name, my little ray of sunshine?" I met Denton's gaze. "Joy."

"I like it."

A talkative and generous math-teacher cowboy? Perhaps if I got to know him, I'd not feel this grinding apprehension. "I have no need for her papers. But I think we should celebrate over a cup of coffee."

"I'll wait out here. It's a beautiful day."

I gave him a mental thumbs-up. "You're a gentleman, and I appreciate it. Please, hold Joy and give me a couple of minutes. How do you drink your coffee?"

"Raven black."

"Strong?"

"Yep. Oh, I have puppy food at my place, and she's had her shots."

Gratitude watered my eyes. "I'll repay you."

"You are with the coffee and possible friendship."

Would he be this friendly if he knew my past?

With only one rocker, Denton and I sat on the porch steps to drink our coffee, and Joy curled up in my lap. I stroked her with shaking fingers. The last time I was this close to a man, I had to fight him off.

But I had dreams like any woman. I longed for a man I could trust—a man I could love and share my innermost thoughts with. He'd feel my presence when I entered a room, and we'd sit for hours content with silence and a love that promised to last through every storm.

Denton stood and climbed the steps. "Sorry. Not my intention to make you nervous." He leaned against the porch post.

I nodded at his perception and took my first sip to regain my composure. "I'm a loner."

"Would you prefer I leave?"

I prayed for guidance. Denton could be a great guy. If he was the enemy, I wouldn't discover it by avoiding him. "I'm okay. We can talk."

"I've been a widower for a couple of years, and it's hard to climb out of the grief. But I'm ready."

Suspicion gnawed at me. "We just met. Why is my friendship important to you?"

"You're a mystery, Shelby. I'm curious."

"And I'm confused."

He waved away my question. "All I want is friendship. Nothing else. Great coffee, by the way."

His warm smile caused me to relax slightly. "I bought it at the same place where I work—Amy-Jo's Café."

"I need to pick up a bag." He pointed to his horse. "Want to meet Big Red?"

"I'd love to."

Denton introduced me, and I petted the horse while cradling Joy.

"I have a soft spot for animals," he said. "My apartment in Houston didn't permit pets. Another reason why I liked it out here. Trust me, as a kid, I pestered my parents for another dog, a cat, and a horse."

"Are you sure you don't want this puppy?"

"Certain. I have my eye on her mama's next litter." We walked back to the porch steps. "Do your parents live nearby?"

I'd rehearsed this type of questioning in prison. "They're east of here. What about yours?"

"Mine live in the Conroe area."

"Are they in good health?"

"Remarkably good and very active. Mom is an ex-cowgirl and RN–turned–trainer for therapy dogs. Dad's a retired police officer and a scoutmaster. He also helps Mom with whatever she needs. They're great parents. I'm lucky."

"Sounds picture-perfect. Siblings?"

"Two brothers, both younger. You?"

"A sister."

"Does she live near your parents?"

I smiled. "I have no idea."

His brow wrinkled. "You aren't close to your family?"

"Not really."

"From what I see, it's their loss."

I hadn't expected his remark, and I could provide a taste of truth. "My fault. I made a few bad choices in my youth and spoiled the relationship with my entire family."

He finished his coffee and set his mug on a table by the rocker. "How about a walk?"

"My parole officer might not approve."

Not a muscle twitched on his face. "The reason for no contact with your family?"

"Yes."

"Number one, the past is behind you. The future is what matters. Number two, I asked for a walk, and I doubt it violates your parole."

For a moment, I wished my new freedom meant more than an unlocked cell. "You might want to google me first. The findings might change your mind."

He shook his head. "If you want to tell me something, the choice is yours."

Denton, like anyone who initiated friendship, shouldn't learn about my past from anyone but me. "I spent fifteen years in prison for a horrendous crime. I paid my debt, and I found Jesus."

"Adversity separates the weak from the strong."

I weighed what I wanted to know about him. His kindness could be a ploy for something deceptive. But how would I learn if I didn't take a chance? Joy snuggled closer to me. While in prison, I was part of a dog-training program. I became attached to a miniature poodle, which in reality was an emotional support animal.

"Where are you?" Denton said.

"I was convicted of manslaughter."

"Okay."

"Does my confession make you nervous?"

"No, ma'am."

"You should be."

"I'm a man who believes in second and third chances. Does Edie know?"

"Yes."

"She believes in you, and that's enough for me."

"All right. She says you're a great guy. I'll take a walk if you promise to look online at my record later."

He nodded. "Shelby, I hope we can be friends."

"The idea is terrifying."

"Understandable. Maybe it's time for a new beginning." He grinned.

Denton was a handsome man with a strong jawline and incredible dark-brown eyes. He appeared sincere in his request for friendship. Yet, his features seemed familiar.

I locked the cabin, and we took the same path as the person I'd chased into the woods. This time, I carried my puppy and enjoyed the spindly pine trees, wildflowers, and musky smell of the earth. A pink wildflower with an oval-shaped petal caught my attention. I bent to memorize each soft curve and how a gentle breeze caused it to nod.

"Want me to snap a pic?" Denton said.

"Yes, please. I'd like to use the shape and colors to design a jewelry piece." Already I envisioned a pendant wrapped in bronze wire or possibly silver. "My hobby."

"I'd like to see them sometime." He snapped it with his phone and handed me the device. He'd captured just the right amount of light.

"Beautiful," I whispered and returned the phone. "Thanks."

"Photography is one of my hobbies. Besides, you're easy to please. Any other photos?"

"Count on it." I laughed.

"Haven't heard such a sweet sound in a long time. You should laugh more often."

Was he intending to impress me? Why? I'd like to think he made the list of potential friends, but trust came at a high price.

Back at the cabin, a box sat on the front porch. Caution snaked through me.

"You have a delivery." Denton moved toward the box. "From the size, it looks heavy. Want me to carry it inside?"

"Let me check the sender first." I motioned for him to stay back and handed him Joy. UPS had delivered the box, and it came from Fire Mountain. Relief raced through me. "The box is from a jewelry supply company."

Denton appeared at my side within seconds and handed me my cuddly puppy. He scooped up the box, and I unlocked the door. "Joy needs to grow fast. You were petrified at the sight of the box."

"More paranoid than fearful." I pointed to the kitchen counter.

He eased it down and turned to me. "I'm sure you want to check out the order, so I'm riding home. Thanks for the coffee, conversation, and walk." He snapped his fingers. "Do you have AirDrop enabled on your phone?"

"What is that?"

He showed me the option and sent the wildflower photos he'd taken earlier. We looked at them together.

"They are incredible." I walked him to the door.

"Hope to see you again, other than dropping by puppy food later. I won't bother you. I had a good time this afternoon."

I didn't encourage him by asking to see his photography. "You promised to find out more about me."

"I will."

Spending too much time with a good-looking man who brought me a puppy and knew a dribble of my past might cause me to make a huge mistake. Time for me to google Denton McClure.

13

DENTON

To say I was confused after spending two hours with Shelby didn't put a dent in my puzzled and frustrated findings. I'd enjoyed my time with her. Too much. And I despised the reluctance in my spirit to condemn her. For years, I'd thought of little else but finding the evidence to prove her guilt in an open case. I liked her, and the thought of being wrong about her rehabilitation or participation in the money theft made me furious. At myself. Tangled emotions weren't my specialty, especially for a woman who'd wrecked my life plans.

I gave Big Red full rein on the winding path to my cabin. Had I betrayed myself? Shelby's smile lingered in my mind, the way her lips curved upward and her soft laughter. Those blue-gray eyes haunted me, drawing me into her world. She admitted her parole status, which caught me off guard, and the crime, giving me an opportunity to back off from friendship. If prison and her statement of faith were legitimate, the penal system had done its job.

Logic and statistics told me old habits seeped into a person's blood and seldom found an exit. Life changes were miracles, not the norm. I believed God existed, but I hadn't gone the route of giving my life to Him. Too much misery in the world to believe in a loving God.

A call from my youngest brother, Brice, interrupted my musings. "Hey, Denton, how's life on the back forty?"

"Great. Fresh air and good people."

"And working undercover? I saw that Shelby Pearce was released."

I knew where this was going. "We've met. Talked."

"Still not too late to resign and join your brothers at Houston PD."

"I'm fine."

"Really? What happened to your wedding?"

"For the record, my engagement was headed south before I chose the FBI."

"She married a cop, our brother."

"Give it a rest, Brice. The past is in the past. Andy and Lisa's marriage has worked for a lot of years." I wish I could accept their relationship . . .

"Know what? You're right. I'm done giving you a bad time, Bro. Andy jumped all over me after I ran you off at Christmas." He drew in a deep breath. "I'm sorry."

"Is that why you called?"

"There's more. I wondered if you planned to be at the barbecue."

"Mom put you up to this?"

"Yes. She said your staying away is my fault. And she's right."

"Never thought you'd swallow your pride." But I couldn't bring myself to dissolve the many times Brice had irritated me with his constant badgering.

"You've had a solid career with the FBI. But not near what you could have accomplished in the police force." After my prolonged silence, he sighed. "Don't forget to call Mom."

Even with an apology, Brice had a way of making me feel like horse manure. When I least expected it, he'd remind me of something stupid I did in middle school or college. Always something. And it always ended with me not going into the family business. Being a police officer.

My thoughts turned back to Shelby. Before her release from prison, she'd been part of a program that encouraged prisoners to bond with dogs while learning how to train them. I understood from my own experience how an animal could be a source of comfort. Now shame tormented me for giving her the puppy as though I had an ulterior motive.

I paced the floor. I'd investigated every inch of this case—repeatedly. Years ago, Shelby's parents grieved the death of a son-in-law and stalwart member of the church and community, as they grieved the loss to their oldest, pregnant daughter. Shelby's high school friends testified to her rebellious and often-dangerous pranks. No one was surprised she'd been charged with murder, except one girl claimed Shelby had put aside her wild ways and chosen to pursue her dreams in fashion design.

Every road I'd followed led to a dead end.

The sensible explanation to my mixed feelings about her today pointed to Shelby playing me for a fool. She'd pretended to be a decent, reformed woman and learned from the past. Had to be a role she played, a ploy of manipulation.

Still, a longing to see her again told me I wouldn't get much sleep tonight. How could I find something good in a murderer?

14

SHELBY

I stood behind the bakery counter and read the article in the *Valleysburg Gazette* for the second time. My parole news was printed on the third page in an opinion column. The information was public knowledge, but reading my release status crushed me to the core. I rubbed my arms. Would the dirt always be there as though I needed a perpetual shower? Someone had taken the newspaper photo the day I met with James Peterson and Sheriff Wendall, further confirming a person or persons wanted me out of the area. My name glared up at me and the crime I'd committed in cold black letters.

Was Officer Randy Hughes responsible? I'd noted the way he and Denton walked and their builds. Neither one resembled the slight man I'd chased into the woods.

Amy-Jo took the newspaper from my hand. "I saw you reading this while I seated a customer. It's trash."

"I'm not finished with the article."

"No need. Nothing you don't already know or haven't read online." She crumpled the paper and pursed her lips. "No one has the right to condemn you. You can reclaim your life and be proud of your accomplishments."

"Maybe I should move on. My job here might damage your business."

"If someone chooses to eat and shop somewhere else, I don't need them. Besides, leaving here is crazy. Edie and I have already talked this morning, and she'll be here as soon as she drops the kids off at school."

"Why? She shouldn't be seen with me."

"More craziness. We were sure of your ridiculous response to one person's opinion. You're in Valleysburg for a reason, to start over."

My mind journeyed to a dark place. "I'd like to know who wrote the article."

"Doubt you'll find out. The person's a coward. Trust me, I know a coward when I see one." Amy-Jo tapped her finger on the glass bakery case. "Are you thinking it's Edie's brother? He's been opposed to her helping you from the beginning."

"He'd sign his name and brag on what he'd done."

She blew out her frustration. "You know him well."

"He hasn't hidden his disapproval or his intention of running me off." I sighed, couldn't stop the response to the heaviness in my soul. "The writer could be someone concerned about me corrupting the community. Could be the person wants me to believe it's Officer Hughes so I don't find out who is really responsible. If I've learned anything during the past several years, it's life can blindside us. People deceive and behave according to what drives them from one selfish motive to the next."

Amy-Jo blinked, revealing teal-and-pink eye shadow. "My late husband used to claim, 'Roaches can hold their breath underwater for forty minutes. No point flushing them down the toilet because they'll crawl right back out.' The writer of this article is a roach. Ignore it and let truth exterminate him."

But I must confront the writer, find out who was behind the threats. "What time does the newspaper office close?"

"Noon on Saturdays."

I'd stop in on Monday after my counseling session with Pastor Emory.

The bell over the café's door jingled, and Edie walked in. Her red face cautioned me to calm her down.

"Good morning," Amy-Jo said, and I waved my greeting.

"I need coffee. Caffeine will help me get the right perspective about this." Her tone showed otherwise.

"Are you okay?"

"My brother and I had a few words."

"And?" Amy-Jo raised a finger.

"He insists today's newspaper article is the consensus of all law-'biding citizens in town. Hard for me to fathom we came from the same parents." A dramatic exhale followed.

"Love doesn't require agreeing with everything a person says and does," I said. "I'll get your coffee with a dollop of half-and-half."

"Surely you're not defending him." Edie's eyes widened.

"He has a right to want the best for his city, family, and friends. My job is to show his taxes have gone to good use." I choked back a sob like a spineless weakling. My emotions centered on Edie and Amy-Jo. These ladies were ready to march to my battlefront and take a hit.

"I appreciate both of you. You support me and neither of you have asked any questions about my ugly past. But the truth is, people judge. People are easily frightened by those convicted of evil things. I have to bear the burden unless someone breaks the law—then it's Sheriff Wendall's or Officer Hughes's responsibility. I need to prove to you, James Peterson, and Pastor Emory that I'm trustworthy. I'd like to stay in this beautiful town, yet I won't put anyone's reputation at risk." I eyed them separately. "You will not suffer for my sake."

"Whoa," Amy-Jo said. "Let's ride this out together. Shelby,

you're right about human nature. But nothing scares me because I've seen the worst of the worst. In my opinion, nothing's changed. Just more people know what brought you here. I'd like to think good will come from this." She patted my arm.

I flinched.

"Sorry to offend you." Amy-Jo stepped back.

"Habit. I was thinking about . . . stuff. I'm not used to being touched unless it's with malevolent intent. My apologies."

"No problem. You know, Randy could decide to like you."

"Seriously?" Edie said. "That might happen on Judgment Day."

I laughed and broke the tension. A regular customer lined up for his blueberry scone. I pointed to him. "Ladies, excuse me, but I have work to do."

The man would make a great Santa during Christmas—his white hair reminded me of a much older version of Denton. "I'll have four blueberry scones, four large cinnamon buns, and a dozen donut holes. The grandkids will soon be up and ready to start a Star Wars marathon."

I slipped into a fresh pair of gloves and packaged his order. "I remember watching those movies with my family. Loved every minute. We all were fans."

A woman behind him glared with large blue eyes. "Did a storm trooper inspire you to blow a hole in your brother-in-law?"

I looked up. What was wrong with this woman? Had she never made a mistake? Sacrificed for someone she loved more than life?

"You're a disgrace to our solid community," she said.

Behind her, Amy-Jo's and Edie's mouths stood agape. But I'd not fall into the condescension trap. "What can I get for you?"

"A dozen of Miss Amy-Jo's lemon tarts. The ladies' mission group is meeting this morning."

I selected the best pastries and placed them in a box.

"Is Mrs. Emory joining you today?" Edie said.

"No. The family's on the mend from the flu, and she's exhausted from caring for the kids, the pastor, and herself. The pastor hasn't felt like working on his sermon, and he needed her to help finish it for tomorrow."

I taped the box closed and handed it to the woman, forcing a smile to cover my anger. "I hope the ladies enjoy these tarts."

"Extra napkins, please."

A flow of sarcasm swirled through my mind. Unleashing my fury only demonstrated my pride.

15

DENTON

My plans for this morning were less than honorable but necessary. I stalled at my cabin until daylight before I walked to Shelby's cabin. She told me yesterday her shift ended at two, offering plenty of time for me to search her cabin.

In the back of my mind, I wanted to come up empty. The war within me waged on.

Picking the lock on her door came easily, and I stepped inside, careful to lock the door behind me. Neat. Clean. The scent of lavender and wood permeated the room. And I planned to disrupt it all with the scent of betrayal.

Joy bounced in her kennel, and I lifted the latch to reach inside and pat her head. Good thing she couldn't talk.

I started my sweep in Shelby's bedroom, opening drawers and sorting through her few belongings. Most drawers were empty. I removed them and felt along the sides and bottoms for anything I might find to use against her. Inside her nightstand drawer, a journal appeared. Many pages were filled, and I wished I had time to read them. I reached for my phone and randomly snapped pics of several entries. No reason why I couldn't return another day if something emerged among her writings.

I moved my rummaging to the bathroom, second bedroom, closets, kitchen, and living room. Nothing out of the ordinary snatched my attention. I returned to her bedroom and surveyed the area with the idea of reading her journal. Her Bible lay on the nightstand, and I picked it up. She'd underlined a lot of passages and made notes in the margins. I held it by the spine over the bed, shook it, and a folded piece of paper drifted to the floor.

Only God knows the truth, and He is Truth.

My mind turned the note inside out. What truth? Her faith, forgiveness, and all the God stuff?

Below it she'd penned a few short lines—

Why do I remember
The sins that stalk my soul?
Why can't I hold on to the
Forgiveness that makes me whole?
Ashes rise to steal my breath.
I choke from drowning fear.
Help me, Lord, to cling to You
In never-ending prayer.

Her words spoke of anguish that God hadn't removed. Why did He promise peace when she obviously lived a self-induced nightmare? Did she have dreams of a husband and children? Ambitions to use her business degree? Make a success of her jewelry design? How could she hold on to God when He'd failed her? I shrugged. God failed people on a consistent basis. I knew firsthand.

A thought lingered . . . What if she had changed?

'The sound of footsteps outside the front door caused me to step between Shelby's bedroom wall and the door. Trapped just when I'd tried to gain her confidence. Maybe she'd forgotten something, and I could stay hidden. I peered through the slim crack between the door hinges and the frame.

A square envelope slid under the door.

Randy Hughes had a few loose screws when it came to Shelby. But invading her privacy while representing the law seemed low for him. I suspected him of sending the last note, except the person who'd left it had raced into the woods. Hughes's beer gut slowed his speed. Of course, I was breaking and entering. What about the man who'd fired into Edie's tire? Ran Shelby off the road and into a ditch?

I hurried to the living room window and saw no traces of the sender. The person had been on foot and obviously headed to the side or rear of the cabin. I drew my Glock as I slipped out the back door, hoping I didn't confront a bullet. The quiet morning greeted me. Man-size boot prints sank into the dirt and led to the woods behind the property. I snapped a few pics of them and wrestled with the idea of trailing him. If the person was armed, the stretch of open field behind the cabin set me up as target practice.

Inside the cabin, the envelope lay on the floor with Shelby's name written in adhesive black letters, like those purchased at a craft store. Tearing off a paper towel, I wrapped it twice around my fingers to grasp the unsealed envelope. I slipped out a card.

To the Pearce family,

> No words can ease your loss
> In the suicide of your daughter
> Or the answer to why
> Or bring comfort in the pain.
> Know you are in our thoughts and prayers
> In this difficult time of grief.

We all will miss Shelby.

I stared at the handwritten personalization at the top and bottom of the card. The sender had a warped sense of humor. My jaw dropped, and the card fell from my hand. What kind of sicko broke—?

Someone wanted Shelby dead and concealed the telltale signs of murder. Her time in prison raised the likelihood of her gaining enemies, and her past left a trail of hate and possibly even vengeance, but what else had she done? What information needed to follow her to the grave?

Were the jagged pieces of Shelby's life even sharper than I'd ever considered? I'd overlooked something vital, and although what I'd witnessed today may not be connected to the missing money, I'd not sign off on this case until I had answers.

I slid the card back into the envelope, yet leaving it for Shelby to find seemed wrong, cruel. What good came from messing with Shelby's mind? That labeled me a worse offender than breaking into her home. If she fell prey to depression again, as her prison records indicated, and she committed suicide, I'd own part of the blame.

I'd taken this journey because I believed in justice. Well, that and restoring my pride. The thought of discovering additional crimes with her name on them challenged my near attraction to her. The unknown drew me forward. I could no more abandon my quest than deny my own name.

No matter what I discovered.

I tucked the paper towel–covered card inside my shirt and made certain the interior doors were locked. Unlikely that fingerprints still existed on the card, but the handwriting could be documented in the FBI database. Enough time had passed for the sender to hoof it back to his vehicle, but clues to his name and purpose lay out there in the soft earth. I followed a trail across the back field.

Only God knows the truth, and He is Truth.

16

SHELBY

Home was often described as a state of mind. How quickly I'd embraced this cabin as my sanctuary. No dank smells, concrete, metal, harsh sounds, or fear of assault. Oh, the thrill of caressing my sweet puppy and designing jewelry.

Except this afternoon I chilled the moment I stepped inside my cabin after work.

Someone had invaded my privacy.

Fury raced through me. I'd had enough of the invasion.

The scent of the outdoors clung faintly in the air, my air. A small clod of dirt led into the kitchen and rear door by an intruder's shoe prints. I quickly scanned the visible areas for signs of an unwanted visitor. Without a weapon, the idea of confronting the person labeled me as stupid.

I rubbed my shoulders and retraced my steps outside the cabin to my path of pine cones and sticks. Some were broken. Two sets of prints caught my attention—one had treads of a tennis shoe and the other looked like a western boot. I made my way to the woods' edge and grabbed a fallen pine branch nearly three feet long. Having the thin wood in my hand gave me confidence that if someone attacked me, I could defend myself. Chances were, an assailant would take the limb and beat me with it.

My life had been plagued with trouble since the bus dropped me off in Valleysburg. I held my frail weapon like a baseball bat and crept through the cabin. In every room an intruder had rearranged my meticulously placed belongings, not by much, but enough for me to detect it.

I despised an unseen enemy.

The memory of my first prison beating repeated in my mind—not the cuts, bruises, and broken arm, but the violation of my spirit. An inmate bribed a guard to give her and three friends ten minutes to persuade me to talk about the missing money. I refused. At the time, I longed to forget the many hands assaulting me. The pain taught me how to avoid those who lived to do me harm. Smartened me to prison degradation. The gang set out to build an empire while I counted each day until my release.

Other beatings occurred, but none like the first.

I stared into my bedroom and at the closed door of the second one. Who did I call when my only evidence lay in dirt on the floor, the shape of the drawers in my bedroom, footsteps in the dirt, and a sixth sense crawling up my spine?

Actually no one but James Peterson or Sheriff Wendall. My suspicious nature told me even they could be behind the threats.

Silence kept its secret.

My phone rang with an anonymous caller ID.

"Shelby," the distorted voice said. "Did you receive my calling card?"

"Yes. Why not come to the door when I'm here and knock like a civilized person?"

The voice laughed. "Are you ready to accept my invitation?"

"Which is?"

"Take an overdose, an easy way out. Your parents despise you. Marissa and her daughter are afraid of you. Give them the peace they deserve."

Love for my family had guided my actions for years . . . but I refused to take my own life. That belonged to God. "I'd rather live and see you arrested."

"Always the selfish one."

I stared at my phone after his final words. One bit of information told me the caller knew more than I did about my family . . . I had a niece. All these years I'd wondered if Marissa's child was a girl or a boy. Now I heard it from a person who wanted me dead.

17

DENTON

I stepped into church three times a year—Christmas Eve, Easter, and Mother's Day. Sometimes I attended weddings and funerals, both as a sign of respect. Today gave me an extra God-star. I'd sacrificed sleeping in on a Sunday morning not to strengthen my faith, but to add a notch in my friendship belt with Shelby.

I assumed Shelby would walk in any minute, a way to start a new week out right after a rotten start. I chose a pew midway on the right side, thinking she'd sit close by. *"Doesn't matter where you sit, only that you listen"* echoed from one of my grandpa's sayings. Shelby didn't hit me as a front- or back-row gal.

Five minutes to ten, Shelby slid into a pew on the left in front of me. Go figure. She wore jeans and a shirt . . . so did many other folks. Out of my upbringing and sparse attendance, I'd dragged out slacks and a sport coat to spend an hour in God's house.

Lots of people filed in at the last minute. Edie and her kids sat in front of me, a boy who looked like his mother and a smaller girl with huge dark eyes. Odd that Edie hadn't chosen to sit in Shelby's company. Randy Hughes must have missed the invite because he wasn't there. Then again, he didn't impress me as the churchgoing type. Had no clue about his ex-wife and teenage sons.

Amy-Jo scooted in next to Shelby. I had no clue of Amy-Jo's last name, and she didn't come across as the churchgoing type either. I swallowed a chuckle. Today her ensemble resembled a peacock . . . head to toe.

Pastor Emory, a broad-shouldered man in his late forties, welcomed everyone and thanked them for their care and concern while his family suffered from the flu. He gave announcements and congratulated a couple on forty-eight years of marriage. At the sound of a guitar and drums, I startled. The contemporary service and the pastor in jeans and red tennis shoes reminded me of my parents' church.

An older man in the front pew stood. "Pastor, the newspaper said we have an ex-con in our community. Shelby Pearce murdered a family member and is living among decent people. How are we to handle such an atrocity? How are we to defend ourselves?"

I glanced at Shelby, and she attempted to stand, but Amy-Jo pulled her down onto the hard bench. The older man must not have seen her sitting among them. Before meeting her, I'd have sided with the man. I expected criticism, but in church, where sinners were supposed to find forgiveness and support? No wonder I kept God at a distance.

Pity for Shelby washed over me, which was odd. How could I have compassion for a woman who'd murdered a family member?

"I read the newspaper article." Pastor Emory sighed. "While I'm not disputing the circumstances, whoever wrote the piece chose to be anonymous." He scanned the crowd. "Jesus would want us to give Ms. Pearce an opportunity to regain her dignity, to feel welcome."

"She's not." The man turned to face the crowd. "A good person lies in the ground."

"I suggest an open mind and heart. Be loving and discerning. If you have any other concerns about the matter, please contact me personally."

Shelby rose to her feet, although Amy-Jo attempted to yank her back down again. Edie gasped in front of me. Her son wrapped his arm around her shoulder.

"Pastor Emory," Shelby said. "I'd like a word, please."

He nodded and gestured for her to step to the pulpit. The older man resumed his perch on the front row.

"No thank you. Here is fine." Her back was the only part visible to me, but she trembled. "My name is Shelby Pearce. I chose Valleysburg to begin my life over after recommendations from the prison chaplain who is familiar with the area. My purpose is not to cause problems with anyone, young or old. I found Jesus Christ in prison. He accepted me, my past, my present, and my future. He is leading my life as my Lord and Savior. I ask the citizens of this town to give me a chance to show I'm sincere." Shelby sat.

Heat rushed into my face—for what I'd done to her, deceived her for my own well-being.

The older man stood and looked out at the congregation. "Ms. Pearce, standing up for yourself takes guts. While I'm apprehensive about you living among us, I commend your courage. Accept my apology, and I will give you the chance you requested." He turned to Pastor Emory. "Sorry to interrupt worship."

"No problem. I hope all of you will reflect Jesus in your actions."

The sermon took over the agenda, and I tuned out Pastor Emory.

Yesterday, I followed shoe prints to a country road where the sender of Shelby's card had driven away in a vehicle. Someone had developed a devious plan to get into her head, but the motives defeated me. What else had the person done? Would Shelby open up to me about other possible threats? As far as I was concerned, she'd never see the suicide-sympathy card unless I deemed it necessary. Except . . . she might recognize the handwriting and identify the sender.

The service ended, and I waited in the rear to ask her to lunch. I had my truck to load her bicycle and plans to drive her home later. The older man exited his pew and nodded at her. He mumbled something indiscernible before he moved on. Edie and her two kids joined Shelby and Amy-Jo. Then the pastor and his wife stopped to chat. After-church conversation might take a while.

◉ ◉ ◉

An hour later, Shelby and I sat at a popular restaurant known for its down-home cooking. My order of chicken-fried steak smothered in pepper gravy with mashed potatoes and buttered green beans didn't match her healthier choice.

I patted my belly. "I see a six-mile run in my future, but it will be worth every cholesterol-filled bite."

"And drop of sweat." A hint of a smile met me, and my heartbeat bolted like a schoolboy's.

"Is this your first restaurant meal after your release other than at the café?"

She lifted her chin. How could one woman display such a picture of beauty and innocence? "Edie drove me through McDonald's after picking me up at the bus station. Fabulous hamburger and fries."

I sighed. "My effort is number two. My ego is under the table."

She lifted a glass of iced tea with lemon to her lips. "Friendship isn't based on ego. And you sounded like you were flirting, which is not up for discussion."

Was I interested in Shelby other than learning about the missing money? "My apologies."

She set the glass back on the table. "We had an interesting church service."

I shook my head. "You mean the man who wanted you tarred and feathered? Or the brave stand you took?"

"Neither. I was talking about the pastor's message."

Great. I hadn't paid attention. "Okay, you go first."

"Faith is a part of my every breath. What about you?"

"God and I have a difference of opinion on how He runs things. I attend church, depending on the occasion."

"He's always in control of what's happening in the world," she said.

"So I hear."

"You were there today."

"It fit the occasion."

She tilted her head and sadness cast a shadow on the moment. "Denton, my guess is you've scoured the Internet and read every post and viewed every video about what I did years ago. You heard the older man in church voice his disapproval. Since arriving in Valleysburg, I've been threatened, and I've promised to keep my distance from Edie. You're aware of these things, and it hasn't deterred you. By being seen with me publicly, you risk your reputation and your safety." She hesitated. "Let's be honest here. What's the real reason for your keeping company with me?"

"Do I need one?"

She folded her hands on the table. "Over fifteen years ago, FBI Special Agent Allen Denton McClure was assigned to track down the disappearance of $500K, part of the case involving the murder of Travis Stover. The state of Texas filed the murder charges and tasked the FBI to help locate the money. Agent McClure and his partner, Special Agent Mike Kruse, failed to recover it. No one did. The missing money remains an open case. Back then your hair was dark brown. No mustache or beard. You got rid of your large-framed glasses, possibly in exchange for contacts. I say that because when we took the walk through the woods, your eyes reddened. I assumed because of allergies. You've gone to a lot of trouble to portray a widower finding his way back from grief."

Pain from my betrayal flashed across her eyes. "Your turn, and I deserve the truth."

I'd underestimated her. Now I looked like a fool. I peered at her. Cover my rear or admit the truth? "How long have you known?"

"Since Friday evening. No one gives a puppy without a reason."

"Shelby, I thought the puppy could be a companion. Nothing else."

"And you expect me to swallow another lie?"

"Is that why you agreed to lunch?"

She shrugged. "I'm curious." She studied me as though I were a despicable specimen under a microscope. "Is this about adding credibility to your résumé? A promotion? Are you and Officer Hughes working together?"

"It's about seeking justice."

She glanced away, then back to me. How did she keep her face so calm? "Have you attempted to locate the money all these years?"

I nodded. "Off and on."

She laughed, but it held no humor. "You've wasted years of your life on a travesty. How sad."

"Prove me wrong."

She leaned in closer. "I've spent years trying to understand what happened to Travis's money. But it doesn't control me."

"So your accomplice made off with it?" Contempt scorched like I'd swallowed acid.

"Good one, Denton. If I'd enlisted someone to help me, the money would be long gone. No fool would wait on a killer who might never be released."

"What about the threats since you've arrived?"

"My vote is for Officer Hughes or you."

"It's not me."

"You're a strange man, rather pathetic." She paused. "At the end of your life, what will you have to show for your quest?"

I'd pondered the same thing. "A life spent seeking truth."

"Maybe you should check your road map. This is what I know.

Three months ago, my parole date was announced as well as my relocation plans. You slither into one of Edie's cabins, set yourself up as a good neighbor, and devise ways to convince me you're a great guy. You used a puppy to win my friendship. Rather low, don't you think? How stupid do you think I am?"

My cheeks burned along with my gut. "Apparently I misjudged your intelligence."

Shelby folded her arms over her chest. "I neglected to mention my compliments to your family's dedication to preserving the law. A dad and two brothers viewed as superhero police officers. And to think you broke the mold to enter the FBI. Impressive."

A female server delivered our food, but my appetite had vanished.

"Miss." Shelby focused on the server with an extra dose of sweetness. "I'd like my order boxed to go, and I'll take the check for my meal."

I raised my palm at Shelby. "This is my bill."

She stood. "No thanks. I neither need your deceit nor a handout. But I'm keeping Joy. I hate the thought of returning her to you."

The server set my plate before me and disappeared.

"I can take you home," I said.

"Not necessary, Agent McClure. I'll relieve you of Officer Hughes's bicycle from your truck bed and be on my way. The day's beautiful, and I plan to sort through information about my FBI neighbor." She slipped a denim purse onto her shoulder. "Question, have you stalked me and broken into my home?"

How should I answer?

"Never mind. You already did. The threatening phones calls had better stop too. Breaking the law for a stellar résumé might land you behind bars. Now how ironic would that be?"

18

SHELBY

Truth could hurt worse than a smack in the face. I knew Denton's identity before I'd confronted him, and still I toggled between anger and disappointment. Why would I confess to a murder and accept the consequences that could have ended my life and lie about a theft?

I pedaled faster. This morning in church when the older man had complained about my presence in the community, I tried to bolt. Amy-Jo grabbed my hand and held it in a viselike grip, forcing me to endure the humiliating torment as though she knew my instinct was to flee. But when I finally shook her loose and chose to address the church, peace flooded my whole being.

On the other hand, Amy-Jo claimed this was the first time she'd attended church in years, but Edie had asked her to sit with me. From what she'd seen from the mouthy old man, Amy-Jo would be accompanying me in the future as my personal body-guard. At times, I wondered about her crusty ways. Maybe like me, she came from a troubled past.

Pastor Emory's message about loving our enemies was aimed at me. Why not title the message "Shelby Pearce is not your enemy. Just love her and everything will be okay"?

I wish. Anxiety reached out to consume me. If I wasn't care-ful, I'd slip into paralyzing depression. My release from prison and my hope of a better future needed more than over-the-top encouragement on the part of the pastor. Surely his faith hadn't overshadowed the reality of having a convicted felon in the midst of his congregation.

I had met Mrs. Emory today, and she appeared not exactly friendly but cordial. She might have objected to her husband's donation to my jewelry business, or maybe the tension about my arrival had moved him not to tell her. How many problems had I caused? Amy-Jo's business seemed incredibly busy, but my observa-tions were before the newspaper article.

Leave it alone.

I was overthinking, overreacting, not weighing the facts, and leaving God out of the picture. Besides, I suspected who'd insti-gated the problems—Officer Hughes or Special Agent McClure.

But bitterness only served to harden hearts and build impreg-nable walls. The people of Valleysburg needed time to accept me just like I needed time to work through many of their glares and remarks. No wonder unforgiveness stopped so many people from ever finding peace. I struggled with forgiving those who'd wronged me . . . even Marissa, who'd shed tears of gratitude when I stepped forward to take the blame for Travis's death.

I was determined to find beauty in small things.

Good things had happened this week—new friendships, an enjoyable job, an unexpected furry companion, and an oppor-tunity to sell my jewelry glistened like precious gems and stones.

A patch of wild daises leaning against a rickety, wooden fence

DIANN MILLS

caught my attention. They nodded in the gentle spring breeze as though encouraging me to stay strong and avoid taking matters personally. Nature . . . I loved it so.

The hum of an approaching vehicle caused me to veer onto the grassy shoulder. I glanced behind me to make sure it wasn't a black pickup. Great . . . Denton had chased me down. But my sights aimed toward home, and I had no inclination to endure whatever his excuse for bending the law in his behalf.

The hot truck engine breathed on me, and Denton slowed. The low whish of the power window reinforced his resolve to get my attention. "Shelby, can we talk?"

Seriously? My stomach craved the lunch nestled in Styrofoam, and irritation pelted me. Neither was decent company.

"Let me take you home."

I pedaled faster.

"I want to hear your side of the story."

How long could I continue biting my tongue? He'd lied to me from the moment he introduced himself as the great guy who lived close by. Denton McClure had much to learn from Mr. Rogers about being a good neighbor.

"Whose idea was it to call me with a shove toward suicide?"

"I haven't made any calls to you."

"Right. That's low, don't you think? Or do you just break and enter?"

"I'd like to explain. I want to believe in your innocence. Can you prove to me you know nothing about the stolen money?"

His plea sounded like a whining boy instead of an immature, annoying grown man.

Every crack and stone in the road caught my attention—anything to keep my mind occupied.

"Shelby?"

"You have all the evidence pointing to my innocence. End of discussion."

He gunned his engine and passed me, spitting a fog of dust and dirt. Once he disappeared, I released the tension in my knotted shoulders.

At the cabin, I scanned the area for signs of unwanted company. The rocks I'd placed on the steps hadn't been kicked aside, and the folded piece of paper stuck between the threshold and door hadn't been moved. Satisfied my privacy hadn't been invaded, I chained the bicycle to the front porch, stepped inside with my lunch, and locked the door behind me. I loved on Joy while each room received a thorough inspection.

I'd worried about my puppy while I was gone. Doubtful the person threatening me would spare my sweet pet. Even Denton wouldn't stoop to such degradation. Officer Hughes? He leaned toward the do-anything mode.

Years had gone by since I was emotional about my own stupid actions. Whoever claimed tears were cathartic hadn't ever been this angry . . . and hurt. I thought I'd hardened to manipulation. Prison tutored the innocent in ways that strengthened or destroyed the human spirit. Those were life skills, not just prison skills. But a part of me wanted to give those on the outside of a locked cell the benefit of the doubt. Officer Hughes had already proved me wrong, and Denton did the same. Why had his admittance to what I'd already discovered cut so deeply? Had I fallen prey to his hypnotic brown eyes and the confidence in his walk?

I'd liked Denton McClure. Past tense.

Shame on me.

19

DENTON

I spent the next eight hours rereading every post and article online about Shelby. Some I'd memorized. Some scratched at my gut . . . like Travis Stover killed at close range. The blood spatters on Shelby's and Marissa Stover's clothes. I reviewed photos and videos in which Shelby displayed no apparent remorse. Her impassiveness matched a coldhearted killer. I'd cut her ruthless image into my mind, despised everything about her.

Now I found myself attracted to a woman I thought I loathed. This afternoon, I had chased her down like a desperate man who longed to be understood. Hogwash, as my grandpa used to say. I glanced at the time—10:02 p.m. Popcorn and Coke had been my supper, and a headache plotted against me.

What had I missed that confirmed Shelby's guilt or pointed to her innocence? Her words poured into my thoughts. *"You've wasted years of your life on a travesty."*

Stretching my shoulders, I headed to the fridge for pimento cheese, bread, and butter. While I grilled a cheese sandwich in a cast-iron skillet, I headed back to my laptop to specifically study photos of Shelby and her family during the trial. Made sense to look for body language. Again. Much of the media had labeled her a psychopath, and I believed it too.

Examining each photo took careful scrutiny until I smelled my grilled cheese burning. I yanked the skillet from the burner and scraped off the charred bits from the bottom. Sorta like how I felt if I'd wasted years of my life attempting to prove false charges.

I ate the sandwich anyway while examining the photos. Near midnight, I zoomed in on Shelby staring at her family on the way out of the courtroom on the day the jury reached a verdict. Softened features indicated a twinge of regret. Possibly fear. Or unbelief. Her cuffed hands were a hindrance to reading some nonverbal communication, but her shoulders slumped over a gaunt body, and she sobbed.

She'd shivered in the courtroom, as though her contemptible actions had hit her heart. The media used her tears to validate her guilt. TV and talk shows ran rampant exploiting teen crimes.

Her prison records noted her severe depression, abuse from gangs, and a refusal to eat. The assessment changed after she became a Christian. Except the gang beatings continued.

I headed for bed, but my restless thoughts churned like a whirlpool. Shelby's intelligence helped her to achieve higher education, and I thought for too many years she'd planned the murder and the theft. Now my FBI instincts pushed me into uncertainty. What simmered beneath the surface? Why did someone want her dead? More importantly, who?

I fought the turmoil. The end of my investigation lay in mere days. Soon I'd get back to my job and bury this mess. But I had no real life to speak of. I'd put dating off until this was resolved, while my family urged me to put Shelby's case to rest. They claimed my obsession with her had become a parasite. Their assessment hit the target. Vacations were spent alone. Holidays with my family teetered between awkward and why had I bothered?

My swirling thoughts persisted and robbed me of any rest. I pursued truth like a madman. At 2 a.m., I gave up my efforts to fall asleep. Wide-awake, I grabbed my laptop and crawled back into bed. The screen came to life, and I dug into the FBI's secure site to find a connection between someone in Valleysburg and Shelby's past.

When nothing snared my attention, I searched the Pearce family to see how they'd moved on with their lives. Her parents, close to retirement age, owned and operated a bakery. Marissa worked alongside them. She had a daughter who attended the local high school and made excellent grades. Typical. The family had chosen recovery instead of wearing the badge of a victim.

My thoughts circled back to Valleysburg and Randy Hughes, a bona fide bully. I hadn't figured out if his attitude pointed to protecting Edie or something else. Since my ongoing investigation had led nowhere, I searched for info about Hughes, the representative of Valleysburg's finest. Spit-polished and squeaky-clean. A classic example of a big brother watching over his widowed sister. Except for a few reports of verbal abuse and one of police brutality. Perhaps the plight of Shelby's sister losing her husband intensified Hughes's motivation.

I closed my eyes, more discouraged than I'd been in years.

20

SHELBY

Trepidation surged through me at the thought of delivering my jewelry to Amy-Jo. What if her response to my craftsmanship sprang from something else? I could handle opposition much easier than pity.

Early Monday morning in the gift shop, I presented her with three necklaces and matching earrings crafted from labradorite stones. The labradorite flashed gold, green, blue, and in the sunlight, some even picked up purple shades. I preferred the dark brass wire and its elegant and vintage feel, but I designed one set using blue stones and silver wire. The intricate cross on the back could actually be worn in the front. Each necklace had a two-by-four-inch white card embossed with a thin copper-colored vine and tied with a white, narrow ribbon—thanks to the advice of Edie's web designer, a high school senior on her deceased husband's side of the family. The card indicated each jewelry piece's name, Hebrew meaning, and Scripture.

"These are breathtaking." Amy-Jo picked up a necklace rich with gold and amber hues and read the card. "This is an *Abigail*. 'Gives joy.' 'Always be full of joy in the Lord.' Philippians 4:4." She gingerly laid the necklace on the display case and examined another necklace in a pale-gray, purple, and taupe stone. "*Bella*. 'Devoted to God.' 'Protect me, for I am devoted to you. Save me, for I serve you and trust you. You are my God.' Psalm 86:2." She replaced the second necklace and lifted the third with a predominantly blue stone. "*Davina*. 'Cherished.' 'People who cherish understanding will prosper.' Proverbs 19:8."

Amy-Jo sighed. "Everything about them is perfect, and I love the fact they are reversible. Who knows? I might have to read a Bible." She chuckled at her own words. "I'll have these sold before you leave today and a dozen orders."

All the while she examined each piece, my heart kept cadence to an invisible marching band. "You're perfect for my ego. I'm working on other pieces, but before I start something new, do you want anything designed differently?"

She pursed her ruby-red lips. "Possibly a few more silver-wire pieces. The younger woman will prefer the silver, but the older and more sophisticated woman will snatch the gold and darker wire. I imagine some shades of stone look better with light than dark."

"I'll have a variety including bracelets and earrings. Some will match other pieces, and some will be separate. But all unique designs will have a name and a verse."

"We have Spring Celebration Days coming up in May. Retail goes nuts then. A huge parade, pet show, talent contest, and people from all over fill the streets. How many pieces can you get done in eight to nine weeks?"

Paying Pastor Emory back ASAP penetrated my thoughts. I calculated the hours needed to create the jewelry and the money left from Pastor Emory's check to purchase any supplies. "I have no idea, but I'll work on them whenever I'm not here."

"Know what?" Amy-Jo twirled a strand of mango-colored hair around her finger. "The celebration will set you up as a local artist, and you'd also have money in your pocket."

"Self-confidence and respect would go a long way," I said.

"You can—"

Officer Hughes marched into the café and headed straight toward us. "Shelby Pearce, where were you between the hours of six and seven this morning?"

Amy-Jo wrapped her arm around my waist. "Right here, Randy. Shelby arrived for work at 5:45 and has been here ever since."

He eyed me as though I were sewage. "You need Amy-Jo to do your talking?"

"No, sir." I dug my fingers into my palms. "Just like she told you, I've been here since 5:45."

"Your work hours don't start until seven."

"Amy-Jo changed them right from the start. Why?"

"Edie called me, said she heard someone messing with her SUV. She grabbed her rifle and chased 'em off."

"And you assumed it was me?"

"Edie had no problems until you came to town. If it wasn't you, then I bet you know who's responsible."

Officer Hughes reminded me of a couple of ominous prison guards. "Did she see anybody?"

"Nah."

"Now you can take your investigation in another direction." I lifted my chin.

The bells over the café door jingled. "We have customers." Amy-Jo motioned to the door. "Shelby, you have work to do." She turned to Officer Hughes. "Unless you're ordering breakfast, I suggest you leave and stop harassing my employee."

His neck and face flamed red. "A little time." He leaned close to me. "That's all you got. Better make the best of it until I find the evidence to lock you up or run you off." Randy stomped out the door.

"He's always been this way," Amy-Jo whispered. "Never understood why when he and Edie's parents were kind people."

I questioned whether police work allowed him to reinforce his bad habits, but I chose not to voice it. "He must be strangely wired."

"Edie told me he's been a bully since grade school. Randy's ways are like a spray bottle of meanness. Somebody has to stop him because he's getting worse."

21

My parole stipulated counseling, and I despised it. My personal life added notches to the lies of my past, present, and future. After work, I slowly pedaled to the church office for the first counseling session with Pastor Emory. I sat across the desk from him and Mrs. Emory, wishing I were somewhere else.

Pastor Emory's jeans and T-shirt topped with a tan sports jacket gave him an average person look—friendly and approachable. His brown hair held a few strands of gray, and he styled it a bit longer than most men. Mrs. Emory reminded me of a pit bull in black pants. She scooted a chair beside him as though she expected the worst from me. Might not hurt if I offered her some of the grace I craved from others. She did have a flawless olive complexion and large green eyes. Seemed like my mistrust for too many people caused me to judge them. Goodness, I didn't even know the woman. After all, Mrs. Emory's presence ensured his protection against gossip and slander, a precaution I respected.

I pushed away my lousy frame of mind and studied the pristine office, containing overflowing bookcases, family photos, and reflections of his faith.

"I appreciate you and Mrs. Emory conducting the counseling."

He leaned back in his chair. "We're glad to help."

Dare I mention his check? Did his wife know about his generosity? The idea of coming between a pastor and his wife sounded deplorable, but I feared the damage had already occurred.

"Thank you for the funds to finance my small business. I'll pay you back in installments, beginning at our next counseling session, around seventy dollars."

"I'm not worried about repayment. The money was a gift to help you get started."

"I think returning the money as soon as possible is commendable." Mrs. Emory squared her shoulders. She'd be an attractive brunette if she would smile. "The gesture speaks well for rebuilding your reputation and future."

Maybe they'd been stung by lending money in the past. "My thoughts exactly."

"Ms. Pearce," the pastor said. "Outside of a few hiccups, are you getting settled?"

"I've experienced good times and not-so-good." I shared with him about James Peterson and how I valued his support as my parole officer. "My goal, and his too, is for me to beat the odds and weave my life into this community."

"He's active in the community, coaches Little League, and is on the school board."

The info revealed a good man. "Sheriff Wendall has also been helpful."

"Not like Officer Hughes?"

I refused to go there. "He's concerned about his community and sister."

"Ms. Pearce, let's speak the truth here. While I must send an overview of our sessions to the parole board, I promise you our discussions are confidential. Randy Hughes isn't on your side."

"Yes, sir. Will he ever be?"

He sighed. "Doubtful, unless God gets ahold of him."

His unspoken words aligned with Amy-Jo's. I tried to pray for whatever misfortune had affected Officer Hughes, but until I could forgive him and mean it, the prayers wouldn't surface. "Do you recommend I avoid Edie at church and stop the sibling arguments about me?"

"Have you asked her?"

"She insists our friendship is important. But we aren't meeting in public."

"Then you have your answer." He opened a legal pad and scanned it. "You received severe beatings in prison, before and after you became a Christian." Mrs. Emory gasped, and he took his wife's hand. "I forgot to inform my wife about those."

"I'm so sorry." Mrs. Emory paled.

"Shelby was hospitalized four times with injuries from a gang," the pastor said. "Broken bones and a concussion."

"I . . . I was horrible when you entered the office." She touched her mouth. "Please—"

"No need to apologize. I understand how I appear in light of my criminal record." This part of the counseling I could handle. I explained the problems in prison were because I refused to admit knowledge of a crime I hadn't committed, and I'd attempted to defend a young woman whom they had chosen to abuse. Other times were a refusal to be part of a gang and to avoid guards' lewd advances.

"How did those occurrences make you feel about God?" Pastor Emory said.

"He promises never to abandon us, and I'm alive."

"Have you forgiven the women and the guards?"

"I'm trying. Just when I think I've moved past it, a memory pops up that brings it all back."

"With a vengeance?"

I nodded. "Discernment and wisdom are lifelong lessons. But sometimes it's all a blur."

"If you're willing, we can work on what happened to you in prison."

The thought of reliving the beatings clawed at my stomach. Some injuries couldn't be healed. "Not sure if I'll ever be able to place them in a locked corner of my heart. Maybe looking over my shoulder is a good habit. Anyway, I'd like to put the ugliness behind me." I meant it, as long as he didn't probe into Travis's death.

"In the weeks ahead, we'll visit those painful moments. Talk through your emotions and pray for healing. Mrs. Emory and I have prayed for you, and we're here to offer friendship as well as guidance."

My twice-broken arm ached. No reason except the vivid details of the beatings jarred my senses. Always did. I could only assume the psychological and spiritual growth demanded courage. Other people's actions in my history included. "External rehabilitation is easier to accomplish than internal."

"But you're not alone, neither have you been since you made a decision to trust Jesus. Who we are stems from examining our past and choosing to move forward with God."

Mrs. Emory jotted something on a piece of paper and slid it my way. "Please call me anytime, day or night."

"Especially if you are hit with depression," he added. "I see that was a problem in the past."

Was my life an open book for everyone to see? "Thank you." Pastor Emory and his wife meant well, but neither could discover the damages beneath the visible scars.

I left the church with one destination—the newspaper office.

⊙   ⊙   ⊙

Some days were met with enthusiasm and others grew sour as the day progressed. Unless I chose joy each morning, I couldn't complain about my day. In prison, I envisioned Marissa, my obedient sister, walked with me, not in the same cell but as an invisible companion to share my thoughts. That was love—conversations of the heart. Today had held its share of good things and challenges. I hoped my next stop before heading home wasn't a mistake.

I opened the door of the newspaper office and smelled what I'd always termed as newspaper ink. An inner door separated the lobby from the printing area, but the odor swirled about. Not offensive, just distinctive. I stared at the receptionist and inwardly moaned—the judgmental woman who'd ordered tarts for the ladies' mission group. I approached the counter with Saturday's edition in my hand.

"We meet again." I mustered cheerfulness into my words.

One quick look and she darkened. "Yes." She focused on her computer.

"I'd like to speak to the owner or editor in charge."

"Do you have an appointment?" Still no eye contact.

"No, ma'am."

"Then there's no point in being here, is there, Ms. Pearce?"

"The associate editor will do. I only need five minutes."

"I assume you don't have an appointment with him either?"

"Correct. Please ask if I can speak to him."

"He's busy."

I pointed to a small seating area. "I'll wait."

She tapped a manicured nail on the counter. "I'll check but I make no promises."

I thanked her and took a seat. Within ten minutes the door opened to a man in jeans and a black T-shirt who reminded me of a rock star minus a guitar.

"Ms. Pearce?"

I nodded, and he joined me in one of the metal chairs. "How may I help you?"

"Yes, sir. Thank you for seeing me. Saturday's paper ran an article on me. I understand freedom of the press, but I'd like to know who wrote it."

"No idea. The article came to me via email, and when I attempted to respond to the writer, I got a mail-delivery error stating the email address was bogus."

"What happened then?"

"I verified the contents and chose to print it." He ran his fingers through three-inch-spiked red hair. "Do you want to write a rebuttal?"

"No, sir. The contents were factual. I simply wanted to talk to the writer."

"Why?"

The thought of telling him I'd been threatened and run off the road nudged me as a mistake. Exactly what I wanted to avoid.

My silence must have made the man uncomfortable because he cleared his throat. "I'm sorry I can't help you. Have you experienced more difficulty because of the article?"

"Some."

He stood. "I'm sorry. Is there anything else I can help you with?"

Summary dismissal could be welcomed or scrape at a nerve, and I refused to cause a scene. I'd find the writer on my own. "No, sir. Thank you for your time."

I left the *Valleysburg Gazette* with a repeated reminder that the same laws informing the public of my prison release had also given me a second chance at life.

DENTON

If I were to learn the truth about Shelby, even if I'd been wrong all these years, I needed to investigate who'd targeted her. Mid-afternoon, I drove into town to talk to Sheriff Wendall. Time to come clean with him.

We met in his office with the door closed at my request. "I need to explain why I'm in Valleysburg."

Not a muscle moved on his face. "What's going on, Denton? Aren't you a math teacher who needed to recover from your wife's death?"

"No."

He moved his Stetson to the corner of his desk and folded his hands. "Whatcha hiding?"

"I'm FBI Special Agent Allen Denton McClure on assignment. Not a math teacher or a widower. I work out of the Houston office." I showed him my ID and continued with my mission to find out where Shelby Pearce had stashed the missing money.

"After all these years?"

"I worked the case as a rookie agent when she was arrested for murder. The money came from the Stovers' nonprofit account."

He shook his head. "I don't have a thing to give you. She's been here a week, and someone is trying to run her off. Is it you?"

Second person to ask me that. "Not my style. But Randy Hughes might be behind it."

"Nah. He wants her out of Edie's life. Claims she made a mistake in renting Shelby a cabin."

"Do you think he'd confess his part?"

"He's not behind the crimes against Shelby. Hughes can be a good cop."

"Can be?"

"He's wading through a few tough times."

The sheriff wasn't going to relay anything personal to me. I couldn't blame him when I'd lied about my FBI position. "How many incidents do you know about?"

Sheriff Wendall frowned. "Three—the shot fired into Edie's tire, the note shoved under Shelby's cabin door, and the attempt to run her off the road. No leads."

"There's more. Yesterday she accused me of making threatening calls. I have no idea what was said to her. Thought I'd ask you to check her phone records."

"Need a warrant."

"Not if she gave you permission."

"And why would she?" The sheriff raised an eyebrow.

"I told you she'd received threatening calls, and they weren't from me."

"Why did she suspect you?"

I told him about Shelby discovering my real identity. "She's not happy with me right now. The other thing . . ." I produced the suicide-sympathy card from inside my jacket and told him how I came by it.

He took the card and snorted. "Let me get this right. You broke into her cabin, and while you're there, someone slides this under the door. You take out after 'em, but you lose the trail and never see the person's face."

"Right." Put that way, my actions sounded worse than I intended. "Take a look at the card's contents." I'd just confessed to breaking and entering, and the sheriff had valid reasons to arrest me.

He read the card and eyed me. "Someone is messin' with her head."

"Her past indicates a propensity to depression."

The sheriff stood and arched his shoulders. He might be small in stature, but his countenance emitted power. "Are you justifying a crime by stating you stole the card to protect her from herself?"

"Guess so."

"Why? Looks to me like you'd be the agent on record if she spilled her guts or if she killed herself, you'd have no money trail."

"Probably both."

"Our line of work means gathering evidence, but this is low. Unethical."

I rubbed my palm on the side of my pants. "I'm beginning to think she has no knowledge of the money."

"That means a lot of your years down the drain. What about your gaining access to her cabin? What's the motivation there?"

"None. I'm guilty."

He sat and laid the card between us. "What do you expect to accomplish by coming to my office?"

"Two things—help to discover if she knows the money's whereabouts and why someone wants her dead."

"Why would I?" He glared at me, a technique I'd used during interrogations of suspected criminals.

"I was hoping you'd pay her a visit, a follow-up about what happened last week. Tell her I gave you my purpose in befriending her and claimed not to have made the calls."

He rolled his chair back and walked to the door. Grabbing the knob, he studied me. "Agent McClure, I don't need the FBI telling me how to do my job. I'll talk to Ms. Pearce because she's the victim here—more than once. But let's get a few things straight. If you step over the line again, your rear's in jail. And if she finds out about your breaking and entering into her home and presses charges, your rear's in jail. If I contact the FBI about your actions, they'll put your rear in jail. In the meantime, I'm talking to Houston FBI about them sending you and not consulting me. Undercover or no undercover, you're not in charge. I'm the law in this town."

"My apologies for taking advantage of you and the community."

He crossed his arms over his chest. "Shelby Pearce is a personal project from your rookie days, and you're a poor loser. Also looks like you're trying to be a hero. Makes me wonder if you two are taking lessons from each other."

Stupidity slapped me in the face with my unorthodox actions. "I'd like the card to run prints and analyze the handwriting."

"Nope. The evidence is mine. I'm capable of conducting an investigation."

"Will you let me know the results?"

"Depends on the findings and my conversation with Houston FBI."

I'd done a great job of making myself look like a rogue FBI agent in a bad movie. But Houston had assigned me to the case and knew where I was living. "Are you going to give Shelby the card?"

"Haven't decided. In the meantime, don't leave town. You're a person of interest in Ms. Pearce's case. Conversation ended."

23

SHELBY

In the past, I knew what my predators wanted. Not so much now. I'd stabbed my finger twice with an awl while twisting wire and working with a tissue wrapped over the cut proved cumbersome. I'd add safety gloves to my next supply order. Hard to focus on designing new pieces with the counseling session fresh on my mind and on the heels of what I'd learned about Denton.

My dealings with most men blurred my vision in shades of gray and black. Dad and I used to be pals, and I'd loved Travis like a brother. Many years had trickled by since then. Denton had shoved a little green into my life, offering hope and healing for a few hours. Rats, focusing on him solved nothing. I was doomed for a colorless existence.

Like a child needing comfort, I sat on the sofa and held Joy. She snuggled close to me.

The fixings for an omelet took over, and I concentrated on

dicing bell pepper and onion. The familiar sound of crunching gravel drew my attention to the window. Sheriff Wendall parked and walked to the cabin. Now what? He knocked in rhythm to my knees. I prayed before I opened the door.

"Evening, Shelby. Hope you don't mind me using your first name."

"Not at all, sir. How can I help you?"

"I'd like to talk to you for a few minutes if you don't mind. Our office hasn't figured out who's been harassing you, and I have a few questions."

I invited him inside. When would someone in a law enforcement uniform no longer churn my stomach?

He nodded at my work area. "I see you're makin' jewelry. My wife brought home a right pretty necklace from Amy-Jo's Café, been tellin' her friends about it. Already makin' a list of what she wants for Christmas."

His kind words relaxed me. "Please give her my thanks." I pointed to the sofa. "Have a seat. Can I get you something?"

"I'm good, and I won't take up much of your time. The counter here is fine." He pulled out a stool and removed his gray felt Stetson. "Have you experienced any more threats?"

I pondered how to answer.

"Your hesitancy confirms what Denton McClure told me today."

"Which was?"

"You discovered his FBI status and accused him of crimes against you, including phone threats. I'd like to know more about what's goin' on." He offered compassion in his demeanor. "Why didn't you come to me about the calls?"

"Because they're threats, Sheriff, and telling you about them potentially puts those I care about in danger. Someone believes I'm a hindrance to Valleysburg, and he or she isn't giving up. Honestly, I'm questioning if I should leave."

"Taking off to another town shows the caller won. And you

aren't a runner. Whoever committed these crimes is breaking the law. If you have any idea who is responsible, I need a name. I've questioned Officer Hughes and Denton. Both claim they're not responsible. Agent McClure is working here on assignment to find out if you are part of an embezzlement scheme from years ago. The FBI claims he has an impeccable record, and for what it's worth, I believe he's only after the truth."

What about his breaking and entering? "Denton and Officer Hughes could be behind the threats, or one of them could have written the article in Saturday's paper."

"I received a call from the receptionist at the newspaper office. She said you'd been there and wanted to know who'd written it. When I questioned her further and talked to the assistant editor, I learned you were well within your rights. If I'd been the subject of that article, I'd want to know who was behind it too." He stared at me, and I could almost see the wheels turning inside his head. "What are the threats about?"

"An encouragement to leave town and not pollute respectable people." I refused to fall into a hole of anyone feeling pity for me. The urgings to commit suicide were a puzzle when I had no idea who'd gain by my death. "Were you able to make any connection with the first three letters of the truck's license plate that ran me off the road?"

"I never read anything of the sort in the report." He frowned. "Did you give the info to Officer Hughes?"

Officer Hughes's negligence came as no surprise. "Yes, but I wasn't able to identify the state."

He pulled a notepad and pen from his shirt pocket. "I'll run what you have and will keep you informed."

My phone rang. The blocked number indicated my anonymous caller, and I wrestled answering it.

Sheriff Wendall slid the phone's screen to him and turned it back to me. "Answer this, Shelby. Put it on Speaker. Prove to me this isn't a legitimate threat."

I pressed the Speaker button. "This is Shelby."

"What's the sheriff doing there?" the distorted voice said.

"Following up on a couple of things from last week."

"So am I. I suggest you let him know this is a friend. If you want your loved ones to be safe, better do exactly what I've told you."

"And if I refuse?"

"Then I start with hurting your friends in Valleysburg and will move on to your family. Suicide makes the most sense, right?"

"Except it makes no sense as long as I abide by the terms of my parole."

"I'm losing patience with your lack of guts. This must be handled soon, or you'll have regrets."

"Then let's have a face-to-face. Are you a twelve-year-old who's mastered voice distortion?"

"You're more stupid than I thought. Who do you want eliminated in your life? Edie? Amy-Jo? Denton? What about the sheriff?"

"I could leave Valleysburg, change my name."

"Leaving won't change a thing."

"All right. Just give me a little time to—"

The caller clicked off.

I laid my phone on the counter and clenched my fists against my legs. What should I do?

The sheriff scratched his head. "Shelby, this isn't going away."

"Why does suicide mean more to my stalker than killing me and not leaving any evidence?"

"The caller is certain you have vital information of some kind. And while the person doesn't have a problem hurting others, they, and I think it's more than one person, draw the line when it comes to killing you."

"No blood on their hands," I whispered.

"And I think you know who it is."

I stared at him, and a name flashed across my mind. I shook away the thought.

The sheriff glanced at his watch. "I need to go. Someone's watching the cabin. Do I have permission to run your phone records?" When I agreed, he continued. "I suggest picking up a burner phone as soon as possible. Use it to contact me and those who might get hurt."

"And you can trace it?"

"Technology offers law enforcement the means to investigate what formerly looked impossible. We can also run the voice through our database. If the person is in our system, we are good to go."

I wouldn't be able to talk to Edie until I bought a new phone. We'd enjoyed texts and calls, and I wasn't ready to let go of our friendship. Although my reasoning was selfish.

Sheriff Wendall walked to the door. "Is there anything here in the cabin or stashed on the property that could be used against you or is of value to someone else?"

"Nothing."

"I want to be informed of everything, no matter how insignificant it seems. But not on this phone."

"Yes, sir." Fear rattled my bones. Intuition told me if I left Valleysburg, the problems would stalk me. Staying here threatened those whom I'd grown to cherish, but according to the threats, I was running short on time. At what point would the caller run out of patience?

A plan swept through my mind . . .

24

After Sheriff Wendall left, weariness settled around me, and hopelessness invited my old enemy called despair to come calling. The person or persons urging me to commit suicide had to stop before depression sent me spiraling. How could I react in a way that would take the satisfaction out of the stalker's game? An idea from earlier in the evening made more sense. The details would take time . . .

Someone pounded on my door. I froze, and a thousand scenarios bombarded my mind.

"Shelby, it's Denton. Can we talk?"

I made my way to the door and leaned my head against it. "Please, I've had enough for one day. Just leave me alone."

"I get it. I'm a jerk. Don't blame you at all. Except I'm asking if you will hear me out. Have I been wrong all these years?"

"Ya think?" But a chilling fear left me pondering if his revelation focused on the money, Travis's murder, or another ploy.

"I won't stay long."

"Denton, I'm tired, furious, and my shift starts at 5:45 in the morning."

"Ten minutes, please. The truth is, I've been involved with this mess almost as long as you have, and in a week's time, you've shaken my convictions. Yes, I lied to you, but I haven't sent you threatening calls."

"Any of your speech include an apology?" I longed to hear him clomp down the porch steps.

"I admitted I was a jerk, and I'm sorry. I'd like to start all over as friends."

"There's that friends pitch again. Why?" I hesitated at Denton's second plea to hear him out. Dare I give him the grace he hadn't shown me? I thought about Mrs. Emory . . . Losing my temper appealed to justice and fairness but not my commitment to faith. As much as I detested my own actions to yield to his request, the metal doorknob twisted in my hand. "All right. Ten minutes."

"Thank you." Once inside, he sat on my sofa, and I slipped into the chair opposite him. A few smile lines fanned out from his brown eyes. "I'll start at the beginning . . . with honesty."

"That's one minute for the past fifteen years, not ten."

He pressed his lips together, no more amused than I. "You remember me as an agent who worked the original case. Your arrest was my first opportunity to investigate a major crime, not the murder charges but the theft. The police requested FBI assistance, and my partner and I were assigned. I desperately wanted to prove myself to the FBI. Instead, I failed and blamed you. My pride took a beating. My dad and two brothers were highly decorated police officers, and earning their approval meant everything to me."

Denton paused. "I was engaged prior to entering the FBI, and she broke it off during my training at Quantico. The same day you were sentenced, she agreed to marry my middle brother, Andy. Sounds weak, but it's the truth. You went to prison, and I continued working other FBI cases, but I always searched for the money and the evidence to pin it on you."

I listened. Did he expect me to feel sorry for him? "So your self-worth is based on your performance?" The moment the words left my mouth, I regretted them. "That was uncalled for. Please continue."

"What I never expected was to like you, and today I realized the girl back then is not the woman today. Something changed you, and if it's the Jesus-thing, I'm happy for you. For whatever it's worth, I don't think you stole the money anymore."

I digested his words and held tightly to concealing my emotions. I'd learned from my online searches that his fiancée married his brother. That must have stung. "You've known me a week. Why would I believe you when this sounds like a tactic to earn my trust and save your ego?" I breathed in deeply for patience. "I'm a convicted murderer, but you want to be friends. How very noble."

"You're right. No reason to believe me. But it's all I have."

"What do you want from me?"

"To tell me if you're hiding any information or protecting the person who's threatened you. Let me find that person behind the crimes."

"I'd be an idiot to trust you."

"True. Guess I'll need to prove my sincerity." His attention bore into me, and his tone softened. "One more thing."

Now what? "Go ahead, Denton. You have five minutes left."

"I broke into your cabin."

I rose to my feet, fury boiling through my body. "So it was you. You found nothing, so you believe I'm innocent? Time to leave."

"I have four minutes left. Please, Shelby, sit."

"I'll stand, thank you. Make your miserable excuse fast." I gathered up Joy from her box. I needed something to hold on to.

"While I was here, someone shoved an envelope under the door. I attempted to follow him or her but lost the trail."

"Where's—?"

"I opened it. Read it, a greeting card personalized to the Pearce family expressing sympathy regarding your suicide."

I was seldom taken aback by the depravity of human beings, but my mouth went dry. "I want to see the handwriting on the card."

"Sheriff Wendall has it."

"You gave my property to him?"

Denton paused, and I assumed he was grappling for words. "Not intentionally. Your past shows an issue with acute depression, and I didn't see any reason to trigger the problem again. I showed the card to him, told him of my FBI position, and he kept it."

I paced the room, too upset to pray. "You're my keeper? Do you think by coming here tonight with this crazy story that I'd believe your nonsense? Or are you concerned if I gave in to suicide, you'd never be able to find the money?"

"Nothing along those lines. I wanted to protect you from making a terrible mistake."

"Really? Is this a new method of FBI interrogation?" The man had hurt me. More like I'd allowed him to crawl inside my head . . . and maybe my heart. "What does Sheriff Wendall intend to do with my card?"

"He's investigating it." Denton walked to the door.

Why hadn't the town's good sheriff revealed that info earlier? "If I had a suspect for the threats, I'd tell the sheriff. You and Officer Hughes are a pair." I gestured him out the door and secured the lock behind him.

I would not get much sleep tonight. My kaleidoscope held so many shades of gray, a mix of life and death, that the idea of adding color to my life faded with each passing hour.

25

DENTON

I had slept hard as though the adage *confession is good for the soul* applied to a weary body too. Not even a dream to interrupt my rest. Except I woke with guilt raging through me like a fever. I rode Big Red for an hour and thought about Shelby. If I were into God like my parents and grandparents, I'd do the prayer thing. But that would mean I'd stopped blaming Him for the mess of the world. The irony of it all lay in Shelby's transformation. Had she morphed into the woman of today because of her own determination . . . or the Jesus-thing?

My horse took me by Shelby's cabin as though I needed to ensure she'd gone to work without any problems. I knocked on the door, and nothing greeted me but singing birds and a distant cow. Now what? If this were a regular case, I'd have my strategy memorized.

Amy-Jo's Café served up a tasty breakfast . . .

An hour later, I sat in a booth and gave the waitress my order. Shelby stood behind the bakery case. Did she feel comfortable appeasing customers like she'd done in her younger days? Or did the memories bring back what she longed to forget? In the midst of the busy morning, Amy-Jo waved at me, and I waved back. Had Shelby told her about my deceit? Probably not, or the woman would have tossed me out of her café.

My attention returned to Shelby. She gave the customer a tender smile, genuine but sad, and melancholia emitted from her blue-gray eyes. Her smooth face and haunting beauty hid her past and present fears. I caught her gaze, and her features tightened. She didn't look my way again, and I couldn't blame her.

I wanted to offer her wisdom and encouragement, but what? How could one woman get under my skin in such a short time? Yet I'd known her for years, followed her every tragedy, new development, and change.

The gift shop carrying Shelby's jewelry raised my curiosity, and I ventured over there until my breakfast arrived. Last night Shelby had been working on her latest design, but asking her about them didn't hit the appropriate mark. A necklace dangled from a display over *Simply Shelby*. The dark wire framing an amber-and-brown stone looked well-crafted to me. Each piece had a name and a corresponding Bible verse. Shelby struck me as a deep soul determined to show a new woman. I admired that.

I returned to the booth and eyed the breakfast before me. Hungry as a growing boy, I finished bacon, eggs, hash browns, and two flaky biscuits oozing with apple butter. The food filled my belly with more satisfaction than I deserved.

Outside in the sunshine, I tried to breathe in the fresh air. But a cloud of remorse for the times I'd upset Shelby hovered over me, and I couldn't leave without apologizing. I retraced my steps and waited until the last customer received his pastry.

Shelby blinked. "What would you like?" Cold and formal.

"I'm sorry. Right from the beginning when we met face-to-face, I'd misjudged you, and I violated your privacy." I paused to pull together a shred of professionalism. "I repeat, I believe you're innocent of embezzlement." I left the café a second time, not need-ing her reply, only to be heard.

I dropped by Sheriff Wendall's office and relayed last night's conversation with Shelby. He complimented me on my adherence to the truth. Not sure how I felt about his attaboy, but I thanked him anyway.

"The card left at Shelby's cabin is minus any identifying finger-prints." The sheriff eyed me with a generous dose of disdain, which I deserved. "For the record, and I'm tellin' you this out of the kindness of my heart, I requested the FBI to do the handwritin' analysis."

I could request the report through my secure access. "Thanks. I'll keep you posted on what happens on my end."

"That would be an improvement." He chuckled and I joined him. "Ya know, Denton, I was raised to believe a man has two choices—right or wrong. Nothin' in between. Officer Hughes will no longer work any incidents related to Shelby."

I understood perfectly.

Outside, Randy Hughes stopped me in the parking lot, wear-ing his typical frown and bad-cop swagger. He had watched too many cop movies depicting law enforcement as worse than the criminals. He nodded at the building housing the sheriff's depart-ment. "Why were you here?"

"Personal."

"My house, my business."

"Not when my taxes pay your salary."

Hughes swore. "I can make life real hard for you."

I turned. "It's FBI Special Agent McClure. I wouldn't advise threatening a federal agent."

Hughes's face reddened while satisfaction swirled through me.

⊙　⊙　⊙

A nudging urged me to call Mike Kruse, my former partner. Fifteen years ago, we worked the embezzlement side of Shelby's case. We'd talked several times over the years—more like I contacted him when I needed his input. He now worked the civil rights division in Dallas. Mike responded on the first ring. We swapped small talk about life, his approaching retirement, family, and golf games until he asked for the real reason I'd called.

"Unless you're dying or getting married, something's speaking louder than your words."

"Shelby Pearce."

He moaned. "How many times do we need to go over this? Have you dug up new evidence?"

"I'm living in the same town as Pearce, working another angle of the case. Perhaps an aspect we missed."

"You've had plenty of years to come up with a dozen. Since you're living there, I'll listen."

I explained the happenings, including the threats. "She had no part of embezzling the money. I'm sure of it."

"Never expected to hear 'innocent' from your lips. Why the change of heart?"

"When she went to prison, parole was a possibility for the future. So why refuse to acknowledge embezzling the money when she might never have access to it? Years ago, you asked me the same thing. Except I wouldn't listen. I believed in the accomplice theory, and I should have listened to you."

"I'm marking this on my calendar—Denton McClure admits he's been wrong. What about her has changed your mind?"

"More than what I could verbalize."

"Try me."

"Another time, Mike, when I'm able to weigh the girl then and the woman now. Looking at what we've learned over the years, what was your gut reaction to her during the trial and interviews?"

"She confessed to murder. But something never seemed right about the theft, and the prosecuting attorney did his best to get a name or her accomplice from her. You've worked this case sporadically since it happened. Anyone else grab your attention? Anyone in her hometown come into a sudden cash flow? I know you've monitored reports from the area."

"No one from Sharp's Creek. Her parents still own the bakery, and her sister works in the family business."

"Who has Shelby kept in contact with over the years?"

"Zilch."

"Do you have suspects for the threats?" Mike continued.

"Possibly a Valleysburg local motivated by a need to protect folks from an ex-con."

"Keep your eyes open, Denton." Mike paused. "Poke around. When you get concrete evidence, call me. Back then we found unidentifiable smudged fingerprints on the murder weapon. Maybe we can find a match."

26

SHELBY

If I could discover my enemy's motivation, I could reverse engineer the reasons and confront the culprit. Tuesday afternoon, thoughts from last night's conversation with Sheriff Wendall and Denton anchored me to explore luring my enemy into a trap. With what had happened since arriving here, I gave the person no leeway—someone had a definite agenda.

Swallowing my pride came at a cost, but this mess had sprawled to affect others.

After locking up the cabin, I walked to Denton's. The jaunt through nature calmed me—the sights, sounds, and cooler temps. He could be the one behind this mess, and if so, my request would add points to his side. I shivered.

Nothing to keep score here. My only goal was to stop the threats.

At Denton's cabin, a little smaller than mine, I knocked on the door. His eyes widened at my arrival. Catching him off guard was well worth humbling myself to request his help.

"I wasn't who you expected?" I said.

"Not exactly."

"Shall I leave?"

"Not at all. Come on in."

"If you have time, I'd like to talk in confidence."

He stepped back and led me to a round kitchen table and single chair, the only visible space not covered with stacks of papers. "Sorry about the mess."

"I'm not here to scrutinize your housekeeping." I hesitated, certain I'd lost my mind, and he'd toss me out. "First of all, thank you for your apology and for the belief in my innocence. I admit I have no idea if I can ever trust you. But all that aside, I need a favor, and you're the only one who has the contacts to help me."

He turned his ear to me as if he hadn't heard correctly. "You're asking *me* for a favor?"

"Ironic, right? This could possibly help you locate the money and right your career. I need to stop whoever is stalking me. The missing money is the only thing that makes sense."

"You're sure Travis Stover's family isn't behind this?"

"Ninety-nine percent sure. They're missionaries, remember?"

"All right, I'm listening."

"I need to discuss an idea with Sheriff Wendall, but I can't use my phone in case mine's been hacked." I took a breath. "Would you call him for me?"

"Easy enough. Must be more. This is too simple." He pressed in a number and handed me his phone.

"Sheriff Wendall, this is Shelby Pearce. I'm using Denton McClure's phone."

"Is he in one piece?"

I laughed despite the circumstances. "Yes. Want to talk to him?"

"Nah, I believe you, little lady. What's goin' on? Another problem?"

"I'd like to meet with you in person. But I'm not sure how to go about keeping it a secret. But if you're agreeable, it needs to be so no one would recognize you."

"Hmm, anythin's possible. We can arrange a meetin'. Let me talk to Denton."

I gave him the phone. "Your turn." The one-sided conversation consisted of "Yes" and "Sure thing."

Denton ended the call. "He'll be at your cabin around eleven thirty tonight."

⊙ ⊙ ⊙

Hours later I closed the blinds and crafted jewelry until a knock at the door and Sheriff Wendall's voice announced his arrival. No doubt my stalker had me in his sights, and the sheriff and Denton had rehearsed whatever was about to unfold. He drove a sedan and wore khakis and a knit shirt, sharing little likeness to the country sheriff representing Valleysburg's law enforcement.

I opened the door. "Can I help you?" The sheriff handed me a business card, and I pretended to read it.

"Ms. Pearce, I represent the district parole office, and I have a few questions regarding your parole." No signs of his usual Southern drawl.

"Is something wrong?"

"It's been brought to my attention that you've violated a condition. I'd like to discuss it."

"Should I contact my parole officer?"

"He's aware of my visit."

I opened the door wider for him to enter. My wild idea to find a resolution to the threats bounced around my brain until my head throbbed, weighing the obstacles and what I'd do if the sheriff rejected my plan. I closed and bolted the door.

"Curiosity is gettin' the best of me."

I offered my sofa, coffee, and a few of Amy-Jo's sea-salt,

chocolate-caramel cookies. He requested two. While I poured coffee and warmed the cookies, he seated himself on the sofa.

"Do you have a name for who's stompin' on your freedom?"

I handed him his warm goodies. "I wish. I want to coax him or her into revealing their identity."

"Should be interestin'. Whatcha got?"

"Just an idea, but here goes. Fake my suicide with a note left on my nightstand that offers clues to the whereabouts of the missing money in the cabin. If it's possible, enlist an ambulance to pick up my body, falsify a death certificate, arrange a newspaper obituary, also plant a newspaper article that shows I'd embezzled the money with the same clues from my suicide note, and establish proof I was cremated. In the meantime, I'll stay hidden for a few days to see who breaks into the cabin."

"Not a bad plan." He rubbed his stubbled jaw. "It would take twenty-four-hour surveillance, and I don't have the officers to spare."

"There's a pine tree that faces my front door. Could a camera be placed there? Another thought is a small camera at my back door."

He nodded. "The other problem is who would pronounce you legally dead."

"Could the coroner's signature be forged?"

"Possibly." He paused. "I could talk to the FBI, but that means lettin' Denton in on what's goin' on."

I grimaced. "Is there another way?"

"Not really. I understand not trusting him after what he's done, but I'll keep him on a tight leash."

"I understand. But involving Denton doesn't mean I like the idea."

"If we did those things and followed through with a trap, how would you explain faking your death to your parole officer?"

"Can Mr. Peterson be trusted?"

"Without a doubt. He's in your corner."

Mr. Peterson's reliability rated higher than Denton's. "Okay. Trust has to start somewhere, and I do trust you."

"And Denton? Since this is part of his assignment?"

I hesitated and told the sheriff what I'd said to Denton earlier in the day. "What if he's the one behind the threats?"

"Denton has nothing to gain by your death. In fact, he has everything to lose."

"You're right." I paced the room. "Does someone have the money and is worried I know his identity?"

"Exactly, Shelby. You were little threat in prison. But now is a different story. You might suspect someone subconsciously, and the person's runnin' scared."

"I'm concerned about Edie and Amy-Jo. They've invested so much time and energy in me. I loathe the idea of deceiving them. How can I show friendship with a lie?"

"How can you live looking over your shoulder? I reckon you don't have a choice. They're in danger too."

"All right. I'll explain and ask for forgiveness when this is over."

"By the way, your phone records showed nothin' but a few calls from burner numbers." He handed me a small phone. "I picked this up so no one could trace you. It's activated."

I thanked him and tried to pay, but he wouldn't hear of it. "Are you helping me because I've become a victim?"

"I am. But it's my job."

"And my friends' lives hang in the balance."

27

DENTON

Nothing alerted me faster to trouble than a visitor at midnight. I opened the door to a man who sounded like Sheriff Wendall but was dressed like an insurance salesman . . . or a mortician. He relayed Shelby's plan to trap the lawbreaker. A bit dangerous in my opinion. "She's not trained in law enforcement."

The sheriff huffed. "She spent fifteen years among the worst. The little lady may look like she just walked out of a candy store, but she's smart and no fool. Give her a chance."

Odd, I'd been obsessed about keeping her behind bars and read the reports about her high intelligence. Now I feared she'd get hurt. "Right. We're on solid ground with Shelby."

"Unless I'm blind, you're fallin' for her."

I braced myself to deny the truth swirling through me like a twister. "Insane. Check out her record. I want the truth and the case closed."

He chuckled. "Famous last words before the big dive into deep water. Are you in or not with the plan?"

"I'm in."

"She walked here through the woods—and is waitin' in the barn."

"You assumed I'd agree before asking."

"And I was right."

I closed the blinds and doused the lights before we walked to retrieve Shelby, who sat in the shadows near Big Red's stall but was no doubt afraid. I'd picked up on her fearlessness in the times we'd been together. Did the courage come from her prison experience or determination to clear herself of suspicion of theft? Or both? I might as well give in. Not only did I believe in her innocence, but I also was guilty of caring for Shelby, a convicted murderer. If I ended up looking stupid, I'd handle it.

We made our way back to the cabin. Once inside, we gathered at my small, round kitchen table.

"How long did you intend to stay out there?" I said to her.

"Until you agreed. Darkness can be a friend."

Sounded like poetry, reminding me of what she wrote on the piece of paper stuck in her Bible.

She smiled at the sheriff. "Thank you for all you've done for me. This is way after hours, and I'm sure your wife and family would prefer you were at home."

"The family's fine, and they understand my dedication to the law. Let's get this plan figured out. As it is, we'll be here most of the night."

"I'll make us coffee." I'd purchased some of Amy-Jo's blend. "We're going to need it."

"I could use a cup." The sheriff adjusted his hat. "Shelby, I'll speak to James Peterson later on this morning."

She nodded. "I work until two if he needs to talk."

"The parole officer is in on this?" I said.

"He has to be in the loop in case this goes south."

"It's not . . . ," she said. "I haven't . . . Never mind."

What did she almost say? It was after midnight, and brain fog had set in. "How do you plan to add credibility to a suicide?"

"Plant the seeds of ongoing depression with Pastor Emory, Amy-Jo, and Edie." She drew in a deep breath. "I hate the ruse when those three have given me instant friendship and support. One of the regular bakery customers is a drug dealer." She shook her head. "I can smell them coming, and I didn't need Amy-Jo to tell me his profession. I'll talk to him where she can see. My death will look like an overdose, and it will play into the threats I've received. I'll leave a note and request cremation."

I just figured out my role. "You want me to find your body?"

"Yes, and help with a few key issues."

"I can make it happen through the FBI," I said.

The sheriff cleared his throat. "This is beginnin' to sound like a movie where I can't predict the endin'."

"The good guys win." I chuckled while pouring water into the coffee maker.

"Hope so. Hey, we need to think through a potential hidin' place for the money."

Shelby shrugged. "I'll work on wording it for the suicide note. I have to make it seem like a depressed person's trying to right past wrongs. Perhaps I could reveal that everything to find the stolen money is in my Bible, and I'll take it with me."

I liked the idea and said so. "The sheriff and I could make it known that we're looking for the money trail, but we can't find your Bible."

"Randy Hughes will be all over this. Count on him to spread the word, just to prove he was right about Shelby." The sheriff drew in a long breath. "If he's guilty, he'll be facing a few years behind bars."

"What does he have against me other than the obvious?" Shelby said. "I expected rejection, but he's downright hostile."

"His behavior has more to do with him than you." The sheriff swung his gaze to me and back to her. "Randy is on a one-man crusade to protect his sister and those around him. I fired him this mornin' for omittin' information on your crime report and lyin' about Edie havin' a problem at her place and accusin' you. Just one of the many times his actions failed to adequately represent his badge. I've given him too many chances."

The timing of his firing coincided with my run-in with him in the parking lot. Randy's attitude was like a loaded gun in a bar full of temper-infused drunks. If he didn't learn to manage it, he wouldn't survive.

Shelby stood and poured coffee for us. Such a wisp of a woman, but she wasn't emotionally frail. "Has he been in counseling?"

"Refused. His ex-wife begged him to get help until she feared for her and the boys' safety. Another thing." The sheriff paused. "Both of you need to be careful. His thinking is off, and if he gets to drinkin', you'll be in his sights."

She nodded and set our cups before us. As if she knew her way around my kitchen, she set sugar on the table and reached in the fridge for half-and-half. "Makes sense for me to return his bike. I don't want to owe him anything. Can I give it to you when we're done here?"

I protested. "How will you get back and forth to work?"

"My legs. I'll buy my own bicycle in another week or so."

"I'll get you one tomorrow," I said.

"No charity. End of discussion."

"We'll talk tomorrow."

The sheriff picked up the conversation. "Randy knows he's on my suspect list. Although endangering his sister indicates how far he might have slid downhill."

"I feel sorry for him," Shelby said. "He must believe his purpose is to protect the innocent. Honorable, even if he's stretched the boundaries."

I tried to unearth Shelby's line of thinking. She'd pulled the trigger on an innocent man, and she knew firsthand the remorse accompanying a horrible crime. Randy could be the one threatening her and still she defended him.

28

SHELBY

In the quiet pre-morning darkness when nature whispered tranquility, I walked to work. Many women would fear the trek to town, but I'd squared off with danger and wasn't afraid. Staying alert had become a way of life. I concentrated on a powerful God who would soon usher in dawn across the eastern sky in yellows, oranges, and sometimes lavender. My way of viewing nature's wonder and worshiping the Creator.

Today exhaustion and "help me" looped in a banner across my mind. Two hours of restless sleep had taken my body by siege. Every muscle fought me like a wounded animal with bared teeth. How sad that Randy Hughes hated me because he couldn't right the world.

Did Marissa feel the same way about me? Had she forgiven herself? I prayed for her, my sweet sister, who'd never made any mistakes. But one.

In the wee hours of the morning, I'd asked Sheriff Wendall

if my dad had called his office fearful for his family's safety. He confirmed it. Since no one from my family had contacted me in years, my past conviction must make me look like a monster in their eyes.

Had I forgiven my family for abandoning me? I hoped so because God expected me to do for others what He'd done for me. But the truth hurt. I never expected Mom and Dad to totally break contact. During the trial Dad had asked me, *"Shelby, did you pull the trigger or was a third person involved?"*

Not going there.

It was useless.

I shook off the past to concentrate on the future. If not, I'd be hit with a boatload of depression.

My burner phone rang, and I yanked it from my sweatshirt pocket.

"This is Denton. I'm leaving the cabin to drive you to work."

"No need. I'm nearly to the three-mile marker. Besides, if we're seen together by the wrong person, it could destroy our plan."

"Walking in the dark is dangerous."

His words touched a part of me long forgotten. Not since my parents had anyone expressed concern for me—although his motives were selfish. Yes, he'd given me Joy, but the puppy wasn't a gift of the heart. "Denton, I appreciate your offer but go back to bed."

"I'm worried about your safety."

Really? "Read my record. The present doesn't change what I've done."

"But you're in a new place now."

If only I were free to tell the truth . . .

◉ ◉ ◉

At the café, Amy-Jo bustled with early morning preparations. Edie habitually stopped in for coffee after she took her kids to school.

I'd met them at church, and they were mannerly. I loved kids as much as I loved puppies. My mind trailed to my fifteen-year-old niece. What was her name? Did she look like Marissa or Travis? She surely hated me for killing her dad, and she should.

When the customer line at the bakery ended, I approached Edie in a booth and told her I had a new phone.

"Has the other one died on you?" She shook her head. "I'm sorry."

"Not at all. Sheriff Wendall suggested a phone that couldn't be traced since it looks like someone is hacking the one you gave me. Please keep this new number to yourself."

"Count on it. Like a book or a movie, you'll use the burner when you don't want the bad guy to know who you're talking to."

"Right." I forced a smile, wishing my reality was part fiction. "Which means we can talk anytime."

She lifted her coffee mug. "I'll drink to friendship all day long. How's the business model?"

"Finished. I have it on my original phone. The Spring Celebration Days in May will be a telling point. If sales are strong, then I'll move closer to getting out of debt and establishing my designs." I hesitated. "I'm tired of dodging verbal bullets."

Edie blinked. "You're doing great. Don't get so down." She took a sip of her coffee. "Got a minute? I need to tell you a few things about my brother."

I checked with Amy-Jo and took a break. Although I suspected I already knew Edie's content, I wanted to hear her version.

"Randy was fired yesterday morning," she said. "Four years too late in my opinion, but Sheriff Wendall showed more patience with him than I ever imagined."

Her story mirrored what the sheriff had relayed to me. "I'm sorry your brother shadows you."

"Randy's belligerent, and I never understood how he convinced his precious wife to marry him. She had no choice but to leave him after he became violent with her and one of their sons."

"Family dysfunction destroys relationships."

"Randy came after her, and their two sons pulled him off." She clenched her jaw. "The younger one called the sheriff while the older one took a beating. The rest is immaterial except for the divorce, and that happened four years ago. And his fixation to watch over me and my kids as well as the community escalated into alienating him from his old friends. Our parents took him to counseling when he was a kid, even had him tested. He had learned how to tell the therapist what she wanted to hear. Nothing chemically wrong with him, just a bullying instinct."

"Have you seen him in the last few days?"

"Oh yes. He stopped by the real estate office right afterward with the news, really angry and irrational."

"He blamed Denton and me?"

"Exactly." Edie glanced at her watch. "One more thing. I told him until he got his act together, not to come near me, the kids, or my tenants. I realize he has no one to talk to, but I pray this pushes him into seeking professional help."

"I'll pray for him too." I paused. "Edie, those who once chose violent means will return to the same behavior if they aren't stopped or learn other means to control their behavior."

She studied me, and I assumed she thought about my past. "Your faith pulled you through."

"Yes. It's all I have." Someday I'd tell her about my journaling. "I asked the sheriff to return the bicycle."

"You walked to work?"

"I found it refreshing."

"You won't in another two months when the temps are a hundred in the shade. I'll get you a bike."

"Please. It's important for me to be self-sufficient."

"What about getting groceries and things?"

I touched her arm. "I'll be fine, and I'll have another bicycle as soon as I'm financially squared away." I stood to take my station behind the bakery counter.

"Which means you'll either walk or pedal to and from the café in suffocating heat." She inhaled deeply. "Randy could be behind your threats, but I guess you've discussed the same thing with the sheriff. He's lost his temper too many times for me to doubt his capability of shooting my tire and whatever else. Be careful, my friend."

"I've learned how to survive. But circumstances are getting harder. Some days I just don't want to go on."

She paled, but it was the response I needed to keep her safe.

29

DENTON

Last night I dreamed I'd missed something vital about Shelby. No idea if the "something" meant good or bad for her. But I couldn't leave it alone. At least I didn't have a stack of paperwork and other cases in my way this time.

Since talking to Shelby before sunup, I fed Big Red, drank a pot of coffee, inhaled bacon and toast, and went over the videos and photos of the trial again.

The sound of a car engine alerted me to a visitor. Randy Hughes slammed the door of his dark-green pickup, and I closed my laptop. He pulled back his shoulders and marched toward my front door. My mind stepped back to my pawpaw's banty rooster that took out after everyone, sorta how Randy looked strutting his stuff toward the cabin. His boots pounded on the steps and porch, shaking the dishes in my cabinet.

I opened the door before he knocked. "Hey, Randy. What's going on?"

"Occurred to me this morning you had a hand in getting me fired."

"You're kidding, right?"

"You might have taken a few things I said seriously and pulled rank with your FBI buds."

"You managed to lose your job all by yourself."

"I'm the best man on the force."

"If you don't calm down, man, you're headed for a heart attack. And my CPR is a little rusty."

"I'll calm down when a few people in this town start listening to me."

"Take a vacation. Clear your head and figure out what to do with your life."

The man before me interpreted the law according to his own views of justice, a miserable and unpredictable man. Pawpaw had wrung the banty rooster's neck, and Mamaw fried him up. Not sure why I remembered the story, except Randy's state of mind might move him to irreversible crimes. He still owned the ability to turn his life around.

I thought he might throw a punch, but he stomped off and sped away in his truck. For sure the man was headed down a precarious road—if someone didn't kill him, his body would give out. Until Randy broke the law or needed medical attention, how could anyone help him? For that matter, did he have any friends or family who cared?

I continued on my repetitive review of Shelby's years before and after prison. No one from her family had visited, only a chaplain. Interesting to find out if Shelby refused to see them or if they chose to write her off. I sent my request through the FBI.

Two hours later, a response landed in my in-box. None of Shelby's family had requested visitation. She refused to see the chaplain until the seventh year of her incarceration. The records included contact information, and I pressed in Pastor Donna Glades's number. I introduced myself.

"Is Shelby okay?" the chaplain said. "She planned to do whatever it took to regain her life."

"She's a survivor. Someone is trying to run her off, even to the point of encouraging suicide."

The woman groaned. "Before incarceration and becoming a Christian, she battled depression. She's emailed me, but nothing about any problems. Then again, I wouldn't expect her to complain. That's not her style. Why is the FBI investigating her?"

I told her the truth. "Aside from recovering the money and if she had a hand in it, she's become a victim. I no longer believe she had a thing to do with the theft."

"Agent McClure, I assure you, Shelby is innocent of stealing from her family. She had told me about the money and how she wished the orphans had received the funds. Shelby told me once she was out of prison, she intended to search for who stole it. She also worried about her sister, Marissa, raising her child alone."

"Have you ever talked to her parents or sister?"

"Her father. According to Clay Pearce, Shelby is dead to him. Her feelings for her family have never changed. She loves them dearly."

"In your conversations with her, was there ever a mention of anyone other than her immediate family?"

"Not at all. Shelby is introverted, incredibly smart, and creative. She's carrying a heavy load and I believe secrets. I have no idea about whom or their nature, but they are destroying her."

"Do you think she'd resort to suicide?"

Pastor Glades sighed. "Her faith is solid, and she knows Jesus, but who can say where the depths of depression could lead her. She internalizes everything."

"A pastor here is counseling her."

"Yes, I've chatted with Pastor Emory, but he hasn't broken confidentiality."

"Those who've befriended her have become loyal in a short while," I said. "The café where she works has a little gift shop.

Her jewelry is there on consignment, and already she has orders. I understand you taught her the craft."

She chuckled. "I showed her the basics, and she did the rest. Shelby has a natural skill in my opinion." The chaplain paused. "If she knew the location of the money, she'd have told the authorities where to find it."

"Do you have any information that could help identify the person behind these threats, someone from prison?"

"Possibly, but I have no proof. I can't state something without backing it up."

"Is there anything you can tell me? I want to eliminate the threats and let her put an end to the past."

"She's a strong young woman and has overcome incredible obstacles. Shelby understands and practices sacrifice. You're an investigator. Look beneath the surface for the truth."

30

SHELBY

Creating something beautiful from raw materials seemed to be my purpose. I felt God's presence, encouraging me to express my love within the context of my heart, mind, and fingers. I polished the stones on two completed necklace and earrings sets. Tomorrow I'd deliver them to Amy-Jo for customers who'd placed orders. The name and Scripture reference for each item gave them meaning. Satisfaction swirled through me, much like in high school when I selected furniture, fabric, and room designs, pasted images of them in a scrapbook, and stored them in my closet for a future in interior decorating.

But the time to fashion a jewelry piece also caused my thoughts to dive into dark places. God helped me there too. My resolve to find out the name and reason someone wanted me dead refused to budge. One of the things I'd learned in prison was those allowed to bully continued their insatiable quest until they were stopped.

My burner phone rang—Sheriff Wendall. I hoped he didn't

plan to stop by. Although the time only read 7:03, I was ready to catch up on the sleep I'd missed the previous night.

"Shelby, I have a bit of bad news for you. Your father called. Your mother is in stage 4 of pancreatic cancer. Critical condition. She's home and under the care of hospice. Askin' to see you."

An image of my strong mother, weak and dying, seemed wrong. A horrible mistake. "Dad chose not to contact me?"

"Yes. I'm sorry."

"He made himself clear of my status with the family a long time ago. My guess is he's against a visit, but Mom's insisting." When the sheriff didn't respond, I took a breath while treasured memories of my mother touched my heart. "I want to see her."

"Okay. I suggest contacting Denton instead of Edie or Amy-Jo to drive you."

"Why? My dad has a mind like a steel trap. He'll recognize Denton's name."

"Does it matter? If anything, Denton's presence means the FBI believes in your rehabilitation."

Then it hit me. "This is an opportunity for Denton to see if the threats are coming from here or Sharp's Creek. We know I'm being watched. But, Sheriff, a smart person wouldn't show his face and risk arrest here or there."

"Depends on the person's desperation."

I thought about Randy's state of mind and the logic of staying away from him. "I'd rather have someone with me who knows how to defend himself."

"We're rollin' along the same road."

His encouragement gave me a nudge toward optimism. I must cling to a better tomorrow. "I'll talk to Denton. I wish I trusted him more. Amy-Jo scheduled my regular day off for Monday. I'll see if anyone will switch Friday with me. With Mom in hospice care, I don't want to wait."

"Good. Work it all out and let me know the plan."

"Yes, sir."

"Get some sleep, and don't open the door to Randy. If he shows, call me. His truck's parked at a local bar, and he doesn't hold his liquor well. I've posted an officer to keep an eye on him."

"What about the safety of his ex-wife and sons?"

"I've warned them and Edie."

At least I understood the enemy in prison. Randy Hughes was a wild card.

"Shelby, what if a trip to Sharp's Creek gave you an opportunity to carry out your fake suicide? Think about layin' the groundwork with Amy-Jo and Edie startin' tonight. Use your original cell phone to contact them. I know it means changin' plans in midstream with little time to finalize, but takin' advantage of the trip sounds good to me."

"Not sure if the drug dealer will be at the café tomorrow. If not, most people won't have a problem believing I had access to his goods. But Edie does know I'm feeling down."

"I'll make sure the right story is spread, and James Peterson is aware."

When the conversation ended, I phoned Denton on my burner and explained the situation. We agreed to leave Friday morning at five. My next call went to Edie as Sheriff Wendall suggested. If my stalker had tapped into my phone, he might hit the overconfidence button and expose his identity. I told her about my mother.

"If I can make arrangements at the café for Friday, Denton will drive me."

"Shelby, I'd like to take you. It—"

"You told your brother you'd keep your distance until this ended. Your kids need their mom."

Edie sighed. "All right. Let me know as soon as you two head home."

"Sure." I paused. "This will be hard. Mom's dying. Dad disowned me, and my sister . . . Some days I struggle to live."

"God's with you. And I'm your un-biological sister. So is Amy-Jo. Hold on tight to that truth."

I sniffed. I'd confessed more truth than a lie. "Thank you, my friend."

Amy-Jo answered on the first ring. One more time I explained about my mother's failing health.

"Don't worry about your shift. One of the gals asked me for more hours, so I'll offer her yours. How are you holding up?"

"I feel like I've fallen into a well, and it's impossible to climb out."

"This might be an opportunity to begin the healing process with your family."

"Unlikely, Amy-Jo. Some relationships are irreparable."

"Do you feel up to working tomorrow? I can get someone to cover you."

"I need to keep my mind occupied."

"Okay, I'll see you in the morning. Call me if you want to talk. I can come out there and spend the night."

"Thanks. You are really sweet." I hadn't lied to my friends about my tendency toward depression. In essence I had two enemies—whoever threatened me and the depression.

With God's help, I'd overcome both.

31

I did nothing to conceal my departure with Denton on Friday morning. His FBI training should allow him to detect someone following us, but I stared at the passenger-side mirror for my own peace of mind.

Fifteen minutes into our drive, I brought up my fake suicide and how Edie and Amy-Jo had been alerted to my dwindling mental condition. "Normally I chat with Amy-Jo and Edie at the café, but yesterday I avoided them. I regret the ruse, but I have no clue how else to credibly expose who's responsible. My Bible is in my backpack, and the note is written and in my purse."

"What if we learn the culprit is someone you know? Like your dad?"

The thought had darted in and out of my mind, unbidden and despised. "We had a strong father-daughter relationship before . . . the shooting. He adored Travis, the son he never had. I don't mean I was jealous. Travis was like a brother to me, kind, funny, and a good listener. Anyway, I won't dwell on Dad either stealing the money or threatening me. The man I remember chose family, honor, and integrity above himself. One vile deed in the family is enough."

"People we trust often fail us. Wants, presumed needs, motivations, greed, and all those deeply rooted internal workings drive us all to consider ourselves first or see life skewed."

He spoke as if he had personal experience. No headlights loomed behind us. Just a dark road. "Selfishness is a human trait. The choices we make show how far we've grown or fallen. Are you a man of faith?"

"Not really."

"When I looked up from my shame, no one was there but a chaplain to show me Jesus. Not since my dad had I experienced caring and acceptance, which is why I refuse to believe Dad is involved. He's a good man."

"Maybe we should hang a shingle outside our cabins saying, 'Counseling Upon Request.'"

"In small print we'd add, 'Therapists—FBI Agent and Ex-Con.'"

"In the finer print, 'Neither trusts the other but you can trust us both.'"

His last statement struck me as funny, and laughter rose from my toes. Denton joined in, and the wall between us dropped a few bricks.

"Your laughter is musical." He sobered. "Do you believe in fate?"

"Depends."

"I wonder why we've been thrown together. Mostly our strange attraction when we should hate each other."

"What are you saying, Denton?" Had he read my mind? Discovered my most personal thoughts?

"Not sure why I said that. Delete it, and I steered us off topic. I've done some legwork too. But I want to hear your thoughts."

"Sheriff Wendall thinks we should use this trip to accomplish the fake suicide. The problem will be avoiding cameras. Public places will video us, and a disappearing act from me looks hard. I think the best solution is to walk away from my parents' house. I could say I need to clear my head before I ride home. Their address hasn't changed, and their neighborhood was starting to run down years ago. It's less likely I'd be seen by home-security cameras. Is it possible one of your undercover buds could pick me up?"

"I prefer an exchange on a back road. I've arranged a safe house for a few days. You'll be okay during the investigation. I'll bring Joy to my cabin until you return."

"Thanks. She's a sweet puppy." I swung my attention his way. "You realize I won't stay at a safe house more than three days. I'm in this with both feet."

He palmed the steering wheel. "Please, Shelby, sit tight while the FBI and Sheriff Wendall trap this guy. You could wind up violating your parole. Have you considered going back to prison?"

"I sat tight for fifteen years. I can handle it. Besides, you're not surprised at my reaction."

"Not in the least." He tossed me a glance. "You're not fooling me. Your voice is quivering. What are you hiding?"

"Nothing!" Had my emotions become transparent? The lie behind the prison sentence? I fought for control. "My life is cursed—of my own making. Leave it alone, please. So how are we doing this?"

"We'll make a transfer with the agents who'll drive you to a safe place. I'll say you took off when we stopped to eat, and you left a suicide note in the car. You could rewrite it to reflect your mother's poor health pushed you to the brink."

"Definitely believable. And I have my Bible with me."

"One more thing—the handwriting on the sympathy card isn't in the FBI's database."

"That means the person responsible hasn't ever been caught or this is his first offense." I repeated what Denton already knew.

A few hours later, we arrived in Sharp's Creek. Heat slid up my shoulders to my face and covered me in a shroud of shame. No one ever questioned my confession because my reputation shouted my guilt.

We passed the Dairy Queen where Dad and I used to share sundae dates. We ate our share of hot fudge with nuts and lots of whipped cream. A former gas station had been transformed into a used-car business. A new Walmart rose on our right where an empty field had once been. The small downtown area showed unfamiliar storefronts and new businesses. Overall, I saw a community who loved their town.

"The small-town setting relaxes me," Denton said. "Sharp's Creek has the feel of family and community that cares for its people. I imagine your sentiments rank alongside a nightmare."

"Bittersweet."

"Good and bad?"

I nodded and scrutinized familiar landmarks like the library that had stolen a little girl's heart. Other constructions had sprung up like dandelions in spring. The stone courthouse still stood as the largest structure in the center of the square.

Denton drove slowly past the worn two-story brick building known for six decades as Pearce Bakery.

"Can we stop for just a minute?" I said.

He pulled in front of the bakery and placed the truck in park. "Thought you might want to reminisce."

The weather-beaten sign bore resemblance to the one Dad had erected when I started high school. "I spent hours here helping after school and on weekends. Dad believed his girls should know every inch of how to run a successful bakery operation. He said whatever we did in life, good business sense would take us far. I loved it. The scent of vanilla and mouthwatering delicacies is a part of who I am."

On the other hand, Marissa avoided the bakery, but her good grades and pleasant disposition pleased Mom and Dad. Marissa walked into a room, and the world became a better place. I closed my eyes.

She and Travis were a good team. Until they weren't.

I smiled at him. "We can go now. Thanks."

The GPS vocalized the directions to Mom and Dad's home, when I could have led Denton there blindfolded. The house looked the same, a modest three-bedroom brick ranch my parents bought new before I was born. Thoughts of yesterday bombarded me worse than I'd imagined.

"You okay?" he said.

"Not really." Memories fought to get the best of me—Mom, Dad, Marissa, Travis, blood, prison. "I'd rather not talk right now, Denton."

He nodded as though he sympathized with my pain. But I couldn't stop the torment. How could he ever grasp the reality of the truth?

Denton parked at the curb, and I prayed for what lay ahead. The years in prison when I'd viewed coming home as a fresh start had been utter stupidity. Seeing Dad took courage when I wanted to fly into his arms. I'd hurt him, and he'd been my advocate until the conviction. Mom often saw through my wild teenage behavior, and many times I appreciated her catching me before I jumped into serious trouble. I needed those boundaries, except when it no longer mattered.

Now telling her goodbye tore at my heart. She'd go to her grave with the belief that I'd murdered Travis. But better me than Marissa. Not sure how I felt about my sister except if given the situation again, I'd do the same thing. She'd shown her love by pushing for parole four times. Travis's parents and Dad rejected the idea. I assumed Mom felt the same.

"Shelby, are you ready? You're pale."

His voice soothed me as I gripped the door handle. "As ready as I'll ever be and feeling sick about it all."

"Thanks."

"For what?"

"For honesty about how this whole thing must be for you."

I swallowed past a lump of dread and opened the truck door. He joined me in the walk to the front entrance. Weeds had taken over the flower beds, and the shrubs had wild shoots. Mom loved gardening. How long had she been sick?

Denton rang the doorbell, giving me a few more moments to gain my composure. Where would I be if I hadn't chosen to take Marissa's place? The alternative of Mom and Dad raising a grandchild could never measure up to a good woman like my sister nurturing her daughter.

The door squeaked open.

Dad stood on the threshold. Less hair. Glasses. A Band-Aid on his cheek in the same spot where he'd been treated for melanoma years ago. Had the cancer returned? Perhaps later I'd ask.

"Dad, I appreciate your letting me see Mom." My voice cracked.

The familiar lines across his forehead etched deep. "Don't upset her. She's not long for this world."

"I only want to love on her. Sit by her side."

"You will not be alone with your mother. It's inconceivable to trust you."

I nodded. "Yes, sir."

Denton stuck out his hand and introduced himself, but Dad kept his hand at his side.

"You're that FBI agent," Dad said. "Why are you here? Are you escorting Shelby because you think she's a danger to someone?"

"I'm here with Shelby in a different capacity."

"Which is?"

"Her transportation and a friend."

Dad huffed, and in a way his orneriness reminded me of Randy Hughes. "Let's get this done before Marissa returns." He opened the door, and I stepped back in time. The smells were the same, except my cherished memories were tainted with medicine.

A small terrier ran to me. The animal must have smelled Joy on me.

"Aria's dog," Dad mumbled.

My thoughts scattered. I wanted to run, but I needed to see Mom.

32

How I longed for my reunion with my mother to be filled with
life instead of death. I followed Dad into Mom and Dad's bedroom. Denton had touched my back, and I viewed it as reassurance as he stayed behind. Shadows deepened around the room.
Mom loved the sunlight, but the hospice nurse must feel otherwise. My mother's hair likened to snow, her body frail beneath a
white blanket, and I doubted even the sun could rid the ghastly
shade of gray on her face.

But her blue-gray eyes were open. "Shelby?" she whispered.

I knelt at her side. "Yes, Mom. I'm here."

A faint smile curved her mouth. "I've been dreaming about
a visit from you." She lifted her hand, and I took it into mine.
Fragile . . . too fragile. The Bible said Jesus was strongest when
we're weak. I feared I'd crumble.

"Are you in pain?"

"Not with you here."

I kissed her forehead. "Can I open the blinds?"

"Yes, please."

"Let me help you." The nurse, a pleasant-sounding woman, allowed streams of late-morning sunshine to fill the room, and I thanked her.

"Wonderful," Mom whispered. "I'd like a few minutes alone with my daughter."

"We talked about this." Dad jutted his jaw.

Mom shook her head. "Clay, I'm dying, and I want time with Shelby. Go, all of you."

"I'll take your purse." Dad held out his hand.

I gave it to him. Did he think I carried something to hurt Mom?

The bedroom cleared, and when the door closed, I turned to her. A tear dripped down my cheek. "I love you, Mom. I'm sorry to have disappointed you."

"I hear you're now a Christian."

"I am. Jesus has my life. I remember when you used to take Marissa and me to Sunday school. You read us Bible stories, prayed with us. I wish I'd found Him back then."

"But you have now." She winced.

"Would you like me to call the nurse?"

"No, dear. The angels have been in my room. They've told me soon I'll be with Jesus. Oh, they are beautiful."

I smiled. "I hope our mansions in heaven are side by side."

She touched my cheek. "My lovely Shelby. I've missed you."

"Missed you too."

"Your dad forbade me to see you or write."

I leaned my cheek into her hand. "It's okay."

"His mandate was wrong, especially when I suspected the truth."

"What do you mean?"

"I'm certain you sacrificed your life for Marissa or someone else."

"Of course not. I—"

Her fingers covered my mouth. "Hush. I must hear the truth before I'm gone. I'm not angry if you paid another's debt. Just sad you took it on." She gasped.

"You need to rest, save your strength." Another tear trailed over my cheek. "I'm sure you'd rather think a stranger destroyed our family, but that's a delusion. You heard my confession and the evidence against me at the trial. Why would you think any differently?"

"You never asked for money. You worked for every penny you spent. Shooting Travis because he denied you a loan makes no sense, especially when you despised guns. Two months before the shooting, you had changed. Your eyes softened. You were kinder, gentler. I remember your asking me about college and how to obtain funding. No more slipping out when we were in bed." She drew in a breath that looked painful. "You took a blame that wasn't yours to take."

"My being here is upsetting you, and I promised Dad I wouldn't do that."

"You aren't. You're giving me joy. Promise me one thing."

I nodded.

"Bring the truth to light. Your dad's blinded by too many things, and sweet Aria is confused about where she fits. Justice is light. Will you make sure your dad—?"

The door opened, and Dad stepped in with the nurse. "Shelby, you've had long enough with your mother."

I fixed my attention on Mom. "I love you."

"And I love you. You'll make sure the truth is made clear?"

I was unable to make a promise I couldn't keep.

"You are the bravest young woman God ever created." She smiled and closed her eyes. "I understand your reluctance."

"Shelby. Now," Dad said.

I rose from the floor and captured Dad's gaze. "Thank you for these moments with her." I turned to the nurse. "And thank you for taking good care of my mother."

He moved away from the door, and I passed by and down the hall. Mom's medication must be fogging her mind and her request, a type of delirium. I hoped she hadn't mentioned anything about her suspicions to anyone else.

In the living room, Denton sat in a high-back chair. Across from him Marissa petted the pecan-colored terrier I'd seen earlier. She bent to the dog and it scurried to Denton's feet and sniffed at my purse. My sister hadn't changed. White-blonde hair to her shoulders and delicate features. She must have sensed my presence because she lifted her head.

Marissa leaped to her feet and wrapped her arms around me. I hugged her back. "Oh, Shelby, I'm so glad to see you. You look amazing. I was afraid I'd miss you." We clung to each other for several seconds. She pointed to my purse at Denton's feet. "Aria's naughty dog knocked over your purse, but I put everything back. I'm so sorry."

"No problem at all. I have a puppy too."

"I hope it's better behaved." She hugged me again. "Thank you for coming to see Mom." She kissed my cheek and held me at arm's length. "So many times I've longed to see you and hear your voice."

"I feel the same way."

She inhaled and glanced over her shoulder down the hall. "Dad gave me a choice of contacting you or finding financial support elsewhere."

"What else could you have done?"

"Nothing really. My daughter and I live here, and Dad has eyes like a hawk. He's about to retire and hand the business over to me." Marissa pointed to Denton. "I never expected to see Agent McClure with you."

I smiled. "It does seem unusual. But we're friends."

"He and I have been talking, and he says someone has threatened you?"

I wish he hadn't mentioned that to her. "Appears so."

My sister shuddered. "The nightmare lives on. I don't know anyone who'd want to hurt you."

"The FBI and local law enforcement in Valleysburg are handling the situation."

"Be safe, Sister." Marissa rubbed her arms. "Hope you don't mind, but I didn't think it was a good idea for Aria to . . . meet you."

"Of course." But my heart ached for the lies separating me from my family.

Footsteps from the hallway alerted me to Dad's presence. "Why are you still here?"

"I'm leaving now."

"Shelby, don't come back." Dad's voice dripped with bitterness and grief. How could I fault him when his life had fallen apart?

Marissa touched my hand. "Can I speak to you privately?"

"I will not allow it." Dad's voice rose. "She's seen her mother. Time for her to leave."

"The 'her' is my sister. I haven't seen Shelby in fifteen years."

"Do I need to remind you Aria is minus a father because of her inexcusable crime? This is for your own good. You're too old to believe there's good in everyone."

"I'm talking to my sister and making a start to narrow the distance between us. She's paid for her crimes. If I can forgive her, why can't you?"

I heard them discuss me as though I weren't there. The humiliation of Denton listening to the dysfunction made me cringe inside. "No need to quarrel. If one of you will call Sheriff Wendall when Mom's time is over, I'd appreciate it. And I'd like to attend the funeral."

"Out of the question." Dad stiffened. "I won't have a celebration of life destroyed by a killer."

Marissa stepped between Dad and me. "Dad, I will speak to my sister outside alone, and I will contact her when Mom passes."

"The consequences of rebellion are ugly. Ask Shelby about the last fifteen years."

Marissa whirled toward him, an action I'd never seen. "Think about Aria gone from your life." She hooked her arm in mine and led me to the front yard. There we faced the street. "I apologize for Dad's rude behavior."

"I hurt him beyond repair. Please apologize to him. You have too much at stake."

"You've always thought of me first."

"I love you, and the world is a better place because you're a shining, beautiful light. Now, go tell Dad he's right, and you don't think I've changed. I'm fine. I have a good job. I'm designing jewelry, and I have wonderful new friends."

"Like Agent McClure?"

"The jury's still out on him. It's a strange relationship."

"Maybe something more than friends?" She tilted her head.

"And how would he explain me to his family full of police officers?"

"Love overcomes a lot of barriers."

I shook my head. "But not good sense."

"Can I have your phone number?" she said.

I gave her my burner info, and she borrowed a pen to write the numbers on the palm of her hand.

"Don't tell anyone you have this."

"I'll keep it secret."

I took her shoulders like she'd grasped mine earlier. "Go. Make peace with Dad."

Marissa made her way back to the house. At the door, she turned and blew me a kiss like we were girls again. Mom's words washed over me. Even in her dying days, she suspected the truth.

The first line of *The Color Purple* swirled through my mind. *"You better not never tell nobody but God."*

33

DENTON

The view of Shelby's and Marissa's backs through the Pearces' picture window hijacked reading any facial expressions. But when Marissa walked toward the house and Shelby stayed at the truck with her face to the street, I assumed the conversation had been smeared with bitterness. Neither woman displayed any sign of cohesiveness.

My noncommunication with Clay Pearce left the room eerily quiet. From his stubborn stance, which I'd seen in Shelby, he'd jump down my throat no matter what I said.

Marissa opened the door and with reddened eyes approached her dad. "You're right. She's more hardened than before. I'm sorry."

"Why did you disobey me?"

"Fear and stupidity. I hoped my sister had changed." She sighed and stepped into his arms. He rested his chin on her head. "Fear for Aria drove me to risk alienating you."

"She made a threat?" Clay said.

Marissa nodded. "The memory of what she did stares back at me every time I look into Aria's face. Out there, I told her never to show her face in this town again, or I'd take legal action."

"I'll initiate a restraining order for all of us." Clay eyed me with the same contempt he'd given Shelby. "Get out of my house and stay away from my family. The best place for Shelby is behind bars."

What had I witnessed? Unless I heard Shelby threaten her sister, I wouldn't believe it. Had I encountered a web of deceit I'd never imagined?

⊙　⊙　⊙

I tried to persuade Shelby to stop for a lunch break, but she merely shook her head. No words, only soft sobs. She had processing of her own to do. I took the long way toward the meeting point with my agent friends, winding around country roads. The investigative side of me analyzed every moment from the time we'd entered Sharp's Creek. Clay Pearce ruled the household with an iron fist. Had he always been a tyrant, or had the tragedy changed him? From what Shelby had relayed, he adjusted to survive.

I waited fifteen more minutes before speaking. "Any surprises?"

She focused on the passenger-side window. "A couple."

"And?"

"Personal, Denton."

"I have a listening ear."

"Right. It's part of your job." She moaned. "That wasn't necessary. I appreciate your offer but no thanks. For lack of a better word, I need a diversion." She massaged her neck. "Did Marissa and Dad work through their argument?"

"Yes. The conversation didn't put you in a good spot, though."

"That's what I'd asked her to do. She needs to stay on Dad's good side. Her situation in raising Aria and her future in owning the bakery rest on keeping him pacified."

"Would you do anything for your sister?"

"Absolutely."

My concern about her possible deceit vanished. I reached across the truck and took her hand. The intimacy lasted two seconds before she pulled back.

"I'm making a new life for myself," she said.

"Not until those against you are stopped."

"Or I'm stopped."

"You're not alone. You have your faith, friends, and for what it's worth, I'm in for the duration."

She focused on me. "Today has been very hard."

She needed time. Both of us did. "While you talked to your mother, I checked in with the agents who'll be handling your protection. We have a transfer in about twenty minutes. Two agents will take you to a safe house about fifty miles from here. I've used it before on cases in my jurisdiction. Sheriff Wendall and I will follow through with our part."

"I suppose it's a good thing. Wish we knew the culprit's name. As it is, I feel I've exchanged one cell for another."

"The temporary housing protects you from the bad guys."

"I'm just voicing my messed-up emotions. Will you check in with me every morning and night?"

"Sure. If I keep you posted, you'll stay put?"

"I can't promise." She reached into her backpack. "Here's the note. I've already rewritten it."

"Read it to me." If the wording needed to be tweaked, she'd have time to make changes.

Shelby opened the folded piece of paper. "'Life has no meaning for me. Mom will soon be gone, and my family refuses to forgive me. Who can blame them? I thought after prison I'd be able to start over. It's impossible. My crimes haunt me day and night. One lie builds on another. Edie, Amy-Jo, and Pastor Emory believe in me . . . my lies. They are dear people and deserve more than my sham. I'm a murderer and a thief. Yes, I took the $500,000 from Marissa and Travis's account. I forged an ID and placed it in an overseas account. The words of my Bible convicted me of the truth. May whoever reads this also find the treasure in that truth.' Rather fitting, don't you think, with all my Jesus talk?"

I asked her to reread it and digested her words. "That works."

"Good. Please give it to the sheriff."

"Will do." I remembered her poem tucked inside her Bible and hoped she'd removed it. "I arranged for hidden cameras inside and outside of your cabin. They'll be installed by the time I drive back."

I sensed her staring at me. "Are you really convinced of my innocence?"

"More with each passing hour."

"Thank you. I appreciate your support today, for being with me to face my family."

I dug deep for a chuckle. "What choice did I have? If Edie or Amy-Jo had driven you, they'd have flattened your dad. Then I'd have to arrest both of them."

She forced a laugh. "What a pigsty that would have been."

"But funny. Your time with your mom went well?"

"We talked, and she knows I love her." Shelby pressed her lips together, and I thought she might cry. "It was worth facing Dad."

"And seeing Marissa?"

I nodded. "Honestly, I wasn't sure what my reception would be. Marissa had a breakdown during the trial, and her parting words to me were filled with hatred, bitterness. I deserved it but living under Dad's thumb had its price too." Shelby leaned back against the headrest. "Denton, when will this be over?"

The weariness in her voice drew me into her lonely world, a place I longed to be to fill the void. And yet she filled an empty spot I thought I'd never fill again. When my plans for marriage and family had exploded in my face, I swore to have a bachelor's life. But I never thought a soft voice with undeniable strength would melt the glacier around my heart. Unlike Lisa, no avalanche of tears to persuade me to her way of thinking or silence that could last for hours.

How did a grown man approach what had been the unthinkable? How did I reconcile her past as a killer? Confusion beat me up. Being attracted to her labeled me a fool or a victim of some cosmic joke.

"Let's take one day at a time," I said. "The person making the threats has grown bold, as though he or she thinks they're invincible. We need them to believe you're out of the picture, so they're free to search the cabin. Then it will be over."

34

SHELBY

Denton assured me the men we were about to encounter had experience and wisdom. But I wasn't convinced. He drove me down a dirt road where we met two older men in a navy-blue sedan. He knew both agents, which gave me a huge dose of comfort. After the two men introduced themselves, Denton and I said our goodbyes, and I slid into the back seat of the sedan.

I expected a black SUV like in the movies and agents who had their real teeth. The car wove in and around country roads until the driver, Isaac Sims, stopped at a rusty mobile home nestled in thick pine and oak trees several feet from the road.

"Home sweet home." His raspy voice indicated a man in his early seventies. He had a round face and black hair, which had to be dyed.

"Is it a World War II tank?" I said.

Both men laughed, and the other agent, Aaron Marod, a man

of basketball-player height and bushy silver eyebrows, pointed to the mobile home. "The last time I was here, I had to clean up varmints from the kitchen before I could put the food away. Denton told me he'd keep this place clean, but he lied to us."

"How long ago?" Suspicions about these two crowded my mind.

Aaron rubbed his chin. "Whatcha say, Ike? Ten years ago? Right after the big scare of the Y2K?"

"Sounds about right."

"That is more than twenty years." I glanced from one man to the other. "Are you two active agents?"

"Retired." Isaac opened the car door. "We're doing this protective detail as a favor to Denton."

"Is he paying you?" How fast could I get Denton on the phone?

"Yes, missy. Private job. Why else would we agree to live out here in this run-down trailer?" He turned to Aaron. "Hold off on bringing in the ice chest until I take a look inside. No point hauling it in until we get the place cleaned up."

Retired agents and a mobile home that looked like it needed to be hauled away? And Denton agreed to pay them? Shock washed over me. *"Private job."* What had this protection detail cost him?

My thoughts trailed back to what he'd done for me since my release. True, he was motivated by finding a link to the five hundred thousand dollars. Later, he changed his tune. Other factors pointed to his being a good man, one who'd gone above and beyond to prove I'd paid my debt to society. He'd been convinced of my innocence. Despite my stained past, he sacrificed his time and money.

Stunned and emotional best described me. So many times, I wished I could tell him the truth about Travis's death.

"I thought the FBI had sanctioned this assignment," I said.

"Investigating it only. But the kid needed more evidence for protection detail, so you're stuck with us." Isaac stepped out of the car, and for the first time, I noted a rounded belly. "We are your best defense. Them young agents have more training than real-life experience. Trip over their own firearms."

Isaac disappeared up wobbly, concrete-block steps and inside the metal structure. I tilted my head to study my "temporary housing," as Denton called the situation. No broken windows, but a screen door rested on one rusty hinge. Weeds grew from under the mobile home as though they tickled its belly, and a thick layer of yellow-green pollen covered every visible inch of grass and metal and foliage. I was allergic to most substances that existed outside, and my inhaler weighed in at nearly empty. At least I had a spare for emergencies.

The structure looked more like it hadn't seen human habitation in decades. I'd say in the last fifty years except power lines were connected to whatever needed electricity inside. An oak tree leaned precariously close to the roof, defying the next gust of wind to blow it down. A crow swept from the treetops and perched on the roof. When the bird cawed, it sounded like a protest against the intruders. A fat tawny cat crept in front of the car, offering a little reassurance to the reduction of mice and rats.

Isaac left the mobile home, shoving the broken screen door back until it broke. His stocky build served him well. He tossed it into the weeds and signaled for us to join him. "Looks like no one's been here since us."

I moaned.

Aaron laughed. "Hey, Ike, I'll get the cleaning stuff from the trunk. And the extra rifle and ammo."

Not their first rodeo.

For the next four hours we cleaned. Isaac tuned in an old radio to country-and-western music, and Aaron took every opportunity to switch to hard rock, which took me off guard. He claimed Def Leppard, Guns N' Roses, and Bon Jovi were the best of the eighties. Isaac argued that Willie Nelson, George Strait, and Kenny Rogers sang the heart of the south.

While I listened to their musical debate, which replaced

thoughts from my own fears and distress, I disinfected the kitchen, top to bottom and inside out. Remarkably, the spotless and disinfected fridge hummed, and cold air swirled from the motor, a miracle considering the dust and dirt now covering most of me. Two out of the four burners on the electric stove burned hot, and the oven, after I wiped up a dozen dead roaches, even worked. I wasn't a stranger to roaches, but I'd never seen so many in one place. . . . Many scurried about, still alive.

My lungs tried my body's patience. Neither had a tolerance for the outside allergens and the inside dust. I bent and gasped for breath until I gave in to using my inhaler.

"Are you okay?" Isaac stood over my air-depleted lungs.

I held up a finger until I could breathe.

"Hope you have plenty of juice in that thing. We may be stuck here awhile."

After a moment's reprieve, I could speak. "This one's empty, but I have another one in my purse." I reached for the spare, but it was gone.

I always carried an extra inhaler. What happened to it?

35

DENTON

I missed Shelby already. Yet the miles from home gave me time to ponder the dysfunction in her family and possible scenarios of who'd threatened her. Clay Pearce was an authoritarian, and although he was supposed to be a churchgoer, I failed to see Jesus in him.

Apparently Clay's daughters bought into his archaic methods of ruling the roost. My suspicions he'd made off with the money vanished given the condition of his bakery and home. His 2006 Honda in the driveway added to his less-than-stellar financial condition. Marissa came across as more sensible, and while she claimed to want a relationship with her sister, Clay squelched that before it moved forward. I wished I'd been privy to the sisters' conversation outside. I always felt better to confirm information firsthand.

In the rearview mirror, I noted a dark-colored, possibly black or deep green, truck on my tail for the past several miles. Adrenaline pumped excitement into my body. I'd chosen to take back roads to Valleysburg for this very purpose.

I swung right at the next county road, and the truck followed. . . . The truck that ran Shelby off the road matched this color. Not sure I could be this lucky. I turned left. Sure enough, the truck stayed about a quarter mile behind me.

I phoned Sheriff Wendall and gave him my location.

"Not my jurisdiction," he said. "I'll contact the highway patrol."

"It's no coincidence the driver's tailing me. I thought I spotted a pickup keeping tabs on me when Shelby and I left Sharp's Creek, but then I lost it well before meeting up for the transfer. Until now."

"Stay connected till the highway patrol arrives."

With one eye on the rearview mirror, I gave the sheriff an overview of the trip to see Shelby's mother. "I have the suicide note in my pocket. I'll let you know when I'm home and walking to her cabin." A question bolted into my mind about the relationship between Travis Stover and Clay Pearce, a matter I'd look into later.

I drove down the same road for another two miles. The truck, which I determined was black, inched closer. At a stop sign, with nothing in sight but fields of new planting, the truck sped up within feet of my tailgate. Front license plate removed.

He bumped me.

I cursed and raced ahead.

"This guy isn't playing around." I pulled my Glock from under the seat.

A second crash shoved my head into the steering wheel. My truck lunged right at a speed reserved for racetracks. I quickly attempted to straighten it without stomping on the brake and flipping the truck.

A pop like a balloon breaking caused me to jump. A bullet grazed the top of my head and embedded in the windshield. My head stung like I'd angered a swarm of bees. The shooter was either a pro or lucky.

A second pop and a bullet zipped by my left ear, sending me into a whirl of disorientation. My foot slipped from easing the brake to the gas.

My truck took flight. Spun. Flipped. More than once. Pain stabbed me like a jolt of electricity down the right side of my body.

My world went black.

36

SHELBY

Most people took each breath for granted, but not those who suffered from asthma. What had happened to my extra inhaler? After I had taken a hot shower, another welcome surprise compliments of the trailer's hot-water tank, Aaron brewed me a cup of herbal tea with honey from their supply of groceries. Mom used to fix the same home remedy for asthma, although it seldom worked. At this point, I'd try anything. As a kid I had made more than one trip to the ER. That's when the doctor insisted I always carry a spare inhaler.

"Let's get a doctor to look at you," Isaac said.

"Haven't a prescription for an inhaler." I wheezed and fought for breath. "I'll be . . . fine."

"You're a far shot from fine."

"I'm hungry. Haven't eaten all day." The sharp pain in my chest caused my eyes to water. "I'll fix chili and corn bread."

Isaac huffed. "Typical woman . . . change the subject when things aren't going your way. If you get worse, I'm handcuffing you and we're heading to the hospital." His voice held a menacing growl, but I appreciated his concern.

"You two are my hero-protectors. I'll keep you posted."

Isaac shook his head. "No need. We can hear it."

Not sure I could tackle any more cleaning with the inhaler operating on fumes. Everything in the trailer looked in order, but my approval had a lot to do with the condition of my lungs. Isaac helped Aaron remake the disinfected beds while I browned hamburger and onion and stirred together jalapeño corn bread. Tossed a salad too. After setting the small table, we scrunched around it together. I could hear and feel my labored breathing.

"Your wheezing is worse." Aaron dug his spoon into the chili.

"I'm all right."

Isaac spread butter over a hunk of corn bread. "What else can you take?"

"I *said* I'm all right."

"In the words of Jon Bon Jovi," Aaron said, "'There's a vintage which comes with age and experience.'"

I coughed, and it resembled a train whistle.

Isaac pointed his butter knife at me. "We're old. Not senile. Your asthma isn't getting any better. One last time . . . what do you need to stop a full-blown asthma attack?"

I'd tried not to think about the inability of a drugstore brand relieving the symptoms. Except hiding my gasps for air and wheezing had met the impossible zone. I took a sip of my second cup of herbal tea. "The best solution is an over-the-counter inhaler. I'm sorry. I always have an extra one, except this time. Must have been my concern about my mother."

"Once we're finished with dinner, I'm driving into town to get you one from Walmart." Isaac snapped his fingers. "I'll call my Teladoc en route, see if he'll prescribe something without seeing you."

"Thanks. But this can wait until morning." When he held up the butter knife again, I veered from opposing him. "How long will it take?"

"Round trip, oh, about an hour and a half. Probably less. Aaron can handle everything here. He's a nicer guy than me."

"You two are angels."

Aaron laughed. "Does that mean you like my rock music over his country?"

I held up a finger. "Not going there. How about more chili and corn bread?"

A short while later, Isaac rinsed his bowl and fished keys from his jean pocket. He patted his stomach. "Good dinner. I'll hurry. Text me if you need anything else."

Tears filled my eyes, and I hugged him. "Thank you for all you're doing. The asthma is making me all emotional."

Once he left, Aaron towered over me with his basketball height and ordered me to my bedroom while he washed the few dishes. Propped up in a twin bed, I clutched my chest and thanked God for Isaac and Aaron, two men with fitting names from the Old Testament. From their language and conversation, faith leaned toward an afterthought for them. But they were a blessing to me. I'd texted Denton to check on his part of the plan, but he hadn't responded. He'd take good care of Joy. Sweet man . . . The asthma tightened my chest, but still I drifted toward sleep.

A hand shook me. My eyes flew open.

"Get on the floor and stay there," Aaron said. "We have company."

"Maybe they're locals," I whispered.

"Night-vision goggles show two men, and local folks aren't armed like these two. Ike's about thirty minutes out. So are the cops."

He closed the door, and I lay flat on the floor. The stench of mold with a heavy dose of bleach sent me scrambling for the inhaler. But it was empty, not even fumes helped.

God, help me. Help Aaron.

Unless I calmed myself, my breathing would worsen. Who was out there? Did they think I had access to the money? I hadn't given up on the stalker driven by Travis's death, but if that were the case, why hadn't a contract for my death been issued in prison? These two wanted a payoff now. Listening hard while the silence seemed to roar in my ears, I counted the moments ticking by.

The crack of a gun broke a window.

Aaron returned fire.

A repeating weapon of some sort rippled along the trailer side, shattering glass. Had it penetrated the metal siding? Did the shooters have night-vision goggles too?

Two shots fired from inside. Then another.

Another round of bullets tore into the side of the mobile home. Then silence.

An engine roared to life. Gunfire from inside broke the night air. Spitting gravel led me to believe the shooters had left.

"Aaron, are you okay?" I called out.

Nothing.

"Aaron, say something."

A moan met my ears. I stumbled down the narrow hallway to the kitchen. Glass crunched beneath my feet. Aaron's form slumped on the floor. Without a light, it was impossible to tell where he'd been hurt. I bent, not knowing where to touch or how to help.

"My side and leg. I let them know we're armed."

I stole a glimpse at the outside through a broken window. Only darkness and silence greeted me. But the shooters could be ready to pull the trigger.

"One jerk got away. But I know I hit the other one, and he's still out there." He groaned. "Get the first aid kit in the bathroom. Towel too."

I hurried back down the hall and felt my way into the bathroom for the items. In seconds I returned to Aaron. I knelt by his side and flipped open the kit, but in the darkness I couldn't see much. Dare I turn on a light?

My lungs fought for air.

"Use the flashlight on my phone." He managed to reach into his pocket, anguish sounding through each excruciating move.

I shone the light on him, a mass of blood and mangled flesh. I pressed a towel onto his right side and leg. How did he stay conscious?

"Call Ike."

Isaac's name was the last number he'd called, and I pressed it in. "This is Shelby. Aaron's been shot. He needs an ambulance."

"How bad?"

Aaron's eyes were closed, and when I spoke his name, he didn't respond. "He's unconscious. I don't think it hit his femoral artery, but I'm applying pressure."

"And you?"

"Struggling for air."

"Take his gun. Use it if necessary."

"I don't know how," I whispered through painful wheezing. I couldn't pass out and leave Aaron to bleed out.

"Better get over that real fast if you want to live."

37

Time dragged like a ball and chain while I fretted over every outside sound and Aaron's wounds. He hadn't regained consciousness, which worried me. With both hands, I applied steady pressure over the gunshots using a bloody towel. He'd lost a tremendous amount of blood, too much in my estimation. My strength dwindled, while my lungs strained to give me life.

I fought for him. I fought for myself.

If the shooter had survived, he'd have broken in and finished Aaron and me off by now. Not that I wouldn't have given him a good fight. The truck had sped away, but what was the likelihood of him or them returning to finish the job?

The day had punched me with one crisis after another. Seeing Mom and telling her goodbye. Facing Dad's hatred. Feeling pity for Marissa and her plight in raising a daughter alone. But someone had learned exactly where I'd been tucked away. Now a good man bled out because of an effort to keep me safe, a man who should be spending his days playing golf or fishing.

Tears stung my eyes for all the people who'd suffered over the years. My lungs burned, and I struggled to breathe. Did all of this really matter? I ached for the truth to surface. It seemed like I'd endured enough, but my longing mirrored selfishness. Love for Marissa had sealed my future, and I had no regrets there. Coming forward with the truth held no purpose, except to hurt my sister and her daughter. Locating the stolen money meant Denton's case was closed and Travis's legacy was established. Nothing I could do about Dad's bitterness. But I would go to my death to find who stole the money for the African orphans.

Mom's words flooded into my senses, the one thing she begged me to do. She suspected I'd sacrificed my life for my sister. *"Bring the truth to light. Your dad's blinded by too many things, and sweet Aria is confused. . . . Justice is light."* If only they could have talked longer, to find out if Mom really knew the truth. She used to say she knew her girls inside and out.

Hadn't I already concluded that Mom's medicine must have altered her thinking?

Sirens grew closer, and I prayed an ambulance was with them. Not sure I could handle anything happening to Aaron.

His phone lit up showing Isaac calling, and I released my pressure on Aaron's wound long enough to press Speaker and answer.

"We're about there. Any more problems?"

"Only my concern for Aaron." My lungs were on fire. My head pounded. "Is an ambulance with you?"

"There's two. Are you shot?"

"No."

"You need medical help for the asthma."

Instead of responding and using what little breath I had left, I collapsed over Aaron's lanky body. He couldn't die because of me.

I must have drifted into a fog because someone lifted me off Aaron and leaned me against the fridge. The person inserted a mouthpiece in my mouth. No need for instructions. I sucked in blessed air, a mist with some kind of beta-agonists, probably albuterol. I swept my gaze over the four paramedics in the small kitchen. Two positioned Aaron onto a stretcher while a third balanced an IV pole. I had dozed while they worked on him.

"Are you okay now?" The female paramedic knelt beside me. "We can transport you to the hospital."

I shook my head and held up five fingers indicating five more minutes. An ambulance left with Aaron. The siren screeched and faded into the distance. Nearly an hour later, the female paramedic removed the nebulizer tube and checked my vitals. The second paramedic jotted down notes.

"She shouldn't be left alone for any length of time," the female paramedic said to Isaac.

"I've talked to a doctor and picked up some meds."

Too weak to respond to their conversation, I mouthed a thankyou to both paramedics, and they left.

Isaac sat on the floor beside me. He opened a Walmart bag. "Here you go. I phoned the FBI doc, and he obtained your medical records. You have the real deal here, two filled prescriptions. One is a reliever inhaler, and another is a corticosteroid for long term. If the reliever doesn't work, your lips or nails turn blue, or you can't speak or breathe, we're headed to the hospital. He recommends you see a doctor when this is over." He opened the prescriptions and showed me the healing mists.

"I'd like to hug you," I said.

He frowned. "You already have but my wife will understand."

"You've saved my life more than once."

"Just doin' my job."

"Shouldn't we follow the ambulances?"

"We're staying right here. If you promise me you won't move, I'll talk to the law enforcement officers outside."

"Go. I'm fine. This floor's clean. I washed it, remember?" My intent to make light of the situation miserably failed.

"Want a pillow behind your back?"

"Yes, please."

Isaac retrieved one from my bed, and I allowed the hum of the old fridge to soothe me. Exhaustion won out, and I drifted off to sleep.

◎   ◎   ◎

The sound of the tank's door squeaking prompted me to open my eyes. Isaac gave me a thin-lipped smile, a rarity in our hours together.

"Highway patrol officers are still here, but we've finished for the moment. Aaron's being life-flighted to Houston."

"Good. What about his family?"

"I talked to his wife, and she and their son are on their way to the hospital."

"I prayed for him," I said.

He squinted. "Not my thing. But if it comforts you, go for it."

I wouldn't push the subject. "What about the shooters?"

"One is dead of multiple gunshot wounds. Doesn't look like all were Aaron's."

"You mean the man who drove off shot him too?"

"Dead men don't talk. Fingerprint records show he has past convictions for robbery and assault."

"Hired assassins?"

"I'm thinking so. But we have a leg up. This old trailer house had a tiny upgrade—a security camera."

"You got his face on camera?"

"Yep. Because I'm retired, my access to info is normally on a need-to-know basis. But we now have a bonus."

"When can we take a look?"

"We?" He tossed his familiar frown at me.

"I'm part of the Three Musketeers."

"In that case, right now." He rubbed his face. For sure the day had aged him. "Our position's been compromised. Highway patrol is parked outside until we leave. But they know I'll review the security camera first, then send a link to Houston FBI."

"Where are we headed then?"

"Hotel near Valleysburg. One more thing. I have bad news."

From the haggard look on Isaac's face, I weighed one critical issue after another. My mother had passed? Another crime surfaced with my name on it? Denton got pulled back to Houston? What about Edie or Amy-Jo?

"Please—" I struggled from the kitchen floor to my feet— "what's happened?"

"Denton's been in an accident."

I gasped.

Isaac shook his head. "Whoa. He's at a hospital in Austin and in surgery. Initial report is a concussion and broken bones. Have no clue if there are internal injuries or if the medical procedure is to set a bone."

I blinked back tears, which solved nothing. "Is he conscious?"

"No idea. If he gave a statement, I don't have it. Most likely, an agent will take one when he's out of surgery."

"Forget this protection detail. Take me to see Denton."

"Stupid idea. Then the bad guys will have both of you in the same place."

I stepped into Isaac's personal space. "My nonconfrontational days that helped me survive in prison are over. Got my rear kicked anyway. Seems to me the hospital would be the best place to be. Are you taking me, or do I talk to the highway patrol?"

"If you don't follow directions, I can't be responsible."

"Drive me to the hospital and then head on home. I don't need a babysitter."

"Denton thought otherwise."

The mention of his name shook me. *Denton is hurt because of me.* "And just look at the condition he and Aaron are in."

"Shelby, you'd drive a man to drink."

"I saw you down two beers at dinner."

"All right. I learned a long time ago the futility of arguing with a woman who has her mind made up. But first, let's check out the security camera."

38

DENTON

I welcomed the serene place in my sleep world where I didn't hurt. I heard my name, but the blissful numbness drew me closer . . .

⊙ ⊙ ⊙

The sound of my name pulled me upward again, and I climbed slowly. The moment I surfaced, pain wrapped me in a tight cocoon. Not yet. Sleep was my new world . . .

⊙ ⊙ ⊙

Someone called my name. My eyes fluttered open, and I clamped them shut.

"Mr. McClure, stay with me. It's time to wake up." The voice was a woman. A nurse?

I remembered driving back toward Valleysburg alone. Shelby was in good hands with Isaac and Aaron. Then a pickup rear-ended me. The driver fired shots. I lost control.

"Mr. McClure?"

I forced myself to gaze up at a brown-eyed nurse. Wide smile. White teeth.

"You're awake. How are you feeling?" She checked my vitals.

"Like—" I swore.

"I expect so. You were in a nasty accident."

"Is any part of me not broken?"

She laughed, or rather giggled, allowing my worry to dissipate. "Oh yes. But from the looks of the photos of your truck, not sure how you survived."

I glimpsed the machines hooked up to me. At least they weren't simply keeping me alive. "Have I been unconscious because my mind's zilch?"

"You're in recovery. You had surgery on your right thigh." She feather-touched my shoulder. "You'll be fine." She told me about a metal pin in my leg, a broken collarbone, broken ribs, stitches, and a concussion. "Two police officers are standing guard outside your door. Are you a good guy or bad?"

"Depends on who's asking. FBI."

"I get it. On a scale of one to ten, what's your pain level?"

"Eight and a half." I closed my eyes, weary from talking.

"The doctor ordered pain medication."

"Double dose."

"Spoken like a man in need. This is fast acting and will make you sleep." She picked up an injection from a tray and stood ready to insert it into my IV. "I'll be checking on you periodically. Sheriff Wendall is in the waiting room."

"Tell him I'll live. Have him come in. I'll take the pain meds when we're done." He'd have questions about the jerk who tried to kill me. So did I. At least Shelby was safe.

⊙   ⊙   ⊙

When I reopened my eyes, Sheriff Wendall stood above me with his arms crossed over his chest. He reminded me of Cowboy Ant-Man. Not sure he'd appreciate the nickname. I must be getting my mojo back.

"You gonna live, Denton? You look like you kissed a semi."

"Feel like it too."

"Ready to tell me what happened? A couple of FBI agents are on their way to take your statement, but I'm here first."

How many times had I done the same thing to a victim? "Trade my story for a few ice chips."

He nodded and disappeared, then soon returned with Nurse Giggle, who carried a cup of ice. She spooned a few cold chips into my mouth and told me I was one handsome man. I laughed but it hurt. Everything hurt. Ah, a taste of heaven's springs quenched my desert-dry mouth.

Sheriff Wendall reached inside his pocket for a pad and a pen. A bit of old-school going on. I preferred using my phone to record interviews.

"Start at the beginnin'." He set his Stetson on the nightstand. "Don't leave out one thing. It's all important."

"I drove Shelby to Sharp's Creek. Met her dad, Clay Pearce . . ."

When I finished, the sheriff paced the floor, pad in hand and the pen behind his ear. He turned to me. "Now that you've given me the textbook version, what's your gut say?"

Apprehension seized control. Whatever I said might be used against me by someone. "I'm still in a brain fog."

"No, you're not. You're avoidin' my question."

I glared. "The Pearce family practices dysfunction like you probe for answers. Shelby, her mom, dad, and sister have secrets. I need to analyze each person's words and body language."

"Fair enough."

I searched for signs of my cell phone. "Shelby will be worried I haven't contacted her."

"No, she won't."

I peered into his face. "You called her?"

"She had her own problems last night. They were at the safe house." He quickly sketched out the details. "Aaron is recovering in a Houston hospital, and Isaac is driving her here. She refused to stay in protective custody."

I hated what the three of them had gone through. "Sounds like her. You say one shooter was killed and another got away?"

"Yep. Isaac and Shelby will be here shortly. I want her story about what happened too."

I loaded my mental Glock with my own questions for Shelby and Isaac. But I needed the pain meds first to process anything.

39

SHELBY

I sat in a chair beside Denton's bed and watched him sleep. Or rather I tried without cringing. His face looked like someone had hit him with a sledgehammer. I'd seen worse in prison, revolting really, but Denton received this because of me. The swelling, bruising, and stitches would take a while to heal. The broken bones a little longer. My memory of it—a lifetime.

I longed to touch his face and run my fingers through his thick, nearly white hair. I'd sworn never to trust a man again . . . Prison had scarred me. But Denton's gentleness and sacrificial giving had chiseled away at my heart, crumbling the self-imposed wall.

Isaac and Sheriff Wendall chatted in low tones across the room. I listened for something that would give me a clue about Denton's and my shooter experiences. They were either conscious of my eavesdropping or deliberately keeping details from me. Probably both.

Aaron had survived surgery to remove bullets from his stomach and thigh. Though listed in critical condition, each hour increased his chances of survival.

Edie texted me on my burner phone with a request to call. Denton still slept, so I stepped into the hallway.

"I'm at an Austin hospital with Denton," I said.

"Is he sick? Hurt?"

"He wrecked his truck." Rats, I despised lying, but ignorance kept her safe. "He's going to be okay. Banged up pretty bad. Broken leg that now has pins, cracked ribs, a concussion. He'll be here at least until tomorrow."

"And you?"

"I wasn't with him."

"Why not?"

How did I answer that? "He had an errand to run."

"I'm so glad you're safe, and please give Denton my best. We'll be praying for him. I picked up Joy last night. She's fine. She misses you, I'm sure." Edie paused, and I heard the hesitancy in her voice.

"What's wrong?"

"Randy's here, and I heard him yell at Timothy and Livy. Hold on while I check this out. I now have three kids to deal with."

I thought she'd told her brother to stay away. She must have given in.

She returned within five minutes. "I banished one of them to his room."

"Which one?"

"Randy. I'm mothering a forty-four-year-old man. Told him to go home until he could behave himself."

"I'm sorry." But I smiled anyway.

"I've been worried about you. Amy-Jo feels the same. Did you lie to us about visiting your mother yesterday, or are you so depressed that you had to get away?"

"I saw my mom, and we had precious time together. Lots of love and closure for us. I'm doing my best to manage the depression."

"What about the rest of your family?"

"As expected." Closing my eyes, I searched for the right words. "Edie, I care about you, and I'll do anything to keep you, your kids, and Amy-Jo safe. If necessary, I'll avoid telling you the truth. The less you know, the better."

"My fears exactly. How will you protect yourself at the cabin? Your parole forbids your having a weapon."

"Maybe I'll keep my location a secret for a while. I have money put aside for the rent, but staying hidden makes sense. Would you consider having your brother stay for your family's protection until this is over? Probably a week. I know he tries your patience, yet the safety precaution is worth his sometimes-disagreeable nature." The caller, if still alive, knew how to find those in the line of fire. "Edie, think about your kids."

She groaned. "No way. He drove me nuts today. But I might have another solution."

"Which is?"

"I'll ask Amy-Jo to stay with us. She can bring her trusty Smith & Wesson."

"Does she know how to use it?"

Edie chuckled. "Without a doubt."

When the week ended, I'd beg her to keep Amy-Jo around until arrests were made.

⊙   ⊙   ⊙

Back in Denton's room, I eased into my former chair. This time I turned away from Isaac and Sheriff Wendall. Tears surfaced and needed to be private. My thoughts trailed to the misery in my life. If not for Jesus, I'd find no purpose. Yet I questioned if He was angry with me. My world continued to crumble, and people close to me met with the same destruction. I knew He was in the business of turning ashes into something beautiful, but enduring trials had to end soon.

"Shelby?" Denton peered at me through sleepy eyes. "I should shake you for refusing protection."

"You're the one who needs a safe house." I swallowed my self-pity and reached deep for a facade of cheerfulness. "Aren't you glad to see me?"

A pitiful, bruised smile met me. "Yeah. You look good."

"Thank you. For the sake of conversation, I doubt your ability to shake me." I touched the side of his bed. "I've been praying for you, thanking God you're alive."

"Thanks, I guess. Where was God when you and Aaron faced shooters and I flipped my truck?"

"Keeping us all alive."

"For what purpose? To smack us again?"

"Trusting God doesn't mean we have to understand why bad things happen."

His face clouded. "Shelby, how can you believe in a God who allows us to suffer?"

"It's about faith in a God I can feel. He's given me peace about the things I can't change. I trust His ways are best even though I don't understand." I peered into his battered face. "And hope for eternity."

"My parents and grandparents are believers."

"You're not, or are you angry because life isn't easy?" When he didn't respond, I ventured one step more and whispered, "What kind of circumstances mold us into stronger people, the easy path or the challenges?"

"How's Aaron?"

I'd hit a nerve, but I refused to retract my words. Instead I kissed my fingers and laid them on his forehead. Isaac and Sheriff Wendall walked to the opposite side of the hospital bed.

"You asked about Aaron," Isaac said. "He made it through surgery and is holding his own. Due to Shelby's quick thinking, she kept him from bleeding out."

The sheriff nodded at me. "I'm not surprised. She's smart and cares about others. Maybe too much."

Denton's gaze met mine. His confusion over God changed to tenderness, and the change penetrated my heart.

"Thanks, Shelby. Aaron's like a dad to me. Him and Isaac. They remind me of the characters in the movie *Secondhand Lions*."

"I saw that movie with my dad. And you're right. Note, we agree."

"Thing is," Isaac said, "I have yet to figure out if I'm Robert Duvall or Michael Caine."

"Maybe the lion." I smiled.

Denton gave me a thumbs-up with his non-IV hand. "While I'm in a coherent mode, update me on the two attacks."

Isaac told him about identifying the shooters from the security camera through facial-recognition software and the dead man's criminal record. "We learned his name was Arthur Shell. You'll probably find more info with your FBI security. Your clearance outranks mine. The driver who took off was Eli Chandler. He drove a dark pickup minus the front license plate."

"Anyone else?"

"Not that I'm aware."

Denton reached for his phone on the nightstand and typed. His impassive look gave no signs of his reaction to what he'd learned. He peered at Isaac and Sheriff Wendall. "I can't share some of what I learned with Shelby, but I have a couple of questions for her first."

My heart thumped. "Go ahead. Then I'll walk to the cafeteria. A Coke sounds good right now."

"Take one of those officers posted outside my door."

"I think you're the center of attraction."

He tried to scowl but it obviously hurt. "Did you recognize the dead man? Or does the name Eli Chandler mean anything to you?"

"No."

Denton showed me a photo on his phone of a dark-haired man. "Ever see this guy?"

"No. Is he Chandler?"

"Right."

"My turn," I said. "Where is he from?"

"Miami."

"Do you think our attacks are connected to the missing money?"

"Maybe it's not about the money," Denton said.

Isaac cleared his throat. "The sheriff and I have been discussing the same thing. The answer could lead to the crimes we've experienced of late."

"I've spent brain cells on this, and I have no suspects." I thought about the possibilities. "I had enemies inside prison, and they were interested in the money. But this doesn't feel right. Too many people involved. But you might be right."

Sheriff Wendall closed the hospital room door. "Can't be Randy unless he's gotten mixed up with the wrong guys. Known him a long time, and he has a short fuse. Sometimes I think he fell off a wagon headfirst—he's all about doing the job, not digging a hole to bury someone else."

Isaac secured our attention. "My opinion is it's a waste of time to consider anything but a situation with the money. While the amount doesn't seem significant in contrast with what's happening, the thief might be worried Shelby can ID him. If he invested it, either legal or otherwise, he has a tidy sum to protect."

Denton closed his eyes, no doubt weary and in pain. "I'll handle the FBI checking everything we've discussed."

"Good," Sheriff Wendall said. "I'll talk to Edie and Amy-Jo about Shelby needing a few days to herself."

I thanked him. "My new friends need protection. I just wish I knew from whom."

The sheriff's phone buzzed, and he read a message. "If that don't beat all. Highway patrol found the truck Chandler was driving. Abandoned about a mile from the trailer. Set on fire, but it matches the description."

"Let me guess," Isaac said. "Wiped clean."

40

DENTON

With Shelby out of my hospital room and sharing the company of one of the officers, I shared some of what I'd learned. "Arthur Shell was a local. In and out of jail. Eli Chandler, on the other hand, is a murder suspect in Florida and California. Not enough evidence to arrest him. Did eighteen months in Kentucky for assault and robbery. Had a string of arrests." I paused. "He gets around, and we lost our chance to question him."

"For now," Isaac said. "I have a personal reason for bringing him in."

Sheriff Wendall paced. "I pulled up that much. What are you keepin' from Shelby?"

"Clay Pearce hired Chandler after Shelby was sentenced. He worked at the bakery for six months."

The sheriff stopped. "Fired or quit?"

"Fired."

"You indicated Clay Pearce is a rule keeper . . . so much his shoes squeak. Is this his cover?"

"Sheriff, if he's our man, he's done a good job of covering it up. I saw the exterior of his bakery, his car and house. Impossible to believe he's linked to a money embezzlement scheme."

The sheriff eyed me. "I used to have a dog, sweetest little boy you'd ever want. But at night he killed my chickens and whittled down my cat population. Thought I had me a coyote or a fox. Took me a long time to figure him out 'cause I didn't suspect him."

He made sense. "I'll dig deeper as soon as I get out of here." Once they left, I'd contact the FIG—Field Intelligence Group— for any and every trace of information available on Eli Chandler and Clay Pearce. And any links between them and Travis Stover.

"Denton, we're taking off." Isaac frowned. "You need your rest and trust me when I say, you look like roadkill."

"I've heard the same thing from a couple of others. Are you heading to Houston?"

"Right. Taking Shelby with me. I can protect her while she's concerned about Aaron. I need to check on him, be there with his wife and son until he's out of the woods."

"Give them my best."

"Sure." Isaac paused. "One more thing. I've been thinking about a remark Shelby made last night. When she called me about the firefight and Aaron's condition, I told her to take his gun and use it to protect herself. She said she didn't know how."

I startled. "Impossible."

"Right. How does a person kill a man and not know how to use a gun?"

"She has the faith thing going on, so maybe she vowed never to touch one again. But her answer was strange." I stuck this tidbit into a process-later file, the one labeled *Unusual Info about Shelby Pearce.*

After Shelby, Sheriff Wendall, and Isaac left, and before I gave in to summoning Nurse Giggles for another shot of relief, Mike

Kruse called me. At first I thought he'd heard about the accident, but his reason to reach out took me down a different path.

"An agent approached me today, an old friend. He's been working on a money-laundering case. Hasn't made an arrest. A woman charged with identity theft offered info in exchange for a lesser charge. She said a money-laundering operation had roots in Sharp's Creek. The agent probed deeper, and she gave a name. That's when he came to me because it concerns one of our old cases."

"Which one?"

"Shelby Pearce. Ready for this? Clay Pearce is a money-laundering suspect."

"Are you kidding?" I told him about my hospital stay, the goings-on, and Eli Chandler. "I was in Sharp's Creek yesterday, drove Shelby to see her mother. She's dying of cancer and requested to see her daughter. Anyway, I don't care for the guy, but if Pearce is involved in money-laundering, he's smarter than I gave him credit for."

"Points to him taking the $500K from Marissa and Travis Stover and cleaning it up for himself."

"Yep. When did he intend to use it? Stuff it in his casket?" I missed something in talking to him, and it aggravated me. "I'd like to see the report."

"Figured so. I'll make sure you get it when we're finished talking."

"Have you talked to Pearce?"

"Another reason for my call. Since we worked the Pearce case, good old Clay might feel more comfortable if we conducted the interview."

"He hasn't won the Most-Likable Citizen Award." I definitely could live my days without talking to him. "When do you want to go?"

"Monday?"

Gave me an extra day to recuperate, possibly get something to manage the pain without the nondrowsy additive.

"It's no coincidence Clay Pearce's name is connected to more than one crime," Mike said. "Where is Shelby now?"

"On her way to a hotel in Houston. Isaac will have an adjoining room." I drew in a ragged breath, accompanied by an agonizing throb in my leg, and gave him the latest news. "Shelby is one stubborn lady. She insists she's okay. Her belief is Isaac's nighttime stay at the hotel is all the protection she needs."

"We obviously have a lot of catchin' up to do. Tomorrow I'll drive to Austin, pick you up, then on to Valleysburg. We'll leave early Monday morning."

I thanked him, and we ended the call. Hard for me to wrap my brain around Clay Pearce as a kingpin in a money-laundering scheme. That was as far-fetched as I could imagine. I replayed my brief encounter with the man who claimed the role of a beaten and grieving man. I'd justified his ill temperament . . . felt sorry for him even if I didn't like him. Something didn't add up, and it would take a lot to convince me Clay had money tucked away somewhere. But I'd follow up. Wouldn't be the first time I'd spent time and energy on a false accusation.

Worn-out and hurting, I hit the call button, and my giggle angel of mercy agreed to pain meds. With any luck when I wakened, the FIG might have the requested information.

41

SHELBY

I despised having nothing to do. The idle time in the hotel room reminded me of prison. Reading, studying, thinking, TV, crafting jewelry in my mind, and occasional online time bored me until I thought I'd go crazy. I paced and hoped the room below me didn't complain to the management.

Last evening, Isaac had checked us in as father and daughter with adjoining rooms. Where he conjured up the fake names was beyond me. I bet in Aaron's and his preretirement days, they were a formidable pair. Still were. They were a bit comical together . . . short, stout Isaac and tall, thin Aaron.

Concern for Aaron nipped at my conscience . . . my fault. He'd made it through the night, a plus for his recovery status. I'd like to see him, thank him for his sacrifice, but showing up at the hospital put him in as much danger as at the tank. His family might not be thrilled to see me either.

Denton . . . how did I feel about him? He occupied way too much of my thoughts. He'd deceived me, but he'd given me a sweet puppy. He'd lied to me, but now he claimed to believe me innocent of taking Travis's money. He'd paid for Isaac and Aaron to protect me. He'd driven me to see my dying mother—and nearly got himself killed.

The compassion in his eyes told me he cared.

He'd hinted at the two of us being an item. *"I wonder why we've been thrown together. Mostly our strange attraction when we should hate each other."*

A ruse?

I shook my head. No point in letting my heart stray until this was over. Denying my attraction to Denton offered no consolation to my plunging emotions.

After checking every TV channel, including Spanish, Asian, and Arabic, I gave up. I tagged myself as officially bored. Descending six floors to the restaurant for dinner crossed my mind, but I'd been there earlier for lunch. If my stalkers were watching, I didn't need to play into their hands.

The last two days crashed against my mind, rolled, and repeated. A ghastly suspicion made me physically ill. Dad had taken my purse before he left me alone with Mom. Had he removed my inhaler? He knew how an asthma attack leveled me. *God forgive me for thinking such a despicable thought.*

I prayed my spare inhaler sat at the cabin or had fallen out of Denton's truck.

Edie had downloaded several e-books on her old phone, so I chose a romantic comedy. Not sure why since happily ever after fell into the same category as fairy tales. The story put me to sleep.

A pounding on the door separating my room from Isaac's jolted me awake. I stumbled to it, but caution stopped me from flinging it open.

"Who's there?"

"Isaac. Were you expecting Santa Claus?" The familiar growl left no confusion to his identity. "Open the door."

I obliged and gasped. Blood spattered his shirt. "Are—?"

"Grab your stuff. We need to get out of here."

As I whirled to snatch my backpack and purse, myriad questions longed to erupt. I slapped my room key on the TV table.

"Now!"

My gaze flew to his face. He swiped at a trickle of blood from the side of his mouth. I hurried through his open door. No need to ask if we'd been found.

Isaac yanked my arm down the hall. "The stairs. One of 'em is on the elevator." We raced toward the red Exit sign. He opened the door and pulled me behind him. We hurried down the concrete stairwell.

One flight to the fifth floor.

Second flight to the fourth. A door above me opened and slammed, and the pounding of footsteps grew closer.

Midway down to the third floor, the stress on my lungs shortened my breathing. The door swung wide in front of me. A man wearing a ski mask bolted through.

A feral scream burst from my throat. I spun to see if the person following us had made it to the landing. A masked man towered above and raised his weapon.

The man in front of us raised his gun.

Isaac pushed me against the concrete wall, and I slid to the step. He opened fire on the man nearest us, then turned to the man who thundered down the steps.

Isaac shot. Grazed the man's arm.

I rolled to the landing beside the man who had a gaping hole in his chest and blank eyes.

Isaac punched the jaw of the man on the steps. He knocked Isaac's gun from his hands, and it fell beside me. I wanted to pick it up, help the situation, but I froze.

"Give me his gun!"

Isaac sent a fist into the masked man's stomach, sending him toppling down the stairs. I hugged the wall on the landing. Isaac jumped over the dead man and retrieved his own weapon.

The man grabbed me. I kicked and hit him. He swung me around with my back slammed against him. The gun barrel pressed into my temple, and his other arm wrapped across my throat. "It's over, old man."

Isaac straddled the dead man. He raised his hands with his gun in his right. "Police are on the way."

"But not before I finish my job. Drop the gun. Slowly."

"No need for this," I said. "You have me—let him go."

"Shut up." The man tightened his hold against my throat.

Isaac slowly bent.

I sank my teeth into the man's arm and drove my fist into his groin. He cried out and jerked me sideways, giving Isaac time to throw his weight into me and the man.

The man released me. I pulled away, coughing. Fighting for air.

The gun fired. The bullet went wild. But Isaac had the advantage and wrenched the weapon from the man's hand while jerking his injured arm behind his back.

"You okay?" He kept his attention on the man.

"Yes." I stared at him for signs of blood other than his face and shirt.

Isaac leaned on his right leg. Blood seeped from his right knee. "Who you working for?" He pulled on the masked man's arm.

"Forget it, old man."

"This old man knows how to make you talk." He yanked harder.

"You're breaking my arm!"

"Answer my question or I'll break both of them." Isaac inched the arm upward. "Who hired you?"

"I have my rights."

"So do the people you try to kill." Isaac slammed his face into the wall, leaving an impression of the man's head. He swung the man around. "Give me a name, or would you like me to break your jaw? I know how to make sure you spend the rest of your life drinking through a straw." Isaac drew back his fist.

"All right! Eli Chandler."

42

DENTON

Old friends are like gold nuggets—they increase their value with time. Mike had driven me home from the hospital yesterday. Hadn't seen him in six years, since he'd been transferred to Dallas, and the few hours in his car gave us time to talk. He'd lost his hair. Also added a couple inches to his belt. I tried to get him to stay with me at the cabin, but he claimed he wasn't a nurse and had work to do, preferably in a hotel room in Valleysburg. As it was, I crawled into bed at four thirty in the afternoon and slept until my alarm went off the next morning.

Hobbling around the cabin on crutches had a learning curve . . . a big one. The face looking back at me in the mirror reminded me of a horror movie. Isaac's comment about looking like roadkill hit spot-on. If the FBI refused to keep me on, I might find a job in Hollywood. No makeup required. Maybe I could scare Clay Pearce into giving Mike and me something we could use. I maneuvered to the stable to feed Big Red. I was sure from the time it took to fill the feed bucket and pump water, he thought we were gearing up for a long ride.

After seeing my condition, Mike had revised the pickup time to seven thirty. Figured we would grab some breakfast on our way to Sharp's Creek. But Mike's internal clock meant he'd be here at seven. I'd learned that mannerism after working as his partner for two weeks. I'd been a slow learner.

Seeing I had fifteen minutes to spare, I checked in with the FIG for info on Eli Chandler and whatever they'd dug up between him, Clay Pearce, and Travis Stover.

Additional information showed Chandler had a reputation as a hired assassin. Besides what I'd read about him yesterday, he'd led an organized-crime group associated with human trafficking, drugs, illegal arms, money laundering, and whatever it took to keep those businesses afloat. While organized crime moved money around the world through various means to clean it up, I questioned if Chandler ran or worked for a syndicate. If he ran an operation, he wouldn't have been on a hit job. The only documented link with Pearce came from the six-month employment years ago. Chandler definitely grew his moneymaking horizons after serving donuts.

Personal background indicated he'd been divorced and signed off on parental rights for three kids to avoid paying child support. His parents and two brothers hadn't seen him in two decades. No current girlfriend or significant other listed. Now he fled the FBI and dodged local law enforcement.

Mike arrived at straight-up 7:00. By 7:05, we were heading east to Sharp's Creek. "We'll catch coffee and breakfast on the way at a McDonald's drive-through."

We'd shared plenty of breakfasts en route to running down bad guys and interviews. At least it wasn't a no-name convenience store without a microwave.

"I have an update on Eli Chandler." I revealed what I'd learned. "He's working for someone. The kingpin wouldn't expose himself and do the grunt work."

"Makes sense that he'd been hired to eliminate Shelby. If only we knew who the boss is and his motive." He glanced at me. "Your face looks worse than last night."

"Thanks. At least I still have hair."

Mike chuckled. "Bald is beautiful. Except your white hair makes you look older than me. What are you now? Forty-two?"

"Forty."

"You'll grow into your white hair."

My turn to chuckle.

"How has Shelby changed?"

Caution rang out an alert when it came to her. "Rehabilitated."

"I've read her prison file. Hope she makes it."

"My bet's on her."

"From the tone of your voice, I'd say she's more than a friend."

"Ridiculous." I shook my head. "She learned her lesson and paid her debt."

"Has the cute, innocent-looking kid grown into a beautiful woman, or has prison life hardened her?"

"Haven't paid much attention."

"Liar." Mike smirked.

My phone alerted me to a call. "Hold on, this is Shelby."

"Why am I not surprised?"

I ignored him and answered the call. "Can you talk?" she said.

"Sure. My former partner and I are driving to Sharp's Creek. What's up?"

"Two shooters found me and Isaac last evening. One man's dead. Isaac's wounded but okay."

"Mind if I put this on speaker?"

"Go ahead."

I pressed Speaker and placed the phone on the console. "Where were you when this happened?"

"At the hotel . . ."

I listened, while my gut seared with the idea of Aaron and Isaac paying a price in this mess. "Have the shooters been identified?"

"Yes, the man in custody is Nick Hanson, and the dead man is Stan Watkins."

"Okay. And Isaac's not in the hospital?"

"He's in the hospital all right. Sitting by Aaron's bed with a bandage wrapped around his knee. I'm at another hotel."

"Address?" I jotted down the location. "Check in with me every hour. A text will do."

"What's going on in Sharp's Creek?"

"A conversation with your dad."

"I'll keep my word to check in if you'll tell me later why you and another agent are paying my dad a visit."

"All right. Will fill you in later."

"Is the agent Mike Kruse, your old partner?"

I glanced at him and he nodded. "Yes."

"The past weaves us all back together, doesn't it? Denton, how's talking to my dad going to figure out anything?"

"Can't go into it."

"Okay for now. I don't want anyone else hurt because of me. Between the two of you, please figure out who's behind this and stop them. The last thing I need is to have Edie, Amy-Jo, or Marissa dragged into a firefight."

"We're doing everything we can."

She sighed. "You're doing far more than I deserve, and I appreciate every painful step."

"The meds help." I laughed when I wished she sat in the car with me.

"I'm not far from a bus stop, so I'm returning to Valleysburg in a couple of hours."

What was she thinking? "Tell me you're teasing."

"This makes sense to me. I'm finished with exchanging one cell for another and endangering others' lives."

Mike huffed and took over. "We'll pick you up once we're done in Sharp's Creek."

"Take a long look at Denton, Aaron, and Isaac. Once I'm back at the cabin, I'll figure out the next step. I don't need you two to pick me up." She clicked off.

I whipped my attention to Mike. "I'm calling Isaac. I want to hear from him what happened."

43

Each excruciating limp to the Pearces' door instilled the need for one of Nurse Giggle's wonder injections. And the need to find who was behind these crimes. Robins sang from a perch on a power line. The sky shone a bright, clear blue. A small boy pedaled a bike down the street, and a woman busied herself in a flower bed.

Isaac had given me the rundown on his exploits with Shelby. The two men who'd attacked him in the hotel's parking lot and then in the stairwell had been identified as low-life thugs. One dead and the other lawyered up.

Clay must have seen me coming because the door opened before I raised a fist to knock. "Morning, Clay. This is Agent Mike Kruse. You probably recall him from Shelby's case."

Mike reached out to shake his hand, but Clay refused. His face hardened. "I remember. What's the reason you're back?"

I took the lead unless the interview went south. "We'd like to talk, ask a few questions."

"About?"

"FBI business."

"Why not a phone call?"

"It's a sensitive conversation to have and one we prefer face-to-face."

Clay stepped aside. "Make it quick. My wife's sleeping, and when she wakes up, I need to be with her."

I clumsily maneuvered my crutches by him and Mike followed. "Appreciate this," I said. "How is your wife?"

The lines deepened in his face. "Not good. She sleeps most of the time. Heavily sedated. Hospice is a 24-7 job."

"I'm sorry. Can't imagine how hard this must be."

Clay gestured into the living room. "We can talk in here, Agents."

"Denton."

"Mike."

Clay nodded and eased onto a worn corduroy recliner where I'd sat previously. We sank onto a threadbare sofa. The tension in the room equaled when Shelby and I were there.

He pointed to my crutches. "How did you get beat up?"

"Rear-ended. Hit-and-run."

"A drunk?"

"Doubtful."

Clay drew in a heavy breath. "Do the questions have anything to do with your accident?"

"I think so. Since Shelby's release, new information about the embezzlement case has surfaced."

He froze. "Is she in trouble?"

"Someone wants her dead. She's been threatened repeatedly, and right now the FBI has her in a safe house, the third attempt to keep her alive. The wrong people discovered the first two and attacked. Two agents have been shot."

"She's okay?"

"Yes."

"The others will recover?"

"One of the agents on protective duty nearly lost his life."

Clay dragged a hand over his face. "She was safer in prison."

"Yes, sir." I noted the distress around his eyes. "The FBI is on it, but progress is slow."

"Where do I fit in this?"

"A shooter claimed Eli Chandler hired him."

Clay stiffened. "Chandler?"

I nodded. "He worked for you six months after Shelby's sentencing."

"I fired him. Found him dipping his hands into the cash register."

I leaned back. My leg hurt but taking a pain pill lessened my game.

"Do the names Nick Hanson, Arthur Shell, or Stan Watkins sound familiar?"

"No, sir."

"Do you mind if I ask you something?" Mike said. When Clay motioned for Mike to go ahead, he continued. "Why didn't you press charges against Chandler?"

"Rough times back then. Shelby had been convicted of manslaughter. My wife had a breakdown. Marissa grieved and was pregnant with Aria."

"The FBI's been investigating a money-laundering case for over three years now. The trail has led to Sharp's Creek."

"Sure your evidence's accurate? This town isn't exactly a hub of criminal or financial activity."

"We've learned in this business not to be surprised by anything. The problem is the investigation provided a name."

"Someone I know?"

"Clay Pearce."

The shock on Clay's face prompted Mike to hold up his hand. "Denton and I volunteered to talk to you because the situation seems like a setup."

"My name's connected with money laundering?" Clay snorted. "Why? Look around you." He gestured at the room. "Am I a man of means? Do you see where I live, my old car, the updates needed everywhere you look? With that kind of money, I'd have paid for my wife to try an experimental cancer treatment."

"I understand." Mike kept his tone even. "When I read the report and talked to Denton, we questioned the validity."

Clay stood. "The thought of the FBI using my tax money in a ridiculous accusation like money laundering makes me furious."

"Would me too. Sit down, Clay. We're friends here." Clay obliged and Mike continued the conversation. "Is there anyone who'd want to destroy your reputation? Someone who holds a grudge against you?"

"No one I can think of. Never had a bad time with anybody but Eli Chandler."

"Consider the person who confiscated the money. He or she might live in Sharp's Creek and plan to keep their crime a secret."

Clay's gaze darted between us. "I'm clueless. If anyone had come to my attention, I'd have gone to the FBI. Although Travis raised the money for African orphans, Marissa could have used every penny over the years. Have you talked to Shelby?"

"She has no idea what's going on."

"You're of the opinion the threats stem from the missing money?"

"The situation has our attention, Clay."

He closed his eyes, a worn man. "My family has suffered enough." He looked at me and shook his head. "You saw my wife and Marissa the day you were here. Why this now?"

"I see how you're hurting," I said. "It appears you're victims again. We need your help to clear your name."

"How?"

"We need a statement and for you to be aware the FBI is investigating you."

"As a person of interest?"

"Yes."

"Whatever you need, I'll do it. Will you keep it between us? Marissa has enough on her plate, and Aria is a good kid. Neither deserve their names dipped in manure."

"I figured you'd cooperate, and we'll keep the situation quiet. Although it's not likely connected, I have a question about Travis Stover." When he nodded, I ventured ahead. "Did you approve of him marrying your daughter?"

"Without hesitation. He was more of a godly man than I'd ever be. He loved Marissa and showed genuine interest in Shelby. His death hit me and the wife hard."

"Thanks. Even after Shelby confessed to shooting him, you claimed she couldn't have killed him."

"Shelby refused to touch a gun. She had a rebellious streak a mile wide, but she drew the line on weapons. We used to spend lots of time together—she was a real daddy's girl. I tried to persuade her to hunt with me, but no use. Her admission to shooting Travis sounded ridiculous. But Marissa swore Shelby had pulled the trigger, and she confessed to it. I thought I knew my daughter better than anyone else, but I was wrong. Marissa told me disgusting things about Shelby."

"What kind of things?" I said.

Clay sighed. "Smoking. Drinking. Using drugs and selling them. Sleeping around since she was twelve. Hard for me to believe." Sad eyes met mine. "I'm a bitter man. My wife's and daughters' lives were destroyed because of one tragic decision. Soon all I'll have left is one daughter and Aria."

Clay's voice softened when he'd spoken about Shelby's and his past relationship. Not at all how he'd responded when I was here before. He loved her despite what she'd done. His emotions must frighten him. That I understood.

44

Between the pain in my battered body and whoever wanted my friends dead, I was in no mood for a smart-mouth. Nick Hanson had no idea how determined a wounded man could be. Mike and I had left Clay Pearce and driven to Houston, where we waited to interview Hanson, the man who'd attacked Isaac and Shelby in the stairwell. Hanson supposedly had no family. No job. No priors. But he had military experience.

"I doubt this is his first offense," I said. "More like the first time he's been caught. According to Isaac, Hanson knew how to handle himself. Why don't you lead the questioning since I look like I got hit by the wrong end of an ugly stick?"

"And lost." Mike gave me a thumbs-up. "I doubt he'll be more afraid of me than you, but I'll give it a shot."

The guard steered Hanson inside. He had the physique of a man who frequented the gym. Isaac was a beast for taking him down.

Hanson sneered. "The Feds, huh? Tell me why I have the pleasure of your company."

Mike offered a slight smile and introduced himself and me. "Nick, you have an impressive military record—two tours in Afghanistan, sharpshooter, covert ops in Syria. Now you're in jail, and your buddy Stan Watkins is dead. Which puzzles me why a man of your caliber took a hit man job from a lowlife like Eli Chandler."

Hanson eyed him. "We were minding our own business when this old guy attacked me and my buddy in the parking lot. We got hot and followed him inside. The old guy shot my buddy, and I surrendered so he wouldn't kill me."

Mike tapped his finger on the table. "The 'old guy' is a Fed. You were wearing ski masks and admitted Chandler hired you. Let's get past the Halloween party. We can talk to the judge on your behalf, but only if you cooperate."

Nick squinted. "How?"

"How long have you and Stan Watkins been working together?"

"About five years."

"Did you recruit him?"

Hanson nodded.

"What about Arthur Shell?"

"Never heard of him."

Mike folded his hands on the table. "Tell us about Chandler."

"That would put me on his hit list."

"You're already there just by talking to us."

"What kind of deal can you offer me?"

Mike eyed him. "Depends on what you give us."

"Never met Chandler. He calls when something needs done."

"Like what? Hit contracts?"

"Errands."

"Give me an example."

"Drive-through Sonic. Pick up his dry cleaning."

Mike stood. "Denton, take over. As far as I'm concerned, Chandler can have him."

I'd played this game before. "Nick, you're wasting our time, and neither of us is in the mood to sift through lies."

Hanson laughed. "Black-and-blue agent thinks he can intimidate me?"

I nodded. "You know the saying 'Don't mess with a wounded animal'? Exactly how I feel. You have a choice—answer my questions or face Chandler."

Hanson swore. "All right. I might have one answer."

"Question number one—how long have you been working for Chandler?"

"Ten years."

"As a hit man?"

"I collect money owed to him or whatever he needs."

"Give us your job details regarding FBI Special Agent Isaac Sims and Shelby Pearce."

"I didn't know the old man was a Fed. The woman had just gotten out of prison and knew something Chandler didn't want her telling."

I held up a finger. "What?"

"No idea."

"Hmm. Chandler wanted Shelby Pearce dead because he was afraid of being blackmailed?"

Hanson shrugged. "He didn't trust her. But the order could have come from Chandler or his boss."

"Name?"

"Never heard it."

"How does the big boss make money?"

Hanson glanced away, and I gave him time to think before I spoke again. "I need more for the judge to look favorably on your charges. Attempted murder and an attack on a federal agent will keep you locked up a long time."

"Money laundering and whatever else is illegal. The big boss stays behind the scenes. I can give you Chandler's number."

I grabbed a pen and paper, and Nick rattled off numbers. "This is progress, unless the number's no good." I sent the number to the FIG and leaned back in my chair to get more comfortable with my throbbing leg.

"What do you know about an attack on another agent and Ms. Pearce?"

"No clue."

"Where do Chandler and his boss base their operation?"

"Miami. I heard the big boss has overseas connections." He shook his head. "I don't know anything else. Neither do I know why they want the Pearce woman dead."

45

SHELBY

Late Monday night, walking the dark road from the bus stop in Valleysburg to home was safer than being with Aaron and Isaac. In the stillness with the peaceful sound of nocturnal creatures, I longed for the comforts of my haven. I also wanted to get back to work. No matter what I encountered there or in the days to come, I planned to fight whoever stalked me. Even if it was Dad. Waiting for something bad to happen made the struggle with depression harder.

"Impossible," I whispered to no one but myself.

My thoughts trailed to the times Dad, Travis, and I took camping and hiking trips to Colorado. Neither Mom nor Marissa enjoyed any part of it, and that was okay. We'd climb a hilly path, and Travis and I would softly harmonize whatever tune hit us, and sometimes Dad chimed in with his deep voice. I missed those special moments.

In my cabin, instead of sleeping with one eye open, I quickly drifted into bliss. Not sure the Second Coming could have wakened me unless an angel blew a trumpet in my ear.

Over coffee late Tuesday morning and while fashioning jewelry, my burner phone rang with an unrecognizable number. A pinch of apprehension hit me. What if Mom had passed? Or had Aaron taken a turn for the worse?

"Shelby, it's Marissa. Are you free to talk?" Her frantic tone alarmed me.

"Is Mom—?"

"No. She hasn't long, but she's still alive." She sighed. "I need to see you in person."

"Out of the question. It's too dangerous."

Marissa sobbed. "Please, I must talk to you before anything else happens."

"Calm yourself and tell me what's going on."

"Aria and I have been threatened."

I swallowed the panic. "Start at the beginning."

"I received a call at the bakery yesterday morning. A muffled voice told me to find out where you hid the $500K. The person warned me about going to the FBI or Aria and I would regret it. I know you have no idea where the money is or even who took it, but what am I to do?"

The stalker had reached his desperation stage. "Marissa, you have no choice but to go to the FBI."

She gasped. "It's too complicated. There's more. Dad told me Denton and another agent came to the house yesterday morning. A money-laundering operation led to him."

"No wonder Denton refused to tell me about the trip. Dad would never—" My mind seemed to explode with reasons against Dad's guilt.

"Shelby, the ones who threatened you, are they after the money too?"

"Not exactly. Maybe."

"Help me understand. I'm confused."

The idea of sparing my sister the truth when she'd been through so much seemed like the right thing. But we were grown women who needed to work out a horrible set of circumstances. "I was told to commit suicide, that my family would be better off."

She burst into tears. "Why?"

"Some people are not good-hearted like you." My sister's innocence needed to stay intact. "They're selfish, greedy, cruel. It's a part of this world you haven't experienced, and I will do whatever's necessary to make sure you never do." The moment the words left my mouth, I committed to my original promise to keep her safe. "You have a fifteen-year-old, and she needs a mother to teach her how to stay away from people who'd hurt her."

"I'm sorry to bother you with this. I didn't know where else to turn. If not for me, you wouldn't have been among the worst people. I promise I will educate myself in the ways of today's world. Aria deserves the best. She's my reason for living. But my resolve doesn't help now. You're the clever one, the sister with a plan. Help me, Shelby. I'm afraid."

Poor, sweet Marissa. "The person who is threatening us has to be someone who followed every moment of the trial and kept tabs on us since then."

"I'm afraid it's Dad."

The dad of my girlhood valued honesty above all things. "If he embezzled the money, why is he living in Sharp's Creek? Why hasn't he left the country or laundered it to improve his life? He's not getting any younger. No, it's not Dad."

"He asked me this morning if he could take Aria on a vacation during spring break. He believes Mom will have died by then, and the two of them could grieve together."

My pulse raced. "He's counting on Mom dying so he can take a trip?"

"I agree it's heartless. When he wanted my permission, I didn't know what to say. I asked him how he could afford a vacation, and he apparently has money saved. I asked where he wanted to take her." She paused. "He doesn't know for sure, but the trip would be a surprise. The worst part is spring break is in two weeks."

Surely Dad hadn't chosen money over his family. "Does Aria suspect anything? Have you told her about the threat?"

"I refuse to frighten her with this." Marissa sobbed. "She should know, right? So she can be on alert?"

"Right. Ignorance doesn't stop a crime."

"Okay. She tells me everything, and she hasn't mentioned a word."

"Has Dad's behavior changed since my release? Has he said anything confusing?"

"He's always difficult, irrational. Hot and cold with his love. But he loves Aria, always has. I think I could rot, and he wouldn't know the difference."

"Not true at all. He loves you." I had to protect Marissa and Aria. "Do you still take a couple of days off occasionally to rest from your rheumatoid arthritis?"

"I haven't for a while. It's impossible to leave Mom or the bakery."

"Take a break. Make sure Aria's with you. I'll talk to Denton to see if the FBI can arrange a safe house."

"I won't leave Mom. She depends on me."

"What about your daughter? There's got to be a solution. Just give me a moment to think."

I prayed for an answer. If Dad stood at the helm of a money-laundering scheme, he'd wasted a lot of years before he took advantage of a leisurely life. Perhaps the years of bitterness held the key. How sad to expect Dad, the one man I loved more than life . . . Unless the person responsible intended to frame him.

"Shelby, I'll tell Dad I need a day off to see a new doctor in Houston. I'll drive to Valleysburg so we can talk in person. He won't hurt Aria."

"Are you sure?"

"I don't know. I'm upset about too many things and it's hard to focus. I'll find a way to bring Aria with me."

"How about Thursday? Please give thought to allowing the FBI to step in and keep you and Aria safe."

"Maybe so. All right, I'll pray about it. I have an idea—I'll tell Dad that Aria needs to be checked for RA. My strain is genetic."

"Is it?"

"No. Thank goodness. I'll tell him the appointment is on Thursday, which gives me tomorrow to pack when he's not around and withdraw what little money I have from the bank."

"If anything happens, call me immediately. Do you have Denton's number?"

"He gave me his card." Marissa sobbed again.

"No one hears about our meeting, okay?"

"Are you talking to Denton? If he goes to the FBI, I'm afraid—"

"No. This stays among sisters."

46

DENTON

My mamaw went through the eighth grade before she quit school to help on the farm. Despite her lack of education, she tutored me through high school algebra. Taught me how to dance. We'd go fishing, and she'd always catch more catfish than me. We'd go hunting, and she'd bring down the biggest buck. Many a night we'd stare up at the sky through a telescope. She'd point out a constellation, and through the stars and visible planets, she'd tell me about Jesus.

Shelby's words about God using hard times to mold us into stronger people haunted me. Because I had to admit every hurdle and tragedy made me wiser, offered deeper insight into behavior.

Memories of Mamaw two-stepped across my mind as I leaned against a post on my porch. Could be the full moon and clear night dotted with stars reminded me of her. Truth was, I craved her wisdom, her soft voice, and sassy ways that guided a young boy before she'd slipped away in her sleep. Pawpaw succumbed to dementia after she died and joined her soon afterward.

Life hadn't gone as I'd planned or wanted—#disappointed. The sweet wife and half a dozen kids lived somewhere else in my mind. I loved my parents, and though I'd isolated myself from my brothers, they were still family. My job had its perks, but the ups didn't bring me the satisfaction I craved.

My heart hurt for relief without a name. I longed for a woman who might not survive. My leg hurt, and the pain meds put me to sleep. Mamaw had a few choice descriptions for whiners, and I fit them all.

Tonight one of Mamaw's comparisons about faith and the universe stuck in my mind. She professed if Jesus created the universe and knew every dark-brown hair on my head, then He'd purposed a divine plan for my life. My role with the FBI—to help stop and prevent crimes—filled me with satisfaction. Volunteering with troubled teen boys packed another hole. But at forty years old, I still craved peace. My spirit wrestled with what I needed to do about blaming God for my disappointments. But anger punched my gut. Over fifteen years of animosity toward God was entrenched in my soul. I wanted it gone—forever. But I couldn't relinquish control.

Unanswered questions about Shelby zoomed in and out of my mind. In the past, difficult cases kept me on task. Nothing drew me away from looming problems. No longer. Shelby had taken root in my heart, and I'd fallen for a convicted murderer, a woman I'd once loathed. What was I supposed to do with that? We'd texted a few times today. Thanks to Sheriff Wendall, he'd positioned an officer to keep an eye on Shelby's cabin.

So many reasons I stared up at the sky and wished Mamaw would offer her sage advice. I breathed in deeply. Her words from long ago repeated in my mind. *"Allen Denton, you need Jesus. Follow Him and you'll feel a whole lot better about yourself and where you're headed."*

I stared up at the Big Dipper and recalled another of her statements. *"If God can hold up the stars in the sky, He'll lead you through the mud that Satan slings your way."*

I was neck-deep in that mud—actually smellier than that. Brice's constant immature comments frustrated me, but the source of my bitterness went deeper. I focused on my pain still evident after fifteen years.

I hadn't forgiven Andy or Lisa for choosing each other.

Their happiness had shoved me into emotional paralysis. I blamed God for my broken heart when He could have stopped the marriage. Their two boys should have been mine.

And Shelby's case . . . I blamed God for stealing my victory there too.

Easing onto the porch step, I fixed my gaze on the stars and planets that existed light-years away. Could a holy God who created the intricacies of the galaxy help me shake off the blame and unforgiveness in my life? Mamaw believed so, as well as my family and Shelby.

I'm tired of fighting life.

Mamaw seemed to sit beside me, and I was a boy again. Words about Jesus and truth rolled through my mind.

The words to Shelby's poem, the one I found in her Bible, seemed to haunt me. Every time I tried to toss them aside, they walked back into my head . . . and heart.

> *Why do I remember*
> *The sins that stalk my soul?*
> *Why can't I hold on to the*
> *Forgiveness that makes me whole?*
> *Ashes rise to steal my breath.*
> *I choke from drowning fear.*
> *Help me, Lord, to cling to You*
> *In never-ending prayer.*

I walked the same misery as Shelby once had.

Six hours later I peered up at the night sky. *Lord, I surrender my life to You. Save me from myself.*

47

Strange how a decision to accept what I couldn't see or touch ushered in optimism. Especially when the world spun on an unbalanced axis. This morning my crutch and swing routine seemed lighter. I made it to the stables faster than the day before. For certain, my light steps were due to my new faith.

I walked inside and leaned against Big Red's stall. Taking my phone from my jean pocket, I pressed in Mom and Dad's number. Mom answered.

"Two calls in a week, Son? This must be good."

"I think so. I became a Christian."

"Oh, my." She wept softly. "Denny, I'm so happy for you. Can't wait to tell your dad. He ran to the post office."

"I figured you've prayed for me for a long time, so you should know first."

"We both have. What brought about the change?"

"The right people and circumstances turned me around."

"A woman?"

"In a way."

"Are you getting married?"

"No, Mom." Then it hit me how much of a role Shelby had played and how much I did care. "Maybe in the future. A lot's riding on our relationship. Some issues need to be worked out first."

"Denny, you have such a kind heart. Whatever it is, don't let another woman break your heart."

"Thanks, Mom. Andy and Lisa are supposed to be together. I'm glad for them."

"Brice is another matter," Mom said.

"It will work out. He reached out to me not too long ago, so I'll call him."

"My dear boy. Your words are like music."

"The Beatles?"

She laughed. "Somewhere between 'Let It Be' and 'Twist and Shout.'"

"Mom, don't ever change. Love you, and I've got to go. Working on a tough case, but when it's over, I'll be home for a visit. Give Dad a hug for me."

My next call to Brice lasted all of three minutes. I told him about my new faith and my desire to be a better part of the family. "I hope we can be brothers again. And friends."

"Uh, sure. Don't know what to say . . . Thanks."

I slipped my phone back into my pocket and checked in with Big Red. "I'm going to see Shelby. Tell her my spiritual life took a boost." He nudged me. "Yeah, I miss her. Sorry you can't take me, but until this leg heals, I'm using a different kind of horsepower. The one and only car rental business in Valleysburg has delivered a compact Chevy, giving me a little freedom. But I prefer you." I patted him and drove the half mile to Shelby's cabin. If Sheriff Wendall saw me driving with one foot and one hand, I'd be ticketed.

She opened the door before I managed to maneuver up the

porch steps. How did she always manage to pull off a sweet country girl look?

"Heard me coming?"

Her face lit up. "Agent McClure, you can't sneak up on anyone."

"Give me six weeks, and I'll be back to fighting form."

"Six?"

I shrugged. "Maybe eight."

She tilted her head. "Are you supposed to be driving?"

"I'm sure short jaunts are fine."

Joy wiggled between Shelby's legs, and she snatched up the puppy. "I want to hear about all your adventures."

"More like swapping stories." An unwelcome surge of pain split my senses, and I jerked.

"Denton, get inside before you fall."

"Yes, ma'am." Jewelry pieces were in various stages of construction all over the kitchen counter. "You've been busy."

"It's therapeutic." She closed the door and locked it. "Please, sit. I have a freshly brewed pot of coffee. Had a feeling you'd be stopping by."

"Oh, so I'm always welcome?"

"Don't press your luck."

I eased onto the sofa, relieved to rest. A small notebook lay open. Four lines caught my attention.

The day swirled in black and white.
The kiss of death and the hope of life.
Good and evil struggle like sibling strife.
Who will hold me safe till heaven's light?

Shelby picked up the notebook. "I've been scribbling."

Her creativity moved me. "I'm not a professional, but I hear the emotional turmoil in your words. Is there anything you can't do?"

She tucked the notepad into a drawer. "When's the last time you popped a pain pill?"

Ah, nice change of subject. She needed to trust me. "Last night. Some Advil earlier this morning. I'm trying to leave the heavy-duty meds alone."

"Don't blame you. Perhaps using one to ease the pain makes sense." She brought me a mug of coffee with fresh bubbles breaking the top and sat with her own in a nearby chair. "You always have a reason for doing things. And here you are."

"Are you ready for news?"

She whirled to me. Alarm clearly written on her face.

"It's positive. At least I think so."

"You scared me. You've found the guilty person?"

"Not yet. This is personal . . . In the wee hours of the morning, I became a Christian."

Shelby rubbed her palms together reminding me of a little girl's excitement. I adored so many things about her.

"What incredible news," she said. "But at the hospital you indicated noninterest."

"Weird, huh? I don't understand it all myself."

"Do you want to tell me about it?"

I shared with her about my mamaw, her influence on my life, and my coming to faith. "Do you think I sound like a kid when I'm a grown man?" Another trait I admired about her—compassion for others.

"I think we're supposed to have childlike faith."

I widened my grin across my bruised face. "Guess I qualify, and I'm confident about my decision."

"Are your parents Christians?"

"Yes, and I called them earlier. Woke them up." I paused, remembering. "Mom had given up on me finding faith."

"My mom and Marissa spent more time at church than Dad and I combined. We were buds back then. No matter what I'd done, he always found time for me."

"Made Friday extra hard."

"Yep."

I stared into her face, so pretty . . . "Missed not seeing you yesterday."

She picked up Joy and avoided my gaze. "I missed you too."

I chose not to tell her about Mom's question of when I planned to get married. Time to get back to business.

"The men who attacked you, Aaron, and Isaac are known felons and have worked with Eli Chandler off and on for the past ten years. The FBI's interrogating the man in custody and the dead men's families and friends. The investigation shows a common denominator—they all worked for the same money-laundering racketeer, a person who remains nameless."

"Has my dad been mentioned?"

I told her about his person-of-interest status.

She worried her lip. "I'm confused. You and Mike drove to question Dad when you should have been at home recovering from surgery. Have you uncovered additional evidence against him?"

"Neither for nor against. Another piece of info came to my attention. The truck abandoned by the shooters at my trailer not only didn't have a front license plate, but it also had the letters *DAT* on the rear plate."

She nodded. "Isaac and I noted from the security camera at the tank that the pickup was missing a front plate."

"The tank?" I thought about my run-down trailer. "Guess you're right."

"Fitting, don't you think? I've been thinking. Probably two men followed you on the way back to Valleysburg. They rear-ended you, then got into the firefight at the tank. Then two more men attempted to finish the job at the hotel. Two men are dead, Nick Hanson is in custody, and Eli Chandler is out there somewhere."

"You got it."

Shelby bored her gaze into an empty wall. "I wish I knew why I had a price on my head." She hesitated. "I have a theory."

"Good because I'm swimming upstream."

"What's been uncovered confirms the threats and attacks are connected to a money-laundering operation. Most likely, the kingpin got started with Marissa and Travis's money, and as long as I stayed behind bars, he felt safe. He's targeted me because he thinks I'll identify him."

"We're on the same page."

"But I have the same three questions. Why not get rid of me in prison? Why initially push my suicide? And what happened to escalate the aggression and risk losing two shooters?"

"The FBI has discussed the same thing."

"I hate to suspect Dad, but he could have reservations about eliminating his own daughter, where suicide . . . doesn't affect him." She shook her head. "Makes me sick to say it, and hearing my own words seems very wrong."

"Uncovering a crime means sifting through dirt. No one wants to think a family member has betrayed her for money."

"The not knowing is unbearable."

I plunged into deeper waters. "Clay and Isaac told me you had an aversion to guns."

"I do. I hate weapons of all kinds. Always have." She hesitated. "I know. It doesn't make sense . . . considering."

"Let's talk about something else. What makes you happy?"

She closed her eyes. "You first."

"Living at the cabin, riding Big Red, taking pictures, enjoying a quiet life." I watched a squirrel outside scamper across the driveway. "I hope when I'm back in Houston, I can return here when life gets overwhelming. Your turn."

"Not yet. Hobbies other than photography?"

"I like high school kids. I volunteer at a youth center." I grinned. "Now, let me hear about you."

"Okay. Creating things and helping others."

"You design jewelry, bake, write poetry, and sing. What am I missing?"

She laughed. "Back in high school, I wanted to be an interior designer in New York City. I dreamed of having an apartment overlooking the busy city."

"You're one talented lady."

"And you're an enigma."

"Is that good or bad?" I said.

"I'll let you know when I decide."

I took a sip of coffee. "What are your goals for the future?"

She stared out the window where the squirrel still played. "Same. Help others, possibly work for a prison ministry. It's a nudging in my spirit, but I haven't talked to Pastor Emory for his thoughts. Build my jewelry business. How about yours?"

I chuckled. "My future changed before six this morning. In your words, 'I haven't processed them all yet.' Back to you. What about marriage and a family?"

"An impossibility."

"Why?"

She shook her head. "No decent man with an ounce of sense would want me."

"You're wrong. When this is over, I'd like to talk about us."

She startled. "Have you lost your mind? Everything about 'us' spells trouble." Her narrow shoulders lifted and fell. "In your processing for the future, ask yourself how to reconcile the fact I murdered a man."

She'd hit me with reality, but the woman before me was not that irrational seventeen-year-old.

Shelby's eyes showed profound sadness. "You've known me two weeks."

"I've known you a total of fifteen and a half years."

"Denton, for nearly fifteen and a half years you've despised me."

"They're similar emotions . . . love and hate."

She sighed. "You've found Jesus, but you've lost your mind."

"Good one, but not the truth. The agent in me hasn't detected your denial of 'us.'"

Shelby's blue-gray eyes watered, and she blinked. "'Us' has too many negatives. Reality is key here. How would you ever explain me? And what about your family? How would they introduce me? And what if they broke contact with you because of me?" She held up a finger. "I'm living the broken family relationship scenario, and it's a miserable existence."

"My family is forgiving."

"You have no guarantee of their reaction. And if we . . . became a permanent thing, what about our kids? Do you think they'd have respect for either of us?" She tilted her head. "Your features have hardened. What are you holding back in our come-to-Jesus meeting?"

Dare I talk about the mess in my own family? "I already told you about my ex-fiancée marrying my middle brother, Andy. What I didn't tell you is my entering the FBI was only one of the problems between us. I put my career above everything else, including her. When she wanted to discuss the wedding, our honeymoon, or even where we'd live, I didn't have time. In short, she accused me of putting my work ahead of her." I shrugged. "Truth is, I did. She turned to my brother for understanding, and he gave her the time of day."

"Another reason to blame me?"

"At the time I needed to blame someone. You and God made sense. Over the years, Andy and I made our peace, but I held on to my resentment. And my younger brother Brice can be an annoying pain." I paused. "He recently called and apologized, so with God's help, we'll mend our relationship."

"Denton, all the more reason for you to think again about us being together. You're wasting brain cells when you have a beautiful life ahead of you with Jesus. Please."

Her pleading stopped me. I hadn't shown up at her doorstep to upset her with my attraction. "Shelby, I'm sorry. We can table this conversation for another time."

"No point, Denton. There can't be a relationship between us.

I have too much respect for you and how I could damage your future."

I grabbed my crutches and stood. "My past is over, and my future is forever changed. I'm falling in love with you, Shelby. Deal with it."

48

SHELBY

How wonderful Denton had given his life to Jesus, but how tragic for him to believe he loved me after he'd warred against me all those years. I watched him hobble to a rental car and drive off. He'd hinted at an attraction on occasion, and I'd done a poor job of discouraging him. I should have stressed more how we could never work. My sacrifice for Marissa touched every area of my life.

In a corner of my heart where no one but God could ever enter, I longed for more than friendship with Denton. His words had added a soft blue to my life's kaleidoscope. I treasured his company, his wisdom, his laughter, the intensity of his brown eyes, and the magnificence of his thick, mostly white hair. Reality hovered over me—with a love-filled dream came the gray. Always the gray.

Avoiding him seemed like the best solution, yet it was impossible until this ended. The only man who'd ever loved me was Dad. I'd ruined his life, and I refused to ruin Denton's. I'd read about his brother marrying his fiancée, but the online article wasn't a trusted source.

The phone rang—Sheriff Wendall. I dreaded bad news from any front. Maybe this time was different.

"Shelby, are you free to talk?"

"Yes, sir."

"Your mother passed yesterday afternoon."

I slid onto the sofa with a mix of sadness, nausea, and yet peace that Mom no longer suffered. "I knew she didn't have long, but the news is still devastating. Has my dad changed his mind about my attending her funeral?"

"I'm afraid not."

"Mom and I shared closure when I saw her. Guess that's the best way to remember her. I appreciate your call."

Alone in my home, I shed tears for losing my mother, for the heartache I'd caused her. For the love and nurturing she'd given me while I was growing up.

Contemplating a walk in the woods, among the sweetness of nature drew me outside. I carried Joy into the canopied shade. Like a child who refused to be comforted, I cried into her silky coat. Talking to Edie tempted me, but the idea of her hearing me sob didn't sit well. I missed Amy-Jo too and her no-nonsense approach to life.

Marissa texted me about Mom's passing and canceling tomorrow's meetup. The idea of Aria and her in danger tore at my protective nature.

The funeral is Friday morning. I'll check in before the weekend is over to reschedule.

Be safe.

I will. Dad's in bad shape. Losing Mom was hard for all of us. Do you need to talk?

Thanks. Aria is upset and needs me. She and Mom were close.

The idea of Dad requesting to take Aria on a vacation after Mom passed tormented me. I once believed my dad held more integrity in the palm of his hand than most people ever acquired in a lifetime, and I couldn't shake it loose now.

49

Edie had become more than a good friend—she was my sister-friend. Thursday morning, her condolences about Mom's entrance into heaven touched me like the love I shared with Marissa.

"I know the funeral's tomorrow," she said. "Sheriff Wendall stopped by my office with the news. I can only imagine how badly you want to be there. The sheriff said you learned about it yesterday. He'd have called me sooner, but he had to be in Houston for a trial."

"Thanks." The lump in my throat thickened.

"Wish I could see you. But we can still talk, and I'm a good listener."

We shared mom memories from her life and mine. We exchanged a few tears and laughter in the process. Loved my sister-friend.

"You've been down," she said. "Anything I can do to help? Life's hit you with too many obstacles."

More like bullets. "It will get better. Is Amy-Jo still staying with you?"

"Yes. She's a character. Offered to teach me how to shoot. I think I'll take her up on it."

"Good idea." I put away laundry while we talked. "What else is going on with you?"

"My kids thought a real-life nightmare was funny."

"Nightmares are never funny. What happened?"

"Laugh, and I'll be knocking on your door. Last night I walked into my bedroom, ready for my pajamas. A bat flew over my head and I screamed. It flew past me again. Trust me, I hit the hysterical level. Timothy came running. All I could do was point to the ceiling fan, where the bat perched on a blade."

"Timothy took care of it?"

"No! He started listing the good things bats do—like eating mosquitoes. I told him bats were rats with wings, and rats carried the bubonic plague. Who knew what the winged demons could do? There is a reason why bats are in horror movies. They belong with the destination of all other fiends of the world." Edie sucked in air. "I'm still upset. Anyway, I escaped under the bed like a two-year-old, not a mother who's supposed to defend her children. Timothy chased it with a broom and hollered for Livy to open the front and back doors. Between them, they chased the varmint out of the house. Me? I was too scared to crawl out from under the bed for a long time."

An image of Edie paralyzed over a bat hit me as incredibly funny, and laughter rolled over me. The best prescription for sadness.

"I figured you'd view my nightmare as comic relief. Goodness, I've probably scarred my kids for life, requiring perpetual counseling."

"Bats are scary. My first experience with a bat happened—" A car door slammed, and I peeked through the window to check on the visitor. Randy Hughes stumbled out of his truck and wobbled up the stony path to my front door. "Edie, your brother's here. He appears to be drunk."

"I'll call Sheriff Wendall. Stay inside. He can be dangerous when he's this way. Hang on while I click over."

I stayed on the line while Randy clomped up a porch step. A second step, then a third.

"Are you there?" Edie said.

"Yes," I whispered.

Randy pounded on the door.

"I heard that. Is he armed?"

"I don't know."

"Shelby, open the door. This is Randy Hughes." He slurred his words. "We need to talk."

While I'd been at the wrong end of angry people before and faced the brunt of their hatred, I knew better than to face him. Irrational behavior shook me to the core. Where was the officer who watched my house? I texted him for help. My only recourse was to talk Randy down until officers arrived.

"Gotta go." I pressed End before Edie could protest. "What do you want to discuss?"

"You caused me to get fired."

Anger fueled my mouth and restraint slipped away. "Randy, I had nothing to do with your losing—"

"You owe me."

The distant whine of a law enforcement siren sounded. "Officers are on their way. Why not sit on the porch? Once they're here, I'll brew coffee to sober you up."

He swore and kicked the door. Although it was thick and sturdy, it had a breaking point, just like everything and everyone else.

Randy punched his fist through the window nearest the door. Glass shattered. Blood dripped from his knuckles. My home should be my sanctuary, not another prison. More glass cracked and fell to the floor. I hurried to the back door and flung it open. Safety lay ahead in the woods and bought me time.

I found refuge behind an oak tree and studied the front of my cabin. Randy had disappeared, and I assumed he was inside. How long should I hide here before moving deeper into the woods? Two police cruisers slid up next to Randy's truck. Four men exited with their weapons drawn, including Sheriff Wendall. Two of them jogged to the rear of the cabin.

"Randy, come on out with your hands up," Sheriff Wendall's voice blared above the sounds of nature. "No reason to stay in there."

No answer.

"Have you hurt Shelby?"

"She took off."

An officer shouted they had Randy. Breathing my thanks, I walked toward Sheriff Wendall.

I was safe. For now.

50

Randy fought the cuffs and swore at everyone around him. "I only wanted to talk, and you're takin' the side of a killer and a thief."

"Shut up," Sheriff Wendall said, "or you'll be facin' more charges than a DWI, breaking and entering, and attempted assault." The sheriff turned to me. "Shelby, are you all right?"

"Yes, sir." Anger, more like rage, burned in my stomach. "At least one of my windows is broken."

"We'll look at the damages in a few minutes. Do you want to contact Edie? She's worried sick."

"Sure."

"Edie won't press any charges against me," Randy sneered. "And she'll bail me out of jail."

"Don't count on it." Sheriff Wendall huffed. "Why were you here when you'd been ordered to stay away?"

"No law against having a conversation."

Sheriff Wendall stepped to Randy, nose to nose. "Looks like

you've broken enough laws to spend several weeks in jail. Maybe you'll dry out."

I trembled, the unfairness of it all pounding in my heart. "I don't think you're the one who's been targeting me, but I think someone hired you. Who?"

Randy spat at my feet. "I never murdered anyone."

I swallowed my pride, took a deep breath. "That's right. Just like I faced charges, a judge, and paid my debt, you will do the same. Know what? For a moment, I nearly stooped to your level." I faced the sheriff and the other three officers. "Thank you. I'll assess my home for damages."

The sight of shattered glass brought hot tears. Thankfully my belongings and Edie's cabin and furnishings had stood the test of Randy's drunken violence.

He reminded me of a male guard who used to corner me with threats if I didn't give in to his advances. He made life behind bars even more frightening, but I was stubborn and never relented.

Valleysburg was my home now, and I intended to stay.

I talked to Edie and assured her Sheriff Wendall and his officers had Randy under control.

"Did he admit to violating your rights in the past?" she said.

Odd choice of words for the gal who'd hidden under her bed to avoid a bat. "No. Who knows what he'll claim when he's sober. I'm sorry. He's your brother, and I should be more considerate."

"Shelby, I've seen him in action. When he's drinking, his violence escalates. On top of that, you're dealing with grief from your mother's passing."

Sheriff Wendall joined me and I ended the call. I valued his concern and all my new friends who cared without knowing the truth. He sat on the sofa, and I took the chair I'd used earlier in the day when Denton visited.

"From here, I'm heading over to Edie's office. In her opinion, Randy needs to be locked up for his own good and the safety of others."

"Maybe he'll get help."

"Kind of you to say so with his latest stretch of the law." He laid his Stetson on the sofa beside him. "Do you have any evidence Randy is behind the threatenin' calls?"

I shook my head. "Outside, I reacted in anger, lashed out. But what I believe is if someone offered him cash to make my life difficult, he'd jump on it."

He pressed his lips together. "Did you let Denton know what happened?"

"Haven't talked to him."

"I'll call him on the way to see Edie and ask him if he's available to stop in. You shouldn't be alone."

Protest jumped into my throat, but I held back. No need to tell the sheriff about Denton's and my last conversation.

"Have you neglected to relay information about other crimes against you?"

"Not sure."

The sheriff frowned. "Not sure? What are you keepin' secret?"

He'd never understand how protecting loved ones ruled every breath. "I'm sure I've told you everything. I'm a little shaken right now."

The sheriff studied me. "All right, but you know I'm available day or night."

He didn't believe me. "Thank you."

"Maybe the guilty person is taking a break until after your mother's funeral. You're right—Randy couldn't be behind all of this."

Dad must have Sheriff Wendall's attention too. I despised all the free time anticipating my enemy's next move or arrest. It boggled my mind, and with Randy Hughes in custody, I sensed the suspect list narrowing.

Activity outside captured my attention. Two officers supported Randy and laid him in the rear of a cruiser. "Sheriff, looks like Randy might have collapsed."

"Probably passed out."

We both rushed outside.

"He's having a heart attack," one of the officers said.

"Get him to the hospital." The sheriff rushed to his car. "Shelby, do me a favor and call Edie."

51

DENTON

Women handled emotional trauma in bewildering ways, and Randy's stunt added to Shelby's burdens. I had no idea if she'd kick me off her porch or let me help. She opened her cabin door wearing an exasperated frown. I'd seen bad guys more excited to see me.

"Have you heard anything about Randy's condition?" she said.

"Partly. He's stable. Edie and Pastor Emory are with him. The mix of high blood pressure and alcohol shoved him into a heart attack."

"Maybe he'll get professional help now."

"He has to admit a problem first." I jumped in with the hard task. "Sheriff Wendall thought you should stay at my place until your window is fixed."

"Edie's already arranged for a repairman. He'll be here first thing in the morning."

"Then I'm spending the night on your sofa."

"You still look like you're the one who needs protection, and I'm not in the mood to cook." She raised her chin, and I saw the little girl who'd given her parents sleepless nights.

"That'll give me a job to fill my time. And if the wrong people show up, I'm mean with these crutches."

Shelby's stomach growled and I grinned. "Are you going to invite me in so I can whip up a semi-gourmet meal?"

"The last two agents who attempted to keep me company were shot."

I stared at my feet for a few beats. "So I hear."

"Another one had surgery and will be on crutches for weeks."

"I heard about him too. I'm one of the good guys, remember?"

"Are you going to behave yourself?" She bit her lip and revealed a spark of humor.

"Nope."

A smile tugged at her lips. "Me either. I'm bored and angry. Neither are a good combo for an ex-con."

After Shelby poured us freshly squeezed lemonade, I suggested we sit on the front porch. "I'd have driven you to your mother's funeral."

Shelby stroked Joy, who'd followed her outside. "I know, Denton." She'd morphed from a rebellious little girl to a sad woman.

"We're spending tomorrow together. I'm not leaving you alone."

She slowly nodded. "I'd like that. It will be a tough day." She stared out at the narrow road. "I'm going back to work on Saturday morning."

"The bad guys are still out there. You'd be easy to pick off on the road. No one would ever know who did it or why."

"Whoever's responsible could have eliminated me on the other days I've walked to and from work. Besides, I've already made a commitment to Amy-Jo, and I'm tired of hiding."

"What else have you vowed to do?"

She gave me a sideways glare. "It won't be a surprise."

"Try me."

"Find who is responsible for embezzling the money, the threats, the shootings, and two hit-and-runs. All I know at this point is Eli Chandler is involved. I want to know how he fits in with my dad."

"Then what?"

"Make sure the guilty ones face a judge and jury."

"We're in this together."

"Next time you might not be so lucky."

I deliberated her words. "I'd rather sacrifice my life to keep you safe than attend your funeral."

She blinked. "What am I to do with you?"

"When this is over, I'll tell you."

That night I lay awake on her sofa, not because of the plywood nailed over the window and the living room chair against the door, but because of my growing feelings for Shelby and the threats against her.

The agony in my battered body caused my eyes to water. Hard to concentrate when I couldn't figure out how to end this. Tonight we'd grilled chicken, tossed a salad, and baked potatoes for supper. We stood much too close for a man who'd admitted the pangs of love. Rather pathetic because I lacked the skill to handle myself personally.

I gave in to taking half a pain pill and slept.

Four hours later, I grabbed my laptop from Shelby's kitchen table. The FIG had my latest inquiry about Travis Stover and Eli Chandler. If the two men were connected before Stover's death, the investigation might lead to the missing money. I wanted coffee, except grinding the beans made too much noise and Shelby needed sleep.

An hour later with sunrise on the brink of bursting across the sky, I closed the laptop and my eyes.

No leads.

Just an aching heart and leg.

52

Working at the café kept my mind off my messy life and those who'd been hurt because of their association with me. Saturday morning customers lined up for donuts and pastries or one of Amy-Jo's Southern-style breakfasts. Later on I rearranged the bakery case for afternoon snackers, which meant a 20 percent discount on everything. Amy-Jo used Mom and Dad's cookbook *Pearce Bakery Favorites*, and the thought of her using recipes I'd memorized as a kid filled me with tender memories of Mom and Dad. Since Amy-Jo had started making Mimi's cinnamon bread, a recipe from Grandma Pearce, customers had to place orders ahead of time or risk Amy-Jo running out.

"Are you Shelby Pearce?"

I glanced over the counter to a slight teenage girl. Her long blonde hair and blue-gray eyes resembled . . . No, impossible. "Yes. How can I help you?"

"I'm Aria Stover."

I forgot how to breathe and gripped the top of the bakery case. Myriad questions littered my mind. Where did I begin? I looked to see if anyone familiar had entered the café.

"Who is with you?"

"No one, Aunt Shelby."

The last two words shook me to the core. "How did you know where to find me?"

"Grandma told me." Aria started to say more but pressed her lips together.

"How did you get here?"

"Some friends were going to New Braunfels for the weekend, and I asked them to drop me off."

A dozen fears for Aria twisted in me. "Your mother must be worried sick."

"She's on one of her rest weekends. I left Granddad a note for when he gets home from the bakery. Normally I'd be there working with him, but I told him I wasn't ready. He left at four this morning, and my friends picked me up at four thirty. He'll know where I'm at, and I have my cell phone."

"He'll be really upset, especially after the funeral. Why have you come, Aria? I don't understand."

"To talk." She punched the two words out. "Can we do that?"

"Of course." I looked at the clock. Fifteen minutes until my break. "Have you eaten?"

"Not today."

I gestured to a nearby table. "Order whatever you want and tell the server the bill goes to me. By the time your food arrives, I'll join you. In the meantime, call your granddad. He deserves to hear from you and be assured you're safe. Tell him I'll notify the sheriff and my parole officer."

Her eyes widened. "Are you in trouble?"

I shook my head. "The sheriff is a friend, and my parole officer must be notified of everything that can potentially be a problem. The communication keeps me out of prison."

"Okay, I will. I'm starved." She gave me a thin-lipped smile. "Grandma told me we looked alike."

I leaned on the counter. She might have weighed ninety pounds, so much like me at her age. "Yes, we do. Aria, I don't know what to say. I'm shocked to see you."

"I feel strange too. I mean, we're seeing each other for the first time, but I had to find you." She sighed. "Grandma said only you had answers."

"About your dad?"

She shook her head. "My mom."

◉ ◉ ◉

I experienced the longest fifteen minutes in history, but I called Sheriff Wendall and James Peterson with the happenings. Finally I sat across from Aria. She poured syrup over pancakes and scrambled eggs . . . I used to sweeten my eggs with syrup too.

"Did you talk to your granddad?"

"Yes, ma'am. He's not happy, but he's glad I'm safe." She stared down at her plate. "He has a worker who will close up the bakery today. He'll be on his way in the next few minutes. Which means you and I have plenty of time together."

I folded my hands and asked God to put the right words into my heart and mouth. "You've been told what happened to your father."

She stared into my eyes, and a mirror looked back at me. "Yes. Mom told me."

"What are your questions? I'm fairly certain Marissa gave you the facts."

She swirled a forkful of pancake on her plate. "She said as a teen you shot my dad and went to prison for it. And she let me read the court transcripts. You were always in trouble and broke Grandma and Granddad's hearts."

How sad for my niece to be aware of the family's black sheep.

"Then you know everything. I'm sorry you've grown up without a father. He was a godly man. You have every reason to despise me, and still you're here. If you're after vengeance or have hate to spew, I understand."

Her face clouded. "I used to hate you until I found Jesus and forgave you. Grandma always took me to church, but I didn't know the stuff I kept inside was hurting me until Jesus and Grandma helped me see it."

"I'm a Christian too."

"Grandma told me." She eyed me with a tilt of her head. Eerily familiar. "You don't understand. There's more going on since you were sent away."

Weird choice of words for *prison*. "I'm listening."

"Mom has never loved me. She's told me I'm a burden. If someone is around, she puts on an act to look like the perfect mom. And it hurts. Always has. Granddad and Grandma raised me since Mom seemed to be sick a lot and needed time away to rest." Aria took a long drink of water. "She's supposed to have rheumatoid arthritis, but she doesn't take any meds. I've looked everywhere. When I asked the name of her doctor, she said it was none of my business. I talked to Grandma about my mom to find out what's wrong with me. Grandma cried. We've always been able to talk about anything."

Aria drew in a breath. "She told me Mom's behavior had nothing to do with me. She said life isn't always what it looks like, and I should seek out the truth—from you."

"Was this conversation before or after I visited Sharp's Creek?"

"Both. She said you promised to find the truth."

I gazed into her young face. I'd always believed Marissa was a perfect mother. So many reasons for her rejecting Aria, from guilt of killing Travis to having me take the blame. But it wasn't her daughter's fault. Maybe Aria had inherited more than my physical likeness. Perhaps my curiosity streak. What else explained her visit and accusations against Marissa?

"Why does Mom make everything about her?"

"I have no idea."

Aria worried her lip. Rats, I did the same thing. Were the similarities why Marissa might have held back on her love?

Aria glanced around us as though someone might be eavesdropping. "I overheard two conversations lately. Mom was talking on the phone and didn't know I'd come home from school early. I have no idea who was on the other end. She said, 'Shelby's release has to be short. Do what's needed to eliminate her.'"

I fixed an impassive expression on my face. Yet my pulse sped. "There's no way for me to judge the conversation without hearing all of it. Perhaps she feared for you or she was concerned I'd try to contact the family."

"The only thing Mom fears is not being the center of attention."

Harsh, but I didn't contradict her.

"The second thing happened when I overheard Mom and Grandma talking. Grandma knew you didn't kill my dad." Aria gasped. "She asked if Mom pulled the trigger."

Mom had confronted Marissa? "Aria, my fingerprints were on the firearm."

She stared at me as though she saw into my soul. Emotions swept over her face—disbelief, confusion, grief. I longed to reach out and hug her, but I dared not. She must be convinced I killed her father.

"Aunt Shelby, I've seen enough movies to know fingerprints can be removed and others added. Can we go to your house when you're off work? I'd like to spend time with you, get to know you better, and see where you live."

Nausea hit me. Had she figured out who really killed Travis? "It's a violation of my parole, and you're underage."

"Mom told me you're not to have communication with family, but I'm the one who came to see you. Doesn't that make it okay?"

Something Marissa had claimed bothered me. I smiled into the eyes matching mine in color. "This has been a hard season for you. Do you have plans for spring break? A vacation for you and Dad?"

"Granddad and I will go through all of Grandma's things, a hard job for both of us."

"Nothing fun?"

"Money's tight right now. We might do a little fishing." She paused. "One of my girlfriends asked if I could spend a night or two with her."

Aria and Dad's plans showed no similarity to Marissa's claim of the two taking a vacation.

The bell rang over the café's door, and Sheriff Wendall walked in. I waved and he approached our booth.

After introductions, Aria peered up at him. "Are you taking me to jail until Granddad drives here?"

He chuckled and she relaxed. "I told your grandfather I'd make sure you were okay. Problem is the café closes at three." He glanced at me. "I took the liberty of requestin' permission for Aria to stay with you until then, providin' Denton is present."

"Who's Denton?" Aria said.

I glanced at the sheriff. "I'll explain it to her. He's an FBI agent assigned to my case years ago. We're friends now and neighbors."

"Weird. But I'm good with it."

Sheriff Wendall nodded, and I pressed in Denton's number. He already knew the situation from the sheriff. "I'll be there in a few minutes. I'm a little slow with the crutches."

I stared into Aria's smooth face. "You'll be spending a few hours with me after all."

Sheriff Wendall excused himself to order a cup of coffee from the take-out counter and visit with Amy-Jo.

Aria watched him leave. "Another reason I'm here is Mom dropped a bomb before she left. She intends to move to Phoenix, where the doctor says she'll do better in a drier climate. I won't be going. Mom says I'm too much trouble. She plans to tell Granddad I'll miss my friends too much, and I'll regret not graduating from Sharp's Creek High School."

"How do you feel about living with him?"

"I'm with him most of the time anyway when I'm not in school. Ever since I can remember, I've felt like Mom wanted me out of her life. This proves it. I love Granddad, but I miss Grandma."

"I miss her too. We can share special times about her."

Amy-Jo joined our table with the sheriff. I introduced her to Aria.

"Shelby, take the rest of the day off. Spend time with your niece."

"But I just got back to work."

"Family time is more important." She pointed to Aria's plate. "On the house, then have a wonderful day together."

Oh, how I'd been blessed with great friends.

All these years, I'd envisioned the circumstances surrounding my first meeting with my niece or nephew. I expected an explosion of blame and accusations. An anticipated response would have been easier than the gentle girl seated across from me, a hurting teen who'd claimed to rely on her grandmother to fill an emotional vacancy.

53

Awkward best described my sensation of sitting on the passenger side of Denton's rental car with Aria in the middle. My walk to and from work seemed to speed by faster than this. Every familiar fence post, clump of wildflowers, and dip in the road brought me closer to dealing with the past. I'd go to my grave wearing lies like another layer of skin.

I'd spent so many years with my own thoughts as a companion that I resembled a nineteenth-century hermit. What did I say to a fifteen-year-old who'd been told I'd murdered her father?

"Aria, what are the plans once you're at Shelby's cabin?" Denton said. "You'll have nearly five hours together."

She swung to me. "You live in a cabin. Cool."

"Yes, it's homey, peaceful. It sits next to a grove of woods filled with wildlife. I've seen deer, a coyote, raccoons, a fox, and lots of incredible birds."

"I love animals. But the only thing on my mind is spending time with you."

Denton tossed me a baffled look. For certain he had questions upon questions about how Aria and I would spend our time together and why she was in Valleysburg.

"We'll figure it out once we're there." If she liked jewelry, I could give her a few tips on how to create a necklace or bracelet. Working with our hands would give us something to do while we talked.

"Aunt Shelby, how did you and Denton become friends? I'd think you'd run the other way since he investigated the . . . you know. But—" She paused. "Maybe it's like you and me. We're better people not to profile each other. Back to my question, when did the friendship start?"

"I'll let Denton answer."

He rubbed his face. "We decided to like each other when we took the time to get acquainted instead of viewing each other as enemies."

"Who took the first step?"

I burst out laughing. Couldn't help it.

"What's so funny?" He frowned.

"Aria's so much like me."

"Laughter at my expense, huh?" He grinned.

"What happened to your leg, face . . . and the rest of you?" Aria gestured from his head to his toes.

"A truck didn't see me."

"Next time wear a neon vest."

"I'll remember your sage advice. Now I have—" His phone rang, and he snatched it from the dash. Reading the caller ID, he answered. "Sheriff, how can I help you?"

I observed every muscle and line on his bruised face for telltale signs of the call's content since we'd just left Sheriff Wendall at the café. Typical agent, couldn't read a thing.

"Who paid the bail?" He scowled. "All right. I'll handle it." He placed his phone on the dash. "Change of plans. We'll stop at Shelby's cabin, pick up anything needed, then head to my place."

I frowned. "Can you tell me what's happened?"

"Randy's out on bail. A friend of his paid it. No worries."

No point elaborating.

"Who is Randy?" Aria looked at me. "And—?"

"Not up for discussion." I used my gentlest tone, although I hadn't had much practice around teenage girls. "Some things are better left alone."

Aria huffed. "In some countries, I'd be married with a kid."

Denton chuckled. "But not in Texas."

At my cabin, Aria inspected every room with compliments. "The green is terrific and so are the touches of yellow and lavender, but a burst of red would make it pop."

So very me. "You have an eye for color. Thanks."

She caught sight of the jewelry on the kitchen counter in various stages of construction. "You made these?"

"Yes, it's a hobby but I'm expanding it to a little business. The café is carrying some pieces."

She peered at a Scripture card. "Simply Shelby?"

I nodded.

Aria gingerly picked up a necklace in labradorite amber, turquoise, and purple wrapped in silver wire. After viewing the cross on the back and running her fingers over the twisted wire, she read the Scripture card. "'Eva, life. "Whoever has the Son has life," 1 John 5:12.' This is beautiful—the necklace, the Scripture." She laid it on the kitchen counter. "They're all beautiful."

I sensed she wanted a necklace, but what could I say knowing Dad would disapprove? He'd already be upset with her, and one of my jewelry pieces paved the way for a nasty relationship between them. Perhaps—"Pick out a stone and wire. We have time at Denton's to make one for you." I showed her a few stones I hadn't used. She selected one in amber, green, and deep blue. "Good, what about a name?"

"My middle name and Grandma's, Grace."

"Aria Grace is beautiful. Do you have a Scripture in mind?"

"Not sure where the verse is in the Bible, but it's the one in Ephesians about being saved by grace because it's a gift."

I wished I'd had her wisdom back then. "Perfect choice. Right now, let's gather up what we need. Who knows? Denton may decide to design a piece too." I sensed him studying us, and I caught his gaze. Curiosity and something else met me, a frightening emotion. I shivered.

Denton hadn't stretched the truth. He cared for me, and the irony of it all was I felt the same for him.

54

Aria rubbed her arms and trembled. "He's here," she whispered, as though Dad's arrival couldn't possibly be true.

He pulled into the stone driveway beside Denton's cabin. The two had talked twice, and both times she'd been in tears.

"You look like two scared rabbits," Denton noted when Dad exited his car.

Aria peered out a window and watched him walk to the door. "He's mad. I can tell by the way his shoulders are like tree trunks. It will be a long ride home."

I remembered the dread of facing Dad when I'd gotten into trouble. "It's not so much he's angry. He's disappointed."

"Worse is, I love him and I feel awful." She sucked in a breath. "But I won't cry. Mom uses tears against him. She's like a water faucet on full power."

Aria had far too many of my traits. I took her hand and squeezed. "Aria—"

Dad's knock stole the moment to hug her just once. But she needed Dad, just like he was my hero at her age. I'd do anything to keep their relationship solid.

Denton opened the door. "Evenin', Clay. Come on in."

Dad thanked him and took a step inside. He stared at Aria and me and startled. Perhaps our similarities hit him hard, the past and the present bubbling into a cauldron of suppressed emotions. Aria trembled beside me. I wanted to push her into his arms, but I might make things worse.

"Aria, I don't know whether to hug you or turn you over my knee," he said. "When the sheriff called, I was afraid I'd lost you."

"I'm sorry," she whispered. "All I thought about was myself instead of how this would hurt you. All I could think about was meeting Aunt Shelby, talking to her."

An angry flash met me. "Are you satisfied your mom and grandparents told you the truth?"

She shook her head. "No. Grandma told me to talk to Aunt Shelby and ask her hard questions."

"And?"

"Her answers are the same as yours." Aria struggled to speak. "But I don't hate her."

He took a deep breath and opened his arms. Aria rushed to him while déjà vu made me shiver. I tore my attention to Denton, who gave me a slight smile. His eyes emitted tenderness, a gift I craved desperately.

"It's just you and me now." The heartfelt intimacy moved me to blink back the tears.

"Mom told you she's moving to Phoenix?"

"She's not coming back." Dad held Aria at arm's length. "She felt it was better not to have an emotional goodbye with either of us."

"Granddad, that's cruel. What about her clothes and stuff?"

Aria had told the truth about Marissa. How horrible.

"She'll send for her things. I'll tell you more in the car." Dad glanced up at me as though he'd forgotten Denton and I were in the room. "We need to get on the road."

"Clay," Denton said, "you're facing a long drive. Why don't you and Aria stay here tonight and get a fresh start in the morning?"

"Can't take advantage of you, especially with the circumstances. You looked after Aria, and you're not in good shape."

"Dad, I'll go to my cabin if—"

"No way." Denton shook his head. "Randy's parked at his drinking hole, talking crazy."

Dad focused on Denton, and I understood how looking at me created bitter memories. "The man who's made threats and caused so much trouble?"

"We think this is a separate issue. He was a local police officer who got fired for a variety of reasons. He blames Shelby and me, and he's already spent a little jail time for acting stupid. The FBI and local law enforcement haven't discounted a connection, but he won't show up here and risk crossing a federal officer. Why not stay at my cabin for supper and rest up before the drive back?"

Exhaustion etched deeper on Dad's face. Thank goodness Aria didn't utter a sound. "Not sure what is best."

"Isn't the bakery closed on Sundays?"

Dad nodded. "We'd be a big imposition."

"Not really. Shelby gave me her mother's recipe for chicken and dumplings. I've got the fixings for a salad, and we have a pecan pie from the bakery."

Dad rubbed his face. The stress of losing Mom, Aria's escape, and Marissa's announcement clearly bombarded his head and his heart. And then there was me, his younger daughter, newly released from prison. If only I could put my arms around him.

"Supper is tempting me." Dad scratched the back of his neck . . . like always when he was indecisive.

His response staggered my emotions. When he'd arrived, I assumed he'd stand on the porch, ask for Aria, and the two would be gone in a matter of thirty seconds.

"Aria and Shelby can share my bed," Denton said. "You can have the guest bed, and I'll sleep on the couch."

Dad raised his brows. "I'll help with the food and take the couch. You need to stretch out so your leg will heal."

"My mamaw would slap me sideways for being inhospitable. In fact, so would my mother."

"That's my condition, and I cook breakfast."

"My job," I said.

A heavy, pin-drop pause sent me scrambling for an escape.

"You and I can cook breakfast together." His raspy voice and watery eyes told me how difficult it was to make his offer of reconciliation.

I swallowed my gratitude. "I accept."

Within an hour, the four of us crowded around Denton's table. Strange and yet wonderful to be surrounded by Dad, Aria, and Denton, enjoying way too much of the chicken and dumplings from my childhood. Dad struggled with his words and mannerisms. We all did, but we'd taken a giant step forward. Conversations, thanks to Denton, were easy topics.

Midway through our second helping, my phone on the kitchen counter summoned me. Not the burner. I captured Denton's attention. It rang a second time. He left the table and gazed at the caller's number.

"Best answer it." He handed me the phone.

I saw the number and escaped to the porch with Denton on my heels. He bent forward to listen to the conversation.

"Took you long enough," the familiar distorted voice said. "Where are you?"

"None of your business. Why don't you tell me what this is all about? Good people are hurt, and two of your men are dead. I'm tired of it."

"You've seen the results of your idiocy."

"What do I have or know that scares you?" Only one person in the world had reason to be afraid of me . . . and the thought bored a hole through my heart. "Tell me where and when to meet, and let's work this out."

"Who's next, Shelby?" The caller hung up.

I held the phone in my hand as though it contained answers to the tragedies unfolding around me. "Dad can't find out about this. It would only worry him."

"But he needs to be cautious. I'll tell him later on after you and Aria are in bed. In the meantime, I'll contact Sheriff Wendall to arrange surveillance."

"Thanks. I doubt I'll go to bed."

"Aria will be suspicious. I'll keep watch."

"I'm so sorry. I was hoping we were past all this. We don't have a choice but to implement my original plan. How soon can we fake my suicide?"

"Tomorrow night when you're home. I'll help you stage it."

Sheriff Wendall's words after he'd overheard a phone conversation from the same caller swept back to haunt me.

"The caller is certain you have vital information of some kind. And while the person doesn't have a problem hurting others, they . . . draw the line when it comes to killing you."

"No blood on his hands," I'd whispered.

"And I think you know who it is."

Who feared and despised me at the same time? Had I been too blind to see the obvious?

55

DENTON

My leg and body throbbed like I'd been attacked by a rabid animal, and I had little worry about falling asleep and missing Randy's retribution. Or whoever else decided to invade my cabin.

My mind spun with conversations and happenings. Tonight I'd witnessed the beginnings of a reunion between father and daughter. But the unspoken bothered me more than the spoken.

A comment Shelby had made to me on the way to meet Isaac and Aaron struck me differently than before.

"Would you do anything for your sister?"

"Absolutely."

Other things poured into my brain, like how the missing inhaler from Shelby's purse had been dumped at the Pearce home. The FBI's money-laundering lead to Sharp's Creek. Aria's insistence that her mother didn't want her. Had I stumbled onto something since Marissa had worked with Eli Chandler at the bakery?

If my hunch was right, Marissa might have taken the five hundred thousand dollars, then used it as seed money to fund her own operation. I pulled up photos and videos taken during the trial. Marissa's victim status had given the media plenty of stories, and a hint of a book and movie contract had surfaced, but neither materialized. Other reports spoke of her deteriorating emotions and mental breakdown—her husband murdered, her sister charged, the fate of her unborn child, her parents' grief, and an uncertain future.

Over the next hour I zoomed in on pics to read Marissa's body language. Visible tears, and she often touched her nose and dabbed beneath her eyes. The video of the scene outside the courthouse after Shelby's conviction drew me to the wounded sister. Something I'd ignored previously. Her parents walked on both sides of her. With the camera on Marissa, she averted her gaze to the sidewalk. Her rounded shoulders indicated a broken heart. Nothing unexpected considering the enormity of the situation.

I searched through more images, and the majority focused on Shelby. In the background of one photo, I zoomed in on Marissa, who'd faded into the shadows with the camera lens on Shelby. Instead of a grieving young pregnant woman, a hint of smugness met me. I wouldn't have seen it if not for a closer view. Did she feel self-satisfaction in the verdict? Who could blame her? Or had she planned a better life at the expense of her sister's conviction?

The quandary about Shelby's dislike of weapons mystified me. How angry had Travis Stover made her the day she shot him?

Suspicions mounted against Marissa. First chance I had this morning after Clay and Aria left, I'd call Mike.

56

SHELBY

If good times were snapshots of blessings, Saturday night with Dad, Aria, and Denton had filled my memory's scrapbook. Aria and I cleaned up from supper while Denton took Dad to see Big Red. I knew the topic of their conversation, but I was confident in Denton's explanation of the phone call. Sheriff Wendall arranged for two off-duty officers to keep an eye on the cabin.

For a little while, I relaxed and allowed normal to seep into my heart and soothe the turmoil. If only I could make these hours last forever. As the evening wore on, Denton suggested a game called Scattergories. I'd forgotten how competitive Dad and I were at games, while Aria and Denton laughed at our antics.

Once in bed with Aria's soft, rhythmic breathing beside me, I tried to stay awake . . . just in case. My body had a mind of its own, however.

Sunday morning, I woke early and tiptoed into the kitchen,

where Dad and I swung into action with breakfast. Coffee sounded really good, so I took the grinder outside not to waken Aria or Denton. A police car was parked not far away.

Comfort, treasured comfort.

A few ideas had occurred to me about once more faking my death. But I had no time to ponder them now.

Back inside, Dad grated potatoes, and I placed bacon into a huge cast-iron skillet. Edie must have thought Denton's cabin needed the skillet to cook for a dozen people. We used Mom's recipe for scrambled eggs, adding sautéed mushrooms and whipped cream cheese.

Standing so close to Dad nearly brought on a gush of tears. "Thanks," I whispered.

"You're welcome. Thank you for letting me feel like a father again."

I swallowed hard. "Are we able to move forward?"

"Hope so." He stopped kneading biscuit dough. "Your mother had plenty to say to me before she died. Things that seemed ludicrous at the time but are making more and more sense."

"I'm puzzled."

He sniffed. "Ever hear knowledge is horizontal but wisdom is vertical?" I shook my head. "For three decades, I used knowledge to live my life. Your mother chased after wisdom." He stared into my eyes, his gaze a torrent of pain and grief. "She believed you loved your sister enough to take the blame for Travis's murder."

My heart thudded loud enough to wake Mom and Travis from the grave. Doubt, worry, and the constant looking over my shoulder pressed on me. I would not put Dad through the agony of danger by admitting the truth.

"You're pale, little girl, and there's no need to say a word. Marissa's history and her abandoning Aria speak loud and clear."

"I confessed, remember?"

"Sacrifice always has a price. Can you forgive this old man for using knowledge and lies instead of wisdom to seek the truth?"

"Dad, we all have a journey to walk. I've never stopped loving you and forgiveness happened years ago. I shouldn't have given up writing you in prison."

He picked up a biscuit cutter and pressed it into the dough. "Reality has hit us hard. Denton told me about last night's call and details about the other threats and shootings. The person responsible will pay." He focused on me, and I flushed hot. "Whoever it is."

My thoughts reached back to my last conversation with Mom . . . Aria's concerns about Marissa . . . and the identity of the one person who feared what I knew and might not hesitate to kill me. If I'd figured it out, how much longer until everyone else realized the improbable was a reality?

"I will have a long talk with Aria on the way back home."

"You might not appreciate what she has to say."

"I don't care." He wiped his hands on a towel and drew me into his arms. "I've missed you."

We sobbed together.

⊙　⊙　⊙

Reconciliation was the most beautiful word in the English language. I leaned against the porch post and watched the car disappear with Aria and Dad. A profound loneliness settled on me, choking me like a thick cloud of dust. Each breath hurt. My chest ached. I'd been blessed beyond earthly understanding, and His favor humbled me.

The door opened behind me. I couldn't pretend emotion hadn't overtaken my heart. Oh, the struggle to keep from crumbling.

I swallowed.

I blinked.

I trembled.

Denton touched my shoulder. "There's no reason for you to go through this alone. The Pearce family took a giant step forward in the last twenty-four hours."

"I will treasure every minute for as long as I live." A longing to face the man who'd inched into my heart coursed over me. Why his caring when my past lay in blackness with no hope for the future?

"Shelby, tears are healing."

I turned and allowed him to hold me. He dropped his crutches and embraced me with both hands. The smell of him, the tenderness, the stroke of his hands in my hair all belonged to a more worthy woman. Not since my childhood and early teens had I experienced genuine caring without conditions attached. The joy and confirmation of no longer enduring abandonment by those in this world filled my wounded heart. He kissed my cheek, and the intimacy burst the dam of pent-up hurts.

I have no idea how long I shed one tear after another, but when I stepped back with spirit-filled renewal, my foot bumped against a crutch. "I'm so sorry. You could have fallen." I retrieved both crutches, and he slipped them under his arms.

"Holding you was worth a fall."

I dug deep for words. "I—"

He brushed my lips with a kiss. "I'm not apologizing."

Fifteen years without a kiss, and none of my teenage memories compared to the warmth of his lips touching mine. "You did tell me to 'deal with it.'"

"I love you." He traced my lips with his finger.

"I'm afraid you love me for the wrong reasons. Denton, you realized I'm not a thief, but I'm still a killer."

"I've determined more, but I'll save it for another time." He smiled. "If you're not in a hurry, let's sit and talk on the porch—not about us. Just a few moments to relax. Oh, Randy had a relapse at the bar last night, and he's back in the hospital."

I eased onto a rocker away from his closeness with a wave of regret over the unknown. "Thanks for all you've done yesterday and today. Letting Aria and I grow close and inviting Dad and her to spend the night. We all invaded your privacy, and I'm so grateful."

He moved a little slower easing onto the rocker and positioning his crutches. "Felt good thinking about someone other than myself. What caused the change in your dad?"

"I wanted to ask him. But when he didn't offer an explanation, I assumed his reasons were personal. Other than the hurt caused by Marissa's move." No way could I go into our conversation without Denton probing into forbidden territory.

"Where are you?"

A loaded question on many levels. Too many things about Marissa didn't add up.

The rhythm of the rocking chair blended with the incredible mellowness flowing through me. "My spirit has quieted from one end of the spectrum to the other."

"I'm listening."

"The longer I believe in God and His grace, the more I feel His love. Growing stronger in my faith has caused me to hold on tighter. This very minute I'm weak, and I hope the renewed relationship with my family keeps the Pearces united. Yet I'm tired of fighting. I want to give up, but I refuse to admit defeat. If I lose, the enemy wins." I gazed into Denton's brown eyes, the ones my heart refused to forget. "In this instance, stubbornness is an asset. There is a way to bring justice to what's happening."

"I have an idea." He grabbed his crutches. "We'll take our discussion inside."

57

DENTON

How could Shelby and I shove her stalker into the open without risking her life? A revisit to the original plan seemed like our best option, and we agreed one more time to implement a fake suicide. Other matters connected with the case bothered me. She agreed to lie low for a few days while the FBI dug deeper into their expanded money-laundering investigation. And I had concerns about Marissa that needed to be analyzed.

Shelby reached across the sofa and touched my hand. "I believe in your plan."

"This time it will work. I'd like for you to stay here through tomorrow."

"For many of our friends, the arrangement looks like we're having an affair."

"Don't I wish."

"Denton, I'm serious."

I wiped away my grin. "I am too." Guessed I needed to restrain my thoughts about sex now that I'd become a Christian. "The sheriff said he'd work with us. Another night of protection gives us time to form a backup."

"Then tonight we put it into place?"

"Right. You can't go to work—"

"But Amy-Jo counts on me, at least for today." She paused. "But this will keep her and others from danger."

I gave her my best encouraging smile. "Where do you go for good memories, happy times?"

"Other than last night with Dad and Aria, I'd say growing up with Marissa. Memories of our childhood kept me sane in prison."

I took her hand in mine and gestured for her to begin.

"All right, but then your turn. She's five years older, and we were close. Even when I was the bratty, irritating little sister, she had patience with me. We'd play school, and she taught me so much. Sometimes she'd dress me in her clothes, shoes, and do my makeup. I could be annoying when her friends were around, but she showed more kindness than I deserved. Marissa had the good-girl, love-Jesus gene, and I embraced trouble with a wild streak. Imagine my surprise when she asked me to be her maid of honor." She paused. "I really missed Marissa living at home." She stopped. "Except I liked Travis. I'm sure that sounds odd."

"No, it doesn't. Go on."

"Although I fought rules and laws, my sister encouraged me to take my love of creativity to the next level, go to college, and settle down. I listened until one day, and then I destroyed her world and mine. She must resent Aria. My fault too."

Had Shelby contrived the story about a loving relationship with her sister? What was I missing in this picture? "When you were small and played school, what did Marissa teach you?"

"Math. She loved word problems. Other times we'd make up stories, little mysteries that forced me to figure out how bad guys conducted crimes and got away with them. Our creative stories became prophetic. Our pretend games fueled my later rebellion." She inhaled. "Even pleasant moments from my childhood have a way of haunting me."

An unexpected chill accompanied a deeper suspicion. "You and Marissa planned crimes?"

Shelby nodded. "She urged me to be more intricate and to look at her scenarios like the hardest jigsaw puzzle in the world."

"When you later acted out those stories, did she have a reaction?"

"Marissa believed our games had become a reality to me, and she blamed herself. Incredibly sad. She forgot I owned my own choices. I hot-wired cars. Snuck out to date bad boys my parents despised. Incredibly stupid behavior."

"Did you read back then?"

"You mean together?"

"Sure."

"When I was five, she read Hardy Boys and Nancy Drew stories to me." She paused. "For my eighth birthday, she read to me Truman Capote's *In Cold Blood*. After that, she and I read true crime together."

Sickening dread chilled me for what Shelby had been exposed to as a child. I had work to do, and I couldn't get to it fast enough. "I nearly forgot to feed Big Red, and I owe Mike a call."

"You haven't told me what makes you happy."

"Being with you."

"Cheesy, Denton." She pointed to the door. "Go ahead, unless you need help. The kitchen needs a little attention."

I grabbed my crutches. "I won't be long. Today starts a new chapter, and I don't want to waste any of it."

58

I sensed I'd stepped into a nightmare, and the only way to resolve it was to take action. I navigated my crutches to the small barn while Shelby stayed inside the cabin. I contacted the FIG with my questions about Marissa. Clay had stumbled onto something too—I could feel it.

Marissa, the role model and older sister, had challenged Shelby with math word problems, which developed analytical skills, creative thinking, and to effectively handle life's problems. Add to that, challenging her ability to solve critical issues in a story setting and her mind expanded to . . . a step-by-step process for whatever Marissa devised for Shelby to do. Just a theory or reality?

I fed and watered Big Red before I yanked my phone from my jean pocket.

Mike answered on the first ring.

"Do you have time for me to run a few things past you?"

He agreed, and I shared the happenings over the last two days.

In short, I questioned if Marissa had everyone fooled and if Shelby hadn't shot her brother-in-law.

"Whoa, you hit me broadside. Have you been drinking?"

"No, Mike, my thinking makes sense."

"When you told me Shelby refused to handle a weapon, I couldn't shake it. Let me get this straight. You're proposing that at an early age Marissa urged Shelby to develop critical thinking by manipulating her to commit crimes under the pretense of games? It's speculation, but I can't discount it either. Then again, if Marissa pulled the trigger and took the money, why wait all these years to upgrade her lifestyle?"

"The high-dollar question," I said. "With Shelby in prison, Marissa might have expanded her business and needed the cover. Or if she is guilty of murder and she took off, would Shelby reveal the truth? If Marissa is driving the threats, I see why she'd encourage Shelby's suicide before moving on to murder. After all, Shelby is her sister and perhaps paid the price with her freedom. The voice distortion could be Marissa's, but I don't think so. If she's behind the crimes, then she'd have someone else do the dirty work, like we've already seen. One more bit of information to process is Marissa's sudden move to Phoenix. Aria mentioned it to Shelby, and Clay confirmed it." I relayed all I knew about Marissa abandoning her family.

"Strange there were no goodbyes or taking personal belongings. Don't you find it interesting Clay made a turnabout with Shelby?"

"Yep. No explanation, and Shelby didn't ask."

"Why? Nervous dear old dad might change his tune, or something else?"

I leaned against a horse stall. "Spot-on, in my opinion. I think he may suspect the truth and it's too much for him to handle. I'll find out."

"Maybe Marissa has met somebody, and she'd rather be with him."

"Except she first claimed to have taken a few days to rest due to her health and abruptly decides to leave the state. Why now? Medical records would give us more insight," I said.

"I'll see about gaining access to her medical history. Interesting your theory indicates Marissa could be a narcissist, a high-functioning psychopath."

"I'd forgotten about your psychology degree."

"Comes in handy." Mike chuckled. "But if true, she would implicate her dad."

"From my one time meeting with her, she's charming and kind. She demanded the right to talk to Shelby and did so, but later she cowered to Clay. Shelby told me she'd asked Marissa to make amends with him. If that was another Marissa ploy, those traits bring cunning to the table."

"Give me a moment to piece this together." Finally Mike spoke. "Sociopaths are very good at what they do, and often victims don't know they've been used until it's too late. But don't jump to this until we have more evidence. We still have the testimony from the woman who identified Clay as part of a money-laundering business, but she could have been under orders to ID him. I'll have her brought in for another interview."

"I contacted the FIG to see if they have anything on Marissa, specifically any links between Eli Chandler and her. The voice distortion wasn't in their database, and Chandler's voice is there."

"Denton, if what you've uncovered is legit, Marissa is the one who should have suffered in prison for fifteen years. I realize that's a no-brainer."

"Glad to hear I'm not losing my mind."

"Because you're falling for Shelby?"

"I'm pleading the Fifth."

"At least you're not in full denial. Have you detected any arrested development issues in her?"

"Such as?"

"Considering her age during incarceration and the need to find ways to cope with the trauma, has Shelby shown you a rough or distant personality? Even another means demonstrating a lack in emotional processing?"

I considered my conversations with her and her behavior. "A little distant or, should I say, cautious at times, but nothing unexpected. She's in counseling."

"Good. Mahatma Gandhi has a saying about women like Shelby, 'The real ornament of woman is her character, her purity.'"

I sobered. "Took me a long time to see that. Thanks. As soon I hear back from the FIG, I'll forward the report. If all this checks out with evidence pointing to Shelby's innocence, I've got to confront her."

I pocketed my phone and hobbled back to the cabin. Having Shelby close brought back all my thoughts of one day having a wife and family.

Later, Denton. Save her life first.

Shelby wore her hair in a ponytail, fresh and downright appealing. Her rare smile tempted me to act on my feelings. But not yet. She might level me, and I'd be no match on crutches.

She worked on her jewelry pieces, intently concentrating. I studied her. A beautiful woman who took my breath away. She must have sensed my scrutiny because she glanced up.

"What?"

"Just watching you in artistic mode. Sorry."

She sighed. "You are so funny."

I scowled, knowing exactly what she meant. "Funny? In what context?"

She tilted her head. "You're so obvious."

"I'll try to do better."

A shadow passed over her face.

"Shelby, has something happened?"

"I'm thinking. Marissa dis—"

My phone buzzed with an email from the FIG.

"Take it. We'll talk when you're finished."

The FIG's fast response surprised me. I entered my secure password and opened the document. When I finished, I made additional requests and forwarded it to Mike before I steadied myself on the crutches. "I've got to make another call."

"Tell Mike I said hello."

I nodded and made my way to the porch, then closed the door behind me.

"Nearly finished reading the report," Mike said. "Back then we searched in the logical places, just not in the right ones. Looks like the FBI has footage of Marissa and Chandler entering Stage 7 restaurant in Miami, the one criminals use for meetings. The surveillance target at the time was Chandler."

"Why hasn't the FBI checked into her background?"

"She's in the background, and I enlarged the image. Opened my eyes to her activities." Mike cleared his throat. "Dinner costs more than a month of her bakery wages. I've requested security camera footage to see if she's been there previously."

"Since I sent you the report, I've learned she's used the name Janae Frosk for flight reservations, hotel, and paid for her and Chandler's evening with a credit card under the same name. We're looking at her dropping several grand."

Mike swore. "Is Janae Frosk simply an alias, or did she assume the identity of someone else?"

"Frosk died twelve years ago. It's near the end of the report." I typed into my phone. "Checking to see how long Marissa has used the woman's Social, match up dates, bank accounts, and see if she's calling the shots for crimes other than suspected money laundering."

Mike drew in a deep breath. "Add murder to the list."

"When Clay and Aria were here, Shelby was happier than I've ever seen her, and I hate to spoil those memories. But she has to know what we've uncovered."

"She was happy with her dad and niece, not Marissa. Think about it. She's thrilled her dad is back in her life, but remember the tough emotions are just below the surface with her mother's death, the threats, all of it. She could view our findings as an act of animosity."

"Right. I need to be careful, to form my words so she doesn't think I'm ganging up on her."

Mike huffed. "Honestly, do you think she'd admit Marissa's part after serving time for murder in her stead?"

"She may have endured enough. Doing time so her sister could raise her daughter and then Marissa abandons her?"

"Stand down, Denton. The timing's not right. Let's dig for more evidence against Marissa."

His insistence went against my resolve. Yet Mike reacted from years of experience, and I had the heart-thing going. We needed solid proof. "I'll hold off. Will call later after I've done more research."

I hesitated before opening the cabin. Shelby faced me, and she'd been crying. "What's wrong?"

"I've lived a lie for so long, wandered through a fog until I believed my own claims."

I frowned. "I don't understand."

She swiped beneath her eyes. "Please call Sheriff Wendall and Pastor Emory and ask them if they'd stop by later on. Tell them it's important."

"Anyone else? James Peterson, Edie, or Amy-Jo?"

"Their support sounds wonderful except what I have to say might put them in the sights of a shooter."

"Have you received another threat?"

She shook her head. "Denton, I've been a fool."

59

SHELBY

Pastor Emory's presence eased my trepidation, but I needed courage to move ahead. The pastor's compassion for others emitted from his every breath, his faith a pillar of strength. The irony of the three gathered in Denton's living room at my request brought a smile to my lips—the FBI agent, the sheriff, and the pastor with an ex-con. What a motley crew. If only the circumstances were a Sunday evening dinner on-the-grounds kind of celebration. Instead, confession of the hardest kind.

Sheriff Wendall pulled a chair from the kitchen. Pastor Emory sat on the sofa beside me, and Denton sprawled out in a recliner, his crutches leaning on the chair arm. These were my friends, and gratefulness washed over me.

God, help me to hold tightly to You.

Coffee and the fixings sat on a trunk Denton used for a table, and I added a plate of blueberry scones.

"I know y'all are wondering why I asked you to meet here this evening." Would they even believe me? "I've called you together for a reason. What too many innocent people have faced has to end before any more blood is shed. I beg of you, what's said tonight must be confidential. If you can't keep my words private, best you leave now. But I hope with what I have to say, justice will be served."

"None of us have any thought of walking out," Pastor Emory said.

The others chimed in and I braved forward. "Thanks. Pastor, would you open us in prayer?"

His words, simply spoken, asked for God to bless their time together and to give everyone wisdom in whatever transpired.

I rested my half-full cup of coffee on the table. Who should I focus on? Denton, who'd been a part of the tragedy for nearly as long as I had? The pastor, whose prayers requested peace? Or the sheriff, who swore to uphold the law?

"Denton, I'm directing my words to you because I owe you my most sincere apology for the sacrifices you've made on my behalf."

"That apology works both ways. I've followed you for years, back when I was a rookie agent and you'd confessed to murder. Later, here in Valleysburg, I've observed you, listened, looked for discrepancies in your actions, and searched online for information about what happened fifteen years ago. In a short while, I've learned to trust you and your statements of faith." Denton faced Pastor Emory. "You'll be pleased to know God and I are squared away. A few days ago, I had a come-to-Jesus meeting, as my grandparents used to say." Pastor Emory congratulated him, and Denton continued. "The four of us have a stake in righting wrongs, and we are people of integrity."

My mouth went dry. My stomach soured. What I planned to say would take me off his admirable list. Maybe I shouldn't confess and break my promise to Marissa. But something whispered to me otherwise.

Denton's brown eyes peered through to my soul. "Something else I noted—Shelby, when I broke into your cabin and read a note in your Bible, you penned 'only God knows the truth.' During the time the shooters unloaded on the safe house, Isaac told me you refused to touch Aaron's gun, even if a killer opened the door. He also said you froze in the hotel stairwell. Isaac had lost his gun, and you couldn't pick it up. Your dad confirmed your aversion to weapons. The incidents kept me up all night. Did you promise God never to touch a firearm again?"

Heat blazed from my neck into my face. I'd relied on deceit for so long that a black hole permeated my soul. Now Dad faced investigation for an inconceivable crime after he wanted me back in his life. Until all the facts surfaced, he'd be a person of interest in a money-laundering organization based on some woman's testimony who'd offered his name in an FBI interview. I sensed everyone's eyes on me.

Once again I was in a cell of my own making.

"Shelby, you're like a daughter to me," the sheriff said. "We have the resources to handle whatever's goin' on. But we need the facts."

"We want to help." Pastor Emory's counseling tone mingled with his prayerlike voice.

At least he didn't say, "The truth would set me free." I'd long abandoned the verse knowing my confession led to harm for those I loved. Did these three men suspect the truth?

"I've lied to all of you," I whispered.

"Your hesitation and pale features show years of suffering and pain." Pastor Emory patted my shoulder.

A torrent of emotions flowed unchecked and challenged me to transparency. To live behind a mask of deception meant eventually the facade became reality. The thought frightened me . . . almost as much as the truth. "Pastor, I made a promise."

"Promises are virtuous and God-honoring if they follow His ways."

I gripped my trembling hands. "And where does unconditional love fit?"

"For every person on the planet. We are instructed to love but not to lie."

"Breaking my promise means destroying the lives of my dad and niece."

Pastor Emory nodded. "What would they say if they were here now?"

The cliché of my heart pounding in my ears fit. While my gaze stayed fixed on him, his face blurred from my tears.

"What haunts you, Shelby?" the pastor said. "How have you lied?"

I breathed in, a prayer for courage. "I didn't pull the trigger on Travis."

Silence swept around the room. The words had never been uttered until now. Yet freedom lifted the burden I'd carried for so long.

"Why confess to a crime in which you were innocent?" Pastor Emory's voice continued to calm me.

"To protect Marissa and her unborn baby. My rebellious past made my confession credible. I was convinced my sister was a good person. She deserved the opportunity to raise her child outside of a prison cell."

Denton took over the conversation. "Was the admission of guilt your idea?"

"No. Marissa begged me to help her. I walked in on her aiming the gun at Travis, but I couldn't stop her before she fired. She told me he threatened to hurt her and the baby, and she panicked. She rubbed her fingerprints off the gun with a towel and gave it to me. The only time I've ever touched a firearm."

"I see. You agreed and took the blame. Back then, Mike and I were unable to identify the smudged prints. Who besides your sister knows what happened?"

"Only you in this room." I gripped my hands tighter and stared into the pastor's face. "Today Denton and I had a conversation about what makes me happy. I told him about girlhood games with Marissa. Voicing them caused me to see my childhood in a different way. While Denton was outside, I remembered the conversation I overheard the day of the shooting but must have blocked out. Marissa had told Travis she'd never loved him and she deserved happiness. He couldn't stop her."

I hesitated but I'd come this far. "The more I thought about her words, the more ambiguity existed between the lines. Yesterday my niece shared with me Marissa's lack of mothering skills. Now Marissa has taken off to Phoenix without telling her daughter or Dad goodbye. Reality of being played is hard for me to admit, but my sister is a manipulator. It's possible she's aware of all the threats and attacks that have happened since my release."

I struggled to say what had shaken me to the core, haunting words I couldn't shed. "Of all the people who have the most to fear and lose from my prison release, it's Marissa."

60

DENTON

I'd been convinced Shelby was innocent of embezzlement and suspected she might not have killed Travis Stover, but to hear it from her lips stunned me. Each time I considered Marissa setting up Shelby for those crimes, the more I saw the older sister's maniacal mind. She must have despised Shelby. From the lack of response from Sheriff Wendall and Pastor Emory, they shared my same shocked reaction. I never expected Shelby's confession to be my way of reconciling her past.

"You believe my story?" Shelby said.

"Yes." Pastor Emory broke the silence. "The moral, spiritual, and legal implications of taking the blame for a horrendous crime you didn't commit have me baffled." He studied me. "Denton, were you aware?"

"Earlier today, she expressed the childhood games that Marissa initiated. The control over Shelby caused me to rethink what might have happened fifteen years ago. But this is news to me too."

Sheriff Wendall stood and paced. "Hold on. What kind of games are we talking about?"

Shelby shared what she'd told me and a few details not spoken of previously. "I've never stolen, but I have sold drugs, not for money but to prove I could get away with it."

"You studied robberies, murders, even kidnappin' to figure out how to commit the perfect crime?" the sheriff said. When she nodded, he blew out his obvious anger. "Little lady, where were your parents?"

"They didn't know. Marissa called our time together secret-sister games."

"More like secret-sister crimes." The sheriff crossed his arms over his chest. So typical. "Your dad deserves the truth."

Shelby's face paled. "He'd be devastated."

I shifted to ease the agony in my leg. "He and Aria planned to talk on the way back to Sharp's Creek. Don't you think from the way he took time to heal your relationship that he suspects at least part of it?"

She covered her mouth and stared over my head into the kitchen. "When I saw Mom for the last time, she asked if Marissa had shot Travis. I stood by my original confession. Mom might have mentioned her doubts to Dad. I'll call him."

I didn't think Clay could handle derogatory info about Marissa. "Not a good idea. Clay Pearce deserves to hear this face-to-face from his daughter. His phone or Aria's might be bugged, putting them in line for a death order."

She leaned back against the sofa, trembling. "If not for Aria's visit and where my thinking led, I'd have continued the ruse. I believed Marissa was perfect." She buried her face in her hands. "I see now how she fostered my rebellion and how she used me to accomplish her own agenda. I'm incredibly hurt . . . and angry." She stared at me. "I have no proof of my innocence."

"You served your sentence. You've been victimized. And now Marissa has abandoned her daughter. The FBI needs your official statement."

"All right."

Sheriff Wendall summoned our attention. "Makes sense Marissa took the $500K and claimed it had been embezzled. Would you recognize your sister's handwritin'? I have the sympathy card, although the FBI didn't find a match."

"I could identify it," Shelby said, "and if it's a match, then the FBI has reason to bring her in for questioning. She's supposed to be in Phoenix as recommended by her RA doctor. Is her medical condition even legit? Aria doesn't think so."

"Maybe not. I've learned more about her actions." I told them about the photos of her and Eli Chandler in Miami, the restaurant's reputation, and the use of an alias in her travel. "I requested medical records for her earlier today, and I'll contact Clay about the dates she claimed to be resting. Doubtful she left anything incriminating behind at your dad's, but the FBI has cause to issue a search warrant and sweep her room."

The sheriff cleared his throat. "Denton, if big sister's on to what you've uncovered, we're low on time. My guess is she's on her way out of the country. Has the FBI red flagged her alias?"

"If she's made flight arrangements using that name, she'll be arrested at the airport."

"No, she won't," Shelby said. "Our games included numerous cover-ups of all kinds. We often made up aliases."

The idea of Marissa manipulating a child fueled my anger. "How many years did you play these games?"

"Years, from the time I was four until I turned sixteen when she married."

"A lot of indoctrination." I wanted to say a lot more, but she might grow hostile.

"It took lots of careful planning on her part, to say the least," she said. "Marissa has my burner phone number, and she's texted me with it. Before Mom passed, she wanted to meet with me about a threat on her life and planned to drive here for us to talk. She asked me to keep the trip a secret."

"When was this scheduled?"

"The Thursday before Mom's funeral. But given what happened, she canceled with the intention of rescheduling. I haven't heard from her since. How noble of my sister to push suicide so she'd not dirty her hands." Shelby lifted her chin.

"We must be careful until we find Marissa or Eli Chandler," I said.

"I know how to end this madness."

"How, Shelby? By doing something crazy?"

"Yes." Her voice held a wild tone.

I tightened my hands into fists. "I don't like the daredevil look in your eyes."

She smiled. "Forget the fake suicide, especially if Marissa can't be found. I can infiltrate her organization."

"Impossible. You know nothing about money laundering, organized crime, or what your sister is capable of doing."

"I agree," Sheriff Wendall said. "It assigns a bullet to you."

"And you think hiding from her hired guns is safer?" Shelby raised a finger. "How easily you forget what's already happened."

Fear gripped me. "Trained agents spend months, sometimes years learning the habits and personalities of a specific money-laundering organization before they're able to work undercover. You have no idea the size of the operation or who else is involved."

"I have an advantage. I understand her conniving thought process." She paused. "I'll contact her, tell her life has gotten too hard, and I want in on whatever she's doing."

My blood pressure shot up. "Pastor, tell her not to take on this investigation."

Up to this moment, Pastor Emory had not offered guidance on her outrageous idea. "With all things considered, Shelby has suffered more than we can imagine with her sacrifices. She acted and reacted out of love, which is exactly how Jesus instructs us. Our faith isn't about allowing injustice to reign over us or watching crimes unfold. Sometimes we have to take a stand. No matter what any of us say, Shelby is going to act. All we can do is pray and help her make this possible. If you want all my scriptural reasons to support her decision, prepare for a lengthy sermon."

"She'll get herself killed!" The roof nearly lifted with my outburst.

Shelby leaned over and touched my arm. "You're letting your feelings show."

"Amen." The sheriff laughed.

The pastor stifled a laugh, but I heard it.

I didn't appreciate their responses. "None of this is funny."

Her eyes stared into mine. "Help me stop Marissa."

"What makes you think she won't kill you anyway? Mike believes she's a sociopath. Can't be trusted."

"I know how to play into her narcissism and warped conscience," she said. "Without me, she wouldn't have anything."

"But that changed when she took off to Phoenix."

"It's a gamble worth taking. My role is to convince her I learned enough in prison to help her now. I claimed faith and kept my nose clean to appease the parole board. For a little leverage, I could threaten to take what I know to the FBI."

"She'll get you alone and blow a hole right through you."

"Marissa is greedy." She lifted her shoulders. "For too long I refused to believe her sweet temperament could possibly be woven with manipulation. The truth is, I let her blindside me."

"You won't be alone in your pursuit." Shelby held my heart in the palm of her hand. "I'll do all I can to get others on board to help." I rarely changed my mind, but she'd turned my life upside down. "Call your sister."

She grabbed her burner phone and pressed in numbers. "Hey, Sis, this is Shelby. We need to talk. Life's gotten harder to manage. Denton, the sheriff, and the pastor who's doing my counseling ganged up on me, accused me of embezzling the money. Call me back as soon as possible. Denton told me the FBI has evidence about your illegal activities and aliases. I don't want to go into why you or Eli Chandler have targeted me, but it's little sister's turn for a piece of the pie."

I hadn't fallen in love with a woman who had a shameful past . . . I'd fallen in love with a martyr.

61

Shelby's words cemented the contract on her life. But she'd been on a hit list for years.

She stood. "I'm making a pot of coffee and putting together sandwiches. Blueberry scones are not brain food. Besides, Marissa won't call right away. She wants me to turn on anxious mode and worry about it all."

"Because of your experiences with her in the past?" I said.

"Yes. My call will shock her since we talked face-to-face before Mom died. Game time. It's her move." She focused on Pastor Emory. "Your family, this community, needs you. Go home and fight my battle on your knees."

I admired Shelby's decision to take control, even if I feared for her life. "She's right. If this goes south, the truth will hold court. I believe it was Aristotle who wrote, 'As often as we do good, we offer sacrifice to God.'"

"Which is exactly why Pastor Emory needs to leave." Shelby's tone morphed into her stubborn mode.

"Sheriff, what's your choice?" I said.

"I agree. My great-granddad was this town's first sheriff. The Wendalls don't back down from any fight. I'm not a prayin' man, but I don't discount a God who helps right wrongs."

The pastor protested, but the rest of us insisted he drive home. At the doorway, he faced us. "Stage an argument."

Confusion punched me. "What?"

"When the sheriff leaves here tonight, stage an argument with Shelby. That ensures whoever is watching—and you know someone is—observes you trying to get information about the missing money from her. Denton, take her home and at her cabin continue the argument."

"Good one, Pastor. What else?"

"Let's pray for divine guidance."

"And for the truth," Shelby said. "I want to know what Marissa's been doing the past several years."

After Pastor Emory prayed with us and drove back to town, I called Mike and updated him. I asked him to contact Houston's FBI and relay our findings. With the new info, the bureau would be supportive.

He thanked me with one of his favorite phrases—not suitable for kids or Christians. "I'll arrange protective custody for Clay and Aria and dig into updates on Marissa. I'll have the assigned agents tell Clay that he and Aria are in immediate danger."

"He may suspect Marissa."

"I'll brief the agents to tell him nothing. If I'm going to spend my days before retirement on a case, you'd better keep me posted. Hourly. I'm leaving for Valleysburg as soon as I throw together a bag."

"Thanks. Appreciate it."

"I'll call you every thirty minutes. I don't like surprises. Look for me at your door."

While the aroma of freshly brewed coffee swirled around me, the sheriff paced, Shelby made notes in her journal, and I . . . I hoped I hadn't lost my mind with a ridiculous plan.

"We need a timetable." The sheriff grabbed a sandwich and another blueberry scone along with a mug of coffee. "How's this goin' to play out?"

"We're looking at digging up facts, evidence, and how to interact with unpredictable people like money launderers—tonight. All based on Marissa contacting Shelby."

"With those odds, maybe we should have asked Pastor to stay. Put in a good word to God," the sheriff said.

We needed all the divine help available on the planet. "Mike is working on gathering intel. As soon as he has something, he'll forward it to me. Basically, I'll take Shelby home. When a plan's in place, she'll leave the rear of her cabin into the woods to a safe location. About six in the morning, I'll check on her cabin with the excuse I was worried about her state of mind. Then I'll call you with a missing person report. Notifying the paper and Amy-Jo of her disappearance gets the word out. One issue is James Peterson."

"My department," the sheriff said. "I'll tell him this is part of a plan to keep her safe, and the FBI is monitorin' the situation."

She frowned. "Where will I go while I wait for Marissa's call?"

"I have a deer lease." Sheriff Wendall crossed his arms over his chest. "Not fancy, but it's a real cozy cabin."

"It's not hunting season, right?" She smiled, but I knew she feared the worst.

"And we intend to keep it that way. Problem is, I don't have time to drive you there and get back to follow up on Denton's call."

"Don't worry," I said. "I've got an idea." Mike would earn his retirement.

62

SHELBY

Timing, the crucial element of every sting operation. An exhilaration in my spirit gave me incredible energy, or perhaps the adrenaline came from my commitment to bring justice to light and honor Travis's memory. With an hour left until I made my exit and met up with Mike Kruse, I showered and dressed.

Alone in my cabin, my mind refused to slow down. I'd listened to Denton talk about money laundering and read FBI articles. I banked on Marissa's delay to memorize what I needed to know.

Marissa had attempted four times to persuade the parole board to review my case. Now I saw her persistence wasn't for my benefit. If she'd taken off while I sat behind bars, I'd have nailed her. So I needed to be out of the picture. As a result she used Mom and Dad's generosity as a cover, like she'd used the family bakery, church involvement, community activities, and at least one alias. Did she work for Eli Chandler or the other way around?

Slow down.

I tossed my inhalers, my journal, and a few clothing items into my backpack. Not a difficult task when my life's belongings could be held in one hand. I'd entered the official world of minimalism.

Not calling Dad needled me, but I'd given Denton my word not to contact him. The FBI were en route to transport Dad and Aria into protective custody. I longed to be with them, to hear their voices, and touch them. Soon . . . First things first.

◎   ◎   ◎

My flashlight kept me company until Mike texted me for the meetup. My God, who held the grand kaleidoscope, promised myriad colors for the future.

The GPS on Mike's car sent us in a northwestern route, an hour away.

His stomach growled. "We should have grabbed some donuts."

I reached behind the passenger seat for a small box. "What's your poison? Because I have a mixed dozen of day-old Amy-Jo's specialties."

"Tempt me."

I pressed the light on my phone and flipped open the lid. "Glazed donuts. Chocolate-filled donuts. Blueberry scones. Sausage-egg bagel. Bear claws. Apple fritters—"

"Sausage-egg bagel, then the apple fritter. Too bad we don't have coffee."

"Next time I'll pack it. Orange juice too." I handed him his early morning breakfast.

"Shelby, you're a brave woman."

"Not really. I'm tired of playing the scapegoat. Praying this time the plan works."

"Relax, you're sitting beside the best of the best."

I laughed. "Typical FBI mentality. But a little confidence is good."

"You must be talking about Denton. The man has fallen hard."

He wasn't alone. "I've tried to talk him down. A supposed relationship has little chance of survival. He deserves a woman without a past."

Mike turned left down a country road. "You mean he needs a woman who's selfish and doesn't make sacrifices out of love?"

"I'm not anything special. Change of subject, please."

He chuckled. "Denton was right."

"About what?"

"You're stubborn."

I could hear Denton saying those very words. That stubbornness had walked with me for as long as I could remember. "You bet. I stand my ground."

"If it doesn't get you killed." He pointed to his phone. "I have a copy of the handwriting on the suicide-sympathy card. Take a look to see if you recognize it." He gave me his password.

"Sure you should have given me your security info?" I said.

He huffed. "I'll change it when we arrive at the deer lease."

I peered at the screen and zoomed in to view it closer. How convenient if the handwriting had been Marissa's. "Nothing familiar." I'd had enough of gloom talk. "Do you have family?"

"I'll play hush-the-agent. Wife, two daughters, and three—" Mike glanced into the rearview mirror and swore. "Just like I suspected, we have a tail."

I swung a look behind us at a pickup gaining speed. It passed us, tossing rocks into the side of Mike's car, raced ahead, then whirled around and blocked the road. Two men flew open their doors and stood on each side of the truck, both aiming rifles at us.

"Brace yourself." Mike stomped the brakes and spun into a one-eighty, heading back the way we'd come. Bullets pinged off the trunk of the car. "They must be tracking us. Did you bring both of your phones?"

"Yes. I'm sorry. I—"

He cursed again. "Keep the burner and toss the other one."

I obliged and craned my neck, expecting to see headlights speeding after us. "You think they know where we are because of my phone?"

"Little late now, but we'll manage."

I'd heard reassurance in the past, and the words always blew up in my face. The last time Denton, Aaron, and Isaac were nearly killed.

Mike turned off his headlights and drove like a drunk teenager. Every road that turned, he took it. His pattern of losing the pickup swung left and right for the next several minutes. Not once did I see a sign of an oncoming or tailing vehicle. He pulled down a dirt road and cut the engine. After reaching across me to the glove box, he pulled out a gun. I said nothing for fear he'd send me walking. Not that I could blame him. Twenty minutes later he started the car.

"We're taking the long way to the deer lease."

I must be cursed. Their narrow escape from death was my fault.

⊙ ⊙ ⊙

Sheriff Wendall's deer lease looked like the perfect hiding place. But it was also the perfect spot to have a firefight without raising any attention. What else had someone tracked on Edie's phone? And how had it happened? Surrounded by mesquite trees and flat land, the rustic cabin provided a look at nature without bringing nature inside . . . like the tank after a huge renovation. The pantry contained staples, and a small freezer held enough deer, in every form, to feed Mike and me for weeks.

My protector for the next several hours or days shared the same cautious gene I'd come to recognize in Denton.

"This area is known for rattlers," he said. "Wear your shoes and watch where you step."

His warning resembled the vigilance of my life.

Mike and Denton exchanged phone calls. I learned the woman who'd named Dad as running a money-laundering operation had

died of a barbiturate overdose. I assumed one of Marissa's hench-
men had forced the woman to take them. I'd grown cynical.

Shortly before 3 p.m., my burner rang with an unfamiliar
number. Mike studied me, as though we knew the caller. I pushed
Record, not that it was admissible in court, but Mike and Denton
needed it to prove my legitimacy to the FBI.

I prayed for wisdom. "Let me guess who this is."

"Are you getting smarter after spending years behind bars?"
Marissa said.

"It's amazing the schemes some of those women shared with me."

"What's this all about anyway? You leave a crazy message about
the FBI having evidence about my so-called illegal activities. Then
you accuse me or Eli Chandler of targeting you? What kind of cash
pie do you think I have?"

I allowed a heavy pause. "I gave you fifteen years to be a good
mother, and you walked out on your daughter."

"Is that why you're hot?"

"Actually, it's the reason I want in your organization."

She laughed. "Organization, as in a business? You've lost your
mind. I've met someone, and I intend to spend the rest of my life
with him. Aria and Dad deserve each other."

"Who is he?"

"None of your business. You know, little sister, I can call your
parole officer and tell him you threatened me."

"He'd have to find me first."

"Are you in the States?"

"None of your business, big sister. I picked up a lot of tricks
from harder women than you'll ever know. But if the Feds get to
you first, then you can have special girl time too. Let's talk about
you. Everything points to you either as ringleader for a money-
laundering business or entrenched in the operation with someone else. Possibly Eli Chandler since the Feds have pics of you at
Stage 7 in Miami. Oh, by the way, they are on to your traveling
alias, Janae Frosk. Denton showed them to me when he was fishing

for leads to the money you stole from Travis's nonprofit." I allowed my words to sink in.

"What do you want?"

"What's owed me. I paved the way for you to make millions."

"Maybe. Maybe I'm calling your bluff."

"Try this on. Arthur Shell and Stan Watson are dead. Nick Hanson is in custody. He said Eli Chandler hired him to eliminate me, and the big boss gave orders to kill."

"I've never heard of Hanson. That doesn't mean Chandler's boss is me."

"I can't help you grow your organization if you aren't honest with me."

"Even if I was interested, any positions I have involve a learning curve."

"Really? Check out my previous address. Who's running your call center? Purchasing leads? Collecting the cash? What are you outsourcing?"

"I can't approve you."

"Yes, you can. Decide soon before I leave the country."

"You'll get picked up at the airport."

"Not a chance. I have my connections too. Call me by ten in the morning if we're going to work this out."

"You're giving me a deadline?" Marissa's voice sliced like a blade.

"I have a good offer in Europe, except they need an answer by eleven. Thing is, I'd rather work with you. We're sisters and understand each other, but that's your decision. You have what, twelve to fifteen people you trust? Or think you trust. You trained me for a lot of years how to get out of tight places, to read people, and commit the cleverest of crimes. We have much to teach each other. Give me a corner, and I won't bother you." I clicked off.

Shaking.

"You did a good job," Mike said. "Convinced me."

"But did I convince Marissa?"

63

For so many years, I'd buried my emotions and attempted to mold myself into someone else to find acceptance. First as a child to gain Marissa's approval, then as a teen to gain my own approval, and on into prison years when I no longer cared. Those were the lost years before I met Jesus. The only approval and acceptance that mattered now came from my relationship with Him. Depression still knocked me down on occasion, but now I knew how to get back up. I'd made mistakes and grown from them. The difference between me and my sister was Marissa had never faced consequences.

After her call, I stepped outside—with shoes on—and talked to God about my fears for my loved ones. And I couldn't turn off my love for Marissa. I vowed to follow through with doing the right thing. I asked for forgiveness for covering up a crime. I prayed for those who'd been victimized and lost loved ones. I breathed out my prayer in sobs—*God, help me bring truth and justice to so many tragedies.*

A memory crept in from when I was six years old. Unbidden, but one I needed to access . . .

"Shelby, here's your puzzle," Marissa said. "We live in a two-story brick house, and your bedroom is upstairs. Mom and Dad alarm our house at 10 p.m. You went to bed at 8:30 but snuck out to play with your friends. It's now 11:15. How will you get back inside without getting caught?"

"Easy. Before I leave, I'll toss a rope out the window so I can crawl back up."

"All you have is a jump rope, and it's not long enough."

"I'll use a bedsheet and tie it to the leg of my bed. Give me a harder one."

"Good job. Here's a cherry Tootsie Pop. Your favorite."

As I grew older, Marissa had confirmed my foolproof plans with more praise. Winnings escalated to more games, nail polish, lipstick, and special time with her. I spent hours creating the perfect crime. The last game before she married pushed the current problem into perspective.

"This may be your hardest game yet. You've robbed a bank and seriously wounded a security guard. All modes of transportation out of the city are guarded. Your face is plastered on the TV screen. Then the security guard dies."

"A little harsh," I said. "Give me a moment to figure it out."

"We're only playing a game, Sis."

I nodded. *"When I planned the robbery, I outlined all that might go wrong. I studied the bank's layout and found the entrance to an attic in a storage closet that also housed the alarm system. The attic exited onto the roof. Late at night, I climbed onto the flat roof. Nothing there to hide under. Disappointing, but I could haul two black tarps up there ahead of time, one to hide under and the second tarp to hide a disguise. If a helicopter flew over, nothing would look out of the ordinary. I chose winter, which decreased daylight hours. I'd rob the bank on a Thursday night when it was open until seven, buying me time and darkness. From experience, few customers or staff are there then. I'd take care of business and disable the alarm. I allotted fifteen extra minutes if I had to remove the opening to the attic. Once on the roof, I'd change clothes and disguise my appearance with what was left under the tarp. Under the other tarp is a portable—"*

"You've used a rope before. You need something different."

"For now a portable ladder." Marissa smiled, and I jumped back into the game. "I make my escape from the rooftop and walk to where a car awaits. I drive to the next state and a city with an airport where I've already purchased a ticket under an assumed name. I'll use my passport under the alias and fly to Denmark, where I'd invest the stolen money and live happily ever after."

"You forgot one thing."

I stared back at her. "Where to invest the money?"

"You'll need to learn about money laundering."

How hard to admit she not only manipulated but also despised me. If Mom were alive, I'd ask her to provide insight into Marissa's behavior. But then again, I wouldn't have risked upsetting her. She had two daughters whom she loved, and my questions would've drawn a dividing line between her affections. Oh, how I longed to spare Dad and Aria.

My stomach growled with a reminder I needed to contemplate supper. Mike had stopped at a small grocery along the way and purchased potatoes, salad fixings, broccoli, bananas, and a gallon of milk—for himself. Not me. Even the color of it soured my stomach.

He met me on the porch. "Did you call Denton?"

"No."

"He's worried about you, and his voice sounded like the look on your face."

I shook my head and connected with Denton. "I'm grilling deer steaks for tonight. Will you be here in time?"

His familiar chuckle relaxed me. "I have enough hot *s-t-a-k-e-s* right here. Amy-Jo suspects we're up to something."

"Were you at the café?"

"No. She paid me a visit. I'd never seen her dressed in black with a baseball cap—or packing. But the pink-and-green eye shadow were all hers. She had a feeling you were in trouble when the sheriff told her about you taking off. She demanded answers to where you'd gone."

"What did you tell her?"

"Said you took off, violated your parole. She called me a liar and drilled me with questions. Relentless. I confirmed a few things of interest about our Amy-Jo. Right now she's clueless, and I'll do my best to keep that intact. We could have drawn her into our plan."

My face burned hot. "Denton, you'd have placed her in danger."

"Let me tell you about her past."

"I'm listening. Better make it good."

"She started the story with the words, 'Honey, I may look like a chubby throwback from the eighties with an intense fondness for Cyndi Lauper, but this lady retired from the Army, rear-deep in black ops.'"

"Whoa. You're kidding, right?"

"I confirmed every word. She backed it up by showing me her S&W and her permit."

I recalled the first time I'd met Amy-Jo—mango-colored hair, purple eye shadow, pink large-framed glasses, and ruby-red lipstick. Eccentric but not ex–black ops.

"Shelby, have you fainted?"

"Thinking about it. What else?"

"We talked about some of the places in Europe where she'd worked, not specifics. She wants you to know she's on your side, and she wished she'd been a part of whatever you're doing. Claims you'd be safe with her, and she's bored." He laughed. "She's ready for more excitement than burning a batch of cookies or stepping on the scales."

Amy-Jo's confession sent me into laughter. Hysterical. Healing. Howling. Laughter.

64

Mom used to tell me nothing good happened after midnight. The clock on the wall displayed that ill-fitted hour, and if my mind listened to logic, it would shut down so I could sleep. Mike and I played Monopoly using pinto beans for houses and black beans for hotels. I lost more beans than I could count, and usually I cleaned up.

"You should get some sleep," he said for the third time.

"Too many cylinders are firing in my brain."

"Try warm milk."

I'd run into people who surprised me with their unpredictable behaviors, like Edie's fear of bats and Amy-Jo's military background, but an FBI agent who wore a milk mustache and played Monopoly?

"I'd rather forgo sleep. When do you plan to rest?"

"I'm used to catching up when I can. Part of the job. You, on the other hand, need your mind and body in gear."

I protested, and we compromised. He'd stretch out on the couch for the first three hours, then I'd wake him. We closed the blinds, and I sat at the kitchen table with a dimly lit lamp from a bedroom. My insomnia gave me time to journal all I remembered about the afternoon Travis had died. Memories of the games with Marissa flowed into my thoughts too.

Through Mike's soft snores and rhythmic breathing, I wrote page after page of recollections until my hand cramped, a small price to pay for weeding out my thoughts. Closing my eyes, I replayed the conversation. Marissa claimed before I entered the house that Travis had threatened her. I hadn't heard those words. In fact, I couldn't remember him ever raising his voice to her.

"Put the gun down," he'd said after her outburst of hate. "We can talk this out."

"Too late, Travis."

I rushed forward to stop her, but she aimed and fired.

I forced my mind to focus on their argument beforehand. Something about he forgave her. Travis had such a good heart. Those three words backed up many things Marissa could have done.

At 4:30 a.m., I nudged Mike awake. By now I was ready to crash. He grumbled about me letting him oversleep, but I ignored him. I gave him my journal and asked that he made sure Denton got it.

The idea of drifting off into oblivion seemed like an illusion. Were Dad and Aria safe? Had Marissa swallowed my story? Did she suspect the FBI were tracking her? If she refused my proposition, I had no idea how to proceed. Would she contact me before ten this morning? I expected her to linger until the last minute. Even so, the slow pace of time passing consumed me.

At 9:59 a.m., Marissa called, using an unknown number, yet I didn't expect her to use the same phone twice.

"I've been thinking about your offer. I need help from someone I can trust. I'm spread too thin, been too hands-on."

Busyness must be her excuse for escaping motherhood. "Where do I fit?"

"First of all, let's be clear about one thing. If you're out to steal from me or turn me in to the Feds, you're dead. That includes Dad and Aria. They appear to be hiding out somewhere, which is useless with my network of connections."

My stomach churned. "No problem. I'd expect it. I'm sure you know Aria showed up where I worked, and Dad retrieved her."

"Bet he unloaded."

"More than once."

"They disappeared soon after. You don't want to know what happened to my man assigned to watching Dad. At first I suspected you arranged protective custody, but the news claims you violated your parole and there's a warrant for your arrest."

"Right. I'm tired of living like this when there's more to life than one paycheck to the next."

"Mom talked to you privately. Anything I should know about?"

"She wanted reconciliation."

"That's our mom," Marissa said. "She accused me of lying about my RA getaways. Other things too. I thought I'd have to eliminate her myself, but cancer took care of the problem. Right now, you have the benefit of the doubt."

Only a monster conceived the idea of murdering her own mother. "Where do we meet?"

"Miami. Once you're here, I'll make contact for the next step."

"Good. I'm incredibly bored."

"I have the perfect job lined up."

65

Mike demanded I review money-laundering facts all the way to a Houston hotel near the airport. He handed me a carry-on containing a prescription for an inhaler with four refills, passport, ID, credit card, extra burner phone, plane ticket to Miami under the name of Ellie Whyte, and a change of clothes with a short, perky dark wig. My new look matched the images on the photo IDs. I'd officially become clandestine.

"Shelby, you don't have to go through with this. You're not trained."

"You're wrong. I've prepared for this since I was four years old. My stupidity allowed her to commit more crimes than we will ever discover." I drew in a breath to calm my shaky voice. "She will face justice for all those she's victimized."

His soft-blue eyes emitted gentleness. "Intel suggests her operation is expanding internationally."

"We suspected she had overseas accounts. How widespread is her network?"

"I'll keep you posted. My point is you're walking into a potential trap."

"The FBI is aware of all this, and I won't be arrested once I land in Miami?"

"You're covered."

"Thanks, Mike. I owe you big-time. I believe God will see me through this. If He takes me home in the middle of it, I'm confident Marissa will be stopped."

"I see why Denton is in love with you. You have many admirable qualities and compassion for others, but don't substitute courage for the role of a fool. And don't get yourself killed before you and Denton can have a life together."

I smiled and kissed his cheek.

Alone in the hotel room until an early morning flight, I called Marissa and updated her on my travel plans.

"What are you wearing?" she said.

"Jeans, yellow T-shirt, short dark wig. Are you picking me up?"

"No. Someone who works for me."

Walking into a trap crossed my mind, a reminder of prison life. "A need-to-know basis?"

"That's how I operate."

Supper held no appeal, but I needed food for strength. I ordered vegetable beef soup and bread, but the taste escaped me. I tried to sleep. A useless endeavor. The circles beneath my eyes resembled craters. Sometime after midnight I drifted off. At 4:45 a.m. the alarm sounded.

Showtime.

Denton texted me with emojis, one with praying hands.

Infiltrating a money-laundering operation frightened me when my knowledge of how it worked resided in games played long ago and online research. I couldn't right any of Marissa's wrongs—or even my own—but I could do my best to stop the crimes.

⊙ ⊙ ⊙

After exiting the aircraft in Miami in the central terminal, I bought coffee and watched the clock. The acid burned my stomach, and I dumped it. Forty-five minutes later, a text instructed me to walk to the west walkway that crossed to the Dolphin Garage from Terminal D.

I sighed, longing for the days and weeks ahead to speed by. Denton claimed working my way into Marissa's confidence might take months. The scales tipped in her favor. She possessed the skills and experience of the operation. The contacts and analysis of when and how to move the money and the intricate, underhanded methods were second nature to her. Could I ever match her in a new game of wit?

I recognized my driver instantly from the photo Denton had shown me in the hospital. Eli Chandler. Thick brown hair and large eyes scrutinized me. Although physical attractiveness meant nothing in Marissa's line of work, I saw him as eye bling for her vanity.

"We meet again." I faced him squarely. "Are we on the same side?"

A wide smile and arctic-white teeth greeted me. "At the moment."

I'd met his kind before in female form. He could kill me and walk away, easily done with a weapon hidden under his jacket.

We crossed the walkway to the Dolphin Garage. Were FBI agents watching me in case Eli pulled a gun? We stopped at a black Mercedes.

"Get in."

We drove to the North Coconut Grove area of Miami, light-years from Mom and Dad's neighborhood back in Sharp's Creek, Texas. Eli slowed in front of a gated condo complex, several stories–high white stucco trimmed in terra-cotta. Eli pressed in a series of numbers, and the gate opened. The driveway led to a parking garage where he wound the car to the top parking area and parked.

So far I'd escaped death.

"You've known Marissa for many years, even worked at the bakery for a while," I said.

He shut down the Mercedes. "We had good times before and while you were in prison."

"But now I'm out and I'm a whole lot smarter than you are."

66

Marissa lived in a world beyond my wildest imagination. But not a fairy tale. Her penthouse overlooked the bay, and the skyline had a million-dollar view. The interior design of white, cream, glass, and chrome oozed with sophistication. Perfectly staged. Perfectly decorated. No hint of personalization. The penthouse resembled what I once had envisioned as my own. I shared those ideas with Marissa, and she'd stolen every detail. Instead of irritation, I felt a deep sense of pity. Could it be my sister always took from others?

Eli opened a glass door from a large open living room, dining room, and kitchen onto a balcony. He gestured for me to step through to the massive area where a light breeze bathed my face. Marissa sat in a robe beneath a canopied table, her attention devoted to something on her phone, or so she wanted me to believe.

"Good morning," I said.

She lifted her head and smiled. Even without a hint of makeup, she rivaled the beauty of her surroundings. "Hey, Sis. Glad you're here. Join me and let's chat." She nodded at Eli. "Thanks for picking up my sister."

He disappeared . . . a deadly errand boy. Two other men, stoic as pieces of furniture, stayed inside. I assumed they were bodyguards.

"Breathtaking view." I took a chair facing her. "Gorgeous penthouse."

"Thanks. It's not my only hideaway."

"This isn't home?"

"Home is where my money grows. My favorite spot is in Cyprus."

My mind quickly drew upon research. Those who fought against money laundering had the eastern Mediterranean island country of Cyprus on their radar. The island hailed as an international financial center inviting foreign clients to operate freely. Although some official reports claimed a crackdown on the practice, the revenue into the city took precedence. "I'd like to see it."

"We will, little sister." She gazed out over the bay. "Feels good without the old pretense. I used to wonder what it would be like to have you with me, to experience the pleasures of life without thought of money. We've led separate lives, and yet this has always been our destiny." She studied me. "Where are your thoughts?"

"With my sister, seeing our girlhood games play out in an amazing story."

"Well said. We have so much to discuss, but I'm hungry. Business matters canceled my breakfast, and I'm incredibly hungry. Do you mind sitting here while I grab some clothes? I'll have my men take us to a phenomenal restaurant for brunch."

"Sounds great, and I'll enjoy the view."

"Anything to drink? Water? Coffee? Soda? The coffee at the restaurant is incredible."

"No thanks."

She peered at me. "You still have the gun issue?"

"Yes. I use brains, not bullets."

"More like fools, not firearms. Time to change your little-girl fears."

"I'm on parole, remember? Can't risk getting caught."

"How about getting killed?" She laughed. "By the way, the taller man is Lee and the smaller is Jess. Outstanding bodyguards."

She disappeared and I wanted to text Denton, but for sure cameras were in place. Memorization was my safest choice. From the balcony, I took in more of the view. A golf course on my left dotted with players and carts. Yachts lined up at the pier, bobbing on sky-blue water like miniature toy boats ready to set sail.

The nagging question persisted about the job Marissa had for me. So much uncertainty. Denton and Mike had warned me she could expect me to deal in prostitution, drugs, murder, or weapon sales. I assumed her sisterly demeanor was in place to trip me up. My new mantra resounded . . .

Be careful.

⊙ ⊙ ⊙

At the age of thirteen, I longed to be an actress. The imaginary accolades and requests for magazine shoots and autographs fueled my desire. In those young teen days, I never imagined acting as a means to save my life.

Marissa's bodyguards transported us to a Miami restaurant. Lee drove.

"Your purse stays in the car," Marissa said. "Always, unless I tell you differently."

Already my sister had orders, but I expected it.

Inside the restaurant, we chatted over brunch at a remote booth. The price for our fancy omelets hovered over three figures . . . without the coffee. My sister's pale-blue silk sundress, hat, and sandals gave her runway style.

"You mentioned needing help with business. Have you experienced problems with the economic downturn?"

She pinched off a piece of a blueberry muffin. "Medical insurance billing. I had a licensed physical therapist who used fake patients to bill for services. Lost revenue. The second loss involved selling vacation properties. Can't sell a getaway when the buyer is out of work."

"Have you recouped? I saw scam possibilities with the census and election."

"I dabbled in some. Fundraising for the election brought in a little money. Amazon offered the best cash cow. When I saw 3.5 billion packages were delivered in 2019, I did my research and jumped in." Marissa's eyes widened, twinkling with the familiar excitement.

I smiled and nodded. My sister had been one of several scammers who'd sent emails to millions of unsuspecting victims, stating they had an Amazon package to be delivered. But first the victim needed to provide a credit card to verify the package. The scammers sent a clickable link that installed malware, allowing them to harvest tons of data.

Marissa examined her veggie omelet and tasted a bite. "Cash businesses provide the least risk. A solid place for you to start."

"Which ones do you prefer—restaurants, bars, casinos, check-cashing stores, car washes?"

She laughed. "I started with donut shops. Took a while to make it profitable, but the business model is safe. I learned how to speak to the owner with what he or she wanted to hear. I'll take you with me on a few calls so you can see firsthand how to work."

I forced interest in my omelet. "I need the experience." Marissa had been at this for over fifteen years, and from what I'd seen of her penthouse, I doubt she still resorted to donuts. I silently thanked Denton for insisting I study money laundering. The operation required placement, layering or moving the money around, and integration or pulling the funds out to use when it was cleaned. "Where do I begin?"

"I'll invest in a decent wardrobe for you. Currently you're an embarrassment." She raised her palm. "Rule number one is always look the part. The last time we were together, your hair looked disgusting. I'll make an appointment for a cut and highlights. I'll purchase wigs and miscellaneous items to change your appearance before you enter my world. The cost of my investment will be deducted from your pay."

I nodded as though her stipulations suited me. "Rule number two?"

"Disguise yourself for each new vein of clients. That allows you to check on the investment without the person's knowledge."

"The check-cashing businesses see one person while the casinos see another. Makes sense. Rule number three?"

"Trust no one. Not me. Certainly not Eli. He'd stab his mother, especially if I gave the order. Along with trust, give those around you various levels of it while always remembering the sacred rule." She sipped orange juice laced with vodka. "Live and breathe those three rules, little sister. Forget them and I'll pull the trigger."

67

Marissa's investment into my new wardrobe made me question in what capacity I'd need to perform to please her. We'd spent two full days shopping at high-end stores I'd heard about but never entered. On those trips, she granted me permission to bring one of my new purses. Various disguises, cell phones, and the clothes meeting Marissa's approval were grouped together according to the client. She'd completed my training with a virtual doctorate in illegal operations.

The two men, Lee and Jess, accompanied us everywhere we went. They never talked, and neither did Marissa speak to them.

Always the ever-present question of why she was making an investment in me. I'd given up thinking she held the keys to my fate out of a sense of debt. Something more. Something beyond a game, something she feared from me worse than my death.

We held no conversations about business inside the penthouse, only on the balcony or at a private restaurant. I'd hidden my phone in my closet where I hoped it wouldn't be found. But I expected her to monitor my every move, body language, analyze my words, and search my few personal belongings when we were out. I studied every potential place for a camera to be hidden. The assumption kept me sharp—and alive.

Friday morning we drank dark-roasted Hacienda La Esmeralda coffee on the balcony. The remarkable taste spoiled me for any coffee I'd ever encounter again, and I imagined the price fell into the same category as the clothes and accessories.

Marissa had instructed me to wear an extremely short printed pink silk dress from Balenciaga with matching hot-pink leather sandals. "You select the jewelry, handbag, but no wig. I want to see makeup that complements the dress. Don't outdo me, though. I have to be the one to turn heads."

The voice of a true diva. "Are we having lunch?"

"Yes, with a business associate, and I will handle the introductions. You will say nothing unless spoken to. Later I'll quiz you."

Thinking quickly no matter the circumstances reminded me of being kids again. We used to play this game at the bakery when it bustled with business. "Ever the teacher," I said.

"The difference is in the results of a win or a loss."

Marissa still despised me. "Sister, I have no intention of losing."

"Hope not. I've made an investment."

"Expect a large return." I shook my head. "Hey, why did you marry Travis? I never understood the mismatch."

She laughed. "I first met Eli. And fell hard. He introduced me to the business world, but I needed more of a cover than the bakery. Dad wanted me to meet Travis, and I played the part." She stared out over the bay. "He bored me, and his church-boy attitude was worse than Mom's."

"When did you break it off with Eli?"

"You're good, Shelby. He bored me too, but I strung him along until I made contacts. I keep him on the payroll and occasionally toss a bone his way." She frowned. "He's made a few stupid mistakes lately, but you're aware of those."

Could he be Aria's father? If so, she might feel obligated to keep him alive. "Another question—why live with Mom and Dad all those years? What a cramp in your style."

"The absolute worse. My RA weekends helped. They adored Aria and put up with my complaining for fear I'd take her and leave. Truth is, I built my assets during those intolerable years."

I leaned in. "Why the contract on my life?"

"It's still out there."

"Why?"

"You were worth more to me dead. Mom planned to ask you about what happened with Travis. She'd talked to Dad, but he refused to listen. I bugged her room and learned she'd requested all the public records on the case. Aria has the curious gene, and she questioned Mom about my preoccupation with other things instead of her. If I took off, the three would put it all together."

"So you waited for Mom's death?"

"I helped it along. A friend of Eli's showed me how to replace her medications so I could implement my plans. I decided to keep you alive in the event you could be of value." She finished her coffee. "Besides, you amuse me. It's like being kids again. You're such a people pleaser. Reminder, today your purse stays in the car."

"When are you removing the contract?"

"As soon as you ace all the tests."

She'd presented me with another reason to find the evidence against her before she bored of me.

In less than an hour, I emerged from my bedroom. Definitely unlike the Shelby Pearce I knew. The clothes, false eyelashes, and makeup changed the outer me, except the determined me existed stronger than before. For a lingering moment, I thought of Denton and if he'd approve of the look. Or any of them. My few days away from him complicated my emotions. I missed him—the laughter, conversations, long walks . . . the way he listened. His love for me seemed like an impossibility. But if I survived this ordeal, he and I might have a chance at happiness.

The conversation with Marissa bumped against my brain. Surely Mom and Dad saw through her ruse. Or maybe they were fearful of losing another daughter and granddaughter.

At the restaurant entrance, Marissa handed a uniformed valet her keys. She'd chosen a sophistication of her own identity and not a disguise. We walked inside, and she garnered admiration from every male, young and old. A trim man standing near the corner caught her eye, and her soft voice rose. "Feng, how kind of you to join me for lunch."

"My pleasure. Who is with you?"

"This is Shelby Pearce, my sister and new assistant." Without turning to me, she continued. "Shelby, Feng owns several restaurants. We've been close friends for a long time."

He nodded. "You never mentioned having a sister or needing an assistant. We have matters to discuss." His obvious annoyance ushered in an uncomfortable pause.

"I trust her implicitly," Marissa said. "Nothing jeopardizes what you and I have together. Or the future."

"All right." He pointed toward a double door. "After you, ladies."

During lunch Marissa displayed another feature of her evolving personality—graceful gestures, respectful and complimentary word choices, and an apparent concentration and attentive focus on Feng. She still played games.

"Will I see you in San Francisco?" he said.

"Just as we planned. Will John be there?"

"He wouldn't miss the opportunity. His offer to us still stands."

"I haven't decided. The decision is complicated." She pursed her lips.

"The meeting is in two weeks. Marry me, Marissa, and we'll build a vast empire."

Marissa reached across the table and took his hand. "I'm afraid, darling."

Why the vulnerability? Unraveling my sister seemed impossible.

In the car, I closed my eyes to mentally seal all I'd observed. Marissa had given Feng my entire name but not his. Always a reason . . . to show she respected his investigation of me but kept his status secret?

Marissa touched up her lipstick. "Time's up. What did you see during lunch?"

I stared out at the busy street ahead and asked the One who had all the answers to guide me. "The use of your first name, dress, and appearance show Feng is aware of who you are. You met him originally in a professional setting, but it moved into a personal relationship. Too soon to tell if he initiated the pursuit or if you saw a benefit in manipulating him for personal gain.

"He has feelings for you that extend beyond the title of his mistress or living together. He wants to own you, and marriage accomplishes his need to control and possess. You play into his affections and lead him on. Might even marry him if he can keep you entertained. But he's smart, and you have to be careful.

"His dark side can be dangerous. He's introduced you to some-one powerful who could add dollars and possibly a safety net to your investments. He flinched when you asked if this man planned to be in San Francisco, as though he suspects a rival. I sincerely doubt Feng is in the restaurant business, most likely a cover." I took a deep breath. "How's my analysis?"

A full twenty seconds passed before she spoke. "You've had an excellent teacher."

Marissa drove home in a brooding mood I hadn't seen in years.

68

Patience wasn't a virtue in my agent's dossier, and the following Friday found me missing Shelby, aching to hear her voice instead of anticipating a text.

After Randy Hughes had suffered a heart attack, he spent three days in the hospital, then voluntarily checked himself into an alcohol detox center not far from Valleysburg. At the residential facility, trained professionals had designed a program uniquely for him to heal his mind and body. By forming new habits, Randy had the opportunity to step back into life with a solid support system. My thoughts for him were noble, and before putting God as a priority, I might not have hoped for his rehabilitation.

But would he agree to see me today after spending a few days in the program?

Inside the rehab office, I stated my purpose, displayed my FBI creds, and requested to see Randy. I waited at a table in a spring-flowering courtyard beneath a canopied table. Red pentas and purple petunias exploded into color alongside a white stone. As a kid, I'd pulled weeds from my grandparents' flower beds with those same plants and colors. I relaxed a bit.

Over thirty minutes later, Randy greeted me without the typical scowl. He'd lost weight, and his skin color reflected a well-paved road to good health, providing he didn't take detours.

"Thanks for seeing me," I said. "They must be treating you right."

"Better than I deserve. Haven't felt this good in a long time." He nodded at my crutches. "Fall off Big Red?"

"A truck ran me off the road."

"Familiar story. Get the plates?"

"The driver forgot to attach the front one."

"Shelby Pearce's enemies?"

"Indications point in that direction."

"Don't say I didn't warn you. She's bad news. Curiosity is getting the best of me. Why are you here?"

His familiar disapproval clouded my intentions. "I have questions."

"Shelby?" He frowned.

"I believe she's innocent of embezzlement."

Randy shook his head. "I've learned a lot about myself since my heart attack. Expect to learn a lot more. But hearing Shelby's innocent? Not anything I expected. Neither do I believe it. Your questions?"

"What have you done since her prison release?"

He shrugged. "Guess it doesn't matter. The same day Shelby arrived at the bus station, I got a call from a man who claimed to be Clay Pearce. He said he'd already talked to the sheriff, but he was afraid Shelby planned to come after him and his family. Needed my help to force her back into prison. I'd already argued with Edie about the idea of taking in an ex-con. Clay Pearce's call cemented my commitment to run her out of town." He lifted a finger my direction. "Yes, he talked to the sheriff about fear for his family, but his call happened a week before her release."

"Did you shoot out the tire on Edie's SUV?"

"Nope. But I placed a tracker app on the phone Edie gave Shelby and gave the account info to the caller."

"What about Shelby's burner phone?"

"Wasn't aware she had one."

"Arrange the first note under her door?"

"Guilty. Hired a young scumbag from one of the local bars to deliver it." He snorted. "I broke the law to protect my sister and her family."

"I need the name of the guy you paid."

He nodded and gave it to me. "Sheriff Wendall asked me about the sympathy card you found. I don't know a thing about it, and I didn't write the newspaper article. I flunked junior English twice."

"Do the names Arthur Shell, Stan Watson, Eli Chandler, or Nick Hanson mean anything to you?" I showed him the men's pics.

"Never seen any of them before. When I got fired, the same guy called the next day. Not sure how the news traveled so fast. Unless we have a mole in our police department." Randy waved at another man who walked by. "He told me Shelby was responsible for my dismissal and offered me ten grand to eliminate her. I refused to commit murder. Then I got drunk and got mad enough to take my own revenge."

"Any other contact?"

"Nope."

"Has Edie been here?"

"When I was in the hospital. My ex-wife is supposed to visit here tomorrow."

"Need a prayer?"

"Nah. If I choose to change, I'll do it on my own. Might not be worth it."

"Any more contact from the caller?"

He eyed me. "No." He pulled his cell phone from his jean pocket. "I tried to call a few times, and it just rang. Maybe you can trace the number. Trust me, someone has eyes on Shelby's every move. Yours too."

69

SHELBY

Sunday morning while Marissa slept, I slipped a note under her bedroom door and found Eli on the balcony. "I'm walking to the coffee shop and taking a little time in the park area. I have my phone."

"The coffee here beats any spot I know."

"True, but I need a change of scenery."

"Why?"

"Look, Eli, I'm a smart woman, and I know my relationship with Marissa is currently in a trial period. Only an idiot would mess up the relationship. You'll find me at the coffee shop or in the park. I've been cooped up too long. Call me if Marissa has plans." The same details I'd written on Marissa's note. "In fact, come along if you like. Caffeine and nature are a good mix."

He waved me away and scowled. "Too hot."

"Suit yourself." I left the condo. Never thought once I left prison I'd have to fight so hard to survive. Although I didn't see either of the two bodyguards, for certain one of them followed me.

Miami's heat and humidity mirrored many of my days in Texas, but this early morning brought a balmy breeze. I strolled to the coffee shop, taking in the sweet scent of tropical flowers, lovely songbirds, and the quiet hum of the morning beneath a blue cloudless sky. Inside the café, an old Bee Gees tune of "Stayin' Alive" met my ears. I casually observed every person. One could be the FBI agent assigned to me, and I selected a likely candidate. I examined the bags of whole bean coffee, bought a book about their coffee beans, and left for the park.

A few joggers and walkers wove around a paved path. Willing my body to relax, I kept my sights on a bench next to a cypress tree near a gazebo. Once there, I opened the book where I could enjoy my latte and contact Denton. I slipped my phone inside the pages of the book and lifted the book to cover my mouth. He answered on the second ring.

"Hey," I said. "Good morning from Miami."

"Miss me so badly you had to sneak away to call?"

"You wish." The sound of his voice spread warmth through me. "Denton, remember when you told me that you were falling in love with me?"

"Nothing's changed there."

I smiled and prayed for much-needed courage. "I . . . I'm falling in love with you too."

He chuckled. "We are a pair."

"What was God thinking?"

"My mamaw always said, 'God's up to somethin' good.'" He paused and perhaps like me, he wished he saw the future. "Are you safe?"

"For the moment. I'm in a park a few blocks from Marissa's condo. I'm sure Eli had me followed. I'll make this short. I shared lunch with Marissa and an interesting man, a business and personal friend. They are involved, and he wants to marry her. Supposedly he's in the restaurant business. I was denied his last name, but she called him Feng. There's a meetup in San Francisco with the two of them and another man by the name of John. He's offered them a business deal that she's hesitant to accept. She told Feng she's afraid."

"We know about him. Marissa's been seen in Miami with a Chinese businessman by the name of Feng Liu, who owns what appears to be a legitimate import-export company dealing in the supply of automobile parts. We suspect Liu's smuggling heroin worldwide and is in tight with a man in San Francisco by the name of John Rudder, who owns an auto parts distribution warehouse. The theory is Rudder is receiving Liu's inferior merchandise and selling to unsuspecting buyers and that heroin is somehow involved in the transactions."

"I have no idea where Marissa's interests are vested other than she got started money laundering through cash businesses and bakeries."

"Are you having second thoughts?"

"No." I forced a laugh—one I didn't feel. "I can't give up. Got to find a way into her head. She's spent thousands of dollars on clothes and disguises for my future with the constant threat of not disappointing her hanging over my head. Why allow me to accompany her to private meetings? Does she think I'd never betray her, still have this sister-loyalty thing? Why groom me for a potential position, then turn around and leave my body in a ditch? I'm sorry. You don't have the answers either."

"Let's get you to a safe place. What you've told me is enough."

"Nothing that will stand up in court."

Denton relayed his visit to Randy Hughes. "Glad he's in a good place, as long as it sticks. Is Eli Chandler often at the condo?"

"Yes. I think he lives in the building. At one time he and Marissa were an item. He's made mistakes, as we already know, but he's still in the picture. Makes me wonder if he's Aria's father."

I glanced above the pages and in the distance, I saw a man who'd been at the coffee shop. "Talk to you later. I gotta go."

I closed the book around my phone and slipped it into my purse. I grabbed another phone Marissa had given me. Pressing in Eli's number, I counted three rings before he picked up. "Checking in. I imagine you're missing me."

"How's the park?"

"I'm near the gazebo reading, and it's relaxing. Is Marissa up?"

"She had an errand."

"Care to join me?"

"Are you hitting on me? Marissa might not approve."

The thought gagged me. "Who says she needs to know? In case you haven't noticed, she's tired of me."

"Imagine that."

70

DENTON

Panic squeezed my mind. Why had Shelby ended the call? Fear of losing her pushed me into working every detail to arrest Marissa. For the next few hours, I analyzed info that appeared to have her fingerprints. I'd sent the FIG several requests centered on Feng Liu and John Rudder. Linking either of them with Marissa furthered the investigation. She only thought she'd outwitted the FBI, and somewhere along the line, she'd slipped. A persistent sting in my spirit told me her actions with Shelby were deliberate . . . and led to a murderous end.

If Shelby were listening to my apprehension, she'd tell me, "God's got this."

A car pulled into my driveway, irritating me when I had work to do. I groaned—Edie and Amy-Jo in their Sunday clothes, an indication I was their afternoon mission project. Amy-Jo carried a bag, most likely yesterday's café sandwiches. Maybe if I'd gone to church this morning instead of diving into the worst-case scenario with Shelby, I might be more optimistic. Their steps on the porch counted down a dread.

"Open the door, Denton," Amy-Jo said. "Can't hide from your friends forever."

I flung open the door. "What brings you lovely ladies out this afternoon?"

Amy-Jo pointed a hot-pink nail into my chest. "Where have you been?"

"Working."

"Mucking out stalls?"

I ran my fingers through my hair. "Actually, I did. Have either of you heard from Shelby?"

Amy-Jo touched my cheek with the same hot-pink nail that had been ready to claw out my heart. "We were hoping you'd located her."

"Take a look around." I stepped aside for them to enter. "Nothing but an empty space."

"Sounds like a bad rendition of a Phil Collins song."

Amy-Jo and her eighties music. "I wouldn't know."

Edie glared at me. "I feel badly for you, but, Denton McClure, you have no excuse not to shower. My twelve-year-old smells better after baseball practice. Have you been sleeping in your horse's stall?"

"I wasn't expecting visitors."

"Trust me. We won't be long." Amy-Jo set the bag on the kitchen table. "You're pale too. The food's still hot."

I thanked her, and we sat.

"See here," Amy-Jo began, "if you're working from home, Shelby has made contact, and you're helping her stop some crime."

"Now—"

"Don't placate me. If she'd simply run off, you'd be furious. If she was in danger, you'd be a wreck, which you are. Bet your laptop is hotter than a firecracker. And we learned one more tidbit of news—Clay Pearce and Aria have disappeared."

Facing the consequences of skipping church wasn't worth these two tormenting me. "Since you have this all put together, why are you here?"

"Seeing you helps me analyze your answers." Amy-Jo stared at me. "Is Shelby with her dad and niece?"

"I don't know."

"In protective custody? Or—?"

"Is she alive?" Edie said.

"I think so."

Edie stood. Must be her signal to leave. "When this is over, I want to learn what's going on."

"Me too." I forced a chuckle but neither of them joined me.

Amy-Jo joined Edie at the door, and I did the proper host thing. "Thanks for stopping by and bringing food."

"Get a shower, Denton," Edie said. "Put your clothes in the washer and turn it on hot with extra soap."

I smiled. "Yes, ma'am."

Amy-Jo pulled a newspaper from her never-ending tote. "Have you seen Saturday's paper? I understand you can't reveal what you know, but this could get her killed."

After they left, I opened the local newspaper. Front-page news . . .

FBI announces nationwide search for Shelby Pearce for breaking parole. Pearce was recently released from prison after serving fifteen years for murdering her brother-in-law. Authorities say Pearce is suspected of running a drug cartel from inside prison and may have left the country. Missing family members indicate she may have committed additional murders. FBI Special Agent Denton McClure, who is reported to have been living in the area, is under investigation. Sources say McClure and Pearce met at the murder trial and continued a relationship during her prison years.

I tossed the paper aside and scrolled through notices on my phone. One missed call from Mike and another from my boss. I'd silenced my cell after talking to Shelby so I could work uninterrupted. The article had been picked up Sunday by nationwide sources with more dirt tossed at Shelby and growing accusations against me and the FBI's credibility.

A great way to discredit Shelby's testimony.

My conversation with Mike was short. Houston needed us in the office tomorrow morning at ten thirty.

71

SHELBY

Sunday night, shortly after darkness covered the city, Marissa told me to change into faded jeans, a plain T-shirt, and the brown chin-length wig. She emerged from her bedroom in slit jeans, eye makeup that rivaled Amy-Jo's, and black hair.

"We have an errand." She echoed Eli's description of her destination earlier today. "Leave everything here. We're going to a party." She slipped a gun into the rear waist of her jeans. "It's a 9mm, little sis."

"How many will be at this party?"

"Enough to have a good time." She handed me a cell phone. "I'm giving you a number to call. A man will answer. Tell him your real name and you want to meet with him tonight. The conversation is urgent."

"Who is he?"

"He's hosting the party."

"I'm not sleeping with this guy," I said.

Marissa laughed. "If I intended for you to earn a little cash, you'd be dressed for it." She shoved the phone into my face. "Make the call. His name is Lance."

I pressed in the numbers, and a man answered. "Hey, this is Shelby Pearce."

"We need to talk tonight."

"I prefer a private meetup. You have a report?"

"An urgent one."

"Okay. Near the gazebo on the south side of the park where you sat this morning. Say, an hour?"

"I'll be there." I gave Marissa her phone and repeated the man's words. "Eli followed me today and observed this guy watching me. I noted a man tailing me too."

"Exactly. I want to know what he's up to. But your job is to confirm it—easy. You go alone, and I'll be watching. Got to keep my sister safe."

Who walked into a trap? The guy named Lance or me?

Shortly afterward, I retraced my steps, minus the coffee shop. Soft lights bathed the perimeter of the park, but darkness clothed the bench from earlier today. I sat and waited, not sure if I wanted Lance to show up.

A tall, shadowed form appeared. When he joined me, I recognized him from earlier in the day.

"Tell me, Shelby. Who told you about me?"

"I have my ways. You followed me this morning, and I want to know why and who you are."

"There's a BOLO out on you. I'm FBI."

Clarity hit me. "Get out of here," I whispered. "You've walked into a trap."

He jerked and blood spurted from his chest before I heard a faint sound. I grabbed his shoulders and helped him stagger backward to the ground. Another bullet whizzed past my head.

My end had come.

"I'm sorry." I pressed my hand over his chest, liquid life oozing through my fingers. A lack of pulse repeated my fear of his death. Where was my final bullet?

"Sis, you did good." Marissa's voice brought anger and terror to the surface. She stood about ten feet from the bench.

I'd vowed to bring my sister and her operation to justice, but I drew the line at murder. "Really? Was this necessary?"

"Do you have blood on your party shirt?"

I shivered in the warm night and walked her way. Grief shoved me into a fury difficult to hide. Marissa had killed before. Many times. I followed her into a darker portion of the park.

"Clean off your face and hands." She tossed me a package of wipes from a plastic bag. "Hurry. I have a clean T-shirt."

I obeyed, swallowing the urge to vomit. She handed me a T-shirt from the same bag. I shoved my emotions into removing the bloody shirt and wiggling into the clean one. She held out the plastic bag, and I jammed both inside.

"Why shoot at me?" I whispered through clenched teeth.

"To show you who's the boss. He followed you today, and you neglected to tell me."

"What clued you in to his identity?"

"After you left this morning, Eli and I followed. We saw him tailing you and put together a plan. Eli asked him if he'd take our pic because selfies were always horrible. I protested, stating I didn't want anyone touching our phones. Eli played the irritated boyfriend and asked the man if he'd use his phone to take the pic and text Eli with it. He agreed. Once done and we had his phone info, I requested him to delete the pic from his phone. He signed his own death warrant."

"Thank you. He'd have arrested me and ruined everything." I despised myself for the insensitive words, the lack of compassion for a dead man.

"Mistakes are a countdown to a bullet. Understand?"

"Yes. Nothing stands in your way."

She pulled the gun from her back waistband. "I need you to take this."

I shook my head. "The last time I took a gun from you, I served fifteen years."

"So you do learn from your mistakes." She replaced her weapon. "No fingerprints. Having you with me in the business gives me a sense of family. Don't spoil it." She pointed to a park light, and we ventured closer. After having me turn around twice, she declared me free of blood. "Eli will clean up the mess back there and dispose of the matter."

Dispose? "Where?"

"I have no idea. He'll tell me later. Are you buckling on me, little sister?"

"Just curious. I saw the news earlier. The FBI is looking for me and McClure is facing an investigation in alleged charges of planning my escape. I imagine you arranged the article."

"All things work for good for those who plan ahead. The FBI's inquiry buys us time to finish up a deal before we leave."

"Leave where?"

"Haven't decided yet . . . Hong Kong, St. Petersburg, or Cyprus."

"I always wanted to travel," I said.

"No problem with a money flow. Hey, Sis. I'm in the mood for ice cream, chocolate cherry cheesecake. We'll have a double-decker on the way to the penthouse, a way of celebrating that you passed the test."

⊙   ⊙   ⊙

I tossed and turned, an image of the dead man's blood covering every inch of me. I showered twice, rubbed my skin raw, but the nightmare repeated. My sister had grown up in a home where our parents demonstrated decency and morals. They helped others and encouraged us to emulate them. Marissa played the good girl, leader, cheerleader, straight-A student in high school and college. Had her tendency for narcissism and manipulation always been a part of her, or had she acquired the traits while growing up? In weighing her behavior tendencies, I accepted Marissa was driven by a lust for money, and eliminating others meant nothing to her. Business as usual. Her attitude grieved me. People were tossed aside like trash.

The moment I started to drift, I relived the scene again. . . . Shadows pulled in around me, and I knelt over the man's body. Blood flowed from his chest, through my fingers, and dripped down my arms. His name was Lance . . .

DENTON

I'd never met Special Agent Lance Mason, the man who'd been found murdered on Miami's north side, but we had a connection through Shelby. I parked my rental car in the secured parking area of Houston's FBI headquarters at 9:30 a.m. and read the latest news before Mike arrived, which should be any time since he was always early.

The FBI said Lance had been briefed about Shelby insisting she work as an informant and using an alias. No reason why he ventured out alone in a rogue attempt to close in on the case that got him killed. Lance's wife reported he'd left their home at 9:30 p.m., but he didn't share where he was going or when he'd be back.

Shelby had sent me a text last night and typed her attempt to infiltrate Marissa's operation resulted in the death of an FBI agent by the name of Lance.

Marissa shot him in the chest, then wanted ice cream. Eli disposed of the body.

Concern for the woman I loved wrestled with how to move forward in my job. Shelby had witnessed her sister commit two murders, and evidence stacked that Marissa had ordered the deaths of others. She'd have no reservations about killing Shelby or anyone who got in her way. But the FBI didn't have enough evidence to make a case against Marissa and pull Shelby away from danger.

Mike pulled into an empty parking spot beside me. He stepped out and leaned against his car. I believed we were on the same page with this case—Marissa and her operation needed to come down and soon. Frustration added lines to his face, and I identified with the same emotion. The possibility rose of those in charge dismissing all we'd uncovered. I wanted Shelby out of the death trap, but I knew she'd never agree to leave until Marissa wore cuffs.

I exited my truck and greeted Mike. "Are you questioning why Lance Mason didn't have backup before he met with Shelby?"

"No clue unless he had doubts she'd show." He crossed his arms over his chest. "I talked to his partner. He wasn't aware of the meetup, said Mason tended to balk at protocol."

"And it got him killed."

"Left a wife and two small kids." He snorted. "I want to cuff Stover and Chandler myself."

I sensed my blood pressure skyrocket. "That's my claim."

He pushed off his car. "Might as well see what the bosses say."

"My guess is a butt-chewing and specifics on how to make arrests."

Behind a closed door inside a conference room, Mike and I positioned ourselves across from Special Agent in Charge Rogers and Assistant Special Agent in Charge Leonard.

SAC Rogers, more Mike's age, expressed the need for arrests. He jotted notes on a legal pad of paper. "We lack sufficient evidence for a search warrant."

"Shelby is working on it." I showed him last night's text. "No one could be more motivated."

Rogers leaned back in his chair. "Have you heard from Ms. Pearce since?"

"No, sir," I said. "All communications have been forwarded to you and ASAC Leonard."

"We assume Stover and Chandler have a deal about to take place for them to stay in Miami for this long. The risk must have millions at stake," Rogers said. "Has Pearce mentioned any more about Feng Liu or John Rudder?"

"Not any more than I've given you."

ASAC Leonard frowned, a grim-faced man whom I'd seen smile once in the seven years I'd known him. "Until Pearce confirmed Liu's girlfriend, we were merely speculating. Word is Stover and Liu are negotiating for a merger, and she's leaving the country. Could be they're holding off until the deal with Rudder is sealed."

"While the danger for Shelby rises." The moment the words left my mouth, I wanted to yank them back. "My—"

"Denton—" Leonard leaned in—"is your relationship with Ms. Pearce a liability?"

I pushed aside my dislike for him. "My apprehension would be for anyone working as an informant and unprepared. A Miami agent's death shows Marissa Stover's capabilities. Shelby is taking precautions with the knowledge that everything in the penthouse is bugged or videoed."

SAC Rogers directed his attention at Mike. "What are your thoughts?"

My old friend hesitated. Correction, my old friend who lived and breathed honesty. "My observations are the two have feelings for each other, and both are determined to bring justice to the case. Shelby has a fearless and stubborn streak that I hope doesn't outweigh her good judgment. She's aware of the critical timing."

"All right." Rogers wagged a pen at Mike and me. "I don't want Pearce dead. She's all we have between the truth and criminal activities. We have surveillance on Stover, Chandler, and Pearce as well as Liu and Rudder. We need to know the details for the San Francisco meeting ASAP."

"Are we needed in Miami?" I wanted to be there, help Shelby in any way possible.

ASAC Leonard huffed. "That hasn't been discussed."

"Yes, it has," SAC Rogers said. "The Miami office had a huge wake-up call, and they want the agents who've worked the case there." His phone rang before he could continue. "Hold on. I need to take this call." He stepped from the room.

ASAC Leonard continued the conversation. "If the meeting between Stover, Liu, and Rudder takes place, the likelihood is Stover won't return to Miami. One more time, she'll be out of reach."

Where did that put Shelby? "Stover's calculating, and she hasn't invested in Shelby without a reason."

"McClure, use your head. She's setting Shelby up for a huge fall that's geared to get her killed. Shelby is an amateur, and Stover is holding the aces."

I despised the reality. "Wish you were wrong. But I'm doing all I can to stop this. A recent report speculates Rudder is selling some of his auto parts with fake packaging. But which orders from Liu contain heroin?"

"We need traceable evidence. Obtained by trained agents, not Shelby Pearce." Sarcasm crested Leonard's words. "How many years have you been on this case? What's the problem with you two that it remains an open case? Looks like fresh eyes are in order."

I made no attempt to hide my ire. "No one knows this case better than Mike and me."

SAC Rogers stepped back into the conference room. "I talked to one of the agents based at the safe house for Clay Pearce and Aria Stover. Aria has disappeared."

73

SHELBY

No matter how many times I rehearsed my reactions to Marissa's behavior, her announcement at lunch sent me scrambling. "Eli's picked up Aria."

"How did you find her?" I valued my ability to show a lack of emotion. Yet I panicked at the danger for my niece. What plans were in place for her?

"Dad's such a fool. He called me from a strange number begging me to turn myself in to the FBI. He believed they wanted to question me about something. I dragged out the conversation, making their location easy to find. I have a tech working for me who can perform a trap and trace."

"Why bring her to Miami? I thought you loathed the idea of motherhood."

"She's old enough to take care of herself." She sighed and tilted her head to the right, a common sign of her seizing control. "Aria is insurance, little sister. In my business, we need leverage. Lots of it."

"Insurance for what?" A burning in my stomach ruined any thought of lunch. "Are you leaving the country with Feng and taking her with you?"

"Good call if I were vested in her future. But there's more to the situation. I have duties for you to complete. Aria assures me those will be done according to my specifications."

"Really? Threatening your daughter's life to keep me in line?"

"Exactly. When it comes to the welfare of others, you're weak. I can handle eliminating whoever gets in my way. Goodness knows I've wanted to get rid of Aria since the day she was born. Now she'll repay me for my time and effort. For me to use you effectively in the business means I have to trust you implicitly."

I huffed. "You need me to kill someone?"

"Count on it. Leadership 101 requires courage in the face of opposition."

My niece deserved a chance to grow up normally. "All right. I'll do what you feel is necessary in exchange for Aria's life."

"The insurance policy has an indemnity clause. If she turns up missing, you're dead. If I learn you're double-crossing me, the same consequences."

"Fair enough. When will she be here?"

"Tomorrow."

I needed to talk to Denton. By now he was aware of Aria's disappearance. "Won't the authorities be looking for her?"

"She'll be staying right here, and no one will find her. Besides, I'm her mother. She belongs to me." Marissa paused. "Unless the whining starts. Then I'll have Eli get her out of my hair."

"How?"

"Let's just say you don't want to know."

"What are you going to do with a fifteen-year-old?"

"I can give her whatever she wants—material things, education, and a life beyond her teenage dreams. That is, if she's loyal and does exactly as she's told."

With Aria gone, Dad would be devastated. I hated the thought for him and her. The clothes and disguises in my closet . . . Did Aria face the same detestable future? What if she refused Marissa's new life? I inwardly shuddered.

"You're not eating." Marissa's cool tone showed no remorse.

I forked a piece of avocado. "Thinking about Aria."

"I'm sure you despise me." The smirk on my sister's face had become commonplace. "You'll discover I'm always right. And I always get what I want."

"No, Marissa, I care about you, and you are far more intelligent than I am."

"I'm sorry. I know you're loyal."

"Will you ever trust me?"

She brought the glass of sangria to her lips. I waited. She swirled the liquid in her mouth. I waited. She took another sip. I waited. "For as long as it takes. You have more tests to pass. When I observe enough loyalty to see you're ready for additional responsibility, I'll give you a heads-up. Your job is to keep Aria in line. I'm finished discussing the matter. We have an errand this afternoon. Wear the blonde wig, jeans, and sleeveless top. I will do the same."

"Is this a test or learning?"

She frowned. "Both."

My mind spun with all Marissa preferred not to say. I wanted to explore all the what-ifs and solutions, but the most critical of her corruption lay in Aria's future.

"In the morning, we're meeting Feng and John Rudder for brunch."

"Rudder must want your answer before the San Francisco meeting."

"He does. But we need specifics for the negotiations."

Alone in my room, I stepped into my walk-in closet and texted Denton with the two updates.

He responded. **I learned this morning Aria had been nabbed. How did M find her?**

Dad called her, and she traced it. Eli is transporting her to the penthouse. Dad must be out of his mind.

Sure of it. What does M want you to do?

No idea. If I fail, I'm dead. I won't let M hurt her.

I know. It's the price you're willing to pay that scares me.

What would you do?

The same.

I dressed to please Marissa, weary of the power game, and now Aria had been brought into this horrible evil. My niece's innocence, a necessity for positive emotional growth, must be protected no matter the cost. Marissa's testing plagued me. I'd set up Lance, unwillingly, but my role in his murder made me an accomplice. No more deaths. Not while I breathed . . . but how could I protect Aria? When had Marissa encountered such a callous approach to life? Even an animal fought for its young.

Lee and Jess drove us to our "errand," which I interpreted as business, and whatever that entailed. We stopped at a Miami-based dinner club known for its South American cuisine and parked in the back near the rear door marked *Deliveries*. According to the marquee, the restaurant opened in three hours. A Lexus pulled in on the right, and a man and woman exited. She looked to be in her late forties, the man much younger. A bodyguard?

"Lee, keep the car running," Marissa said. "Jess, you're with us. Be alert. Shelby, watch and listen."

The moment we stepped from the car, the woman unlocked the delivery door and gestured for us to enter. We followed her to a plush office furnished in rich mahogany and vibrant red and turquoise. Two leather chairs were positioned in front of a desk.

"Please, sit." The woman gestured, but she trembled. "Lynn, who is your guest?"

Marissa nodded for me to take the chair on her left, and we obliged. Jess and the other man took positions near their charges. The situation seemed surreal, as though I were a part of a movie cast.

"This is my associate, Ellie Whyte," Marissa said. "I'm training her to take over some of my accounts."

"Mine?" The woman tensed.

Marissa smiled. "Of course not. We've been friends for too long."

The woman relaxed. "You and I have made a good living."

"I look forward to the restaurant's expansion. I've studied the plans and financial picture." Marissa crossed her legs. "I approve the project going forward, with one stipulation." She paused like she'd done with me, intimidation tactics. "You're behind in payments, and the situation isn't improving."

The woman's jaw tightened. "After the economics of late, I needed to recoup my losses."

"We all did. But in order for me to benefit from the new construction, I'll be managing all finances until we are in the black."

"Why? I've always kept my word. This is a personal affront against our relationship and my integrity."

Marissa's placid features demonstrated her control. "This is business. I need three hundred and twenty-five thousand dollars up front to continue. Now."

"I don't have it."

Marissa reached into her purse and aimed a gun at the woman. "Which is it?"

Jess held a gun on the other man.

"Lynn, I can give you two hundred thousand cash now."

"Where's the rest?"

"My house."

"Open your safe and Ellie will see if you're bluffing."

The woman scooted back her chair and opened a cabinet door, pressed in numbers, and stepped back.

"Ellie, go ahead."

I found more cash inside the safe than I thought possible. I counted the wrapped bills, ranging from tens on up to hundreds. I repeated to confirm the amount and faced Marissa. "One hundred and ninety thousand dollars."

"Short and a lie." Marissa still held a firearm on the woman . . . I didn't even know her name.

"I can have the balance delivered to you."

"Unnecessary. We'll send our men and chat until they return."

The woman nodded at her bodyguard. "Get what's needed."

"And leave you alone?" he said.

Marissa waved the gun at him. "You have one hour. Any longer and I'll start eliminating fingers, beginning with the one hosting diamonds and sapphires." My sister glanced at a clock on the woman's desk. "Time starts now."

Sixty-seven minutes later, Jess and the woman's bodyguard returned. Marissa counted the money and stuffed it inside her bag.

"Thank you." She smiled at the woman. "I hope you understand doing business with me means keeping your end of the bargain. Deceit never works." Marissa stood and gave her attention to Jess. "Ellie and I will meet you at the car."

I trailed after her, only wanting to leave. Once outside, I heard a gun fire twice.

"He shot them?" I gasped. "You have your money."

"Get over it, little sister." She opened the passenger side of the car and slid in.

I stared at the delivery door. Those shot needed help. If they weren't dead.

"What are you expecting to see? She understood the stakes when she asked for a financial partner. In the car, or you'll regret it." She pulled her gun. Like an old Western, the weapon did her talking.

I took slow, unsteady steps to the opposite side of the car. *God, when will this be over?*

I watched the delivery door. Jess emerged, carrying a blood-soaked tissue. My head pounded. Prison life showed more sympathetic women than my sister. He opened Marissa's door and displayed the woman's severed finger, bright-red polish, the diamond-and-sapphire ring, and blood. "Situation handled."

"Jess, I wanted the ring, not the finger. Did you have to cut it off?"

He grinned. "I carry a sharp knife for a reason."

"Gross. Give that thing to Shelby for her to clean up."

I opened my door and vomited.

74

I'd seen violence in prison, plenty of it. Travis's blood-coated body at the hand of my sister had affected me physically, and I vomited then too. Years ago, Marissa used paper towels to clean me up. This time she tossed me two tissues.

"Get yourself together."

I wiped my mouth and closed the door seconds before Lee sped from the scene. Plenty of accusations longed to surface, but if I slipped, she'd maim or kill me. Who'd be left to help Aria? Swallowing my revulsion for my sister, I picked up the finger and ring wrapped in bloody tissues on the leather seat beside me.

"About time you showed a little guts," Marissa fumed. "When we get back to the penthouse, go directly to your room. I'll have Eli bring you a jar of jewelry cleaner. Once you're finished, bring the ring to me. By then, I'll be on the balcony with Aria."

Eli met us at the door when we arrived. Aria was nowhere in sight, and neither did I hear her. For the past several days, I'd done exactly as Marissa instructed. Not sure how I could continue.

Be strong. This isn't about you.

In the confines of my bedroom, I released my grip from the blood-soaked tissues holding the dead woman's finger and ring and laid the wadded mess on the bathroom marble countertop. I fought the urge to sob and throw up again. No doubt cameras and recording devices would send a feed to Marissa. How would I ever be a part of her inner circle when witnessing her business practices made me physically ill? Nothing in the scenario from yesterday, today, or tomorrow looked good. I had to trust God. The adage sounded easier than practicing it. In prison, I expected nefarious behavior, but not from Marissa. Witnessing her methods shook me, and yet I must gain control.

A tap at the door told me Eli had arrived with the cleaning solution. I took the jar, paper towels, and small brush without addressing him. He chuckled.

A woman and a man lay dead because of an unpaid debt.

◉ ◉ ◉

Through the glass doors onto the balcony, I saw Aria in tears seated at the table across from Marissa. I wrestled with how to handle the situation—play into Marissa's hand or show how much I cared for Aria's plight? My niece had intelligence going for her, and I had to believe she'd see through my callous response to her . . . and see God's sovereignty.

"What's the hesitation?" Eli said.

"Aria's upset and she may need more time with Marissa."

"Doubt it. Marissa would rather have the ring. The kid gets on her nerves."

I stepped out onto the balcony and captured Aria's gaze. She hurried to me and fell into my embrace. Her lip bled, and a bruise rose on her right cheekbone. My fury rose for what Marissa or Eli had done to her.

The necklace we'd made together dangled from her neck.

"Trust me. We'll get through this," I whispered and pushed her away. "Really, Aria? Time to grow up."

She lifted her chin. "I don't want to be here."

"You want to be with your granddad baking donuts?"

"Yes!"

"Take my advice and listen to your mom. She just might have your best interests in mind." I brushed past her and handed Marissa the ring. "Sorry about my reaction earlier."

"I make allowances for your learning curve." Marissa slipped the ring onto a right finger and admired it. "A little big, but that's an easy fix." She nodded at Aria. "Sit down so the three of us can talk."

Aria sat across from her mother. "All right, I'll listen. Mom, I thought you were in Phoenix."

"I changed my mind. The truth is, I'm in a position to provide anything you might want. But in order for you to benefit from my generosity, I require your respect and obedience."

Aria took a deep breath. "I'm listening."

Good girl, play the part.

"I've found a boarding school in London. Exclusive. You'll have the finest education. Clothes. Jewelry. Vacations."

"Why didn't you ever tell me you had money?"

"My secret."

Aria bit her lip. "I have so many questions, Mom."

"First of all, call me by my first name. From this moment on, no one is to find out I have a daughter. The paperwork is completed for a last name change to Pearce."

"What's your job?" Aria said. "Your clothes and makeup aren't from Walmart."

"I own my own business, a lucrative one."

Aria leaned forward. "Which is?"

"Again, my secret."

"So it's illegal?"

Marissa raised an eyebrow. "Does it matter?"

"What if I refuse and want to live with Granddad?"

"Shelby has witnessed what happens when I'm displeased. Anger me, and you'll regret it for the rest of your life."

"Why am I here?"

Marissa uttered an expletive. "Last question. You're with me as a guarantee Shelby follows my orders."

"Mom—"

Marissa slapped her hard across the bruised cheek and lower eye. "You broke rule number one. My guess is boarding school is starting to look good."

Aria touched her cheek. "Yes, ma'am."

"Shelby will escort you to the spare bedroom. Shower and throw away everything you're wearing. I've done a little shopping. New clothes, makeup, and two wigs are on the bed. I'll have dinner and lemonade brought to you. Meals will be in your room unless otherwise instructed. One of my bodyguards is always here for our protection. We're finished."

"Thank you."

"The tap of generosity flows as long as you behave."

75

DENTON

While the rest of world slept and neglected to anticipate a new day, I drove to Clay's safe house. The idea of seeing him made more sense than a phone call. He'd experienced the loss of his wife, the reality of Marissa's deviance, threats against Shelby, and Aria's kidnapping. Not likely he'd hide his anguish in a face-to-face. Maybe he knew more than he'd shared.

I took a gulp of hot coffee, burned my tongue, and uttered a curse word, a habit I needed to break. The highway stretched out before me with an occasional vehicle in my sights. Lots of think time, as if I hadn't fired all my brain cells on this case. Questions formed, and my speed matched my insistence to get answers.

My arrival found Clay and the two agents finishing up breakfast. I leaned against the kitchen counter with my crutches and noted the lines in Clay's face had deepened since our last meeting. His plate of eggs hadn't been touched.

"Did those making threats against Shelby kidnap Aria?" Clay's features tightened. "Did they see my granddaughter in Valleysburg?"

"What I know is Eli Chandler kidnapped Aria per Marissa's orders and is transporting your granddaughter to Miami, not Phoenix. Mike and I go wheels up in the morning."

Clay shoved back his breakfast. "I'm confused about all of this. I don't understand why Marissa wants her daughter now when she had no problem leaving her in the past."

"I wish I had solid intel for you, but we're working on it." I addressed the two agents. "Do you mind if Clay and I talk privately?"

The two grabbed their coffee and walked outside. Clay watched them leave. "What's the bad news?"

"Nothing to report along those lines. You're worried, and I am too. Here's what I can tell you, some of which you already are aware. Shelby volunteered to find evidence that would hold up in court and prove Marissa is part of a money-laundering organization. Meantime, indications of other illegal activities leading to Marissa have come to our attention."

His eyes reddened. "My wife told me before she died about Shelby taking the blame for Travis's murder. I assumed the pain medications were talking, and I refused to listen. Then Aria claimed horrible things about Marissa, inconceivable things. I've thought of little else since. Memories repeat of my daughters as girls and of Marissa during the time Shelby spent in prison. But is it true? Did Shelby take the blame to protect her sister?"

"Yes."

He clenched his fist. "Is Marissa behind the threats on Shelby's life?"

"We believe so."

"I want the chance to love on Shelby like she deserves and get Aria back. I love Marissa, but how could she do these horrible things?"

Clay needed to hear what he was up against. "Marissa has legal rights to Aria. Instructing Chandler to pick her up and transport her to Florida isn't against the law."

"Unless he hurt her. Aria's disappearance is my fault. One of the agents left his phone on the table. I used it to call Marissa, to find out the truth behind her abandoning Aria."

"She had it traced. What do you remember about the conversation?"

"I didn't accuse her of anything, but I begged her to reconsider what she was doing to her daughter. She cried, her typical response. Claimed she missed Aria but believed her daughter was better off with me. Shelby had threatened her until she had to run, and some guy offered to help her get settled in Phoenix. No admittance of wrongdoing." Clay shook his head. "Now I learn she's in Miami. Why there when she insisted a need for a dry climate?"

"Her medical records are clean. She has no known health issues."

He gasped. "But she has rheumatoid arthritis."

"No, Clay. It's a fabrication."

He swallowed hard. "Before the FBI picked us up, I searched every inch of Marissa's room and the bakery for information about her RA. Nothing. I've been a fool. Tell me how to make this right. I'll do anything."

"Shelby is risking her life to usher in truth, and she'll protect Aria. The—"

"They'll both be killed! I have to do something. You can't expect me to sit here while my daughters wage war against each other. I've been blinded by lies. When and how did Marissa become the epitome of evil?" He rubbed his hand over his face. "You should be asking me that."

Motive came in different layers, and the origin of Marissa's ambition mixed a deadly brew of when and why. "I drove here for another reason—to talk through what led up to Travis's shooting. Think back to when your daughters were small. How was their relationship?" I eased onto a chair and stretched out my injured leg.

"The wife and I thought we'd never have another child after Marissa, but five years later, Shelby arrived. We were happy with another little girl, healthy and so good."

"And Marissa?"

"She seemed excited until she realized Mom and Dad's attention were on two girls instead of one, and she was miserable. She stopped eating and acted out. The typical jealousy of an only child when another child enters the home. It got so bad, we took her to the doctor. Although we divided our time and included Marissa in Shelby's care and added dance lessons to her schedule, it took a long time for her to adjust. We had to keep an eye on our girls because Marissa's jealousy had a violent streak."

"How?"

He sighed. "She lifted Shelby from the crib and attempted to toss her across the room. My wife discovered it before it was too late. Another time, when Shelby was crying, Marissa placed a pillow on Shelby's face."

"Marissa grew out of the jealousy?"

"We thought so. She changed almost overnight. One morning when Marissa was eight, she apologized for not believing we loved her as much as Shelby. My wife claimed God had answered our prayers. Marissa showed interest in her little sister and wanted Shelby to be a part of her life."

"The new relationship must have been a huge relief."

"For sure. Marissa showed patience and played with her little sister. As they grew older, they became very close."

"In what way?"

"In the beginning, Marissa played teacher and showed Shelby how to dress herself, brush her teeth, comb her hair, and tie her shoes. As they grew older, Marissa taught Shelby how to dance and bought her gifts for no special reason. We were very pleased. Later on when Shelby went through her acting-out stage, Marissa took up for her. Made excuses and begged us not to be too hard on her."

"Were you aware Marissa made up mysteries and challenged Shelby to think like a criminal to outsmart the law?"

Clay startled. "What? I never heard a word of it."

"Marissa asked Shelby to keep their games secret."

Clay stared out the window, as though his thoughts were far-reaching. I let him process. The truth hurt . . . I knew firsthand with my brother's betrayal.

"Shelby idolized her sister," he finally said. "She'd never betray their relationship. That's got to be why Shelby took the blame for Travis's death."

"Marissa asked for her help, and she agreed. I'm questioning if the problems in Shelby's teen years correspond to Marissa's prompting."

"I'm afraid it makes sense. If I'm putting this all together right, Marissa never got past her jealousy. Instead she chose other ways to make herself look good and show Shelby as rebellious."

"I'm not a psychologist, Clay, but my thoughts are the same as yours. If we are to end Marissa's crime spree, then we must consider the worst-case scenario. She and Eli Chandler have been together for years."

"Are you saying all the time she and Travis were married?" he whispered, the torment evident in his tone and on his face.

"Yes, according to what she told Shelby."

"Aria could belong to Chandler."

"Clay, leave it alone. You're beating yourself up for something out of your control. If Chandler is Aria's father, it doesn't make her any less your granddaughter. What's important is getting her and Shelby out of this mess safely."

"You're going to a lot of trouble to help Shelby and this family."

"Sir, I'm in love with her."

He peered at me. "I'm glad she has you on her side. But I'm still head of this family, and I'm not spending another hour here."

76

SHELBY

Aria's first day at the penthouse showed me a teen who had no illusions about her mother's evil nature. The girl didn't visibly shed tears, but her eyes were red. Most of the time she stayed in her room. There I heard the sobs.

Marissa told me to ready myself for brunch, not a surprise since I'd already met Feng Liu. I chose a black sleeveless dress, and Marissa wore bloodred. Lee drove us to Stage 7 restaurant. I found the meeting place risky. With all the happenings, why would my sister risk both of us being seen in a public setting known for catering to criminals?

"We leave our phones in the car," she said. "The men have theirs."

"Why when you know them?"

"You'll find out. Do you drink?"

"Not anymore."

"Good."

Paranoia took hold, and I tamped it into place.

My sister never approved of spontaneity, and this morning had a purpose beyond meeting with the two men. If only I had the mental capacity to figure it out instead of faking confidence. One thing for sure, her reasons would benefit only her.

"Listen and learn." Marissa tapped my arm. "Rudder will come on to you, and I need you to play along."

At the restaurant, Lee stayed with the car, and we were ushered to the rear of the dining area. Heads again turned when Marissa walked past. My sister held a striking pose with her white-blonde hair and curve-hugging dress. She thrived on attention. Always had.

In a private room, Feng and another man drank amber-colored whiskey at ten thirty in the morning. Both stood and Feng introduced John Rudder to me, a sandy-haired man with boyish features and startling blue eyes.

"You weren't kidding," Rudder said. "Shelby's gorgeous."

I thanked him with my best "I'm impressed" smile. We were seated, and the games began.

Casual conversation dominated behind closed doors. A server delivered wine for all of us and took our food orders.

The talk continued during brunch until Marissa placed her utensils crosswise on her plate. "Ready for business?"

"You're such a coldhearted woman." Feng gave her a dimpled grin.

"But I have an affair with money."

"And me?"

She patted his hand. "You are my priority. Oh, I'd like a word in private before we discussed John's offer."

"Take all the time you need." Rudder waved them away. "Gives me a few extra moments to get acquainted with Shelby." He opened the door to their small room and requested their server. She stepped inside. "I'd like more wine. My—"

"You've had enough," Feng said. "We have business to discuss."

"You're telling me how much to drink?"

"John—" Marissa pointed to me—"take Shelby's wine. She doesn't want it, right?" She smiled at Feng. "Is that okay?"

"Yes, but not more."

I set the glass in front of John. His glassy eyes indicated his advanced alcohol level.

The server disappeared with Marissa and Feng. Rudder moved his chair closer to me. "For an ex-con, you steal the show."

I feigned a smile. "I assume that's a compliment."

"Always. I've been with the best. Makes me wonder what it would have been like to share a cell bunk."

"I'm sure we'd have kept the guards occupied." I paused. "Who told you about prison?"

"Feng. You pulled the trigger on Marissa's husband, but she didn't mind."

I tilted my head. "True."

"Dangerous women intrigue me."

I propped my chin in my hand. "Are you a dangerous man?"

"Some think so." He leaned over and brushed a kiss across my lips.

I despised what I was doing. But I'd made a vow and I'd play the part.

"Do you really never drink?"

"Learned the hard way when I was younger. I want to be aware of what's happening at all times."

"Your preference could be a plus." He pointed to my wine. "You really don't want this?" He slurred his words. "I hate to see it go to waste."

"It's all yours."

He took a sip. "What are you doing later?"

"John, I'm picky. Very picky."

"What's not to like about me?"

"I'm worth more than another name on a long list."

He smirked. "We'll see. Marissa trusts you. She never brings anyone to a business meeting."

"She has good reasons. I saved her rear."

"She owes you?"

"She's my sister. Nothing's owed." I assumed a bug recorded our conversation, another one of Marissa's tests.

"Are you in favor of the business expansion?"

"Depends on what's in it for me."

"Heroin sales are up, and I'm Liu's biggest client." He downed the wine. "Love what's inside those boxes of spark plugs and washer blades. What's more important than money?"

"Who's managing it and where it's invested."

The door opened, and Marissa and Feng returned. Maybe now I'd learn what they planned together. Feng closed the door, and the two joined us at the table.

"John, we've come to an agreement," Marissa said. "Are you ready to address the details?"

"Let's order another bottle of wine and make a toast first."

Marissa slid into her chair. "We'll toast when there's reason to celebrate."

"What are the stipulations?" John massaged his temples. "I have a horrible headache. Feel sick." His body twitched and convulsed.

I scooted back my chair and attempted to stand, but Marissa grabbed my arm. "Where are you going?"

"He needs help." The words left my mouth the instant *murder* bannered across my mind.

John's face fell onto the table, his mouth agape with white foam oozing out.

"Feng, would you contact the manager." Marissa showed no more emotion than what I'd seen when she killed the agent. "I think John's proposal just expired."

77

DENTON

I couldn't get to Miami's FBI office fast enough. Mike and I grabbed our tagged bags before leaving the airport in Miami and hailed a taxi.

Our phones fired a notification at the same time. Never a good sign or I'd allowed my poor attitude to call the shots.

I read the info from FBI Houston's office.

FBI arrests Shelby Pearce for the murder of John Rudder. Evidence linked to cyanide poisoning.

Mike cursed. "You've got to be kidding."

I stopped along the hallway leading to the car rental exit and pressed in ASAC Leonard's number. The guy annoyed me, but he had answers. "What's the deal with Shelby?"

"I'll send you and Mike what we have. Your Ms. Innocent was the last person with Rudder. A server says she gave him her glass of wine, which we've learned had been laced with cyanide."

"Where did this happen?"

"Stage 7 in Miami. Marissa Stover and Feng Liu were with them. According to Stover and Feng, they excused themselves from a private dining area to chat, leaving Shelby alone with the victim. When the two returned, Rudder showed immediate signs of poisoning."

"Two suspected kingpins in money laundering and drugs are valid witnesses?"

"They are when evidence points to an ex-con committing another murder. As far as I'm concerned, all three are guilty, but your girl has the least going for her."

"This has setup smeared across it. We're on our way to the Miami office." I slid my phone into my pant pocket while informing Mike of the conversation.

Miami's FBI proved more cooperative. Agent Kyle Van Dyke, Lance Mason's partner, met with Mike and me. Van Dyke, barely out of his twenties, reminded me of myself years back.

"Ms. Pearce has been cooperative. She gave us a clear picture of what might have happened. What are the chances her sister learned she's an informant?"

"High. Shelby's not trained and believes her room's bugged. Marissa claimed Aria was picked up to keep Shelby in line." I fought the tension in my neck and shoulders. "We have no evidence other than Shelby witnessed Agent Mason's murder."

"When I interviewed her, she requested a polygraph." Van Dyke pointed to a file in front of him. "We conducted the test, and no indications of deceit were present."

Mike cleared his throat. "I assume you're letting her go, but what's the point of sending her back to her sister? So far she hasn't been able to access any evidence that leads to Marissa's criminal activities."

"She's asked for more time." Agent Van Dyke observed me as though he knew of my feelings for her.

"I'm not surprised," I said. "She has stubborn tenacity, and now her niece has been thrown into the fire."

"Before we bring her back into the interview and discuss how to proceed, we've uncovered more information on Rudder. Some of the generic auto parts he purchases from Liu have made him a little cash. He slaps big-name packaging labels on the auto parts and sells them to make him a hefty profit. That conviction would have cost him, but we've been holding out for the big payoff."

"I assume Liu didn't care. Not worth killing a man when he's making millions from him. Rudder's paid a hefty price for auto parts."

Mike spoke into the conversation. "But Rudder might not have been careful in other areas, and some of his practices could have made him a liability, especially in dealing with heroin." He nodded at me to continue.

"Mike and I have a theory about the heroin. Liu is known for making his millions with it, and we're sure he'd been supplying Rudder. Problem is, without proof of him shipping the drug with the auto parts, we didn't have a case. Neither do we know if the heroin was packed in specific boxes of auto parts or a mix."

"We need to find out who's in control of Rudder's business now that he's dead. I'll keep you two updated," Van Dyke said.

An agent escorted Shelby into the interview room. Her pale face alarmed me. I didn't understand God allowing this. I wanted to hold her . . . want and necessity were at opposite ends of the pole. I heard her wheezing. "You don't have your inhaler?"

"No." She eased onto a chair and greeted Mike and me. "Glad you're here. The situation has escalated, and I know you two have reservations about my part, but I can't give up with Aria involved. I have an idea."

"Let's hear it."

She smiled at me. "Agent Van Dyke says the FBI will release me, but I want to remain in custody until tomorrow. My person-of-interest status keeps Marissa satisfied. She won't leave the country until she knows my fate. Besides, a sudden disappearance stacks the guilt against them after Rudder's death. I assume she has a passport for Aria, so time is critical."

"Your plan?" I said.

"I'll lift my sister's purse while she's sleeping, take her phone, which has all her dealings and contacts, and get Aria out of there."

My blood pressure rose. "How do you plan to walk past Marissa and the bodyguards?"

"I'm not finished." She punched each word. "Every night, Marissa, Eli, and the two bodyguards have a drink before she goes to bed. If I have a few strong sleeping pills, I can make sure they're drugged."

"That's crazy. You'll never get away with it."

She stared at me, those blue-gray eyes resembling thunderclouds. "Do you have a better idea? Marissa and Liu set me up to take the fall for Rudder. Why else use cyanide when it's easily detected? In the car, she told me not to drink at the restaurant. There Rudder was already drunk. He wanted more wine, and Liu told him he'd had enough, and Marissa offers my full glass."

I ground my teeth. Shelby couldn't go back there. "What are the chances the FBI will hand you a controlled substance?"

"None. But they know the people on the street who could get them for me."

"I have a prescription," Mike said.

I shot Mike a glare. "What? Aren't you the agent who follows protocol like an addict chases heroin? You can't give Shelby sleeping pills."

"I have a prescription. But I didn't say what kind. Neither did I say I'd give her anything."

Van Dyke ran interference. "Agents. Back to business. We haven't been successful in hacking into Stover's or Liu's devices. Rudder's missing phone must contain incriminating evidence."

"When I went for help at the restaurant, Marissa and Feng stayed behind. If my sister has the phone, I'll find it." She leaned into the table. "You need evidence to make arrests. I want the murders solved, and my niece free to live without fear."

"Shelby, this is—"

"And I never requested your help. One more bit of information. Rudder liked to talk about himself. He claimed to be Liu's largest heroin buyer. He mentioned loving what was inside those boxes of spark plugs and washer blades. Or he could have been speaking figuratively."

"Rudder must have gotten greedy and demanded more money," I said. "Look, we have enough with his murder to request a search warrant into his business. No reason for you to go back."

She shook her head. "No point arguing with me. My mind is made up."

78

SHELBY

The look on Marissa's face when I entered the condo the following morning hit the top of the startled list. Priceless, but I kept the smug satisfaction to myself. For certain I looked a mess after spending a night in jail.

I was thankful Denton arranged for me to receive an inhaler. He always seemed to have my best interests at heart, even if he did border on overprotective.

"Shelby, you're a wreck."

"I spent a night behind bars."

"Was it déjà vu?"

Fury raged through me, and the impulsiveness I'd given to God vanished. Ten feet between us slipped to one. I jabbed my finger into her chest. "You've messed me over for the last time."

She grabbed my finger. "Sis, I called my attorney the moment the police arrested you."

"When would your attorney take action? In fifteen years?"

"I might have had that coming."

I stepped back out of her reach. "I have questions."

"I'm sure you do." Marissa asked Eli and the two bodyguards to step inside while we talked on the balcony.

The glass door closed, and still I couldn't control the anger spiraling through me. "You poisoned my wine, offered it to Rudder, then made sure the police knew I'd given him my glass."

"I could have you killed."

"But you won't because it drags your name through the mud, and you won't risk an investigation until you're ready to disappear. Aria would turn on you, tell the wrong people about her mother. That means eliminating your own daughter or convincing her a new identity overseas is best."

Marissa laughed. "You think you've figured me out?"

"No, just making sensible observations. Why poison Rudder?"

"He knew too much. My business thrives on me being smarter than those around me."

"Feng?"

"He's different. A genius. We're a good match."

"And how will you recoup your cut of the revenue?"

"The car parts business now belongs to me."

I assumed she'd formed a shell company to handle ownership. "Marissa, you have no need for me. So why am I here? You and Liu have a good thing going on."

"I've told you all along I need someone to help me oversee business, and I'm constantly expanding."

"Here in Miami?"

She shook her head. "I have a flat for you in London where you can keep an eye on Aria. You two behave, and you both live."

"I see. And where will you be?"

"Anywhere I choose." She reached into her shoulder bag. "Here's your purse back. Congratulations, you've passed all my tests. Glad to see you finally have the guts to call me out."

"What's my cut?"

"To be determined." She touched my cheek. "You've seen what happens to those who displease me. I used to think your aversion to weapons would be a detriment. But no more. Who expects a woman of organized crime who won't touch a gun? I've found a couple of bodyguards who'll ensure your orders are followed."

"Your orders or mine?"

"As you've observed, I have my tentacles in everything."

Did Marissa think she had me fooled into believing Aria and I were safe?

79

My original burner phone from Sheriff Wendall remained turned off and concealed inside the wig I'd originally worn to Miami and left on my closet shelf. I checked to see if someone had discovered it while I'd been a guest of Miami PD and the FBI. Nothing appeared out of place, and I'd memorized every item's location in the drawers and the closet. I'd see Denton around one in the morning, and I wouldn't sabotage my plan by contacting him. I'd taken enough risks and put friends and family in danger.

Aria lived behind her bedroom's locked door. Not sure how the poor girl survived, but the distant sobbing tore at my heart. At least I could talk to her from the hallway, although anyone could hear our conversation. Marissa allowed her out for some meals, and she'd taken her shopping with Lee and Jess. Entertainment consisted of downloaded music and movies on an iPad—minus Internet connectivity.

I'd seen my sister slide the key to Aria's room into a zippered compartment of her purse. Hopefully she hadn't moved it. If not, I'd use a paper clip. Denton had given me a handful this morning. Years had passed since I'd picked a lock, but I'm sure it was like riding a bike.

I had spent the evening on the balcony chatting with Marissa, Eli, and the guards. I made fun of the FBI agents who'd interviewed me, even Denton and Mike. At ten thirty Marissa asked Eli to bring their drinks from inside the condo.

"I'll go with you," I said. "A Diet Coke sounds good." In the hollow heel of my sandal, I'd hidden sleeping pills that Mike had given me. Denton hadn't been pleased. Now to distract Eli for a few seconds.

In the kitchen, Eli grabbed the liquor from the counter, and I pulled glasses from the cabinet. I'd examined various places where Marissa could have installed a camera, and I stood with my back against the one I'd noted. While Eli poured shots of liquor, I pressed the ice dispenser button, allowing several cubes to drop to the floor. "Rats. Would you help me?"

"I've got them." Eli bent to pick up the ice, allowing me enough time to retrieve and drop the pills into the liquor glasses.

We carried the drinks to the balcony. Marissa stood and took hers. "I'm going to bed."

"Me too," I said. "Tonight's sleep has to be better than last night's."

"We have plans for tomorrow." Marissa stifled a yawn. "Many details to work out."

"Looking forward to it." I toasted my Diet Coke to the men before I headed inside the condo.

At twelve thirty I crept from my room. Lee and Jess had disappeared, and Eli must have gone to his own condo. A mix of adrenaline and downright fear kept me on alert. In the shadows, I moved to the far side of the penthouse to Marissa's suite. She took her privacy seriously, and I'd not been inside her bedroom.

I needed clarity to find her purse and get Aria and me out of the penthouse undetected.

I slowly turned the knob on Marissa's bedroom door. Locked. I pulled a paper clip from my jean pocket and bent it, allowing me to insert into the keyhole. My stomach churned as I probed and twisted. A faint click released the lock. Holding my breath, I grasped the knob, and the door opened to a shadowed room. From what I could tell through shadowed lights from the street below, Marissa's suite looked out onto a private balcony area. I searched for her purse.

Moving about chanced knocking something over and startling my drugged sister. But I had no choice. Time ticked away.

Inside the bathroom, her purse sat on the marble countertop. I stared into the mirror—my profile frightened me. I felt inside her shoulder bag and wrapped my fingers around two phones and the key to Aria's room. One had to belong to John Rudder. Gripping the handles like a lifeline, I crept from the room.

Emotional paralysis took control. Had tonight been too easy? I shoved the nagging thought aside.

I made my way to Aria's room. This time I had a key. Silence ruled the moment, for I didn't need my niece to scream. Once in her room, I closed the door and tiptoed to Aria's bedside. I covered her mouth, instantly wakening her.

"This is Shelby," I whispered. "We're getting out of here."

She nodded and relaxed.

"Dress quickly. Don't make a sound."

While she slipped into clothes, I checked both phones in Marissa's bag. Thank goodness, I had hers and Rudder's. I handed Aria the bag. "Take this in case anything happens. Evidence is inside the phones to end these crimes." I checked the time. "Denton and his partner are waiting on the first-floor entrance. Other FBI agents and police officers have the building surrounded."

Aria blinked. "Mom or one of those guys will kill us."

I shook my head. "I slipped sleeping pills into their drinks. The problem is I don't have the password for the alarm system. At best guess, we have thirty to forty seconds before it jars them awake. We'll take the stairs on the left side of the hallway. You go first, and don't look back. Just keep running until Denton has you safe."

"Okay," she whispered.

I slipped Marissa's purse over Aria's shoulder, and I grabbed mine. "I love you. Keep praying."

In the foyer, I opened the door to freedom and pushed Aria into the hallway. I raced behind her toward the steps.

"Aria, stop or I'm pulling the trigger on Shelby."

Marissa's voice slowed my niece. "Keep running," I said.

Aria didn't take another step. She faced me. "I won't let Mom . . . Marissa hurt you."

"That's my girl." Marissa rushed toward us with her gun aimed, yanked her purse from Aria's shoulder, and grabbed mine.

"This is over." I stepped in front of Marissa's face. "Feds have the building surrounded. You have nowhere to run."

"That's what you think. Lee already told me. Head up the steps to the roof."

"Please, let Aria—"

"Now!"

I climbed the steps behind Aria and recognized the whir of helicopter blades. The advantage of a top-floor penthouse and a landing pad made a getaway easier. How had this happened when I'd drugged them?

Where were we going? Why not kill me, then make her escape? Aria deserved much more from life than the hand dealt to her.

My mind twisted with my failure. Had I heard wrong? I'd believed God stood with me in finding the evidence to arrest my sister.

Aria opened the door to the rooftop, and a chopper sat on the helipad ready for departure. I expected the noise to be deafening, yet I still heard Marissa order us inside. Why hadn't I planned for Marissa having a helicopter at the ready?

Aria and I slid into the rear passenger seats, and my sister took the left side beside the pilot and put on a headset. I hadn't seen the pilot before now, a stranger. In seconds, we lifted into the air and headed northwest. Marissa waved a gun in front of my face and ordered both Aria and me to put on our headsets. We complied.

"Don't even think about trying anything stupid. I have always been ahead of you." She laughed. "Do you like my pilot? He's on duty 24-7, ready to take me wherever I want to go in ninety seconds."

"Marissa." Aria sounded so frightened. "We won't tell anyone about what you're doing."

She sneered. "Little girl, you have no idea what all I've done. Take a look below us. The area is swarming with cops and Feds."

"You can't go on like this," I said. "Turn yourself in."

"You must think I'm stupid. No one knows the real me. Oh, some think they do. And you're aware of far too much."

"Actually, you're brilliant. A good lawyer would go to bat for you."

"No thanks."

"Where are we going?" I fought my fury to think.

"You'll find out soon enough."

80

DENTON

Miami FBI agents had placed the penthouse building under surveillance since 7 p.m., and the police department monitored all floor exits from the building. Quiet permeated the watch, as though the calm before the storm. The time neared 1 a.m., when Shelby had timed to make her escape with Aria.

A voice in my earpiece reported hearing the start-up of a helicopter's turbine engine from the building's roof. From the pinched look on Mike's face, he'd been told the same. I raced up the stairs toward the top floor with my firearm in hand. Mike stayed on my heels as he called for backup.

I needed to run into Shelby and Aria on their way down as scheduled. But the possibility of finding them in a pool of blood hadn't escaped me. I rounded one set of stairs to another until I reached the eleventh floor. Out of breath but undeterred.

Down the hall, the main entrance to Marissa's penthouse was

closed. Mike and I took a position on each side of the door. Mike took aim, and I pounded our arrival. "Open up. FBI!"

I twisted the knob. Locked.

Mike and I kicked in the door, much like some of our antics when we were younger.

A quick sweep showed an empty penthouse. Why hadn't I followed my gut and stopped Shelby from playing a hero? Where were they?

81

SHELBY

Within ten minutes, the helicopter landed atop a parking garage. Two vehicles sped to the chopper's side. A black SUV and a cream-colored Lexus. Both had dark-tinted windows.

Marissa lifted her purse onto her shoulder. "Shelby, you and Aria get into the back seat of the SUV. Eli's driving."

No point in arguing. I nodded at Aria, and we climbed out of the chopper and into the vehicle. Marissa slid into the front passenger side. Her door closed and both vehicles bolted toward the garage's exit ramp. The chopper rose to the sky and navigated northwest.

How would anyone find us?

"Where to now?" I said.

"None of your business. I'm putting my gun here beside me. I won't hesitate to use it. Understand?" When we nodded, she laid the firearm within her reach. "Want to know how I found out you'd drugged our drinks?"

"I assume a camera in an area I missed."

She smiled. "Right above the refrigerator. I have them everywhere. Even in the bathrooms and closets."

"Everything's been a game?"

"Precisely. You were a worthy opponent until you came to Miami. I tried the suicide route, but you outmaneuvered me. I thought I could mold you into a solid partner. Looked like you'd gotten smarter in prison, but I couldn't be sure. Once you were here, I had my eyes everywhere." She cursed. "You sold me out. The clincher was the FBI's release when I set you up to take the fall for Rudder. Your rear should still be in jail, which proves your agent boyfriend thinks more of you than his job. Doesn't matter. Having you and Aria as hostages keeps my plan in motion."

I'd viewed my sister in various moods, and I hadn't discerned which one was the deadliest. What simmered below the surface kept her in a leadership position to bring in more money and eliminate opposition. Had she calculated every step since before Travis's murder, possibly with Eli's help? Poor Aria. If she survived this, her emotional and mental health might take a lifetime to restore.

My breathing came in short gasps, and my chest ached. Marissa pulled my inhaler from her purse. "Use it but give it back to me. In case you have any thoughts about trying something stupid."

I took two puffs and returned it. What else was in her arsenal? "Really, Marissa? Am I to take the blame for another crime? Do you plan to put me and Aria in the middle of a firefight?"

"I've worked hard to build my operation, and no one will take it from me."

I listened, reaching deep for restraint. "What's your strategy?"

"Considering tomorrow is Aria's birthday, I thought we'd enjoy some girl time before I leave the country."

Eli whirled to Marissa. "Tomorrow is Aria's birthday?"

"Are you stupid? Didn't you hear me?"

He pulled onto the expressway and drove northwest. "Don't

call me stupid when I'm the one who taught you the business. I've protected you for a lot of years, and most of the time you've treated me like dirt." He banged the steering wheel with his palm. "Just did the math, and Aria's mine, not your dead husband's."

I reached across the seat and took Aria's hand. What I suspected held credibility.

"You're a fool, Eli." Marissa spat the words. "This is not the time to discuss Aria's paternity."

"Explain how we were together for the weekend, and you have a kid nine months later."

"Took you a lot of years to figure it out."

"Please!" Aria shrieked. "Is Eli my dad?"

Marissa twisted her body and slapped Aria's cheek. "Not one more word. In fact, all of you keep your mouths shut."

"Don't you ever lay a hand on her again." Eli's words seemed to blow the roof off the car.

"Since when did you start caring about one of your kids?"

"For the record, you promised me a whole lot if I gave up my other three."

"Worked, didn't it?" She aimed her firearm at him. "Drive. I have someplace to be."

We stopped at a gas station with an accompanying McDonald's long enough to switch the SUV for a Toyota and fill it up with gas. I begged for a bathroom break, and Marissa insisted Aria go with us. Made me wonder if Eli might set her free. Inside, I looked for anything to write on or with, a way to let Denton know our location. Verbally alerting anyone invited Marissa to open fire.

Nothing.

In the restroom, Marissa watched Aria wash her hands. "Hurry up."

Aria stuck her hands under the air dryer. My sister kept her hand positioned inside her shoulder bag. No doubt her forefinger rested on the trigger.

An employee entered the restroom, and Marissa kept her focus on Aria. I caught the young woman's attention and mouthed *help*. The girl rolled her eyes and entered a stall. Hope shattered. How would Denton and Mike find us?

If at all.

Or alive.

Marissa ordered us back to the car. Except Eli was nowhere in sight. She visually swept the area and cursed. "Coward. He always runs when he's mad. But I'm not in the mood for his games." She slid into the driver's seat of the Toyota and pressed the engine to life.

Eli had abandoned us with the keys in the ignition.

82

DENTON

Radar surveillance and security cameras confirmed the helicopter
had landed on the roof of a northwest Miami parking garage,
obscuring the view of two fleeing cars: an SUV and a Lexus sedan.
The camera footage showed Melissa, Shelby, and Aria had been
on board the chopper, but we didn't know which car or cars they'd
entered before escaping the scene. The two bodyguards had disappeared . . . finding them could provide the info we needed.

Hours later, roadblocks were in place, but both vehicles had
been found in opposite directions. One was abandoned near Coral
Springs and the other south near Sweetwater. No cameras were
in either area. An intentional and preplanned effort. We had no
option but to rely on the public taking notice of a BOLO, which
listed Shelby Pearce and Aria Stover as kidnap victims. We added
Marissa Stover and possibly Eli Chandler and Feng Liu as armed-
and-dangerous suspects.

The BOLO expanded to surrounding states, including public and private airports.

I paced the Miami FBI office. "Where's Feng Liu?"

"In the wind."

"True. My guess he's in on this, and he and Marissa could have plans to leave the country together. Shelby and Aria serve as hostages, but what happens when their usefulness disappears? And where does Eli Chandler fit?"

"Denton, we know the answers. Marissa doesn't leave survivors. Why are they traveling by car? Marissa could have left the country by now and is over international waters."

Midafternoon, a call from the sheriff's department from the western coast of northern Florida gave us a lead on a Toyota Camry. A McDonald's employee claimed she saw two women and a teen in the ladies' restroom who fit the description of the BOLO. One of the women had mouthed *help*. The employee's manager had shared with the morning shift about a manhunt underway in the state, and the employee realized she might have encountered them. Police reviewed camera footage and spotted Eli pumping gas and the three women leaving the McDonald's, then taking off in the Toyota. We had a partial on the license plate, but why had Chandler walked away leaving Marissa to drive?

Within twenty minutes, we'd boarded a helicopter and followed the license plate number. All the things I wanted to tell Shelby swirled through my mind. More than swirled but slammed against every cell of my tormented body.

Shelby would seize opportunities to free Aria, sacrifice herself if necessary. She'd look to Jesus for strength and try to persuade Marissa to give herself up. From what I'd discovered about Marissa, she'd murder repeatedly until someone stopped her, and I doubted Shelby could manage the task.

"Be prepared we might not find them," Mike said. "Or they aren't alive."

"I can't think about that. We'll find them in time."

Mike flashed a worried glance my way. Losing my fiancée was tough, but I wouldn't survive losing Shelby.

83

SHELBY

Marissa took a single dirt road that led to a small, weed-infested landing strip. Obviously it was seldom ever used.

"Feng picking you up?" I said.

"For a better tomorrow." She pressed in a number, and I gathered he'd been late leaving Miami. "Okay, honey, see you in twenty minutes or less. I'll be looking for your plane."

Dear God, help me find the right way to stop this.

"I'm ready for the truth," I said. "Why set me up to take the blame for Travis's murder?"

"We have time for a five-minute chat." Marissa didn't need prodding to talk about herself. "Think about it. I always got what I wanted by giving you ideas to feed your wild ways and by playing the good girl. I had everything before you came along. I chose to get even. I set you up time and time again, and you fell for it . . . Remember our sister games? When Travis took over a charity for

African orphans, I saw my chance to hack into the account and invest the money overseas."

"What happened?"

She swore. "I didn't expect to get pregnant. An abortion made sense, but I figured out how to use the situation to my advantage—more trips away to rest and take care of business. Eli often joined me. He helped me devise a plan to leave the baby with Travis and lose myself in Europe."

"But why shoot Travis?"

"He found out I'd been embezzling his poor orphans' money. His accusation threatened to ruin my future, and while I aimed a gun at him, my mind danced with how to cover it up with my grandest scheme ever—a glorious means to keep my good-girl facade."

"And I fell right into it."

"You became my scapegoat, my sweet rebellious sister. You swallowed a pregnant woman's desperation, and the rest paved my golden road to millions."

"After my prison release, you sent your dogs after me. Why, after I paid your debt? I honored the request to stay away from all of you."

"Couldn't risk losing all I'd built. I needed your death to permanently lock away the past so I could make my escape."

I hid my anger and grief. "Whose handwriting was on the sympathy card?"

"Eli found a maid from a Miami hotel."

"And what of Aria?" My lungs warred against me. I struggled to keep my strength and sucked in air.

She sneered at me. "Do I look like I want to be chained to a fifteen-year-old? She makes me crazy. Transforming Dad into a Shelby-hater took time. He denied your guilt for a few years." She clenched her jaw. "Aria and Mom were at church every time the door opened. I went to keep up the facade. Utterly disgusting." She laughed, a hysterical high pitch. "Aria looks and acts like you.

You should see yourself. You can't mask your revulsion of me. And I worked so hard all those years to teach you how to hide your body language."

"My hatred is for what happened to you as a child."

"Marissa," Aria said. "I'm sorry I stood in your way."

"Shut up. You and Shelby make me sick."

"Are you going to kill us?" Aria whispered.

"You had doubts? I don't deal with liabilities."

The sound of an approaching vehicle seized Marissa's attention.

84

Eli sped to the side of the car in a battered pickup and stepped out, gun in hand. "Marissa, we need to talk."

She opened the car door and aimed her gun, sending a bullet into his left shoulder directly above his heart. Eli fell back and didn't move. "Another problem resolved." She whirled to us. "Out of the car. Time's running out, and I don't need anyone reporting gunfire."

We exited the car, and she gestured to the front of it. A gust of wind blew, and droplets of rain hit my face . . . like the day I was released from prison. Then it was morning, now we faced sunset.

"Leave Aria out of this. Do this one good thing. She deserves a full life." I softened my voice. "I know you want your daughter free of the hurt you've felt all these years."

"Fat chance."

The whir of helicopter blades sounded. Marissa had specifically said a plane was coming. The helicopter hovered closer over the landing strip. A bullhorn sounded.

"Marissa Stover, this is the FBI. Lay your weapon down now."

Denton. Hope fluttered inside me.

"How did they find us?" Marissa's anger erupted in a shriek. She stared at the car and quickly searched the sky. "They won't shoot up the place as long as I have you two." She pointed the gun at Aria and me. "Besides, I won't go down alone."

Aria and I knew where we'd spend our eternity. "Marissa, God doesn't want you miserable. He—"

"Preaching to me is a waste. I know God wants me happy. I'm blessed. I have money tucked away all over the world. Even here."

Aria trembled. I'd do anything to save my niece.

She aimed the gun at Aria, and I stepped between them.

"Marissa." Eli stood, grasping his gun and staggering. Blood soaked the left side of his shirt. "I told you never to lay a hand on Aria again."

Fury etched on my sister's face. She faced the man and the gun aimed at her. Denton, Mike, and two more men hurried from the chopper, their firearms drawn.

"I . . . loved you," Eli managed. "For seventeen years, I catered to your every whim. Didn't protest when you slept around, thinking it was for the good of the business. I believed your lies." He raised the gun higher. "I still love you, but I won't let you murder my daughter."

"Eli, we can talk—"

He fired into her left chest.

Marissa fell.

Aria screamed.

Heat flooded me. Was my reaction terror? Relief? I rushed to Marissa and bent beside her still body. I gingerly turned her over and lifted her head into my lap. The light in her blue eyes had vanished. Sobs met my ears, but it seemed as though the sound came from someone else. I kissed her cheek and closed her eyes.

"You didn't have to walk the future alone," I whispered. "I wouldn't have abandoned you."

"Mom," Aria whispered. "I'm sorry." She peered at Eli, who'd fallen, and moved to his side. I didn't hear her words other than "thank you."

A hand touched my shoulder, and I sensed Denton beside me. "You can't do anything to help your sister."

I swallowed the acid rising in my throat. My lungs ached to breathe. I was drowning in a whirlpool of grief. "I want to make it right between us. She needs to know I love her."

He knelt beside me. "Tell her how you feel. We're not in any hurry. An ambulance is on its way."

I attempted to wipe some of the blood from Marissa's face. I kissed her cheek again. "Will you make sure they take good care of my sister?"

"I promise," he said.

"It's hard to say goodbye, Denton. I loved her so much. Nothing could ever change how I feel."

He wrapped his arm around my waist. "I love you, Shelby."

My chin quivered. "And I love you."

"I'm staying right here. You won't take this journey alone."

EPILOGUE

THREE MONTHS LATER

Not a day went by that I didn't think about Marissa and how I could have done more to stop her tragic end. The loss was immeasurable, and depression still took a bite out of my heart. I knew the path of sorrow took time, and I pray through each debilitating moment. I'd never know why she'd been so eager for me to join her in Miami, and I'd never be convinced my presence with Aria was her insurance. She needed me . . . maybe one last desperate plea for help. My sister's behavior would remain a mystery, but I truly believed she fought to remain in full control of her life to the very end, and I must try to make peace with her decisions.

The FBI arrested Feng Liu at the landing strip. He and Marissa were headed to Hong Kong in his private plane. Liu had powerful attorneys who'd probably get him released on a technicality. Marissa's bodyguards hadn't been located. My guess was they left the country when the fire threatened to burn them.

After Eli had pulled the trigger on Marissa, he bled out. I didn't think he had a will to live. Aria witnessed both her parents' deaths, and the nightmare culminating in horror pushed her into shock. She still met with Pastor Emory five days a week for counseling. She adored him. Mrs. Emory had homeschooled her the last month of school with her own children. Although Aria was enrolled in the local high school for fall, she hadn't decided if facing a new environment and the possibility of other kids viewing her as a freak made sense. I understood her reservations—the past stalked me fiercely.

Pastor Emory counseled me weekly, and Dad had taken advantage too. One trait about myself had risen to the surface, and Pastor Emory termed it arrested development.

The State of Texas presented me with a full pardon, a bright spot in my life. A Hollywood producer wanted to do a movie about my life, but I refused unless he wrote my faith into the script with a focus on forgiveness. We were still discussing it.

The FBI had found four hundred thousand dollars in Marissa's shoulder bag. As of yet, the authorities couldn't determine where it had originated, so for now it sat in a trust account for Aria.

Each day drew me closer to healing, thanks to God, my dear Denton, and my beloved family and friends. I glanced around Amy-Jo's busy café, taking in the sights, smells, and sounds of normalcy. Customers filled the booths and tables, and servers jotted down and delivered lunch orders. Not much call for pastries until dessert time. *Simply Shelby* had done well, thanks to Edie's help with my business model.

From the kitchen, Dad carried an order. He seemed to sense my gaze on him, and he smiled, an unspoken reassurance of love. We'd get through the tragedy. He'd sold the bakery in Sharp's Creek, allowing Aria and him to move to Valleysburg for a much-needed fresh start. The sale provided funds to take part ownership in Amy-Jo's Café. The two owners had struck up a friendship and often went fishing and hunting together. Our customers learned

Dad's mother had created Mimi's cinnamon bread, and the orders doubled.

Once the truth hit the media, the people of Valleysburg treated me much better, with forgiveness flowing on both sides. I learned Denton had a heart for troubled teens, so we regularly visited the town's youth center. Randy received weekly visits from us at the rehab. He'd lengthened his stay, said he didn't want to do a repeat later. He had yet to apologize to me, and unless Jesus got hold of him, he probably wouldn't ever admit wrongdoing. Pride had a way of destroying us all.

My sweet Joy proved to be an affectionate companion. Potty training was much easier than I expected, especially since I was new to the world of dogs.

The bell rang on the café door. The love of my life walked in wearing a grin as big as Texas. Did he have any idea how many women's heads turned at his handsomeness when he entered a room? And he was spoken for. He jammed his hands into jean pockets and approached the bakery.

"And what would you like today, sir?" I said.

He leaned over the glass counter. "Nothing in the display case could be as sweet as you."

I rolled my eyes. "Flattery, sir, doesn't get you anything free."

"True. But I have you for life. Want to go with me later to take pics of a baby colt? One of the boys at the center invited us."

"I'd love it."

He looked around us like a mischievous little boy. "Can we sneak into the kitchen for a kiss?"

No one was in sight. "How about two?"

Denton and I planned to be married on December 22, a Christmas wedding. From the first moment I met Denton's family, they treated me like a queen, and I saw the premature white hair in his dad and brothers. Denton and Brice took a long walk and returned laughing. Andy and Lisa went a bit overboard making me feel welcome, but their words and gestures were sincere.

Edie and Amy-Jo helped me select the perfect dress, a simple satin-and-lace princess style. Our loved ones would be there to share in the celebration. Yes, I was excited to walk down the aisle with Dad and pretend Mom and Marissa were there too. Aria would be a bridesmaid and Edie, my matron of honor.

Denton had retired from the FBI and decided to teach math and coach sports at the local high school. "I don't need to prove myself to anyone but God," he'd said. "And I enjoy kids. I want to help them find hope."

We'd enjoy a wonderful future together, God willing. How strange God had worked on both of us and then brought us together for the gift of love.

My journal was full, and I was ready to begin a new one. This one would be different because life changed, and we were all changing with it. I might not understand God's timing or purpose, but I'd learned to wake each morning seeking His will. The colors of my life were filled with love and healing for today and tomorrow.

CHAPTER ONE

Vacations offered a distraction for those who longed to relax and rejuvenate, but FBI Special Agent Heather Lawrence wrestled with the decision to take an overseas trip alone. Normally she arrived for a flight at IAH eager to embark upon a new adventure. Not this time. Her vacation expectations had bottomed out over four weeks ago after Chad had slammed the door on reconciliation. Was she working through her grief or avoiding the reality of a husband who no longer wanted her?

She waited to board the flight in a designated line at the gate. The hum of voices blended with airport beeps, and announcements swirled around her as though enticing her to join the enthusiasm. In the line beside her, passengers shifted their carry-ons and positioned their mobile devices or paper boarding passes. Ready. Alert. People eager to be on their way.

Heather offered a smile to those nearest her. An adorable little blond boy with an older woman found it hard to stand still. A middle-aged couple held hands. The bald head and pasty skin of the man indicated a medical condition. He stumbled, and the woman reached for him. A robust man held a violin case next to his heart. A twentysomething woman with pink hair and a man behind her with a scruffy beard exchanged a kiss.

Chad used to steal kisses.

If she pinpointed the exact moment when he chose to separate himself from her, she'd say when he returned from a third trip for Doctors Without Borders late last fall. He'd witnessed suffering and cruel deaths that had scarred him. She'd encouraged his desire to help others, not realizing their future would take a backseat. While he drove toward success, their marriage drifted across the lanes and stalled in a rut.

The boarding line moved toward the Jetway. Each step shook her to the core as though she should turn and try to reverse the past seven months. She'd ignored her and Chad's deteriorating relationship in an effort to make him happy. A huge mistake. But she didn't intend to add the labels *beaten* or *weak* to her dossier.

A cell phone sounded, and a man boarding in front of her stopped to answer it. His shoulders stiffened under a tan sports coat, and he talked in hushed tones. Heather dug her fingers into her palms and forced one foot in front of the other while the man pocketed his cell phone and proceeded into business class.

A flight attendant greeted her, a dark-haired young man wearing a wide smile, relaxed and genuine, an obvious sign he enjoyed his job. She returned the gesture. His black jacket with two rows of silver braid on the sleeves and black trousers were magazine perfect.

Heather walked to a rear aisle seat in business class and hoisted her tote bag into the overhead compartment. Although it held essentials for every emergency in case her luggage was delayed, the bulging piece weighed less than the burden on her heart.

Easing onto her seat, Heather pulled the brochure from her shoulder bag describing Salzburg's music festival, a celebration of musicians past and present. First a layover in Frankfurt and then on to her destination. She'd rented an apartment for ten days within walking distance of the historical center. The flexibility allowed her to choose her itinerary and cook or dine out. From the online photos, the centuries-old building had just enough updates to be comfortable without damaging its historic charm. She'd have hours to explore Mozart's roots, museums, the many churches, immerse herself in the culture, and think.

A female passenger, sporting red spiked hair and chin-length hooped earrings, stopped beside her. The woman carried a Venti Starbucks. "Excuse me." Her German accent a reminder of the destination. "Would you mind holding my coffee while I store my carry-on?"

"Of course." Heather held the cup while the woman shoved her small suitcase into the overhead bin.

"Sorry for the inconvenience. I wasn't thinking when I bought the coffee."

"It smells heavenly." Heather stood to let the woman pass and then handed her the cup.

"Thank you." The woman blew on the lid and took a sip. "I'm Mia."

"I'm Heather."

"Long flight ahead but soon I'll be home." She pointed to Heather's brochure. "Salzburg?"

"Yes. For a much-needed vacation."

"I'm from Frankfurt. Really missing my daughter and husband."

"You'll see them soon."

Mia broke into a wide smile. "We've done FaceTime and texted, but I want to touch their faces and hug them."

Heather continued to read the Salzburg brochure to avoid any personal comments from Mia, like whether she was taking a vacation solo. An elderly man wearing a straw fedora and a white mustache sat in the aisle seat across from Heather. He pulled his phone from his pant pocket and used his thumbs on the keyboard like a kid.

Mia placed her coffee on the tray and made a phone call. *"Wie geht es meinem kleinen Mädchen?"*

Heather translated the German. *How is my little girl?* The woman's excitement resonated through every word. Love. Laughter. Priceless commodities that Heather didn't possess. Yet this trip offered an opportunity to rekindle her faith in God and chart a course for the future.

While the attendants made their way through business class with drink orders, Heather longed to have confirmation she'd made the right decision to take this trip. No one knew of her vacation plans except her parents and Assistant Special Agent in Charge Wade Mitchell in Houston. No one needed to know the why of her trip until she made a few decisions.

Stuffing the Salzburg brochure into her bag, she snatched the aircraft's information and confirmed the layout for 267 passengers, restrooms, exit doors, in-seat power, on-demand entertainment, and three galleys. She always noted the details of her surroundings, another habit of working so many FBI cases. Always be prepared for the unexpected.

If the trip had been FBI sanctioned, her present circumstances might not hurt so much. How ironic she worked the critical incident response group as a behavior analyst, and she wrestled to understand her own life.

Right on time, the flight attendants took their assigned posts while miniature screens throughout the plane shared the aircraft's amenities and explained the passenger safety instructions. The captain welcomed them moments before the plane lifted into the clouds.

On her way. No turning back. She prayed for a safe journey and much-needed answers.

Food smells from business class caught her attention, a mix of roasted chicken and beef. Too often of late, she forgot to eat or nothing appealed to her. To shake off the growing negativity, she paid for Wi-Fi and grabbed her phone from her bag. Time to concentrate on something other than herself.

She glanced at the incoming notifications. No texts. Her emails were an anticipated list of senders when she longed for a change of heart from Chad. Sighing, she closed her eyes. Between her job, Chad, and stress, too often she fought for enough pillow time.

Two hours later, she woke from a deep sleep to the sound of a woman's scream.

CHAPTER TWO

Heather whirled toward the ear-piercing cry behind her. She released her seat belt and rushed back to the economy section. The overhead lights snapped on to reveal the middle-aged couple whom she'd seen at the gate. The panic-stricken woman beside him held a tissue to his nose. Blood dripped beneath her fingers and down her wrist.

Not a muscle moved on the man's face, and his eyes rolled back into their sockets. Heather approached him in the aisle seat. Before she could speak, the woman gasped, a mix of sobs and a struggle for composure. "Help me. I can't stop the bleeding."

Heather used tissues from the woman's lap to help block the blood flow. "Try to stay calm."

The woman nodded. "I shouldn't have let him talk me into this trip. He's been so weak."

From the front of the plane, the male flight attendant who'd greeted passengers earlier rushed their way. He carried two kits, one labeled first aid and the other biohazard. A female attendant trailed after him.

"Help is here," Heather said to the woman. She moved aside for the attendant to administer aid. She prayed the ill man was undergoing a minor problem—an easily resolved issue—and for the woman's comfort. But his lifeless face showed a grim reality.

"Sir, how do you feel?" Not a sound or movement came from the man. Blood flowed from Heather's mass of tissues.

The male attendant twisted off the seal of the biohazard kit and searched inside. He drew out a pair of nitrile gloves and wiggled them on. The female attendant opened the first aid kit, ripped into a gauze package, and handed it to the male attendant, who applied it to the man's nose. She opened the biohazard waste bag to dispose of the soiled materials.

The male attendant captured the woman's attention. "Ma'am, I'm Nathan. Is this your husband?"

"Yes. He's very hot."

Nathan touched the man's forehead. "How long has he been feverish?"

"He was fine when we boarded. Perhaps over an hour into the flight?" Her sobs subsided to soft cries. "Do something. Blood's coming from his mouth."

Heather touched her shoulder with a clean hand. "Take a deep breath."

"How can I? Roy's not breathing."

"That's his name?" His gentle voice ushered in compassion.

"Yes. I'm Catherine."

He bent to speak to Roy. "I'm Nathan. Give me a few minutes to administer first aid." He replaced the gauze on Roy's nose for the second time and turned to the female flight attendant, who'd paled but didn't tremble. "Leave the kits. Call the flight deck and tell them what's happening."

She rushed to the front of the cabin.

"This is my fault." Catherine held Roy's hand. "He finished

chemo and radiation for lung cancer, but his doctor hadn't cleared him for the trip."

"Catherine," Nathan said, "I know you're worried, but try to stay calm. Has he experienced these symptoms before?"

"No."

A voice spoke over the interphone. "If a licensed medical professional is on board, we have a medical issue. All other passengers, please remain in your seats."

Within moments, a lean man arrived from the right side of business class carrying a leather case. "I'm a doctor." Heather stepped back while he examined Roy and spoke to Nathan.

While the doctor stood over Roy with his back to Heather, Nathan turned to her. "We've got this handled. Please return—"

"No, please. Let her stay," Catherine said. "If she doesn't mind."

Nathan frowned. "Okay, for the moment. Our manual states we have to keep the aisle clear around the patient."

"I understand," Heather said. "I'd be happy to sit with her, and I'm Heather."

"Miss, if the pilots call our med service on the ground, I'll need you out of way so we can relay instructions."

The doctor and Nathan lowered Roy to the aisle and treated him. They blocked Heather's view of the procedure, but the doctor rummaged for something inside the leather case. For the next ten minutes, she waited for the doctor to reassure passengers of the man's recovery.

Catherine's hysteria spun in a cloud of uncertainty that left unchecked often spread panic. She unfastened her seat belt and rose on unstable legs. "Please, tell me my husband is all right." The female attendant gently urged her back onto the seat.

The doctor eased up from Roy and spoke reassuring words to Catherine. He peeled off his blood-covered gloves and tossed them into the bag. Had Roy succumbed to the lung cancer or a complication?

Nathan walked to a galley area. "Ladies and gentlemen, I am

Nathan Howard, your lead flight attendant on board your flight today. We appreciate your concern for the man receiving medical attention. We will transport him to the rear of the cabin, where he'll be comfortable. A doctor is tending to him, and the medical concern is under control. Thank you."

Heather supported the airline's protocol designed to keep everyone from alarm and terror while the crew addressed issues. Yet a few people craned their necks to watch the scene as though it was a morbid form of entertainment more interesting than the recycled movies on the screens in front of them.

Nathan returned to Catherine. "I know you'd like for the young woman to sit with you, but it would be easier for the flight crew and safer for her if we placed an attendant here. Can we do that?"

"I guess." Catherine's lips quivered.

Heather bent to speak. "I'm not far." She understood how Catherine had latched on to her, a stranger, for moral support.

Nathan and the doctor picked Roy up and carried him to the rear. Roy was either unconscious or dead.

The female flight attendant sat in Roy's seat and held Catherine's hand. "I'll stay with you for as long as you like."

"Can I join my husband?"

"When the doctor is finished, I'll escort you back."

Heather returned to her seat—her mind weighed with concern.

"Gott hab Erbarmen," Mia said.

"Yes, God have mercy."

"You speak German?"

"A little. Spent a year in Frankfurt when I was in college."

"The sound of it makes me long for home." She hesitated. "What's wrong with the man?"

"His wife said he'd recently completed chemo treatments for lung cancer. I'm sure the doctor is doing all he can. The airline has doctors on the ground, and they'll consult with the doctor on board. Between them, they'll figure out what's best."

"Do you work for the airlines?"

"No." Heather smiled. "I'm with the Department of Justice."

Mia rubbed her palms together. She'd already stated her desire to see her family. "Will the flight be diverted?"

"It depends on lots of factors. The man may just require rest." Heather wasn't going to state the excessive blood from Roy's mouth and nose pointed to his death. By now the doctors at Medi-Pro-Aire, an advisory service for airlines, had been contacted and put in communication with the pilot.

"I read the airline's cost to emergency divert range from $10,000 to upwards of $200,000," Mia said.

"I don't doubt the cost, but with this airline, the safety and welfare of the passengers always come first. They don't blink at the cost of diversion. It's on management's mind post-action."

"Can the pilots be called to the carpet for making a safety decision?"

"I'm sure their procedure is in place to protect the passengers." Heather forced comfort into her voice. "We'll be okay."

Muffled voices around her prompted alarm.

A man shouted for help. "My wife has a terrible headache."

A man in business class vomited.

"My son has a fever," a woman said.

"Please, the man beside me has a nosebleed, and he can't stop it."

"What is going on?" Mia whispered. "All these people are suddenly sick. Frighteningly sick."

Heather wished she had answers while horror played out around her.

"I'm afraid." Mia's face turned ashen.

"We have to stay calm." Heather craved to heed her own advice.

Throughout the plane, people complained of flu-like symptoms. Another person vomited. Heather touched her stomach. A twinge of apprehension crept through her.

Nathan spoke over the interphone. "If you are experiencing physical distress, press your call button. Flight attendants will be in your area soon with damp paper towels. Use these to cover your mouth and the tops of beverages. As always, remain in your seats."

Heather messaged ASAC Mitchell in Houston with the medical emergency report, including the symptoms.

He responded. **The FBI, TSA, CDC, and Medi-Pro-Aire are on it. Are you okay?**

Yes. People's symptoms indicate a serious virus.

The doctor on board has given a similar conclusion.

She trembled as she typed. **Looks similar to what Chad described in Africa.**

The doctor said the same. Is the man dead?

I think so.

How many others are sick?

Heather surveyed the passengers within her sight and typed. **From my seat, I see around ten in business class, and I hear the sick in economy. Will the plane divert?**

No decision yet. Keep me posted. You are our eyes.

Beyond what the doctor on board relayed to those on the ground, ASAC Mitchell must believe she held the voice of reason and objectivity. The irony of their interpretation. The viruses were usually zoonotic or caused by insects, and the symptoms created intense suffering. She blinked to clear her head and not ponder the worst.

With panic gripping her in a stranglehold, she imagined what others were feeling. A man questioned why the plane hadn't landed. A woman bolted to the galley and held her mouth. The man who held the violin marched to the business class restroom but fell face-first and vomited.

The elderly man across the aisle from her coughed. His nose trickled blood.

Heather grabbed tissues from her bag and handed them to him. "Will this help?"

"Tell me this is a nightmare." He gripped her arm—fiery hot.

HOPE OF SUDAN

STAND-ALONES

DISCUSSION QUESTIONS

1. Shelby Pearce hasn't been in touch with her family since she went to prison fifteen years ago. She notes that she and her sister "were raised with the knowledge of unconditional love, but I learned some deeds were unforgivable." How does Shelby handle her family's estrangement? What justifications does her family make for keeping their distance? If you were in their shoes, would you think Shelby's crime is "unforgivable"?

2. What makes Denton McClure so convinced of Shelby's guilt? What begins to change his mind? When did you realize there was more to Shelby's story?

3. Early in Shelby and Denton's relationship, she asks him: "At the end of your life, what will you have to show for your quest?" How does Denton answer that question? How would Shelby answer it? Do their answers change over the course of the story? Think about your own life. What will you have to show for it?

4. Shelby's presence in Valleysburg creates friction among the townspeople, even within the church. What objections to her are raised? Who comes to her defense? How do you think your church might respond to an ex-con in the congregation?

5. On the way to her family's house, Denton tells Shelby: "People we trust often fail us." Who failed Denton? Who failed Shelby? How do Denton and Shelby reconcile with those people? Has anyone failed you? When is it important to forgive? Is there ever a time a person should just move on from a relationship?

6. When Denton lands in the hospital and Shelby and a couple retired agents are targeted at a safe house, he asks her how people can believe in a God who allows bad things to happen. What does Shelby say about this? How would you answer Denton's question?

7. Denton has fond memories of his grandmother, especially nights they spent studying the stars in the sky. In what ways was she planting seeds of faith in him? Who else contributes to seeing those seeds sprout? Is there someone in your life you've planted seeds with or watered those seeds for?

8. What reasons does Shelby have for hesitating in starting a romantic relationship with Denton? How might her objections be overcome? What happens in relationships after mistakes are made? Is it always possible to start over or are some mistakes fatal?

9. Shelby's niece reminds her that sometimes it's better not to profile other people. Who has the hardest time with prejudging in this story? What lessons can be learned from them?

10. Clay Pearce asks Shelby: "Ever hear knowledge is horizontal but wisdom is vertical?" What is he trying to communicate to Shelby? What does this maxim mean to you?

11. Clay also reminds Shelby that "sacrifice always has a price." What sacrifice does Shelby pay and what does it cost her? What does she gain through her sacrifice? What have you sacrificed, paid, and gained?

12. By the end of the story, Shelby understands that she can't "right any of Marissa's wrongs—or even my own," but she determines to stop the crimes. Who is the only One who can right our wrongs?

ACKNOWLEDGMENTS

Lynette Eason—Our brainstorming sessions are more fun than work!

Debbie Fowler—My sister who was willing to share her bat experience. I still think it's hilarious!

Guy J. Gurley—My characterization is always stronger after meeting with you and posing questions about behavior.

James Hannibal—Your insight into writing challenges me to do a better job.

Karl Harroff—One more time you helped me sort out weapons for my characters.

Heather Kreke—Thanks for helping me figure out a plot twist.

Mark Lanier—Thank you for always answering my questions. Your outstanding teachings influence my characters and their decisions.

Edie Melson—Your encouragement and accountability keep me focused . . . and laughing. I treasure our friendship.

Romantic Suspense A-Team—I love how we support each other!

ABOUT THE AUTHOR

DiAnn Mills is a bestselling author who believes her readers should expect an adventure. She weaves memorable characters with unpredictable plots to create action-packed suspense-filled novels. DiAnn believes every breath of life is someone's story, so why not capture those moments and create a thrilling adventure?

Her titles have appeared on the CBA and ECPA bestseller lists; won two Christy Awards; and been finalists for the Golden Scroll, Inspirational Reader's Choice, and Carol Award contests.

DiAnn is a founding board member of the American Christian Fiction Writers and a member of Advanced Writers and Speakers Association, Mystery Writers of America, Sisters in Crime, and International Thriller Writers. She is the director of the Blue Ridge Mountains Christian Writers Conference and Mountainside Retreats, where she continues her passion of helping other writers be successful. She speaks to various groups and teaches writing workshops around the country.

DiAnn has been termed a coffee snob and roasts her own coffee beans. She's an avid reader, loves to cook, and believes her grand-children are the smartest kids in the universe. She and her husband live in sunny Houston, Texas.

DiAnn is very active online and would love to connect with readers through her website at diannmills.com.

CONNECT WITH DIANN ONLINE AT

diannmills.com

By purchasing this book, you're making a difference.

For over 50 years, Tyndale has supported ministry and humanitarian causes around the world through the work of its foundation. Proceeds from every book sold benefit the foundation's charitable giving. Thank you for helping us meet the physical, spiritual, and educational needs of people everywhere!

Tyndale | Trusted. For Life.   **tyndale.com/our-mission**